Praise for **THE FIRE CHRONICLE**

★ "Irreverent humor and swashbuckling adventure collide in a fetching fantasy." —*Kirkus Reviews*, Starred

★ "This is a roller-coaster ride of a story. . . . Fans of the first book won't be disappointed, and will eagerly anticipate the next one. *The Emerald Atlas* was very good. This one is even better."
—*School Library Journal*, Starred

★ "Fans of *The Emerald Atlas* will find much to love: the adventure-driven plot, a scattering of deliciously scary moments, and Stephens's offbeat take on Tolkienesque dragons, dwarves, and elves are sure to delight." —*Publishers Weekly*, Starred

Praise for **THE EMERALD ATLAS**

"A great story is all in the telling, and in *The Emerald Atlas* the telling is superb." —*The Wall Street Journal*

"A new Narnia for the tween set."
—*The New York Times Book Review*

"Rich with wonder and personality, *The Emerald Atlas* is a terrific read. I wholeheartedly recommend it, and look forward to more."
—Brandon Mull, #1 *New York Times* bestselling author of *Fablehaven* and the Beyonders series

"The novel's high energy and humor lighten the tone while still honoring the heartfelt quest for family." —*The Washington Post*

★ "Debut author Stephens has created a new and appealing read that will leave readers looking forward to the next volumes in this projected trilogy." —*School Library Journal*, Starred

Also by John Stephens

The Emerald Atlas

BOOK TWO ❖ The Books of Beginning

THE FIRE CHRONICLE

JOHN STEPHENS

A YEARLING BOOK

This is a work of fiction. Names, characters, places, and incidents either are the product of the author's imagination or are used fictitiously. Any resemblance to actual persons, living or dead, events, or locales is entirely coincidental.

Text copyright © 2012 by John Stephens
Cover art copyright © 2012 by Jon Foster
Chapter-opening art copyright © 2012 by Grady McFerrin

All rights reserved. Published in the United States by Yearling, an imprint of Random House Children's Books, a division of Random House LLC, a Penguin Random House Company, New York.
Originally published in hardcover in the United States by Alfred A. Knopf, an imprint of Random House Children's Books, New York, in 2012.

Yearling and the jumping horse design are registered trademarks of Random House LLC.

Visit us on the Web! randomhouse.com/kids

Educators and librarians, for a variety of teaching tools, visit us at RHTeachersLibrarians.com

The Library of Congress has cataloged the hardcover edition of this work as follows:
Stephens, John.
The fire chronicle / John Stephens. — 1st ed.
p. cm. — (The books of beginning ; bk. 2)
Summary: In the second book in the Books of Beginning Trilogy, Michael and Emma must track down the Chronicle of Life, while Kate must find a way back to present day from the year 1899.
ISBN 978-0-375-86871-9 (trade) — ISBN 978-0-375-96871-6 (lib. bdg.) —
ISBN 978-0-375-89956-0 (ebook) — ISBN 978-0-449-81015-6 (international tr. pbk.)
[1. Brothers and sisters—Fiction. 2. Magic—Fiction. 3. Space and time—Fiction.
4. Identity—Fiction. 5. Monsters—Fiction. 6. Prophecies—Fiction. 7. Books and reading—Fiction. 8. New York (N.Y.)—History—1898–1951—Fiction.] I. Title.
PZ7.S83218Fir 2012 [Fic]—dc23 2012016139

ISBN 978-0-375-87272-3 (pbk.)

Printed in the United States of America

10 9 8 7 6 5 4 3

First Yearling Edition 2013

Random House Children's Books supports the First Amendment and celebrates the right to read.

For Arianne

CONTENTS

THE FIRE CHRONICLE

The boy was small, and new to the orphanage, which meant he had the worst bed in the dormitory, the most uneven, the saggiest, the strangest-smelling; it was little more than a cot, jammed into an alcove at the back of the room. And when the scream came—a scream unlike any the boy had ever heard, the way it seemed to reach into his chest and crush his heart—he was the last of the frightened, shrieking children out the door.

At the bottom of the stairs, the mob of children encountered a dense fog and turned right, stampeding down the hall. The boy was about to follow when two figures emerged from the mist, close on the heels of the children. They were black-garbed, with burning yellow eyes, and held long, jagged swords and stank of rot.

The boy waited till they passed, then fled in the other direction.

He ran blindly, with fear thick in his throat, knowing only that he had to get away, to hide. Then, somehow, he was in the director's office, and there were voices in the hall. He dove beneath a desk, tucking his legs up close.

The door of the office banged open; a light snapped on. A pair of green slippers backed into view, and he heard the orphanage director, a dull bully of a man, begging:

"Please—please, don't hurt me—"

A second man spoke, his voice strangely cold and lilting. "Now, why would I do a thing like that? It's three children I came for."

"So take them! Take three! Take ten! Just don't hurt me!"

The other man stepped closer, the floor groaning under his weight.

"Well, that is generous. Only it's three very special children I'm after. A brother and two sisters. They go by the lovely names of Kate, Michael, and Emma."

"But they're not . . . they're not here anymore. We sent them away! More than a year ago—"

There was a strangled gurgle, and the boy watched as the slippered feet rose, thrashing, into the air. The other man's voice was calm, without a hint of strain.

"And where did you send them? Where do I find them?"

The boy pressed his hands to his ears, but he could still hear the choking, still hear the man's lilting, murderous voice. "Where are the children . . . ?"

CHAPTER ONE
The Letter in the Tree

Kate finished writing the letter, sealed it in an envelope, then walked over and dropped it into the hollow of an old tree.

He'll come, she told herself.

She'd written to him about her dream, the one that had yanked her out of sleep every night that week. Again and again, she'd lain there in the dark, covered in cold sweat and waiting for her heart to slow, relieved that Emma, lying beside her, hadn't woken, relieved that it had only been a dream.

Except it wasn't a dream; she knew that.

He'll come, Kate repeated. When he reads it, he'll come.

The day was hot and humid, and Kate wore a lightweight summer dress and a pair of patched leather sandals. Her hair was pulled back and cinched with a rubber band, though a few loose strands stuck to her face and neck. She was fifteen and taller than she'd been a year ago. In other respects, her appearance hadn't changed. With her dark blond hair and hazel eyes, she still struck all who saw her as a remarkably pretty girl. But a person did not have to look closely to see the furrow of worry that was etched into her brow, or the tension that lived in her arms and shoulders, or the way her fingernails were bitten to the quick.

In that respect, truly, nothing had changed.

Kate had not moved from beside the tree, but stood there, absently fingering the gold locket that hung from her neck.

More than ten years earlier, Kate and her younger brother and sister had been sent away from their parents. They had grown up in a series of orphanages, a few that were nice and clean, run by kind men and women, but most of them not so nice, and the adults who ran them not so kind. The children had not been told why their parents had sent them away, or when they were coming back. But that their parents would eventually return, that they would all once more be a family, the children had never doubted.

It had been Kate's duty to look after her brother and sister. She had made that promise the night her mother had come into her room that Christmas Eve so long ago. She could picture it still: her mother leaning over her, fastening the golden locket around her small neck, as Kate promised that she would protect Michael and Emma and keep them safe.

And year after year, in orphanage after orphanage, even when they had faced dangers and enemies they could never have imagined, Kate had been true to her word.

But if Dr. Pym didn't come, how would she protect them now?

But he will come, she told herself. He hasn't abandoned us.

If that's so, said a voice in her head, why did he send you here?

And, unable to help herself, Kate turned and looked down the hill. There, visible through the trees, were the crumbling brick walls and turrets of the Edgar Allan Poe Home for Hopeless and Incorrigible Orphans.

In her defense, it was only when Kate was frustrated or tired that she questioned Dr. Pym's decision to send her and Michael and Emma back to Baltimore. She knew he hadn't really abandoned them. But the fact remained: of all the orphanages the children had lived in over the years—one of which had been next to a sewage treatment plant; another had made groaning noises and seemed to be always catching on fire—the Edgar Allan Poe Home for Hopeless and Incorrigible Orphans was the worst. The rooms were freezing in the winter, boiling in the summer; the water was brown and chunky; the floors squished and oozed; the ceilings leaked; it was home to warring gangs of feral cats. . . .

And as if that weren't enough, there was Miss Crumley, the lumpy-bodied, Kate-and-her-brother-and-sister-hating orphanage director. Miss Crumley had thought she'd gotten rid of the children for good last Christmas, and she had been less than pleased to have them turn up on her doorstep a week later, bearing a note from Dr. Pym saying that the orphanage at Cambridge Falls had been closed due to "an infestation of turtles," and would

Miss Crumley mind watching the children till the problem was resolved.

Of course Miss Crumley had minded. But when she'd attempted to call Dr. Pym to inform him that under no circumstances could she accept the children and that she was returning them on the next train, she'd found that all the information Dr. Pym had previously given her (phone number for the orphanage, address and directions, testimonials from happy, well-fed children) had disappeared from her files. Nor did the phone company have any record of a number. In fact, no matter how much she dug, Miss Crumley was unable to find any evidence that the town of Cambridge Falls actually existed. In the end, she'd been forced to give in. But she let the children know that they were unwelcome, and she took every opportunity to corner them in the hallways or the cafeteria, firing questions while poking them with her pudgy finger.

"Where exactly is this Cambridge Falls?"—*poke*—"Why can't I find it on any maps?"—*poke*—"Who is this Dr. Pym fellow?"—*poke, poke*—"Is he even a real doctor?"—*poke, poke, poke*—"What happened up there? I know something fishy's going on! Answer me!"—*poke, poke, poke, pinch, twist.*

Frustrated at having had her hair pulled for the third time in one week, Emma had suggested that they tell Miss Crumley the truth: that Dr. Stanislaus Pym was a wizard, that the reason Miss Crumley couldn't find Cambridge Falls on a map was that it was part of the magical world and therefore hidden from normal (or in her case, subnormal) humans, that as far as what had happened there, the three of them had discovered an old book bound in green leather that had carried them back through time, that they'd met dwarves and monsters, fought an evil witch, saved an entire town, and that pretty much any way you looked at it, they were heroes. Even Michael.

"Thanks," Michael had said sarcastically.

"You're welcome."

"Anyway, we can't say that. She'll think we're crazy."

"So what?" Emma had replied. "I'd rather be in a loony bin than this place."

But in the end, Kate had made them stick to their story. Cambridge Falls was an ordinary sort of place, Dr. Pym was an ordinary sort of man, and nothing the least bit out of the ordinary had happened. "We have to trust Dr. Pym."

After all, Kate thought, what other choice did they have?

Faint strains of music were drifting up the hill, reminding Kate that today was the day of Miss Crumley's party, and she looked down through the trees to the large yellow tent that had been erected on the orphanage lawn. For the past two weeks, every child in the orphanage had been working nonstop, weeding, mulching, cleaning windows, trimming hedges, hauling trash, collecting the carcasses of animals that had crawled into the orphanage to die, all for the sake of a party to which they were not even invited.

"And don't let me catch you peering out the windows at my guests!" Miss Crumley had warned the assembled children at breakfast. "Mr. Hartwell Weeks has no desire to see your grubby little faces pressed against the glass."

Mr. Hartwell Weeks was the president of the Maryland

Historical Society, in whose honor the party was being given. The society ran a weekly bus tour of "historically significant buildings" in the Baltimore area, and as the Home had been an armory in some long-ago war, Miss Crumley was determined to see it added to the list. She could then—Miss Crumley had this on good authority—charge groups of hapless tourists ten dollars a head for the privilege of stomping through the orphanage grounds.

"And if any of you mess this up"—she'd taken particular care to glare at Kate and her brother and sister as she said this—"well, I'm always getting calls from people who need children for dangerous scientific experiments, the sort of thing they don't want to waste a good dog on; I could easily volunteer a few names!"

The guests were now beginning to arrive, and Kate watched as men in blue blazers and white pants, women in creams and pastels, appeared around the side of the orphanage and hurried toward the shade of the tent. In truth, she was only half watching. Once again, she was thinking of her dream. She could hear the screams, see the yellow-eyed creatures stalking through the fog, hear the man's voice saying her and her brother's and sister's names. Had the events in her dream already happened, or were they about to? How much time did she and her siblings have?

She trusted Dr. Pym; she really did. But she was scared.

"Well, she's done it again!"

Kate turned to see her brother, Michael, huffing up the slope. He was red-faced and sweating, and his glasses had slipped down to the end of his nose. A tattered canvas bag was slung across his chest, the pouch resting on his hip.

Kate forced a smile.

"Done what again?"

"Gotten in trouble," Michael said with put-on exasperation. "Miss Crumley caught her trying to steal ice cream meant for the party. I thought she was going to have a heart attack. Miss Crumley, I mean, not Emma."

"Okay."

"That's it? You're not angry?" Michael adjusted his glasses and frowned. "Kate, you know Dr. Pym sent us here to hide. How can we keep a low profile if Emma's always getting into trouble?"

Kate sighed. She had heard all this before.

"She needs to learn to act more responsibly," Michael continued. "To use her head. I can't imagine I was so careless at her age."

He said this as if he were referring to some distant era in the past.

"Fine," Kate said. "I'll talk to her."

Michael nodded his approval. "I was hoping you'd say that. I've got the perfect quote. Maybe you can slip it in. Just a moment. . . ." He reached into his bag, and Kate knew without looking that he was taking out *The Dwarf Omnibus*. Just as she clung to her locket, Michael treasured the small leather-bound book. The night they'd been taken from their parents, their father had tucked it into his son's blankets, and, over the years, Michael had read and reread the *Omnibus* dozens of times. Kate knew it was his way of staying close to a father he scarcely remembered. It had also had the effect of giving him a deep appreciation of all things dwarfish. This had come in handy in Cambridge Falls when they had helped a dwarfish king claim his throne. For that service, Michael had been given a silver badge by King Robbie McLaur, and named Royal Guardian of All Dwarfish Traditions and History. More than once, Kate and Emma had come upon him, silver badge pinned to his chest, staring at himself in the mirror and striking somewhat ridiculous poses. Kate had warned Emma not to tease him.

"Honestly," Emma had said, "it would be too easy."

"Now, where was it. . . ." The *Omnibus* was the size and shape of a church hymnal, its black leather cover worn and scarred. Michael flipped through pages. "Oh, here's a story about two elf princes who started a war over which one had the shiniest hair. So typical. If I was an elf, I think I'd die from embarrassment."

Michael had a very low opinion of elves.

"Here we go! It's a quote from King Killin Killick—that's his real name, K-I-L-L-I-N, not a nickname because he did a lot of killing, though he did that too. So he says, 'A great leader lives not in his heart, but in his head.'" Michael snapped the book shut and smiled. "Head, not heart. That's the key. That's what she needs to learn. Yes, sir."

His argument made, Michael settled his glasses once more upon his nose and waited for his sister to respond.

Michael was nearly a year older than Emma. Nearly, but not quite, which meant that for a few weeks every year, the two of them were technically the same age. And every year, it drove Michael a little crazy. Being the middle child, he clung to his sliver of superiority. It didn't help matters that he and Emma were frequently mistaken for twins. They had the same chestnut hair, the same dark eyes; they were both small and scrawny-limbed. Kate knew that Michael lived in fear of Emma getting a growth spurt before he did. Indeed, for a while, she'd noticed Michael trying to hold himself as straight and rigid as possible, as if hoping to give at least the appearance of greater height. But Emma had kept asking if he had to go to the bathroom, and finally he'd stopped.

In five days, he would be thirteen. Kate knew he couldn't wait. For that matter, neither could she.

"Thanks. I'll remember that."

He nodded, satisfied. "So what were you writing to Dr. Pym? I saw you put the letter in the tree."

This was how they communicated with the wizard. Letters placed in the hollow of the tree would reach him immediately. Or so the children had been given to believe. As they had not heard from the wizard since arriving in Baltimore, Kate sometimes wondered if all the notes she'd dropped in the tree were sitting there, unread.

Kate shrugged. "Just asking how much longer we'll be here."

"It's been almost eight months."

"I know."

"Seven months and twenty-three days, to be precise."

Seven months and twenty-three days, Kate thought. And suddenly she remembered waking up on Christmas morning, having just returned to the present, and being told that Dr. Pym and Gabriel had left in the night, that Cambridge Falls was no longer safe, that the three of them were being sent back to Baltimore.

On some level, Kate hadn't been surprised. The night before, alone on the witch's boat, she had learned enough to know that their adventure was far from over. She'd tried to explain the situation to Michael and Emma, gathering them in the mansion library, and reminding them how the *Atlas*, the emerald-green book that let them move through time, was only one of three legendary Books called the Books of Beginning.

"It turns out there's a prophecy. Three children are supposed to find the Books and bring them together. Everyone thinks we're the children. They'll be looking for us."

"Who will?" Emma had demanded, still upset that Gabriel, her friend, had left without telling her. "The stupid witch is dead! Her stupid boat went over the waterfall!"

That was when Kate had told them about the Countess escaping from the boat at the last moment, how she'd lain in wait for fifteen years and had attacked Kate when they'd returned to the present, how Kate had used the *Atlas* to take the witch deep into the past and abandon her.

"So I was right," Emma had said. "She's dead. Or as good as."

"Yes. But it's not her we have to worry about."

And Kate had told them about the Countess's master, the Dire Magnus. She'd described the violin that had heralded his arrival, how he'd taken over the Countess's body, how even Dr. Pym had seemed in awe of his power. The Dire Magnus needed them, she'd explained, for only through the three of them could he find the Books.

Snow had been falling past the library windows, the world outside silent and white. Kate had had to force herself to go on.

"There's one more thing. For the past ten years, all this time we've been going from orphanage to orphanage, the Dire Magnus has been holding Mom and Dad prisoner. It's up to us to free them. But for that, we'll need the Books."

The next day, the children had packed up their few possessions, Kate stuffing the *Atlas* deep inside her bag, and returned to Baltimore.

Now, standing there on the hillside, with the late-summer air warm and heavy against her skin, Kate thought of the *Atlas*. By the end of their adventure in Cambridge Falls, she had learned to command its magic at will. She knew she could make it carry her and Michael and Emma through time and space.

If Dr. Pym doesn't come, she told herself, I can still save them.

"Hey, I almost forgot. Did you hear what happened at St. Anselm's?"

Kate whipped her head around. "What?"

"I heard some kids talking. Some sort of gang or something broke in last night. They're saying Mr. Swattley—remember him?—they're saying he was murdered. Hey—what's wrong?"

Kate was trembling. St. Anselm's was the orphanage the three of them had lived at before first coming to Baltimore. It was also the orphanage from her dream.

"Michael . . ." She tried to keep her voice steady. ". . . I can depend on you, right?"

"What do you mean?"

"If I weren't here, I could depend on you to look after Emma. To be patient with her. To be a leader."

"Kate—"

"Just promise me. Please."

There was a long pause, then he said, "Of course."

And she opened her mouth to tell him about her dream, about all her dreams, not just the one she'd been having that week, but she saw that Michael was looking past her, away through the trees. She followed his gaze.

All summer long, it had scarcely rained, day after cloudless day. But there, massed along the horizon, was a range of thick black clouds. They were moving; they rolled toward the children, growing larger and darker with each passing second. It seemed to Kate that a great dark curtain was being drawn across the sky.

She said, "We need to find Emma."

CHAPTER TWO
The Storm

Michael and Kate came sprinting down out of the trees and onto the asphalt of the orphanage playground. To their left, beneath the yellow tent and a clear blue sky, Miss Crumley's party continued undisturbed. To the children's right, the black clouds were closing in fast.

Michael stopped.

"What're you doing?" Kate demanded. "We have to—"

"Emma! She's locked in Miss Crumley's office! For stealing the ice cream! We need the keys!"

Kate stared at him, her mind working feverishly. Their enemies had found them. She had no doubt about that. Only the *Atlas* could save them now. But it was hidden—

"Can you get them? If I get the *Atlas*, can you get the keys?"

Michael seemed frozen, his assurance of moments before now gone.

"Michael!"

"Y-yes," he stammered. "I can get them!"

"Then meet me at her office! Hurry!"

And Kate turned and ran for the orphanage.

When she crashed through the doors, Kate saw children clustered at the windows, oohing in amazement as the clouds rolled toward them. She didn't bother telling them to get back. Once she and her brother and sister were gone, the other children would be safe. Kate raced along the hall to the basement stairs, leaping down the steps three at a time. On returning to the Edgar Allan Poe Home for Hopeless and Incorrigible Orphans, the first thing Kate had done was to wrap the *Atlas* in two heavy-duty plastic bags and, with Michael and Emma standing lookout, sneak down to the basement. Using a spoon from the cafeteria, she had pried out three loose bricks from the wall behind the furnace and placed the *Atlas* inside.

The basement was empty, and Kate retrieved the scarred spoon from under the furnace and began to pry free the bricks. At first, Kate had come down regularly, in the middle of the night, to check that the *Atlas* hadn't been disturbed. But she had not visited the basement in months. The truth was, no matter where she was, Kate could feel the presence of the *Atlas*. She was bound to the book; it was a part of her now. And as she dropped the last brick onto the floor and drew out the heavy, plastic-wrapped package, her hands trembled with excitement.

There were perhaps forty men and women gathered beneath the tent, the sun shining through the yellow canvas giving them a distinctly malarial hue. The men wore blue blazers with gold buttons and had identical red turtles sewn onto their breast pockets. The women favored long, shapeless sundresses and broad-brimmed hats, all of which were in various states of floral explosion. There was a table set with plates of gelatinous yellow cake and bowls of liquefied ice cream. Another table offered pitchers of iced tea and lemonade. A string quartet, sweating through their tuxedos, played languidly in the corner.

Michael immediately spotted Miss Crumley through the crowd. The orphanage director was wearing a dress the color of egg yolk and talking to a woman with the longest, thinnest neck Michael had ever seen—her head looked as if it were balanced atop a noodle—and a short, doughy sort of man. He had doughy hands, doughy cheeks; even the rolls of skin at the back of his neck had a white puffiness, as if he were only wanting another half hour in the oven and he would be cooked and ready to serve. The man was talking loudly and waving his fork, and from the way Miss Crumley hung on his every word, Michael guessed that this must be Mr. Hartwell Weeks, president of the historical society, in the doughy flesh.

"Reenactments!" he announced, twirling his fork. "Reenactments, my dear Miss Crummy—"

"Crumley," the orphanage head corrected.

"—that's how you sell history to the masses! You want to join the bus tour, you need a high-class reenactment!"

"Yes, quite," cooed the noodle-necked woman as her head swayed this way and that.

"Re-*what?*" Miss Crumley leaned in. "I don't understand."

Michael came up behind the group, nervously gripping and regripping the strap of his bag. How was he supposed to get her to give him the keys to her office? Should he say there'd been a fire? Or a flood? He had to think of something fast.

"Reenactments! Pick a historical event and act it out! Put on a bit of a show! Now, your place here"—the man flicked his fork in the direction of the orphanage, accidentally tossing a bit of cake onto the hat of a nearby woman—"why is it historically significant? Hmm? What's it got going?"

"Well, it was built in 1845—"

"Boring! I'm asleep already!"

"Then it served as an armory during the Civil War—"

"Better, better. Keep going, Crummy! This is the stuff!"

"And it was attacked by Confederate forces!"

"Ha! Jackpot!"

"Oh yes!" Michael could see Miss Crumley warming to her subject, a mustache of sweat glistening on her upper lip. "And can you believe it, those beasts shot cannonballs at the north tower! That's where I keep my office! Why, just imagine if I had been there!"

She did not explain how this might have been possible.

Michael felt a cool breeze brush the back of his neck. The storm was coming. By now Kate would have the *Atlas.* He was running out of time. . . .

"Perfect!" Mr. Hartwell Weeks squatted down, his doughy

palms held out before him. "I see it now! The battle for the orphanage! The heartless rebel forces! The roar of cannon fire! *Boom! Boom!* Dead orphans litter the ground like confetti! You stage it, Crummy—"

"Crumley, please. And it wasn't an orphanage then—"

"Don't let details ruin a good show! You stage the battle and we'll put you on the tour! I've got the Confederate uniforms. I can get you a deal on the cannons. You'd only have to provide the dead orphans!"

"Yes, quite," clucked Noodle Neck.

"Not real dead orphans, of course. We're not savages."

"Miss Crumley," Michael said.

The orphanage director didn't hear him. Her mind was lost amid visions of mock carnage and the busloads of dollars that would soon be arriving at her door.

"Mr. Weeks"—she rubbed her hands together greedily—"doesn't ten dollars a visitor seem a bit cheap? Isn't twelve more appropriate—"

"Twelve? Ha!" The doughy man prodded her stomach with his fork, forcing out a giggle. "You're a hungry one, aren't you? All right then—"

"*Miss Crumley!*"

Conversation around them stopped. Michael saw Miss Crumley stiffen. The spaghetti-necked woman peered down at him, the curve of her neck forming an upside-down U.

"Crummy," drawled Mr. Hartwell Weeks, "I think you've got a dead-orphan volunteer."

Miss Crumley turned slowly about. Her smile had remained

frozen, but her eyes betrayed the fury that was coursing through her. She said, in an only moderately strangled voice, "Yes, my dear?"

"I need the keys to your office," Michael said, nervously adjusting his glasses. "Something . . . very bad is about to happen."

In the end, that was the best he could think of.

"Did you hear?" Mr. Weeks bellowed to the party. "Something very bad! Like what, boy? You think Johnny Reb is going to attack again? By gum, I wish he would! I'd show those rebel dogs a thing or two! Ha! Like that!" He jabbed his fork at an ancient man who was supporting himself on a pair of canes, shouting, "Go back to Dixie!" as the old man tried to hobble away.

Miss Crumley brought her face down to Michael's, lowering her voice so that only he could hear.

"Listen to me, you little fiend, you turn around right this instant and go back inside. You hear me?"

"No, you don't understand—"

"I said turn around!" She was hissing, showering Michael with spittle. "Unless you want the same treatment as your hoodlum of a sister—"

Suddenly, a woman's hat blew off her head and cartwheeled across the lawn. Then a pile of napkins, stacked neatly on a table, blew away, first one by one, then in twos and threes, and, finally, in a great fluttering mass, like a flock of birds taking flight.

"I say, Crummy"—Mr. Hartwell Weeks was pointing with one doughy finger—"those are some nasty-looking clouds."

And the entire party turned to look just as the tide of black clouds blotted out the sun. It was as if night had fallen in an instant. There was a collective gasp, and Michael's heart sank as he saw the clouds swelling higher and higher, like the gathering of some great dark wave. Then he smelled the tang of ozone and looked to see a gray wall of rain sweeping toward them from across the playground, swallowing up everything in its path, and Mr. Hartwell Weeks, scourge of the Confederate army, shrieked, "Run for your lives!" and the party exploded into chaos. Rain pummeled the tent. Michael was knocked to the ground, and, as he struggled to rise, he could hear the orphanage director screaming, "It's just a shower! It will blow over! I have gelato!" But the guests were running across a swampy lawn already littered with dozens of trampled sun hats, and no one paid her any mind.

Michael had just gotten to his feet when he was seized by the arm and wrenched around.

"This is all your fault!" Miss Crumley's hair was a sodden wreck. Lines of green mascara streamed down her cheeks. Her guests were gone. Even the musicians had run away, clutching their instruments. "I don't know how, but I know this is your fault!"

It occurred to Michael that for once the woman was absolutely correct. But before either could say another word, a gust of wind whipped across the lawn, and the tent, which had broken free of its anchors, rose into the air like a giant yellow sail. In a panic, Miss Crumley released Michael and grabbed at one of the loose ropes. She was lifted off her feet and carried along, with a hard bounce here and there, till she finally let go and dropped, face-first, into a puddle.

Michael immediately ran to her side.

"Help me up!" the woman commanded. She was covered in mud, she'd lost both shoes, and her dress was ripped. "Help me up, you villain!"

"I'm sorry about this," Michael said. "Honestly." And he reached into her pocket and pulled out her keys.

Miss Crumley's cries of "Thief!" followed him to the door of the orphanage.

Inside, it was pandemonium. Children ran about in the darkness, shrieking with delight at the wildness of the weather.

"Michael!" Kate appeared out of the crowd, breathless, her eyes wide with alarm; she was holding the *Atlas* tight against her chest, not caring who saw it.

"Did you get—"

"Yes!"

And it was then, as Michael held up the ring of keys, that they heard the first scream. It came from outside, still some distance away; but it cut through the rain and the wind and froze every child in the hall. Michael looked at his sister; they both knew what had made the sound: a *morum cadi*—a Screecher— one of the reeking, half-alive monsters they had fought in Cambridge Falls. And now, as the cry tore through the orphanage, Michael felt the familiar suffocating panic.

It's really happening, he thought. They've found us.

The scream died away. The children in the hall came back to life; but the fear was on them, and they clung to one another and cried. Kate snatched the keys from Michael's hand and took off running down the hall, shouting for him to follow.

Miss Crumley's office was in the north tower, atop a steep

corkscrew of stairs. Michael and Kate raced upward in darkness. Soon, they could hear Emma above them, hammering at the office door, crying, "Let me out! Let me out! Someone help!"

"Emma!" Kate shouted. "It's us! We're here!"

She found the keyhole by touch, and a moment later, the door was open and Emma, the youngest of the family, their little sister, was in her arms.

"You're okay?" Kate asked. "You're not hurt?"

"I'm fine! But did you hear the scream?"

"I know." And Kate stepped into the office, motioning for Michael to follow her and shut the door.

Miss Crumley's office was a small, round room with four windows spread out evenly from the door. There was a desk, two chairs, a steel filing cabinet, and, propped against the wall, a chipped wooden wardrobe.

"Kate!"

Emma was at one of the windows; Michael and Kate rushed over as lightning shuddered across the sky. Far below them, three figures had emerged from the woods and were moving across the asphalt yard toward the orphanage. The children recognized the Screechers' jerky gait. All three of the creatures held naked swords.

Kate quickly told them her plan. She would have the *Atlas* take them to Cambridge Falls. If they left, the other children at the orphanage would be safe.

"Hurry," Kate said. "Take—"

Just then the window shattered, and a half-decayed gray-green hand reached in and seized Kate by the arm. Emma screamed and grabbed Kate's other arm, the one that was holding the *Atlas*. Through the broken window, Michael could see the black shape of the Screecher as it clung to the wall of the tower.

"Michael!" Emma shouted. "Help me!"

Michael jumped forward, hugged Kate around the waist, and began pulling her away from the window. Gusts of rain blew into the office. For a moment, Michael thought they were gaining ground; then he looked and saw that the creature was still gripping Kate's arm and had actually begun to crawl into the room.

"Stop!" Kate said. "You're just pulling it in! Let me go!"

"What?" Michael's face was still buried in her side. "No! You—"

"Let go! I know what I'm doing! Now! Do it!"

There was such command in her voice that Michael and Emma both released her. The Screecher had half its body inside the room, its fingers digging into the flesh of Kate's forearm. A deep hiss gurgled from its throat. Michael saw his sister work several fingers between the pages of the *Atlas*, and he realized what she was going to do.

Kate looked at Michael and their eyes met.

"Remember," she said, "whatever happens, take care of Emma."

"But—"

"Remember your promise."

And then she and the creature both vanished.

"Kate!" Emma cried. "Where'd she go?"

"She . . . she took it into the past," Michael gasped. "Like she did with the Countess. She took it into the past to get rid of it."

His heart was hammering in his chest. He placed a hand on the desk to steady himself.

"So why didn't she come back?" Emma's face was wet, whether from rain, or tears, or both, Michael didn't know. "She should've come back right away!"

Emma was right. If the *Atlas* had worked as it should have, and Kate had left the Screecher in the past, then she should've returned to the exact moment she'd left. So where was she?

The cry of a Screecher echoed up the tower, and they heard boots pounding on the stairs, growing closer and louder. The children backed away from the door.

Michael heard Emma shout his name.

What was he supposed to do? What could he do?

Then the door flew open, revealing the dark, ragged form of a Screecher, and at that same moment, a pair of hands seized the children from behind.

CHAPTER THREE

The Devil of Castel del Monte

"And here we are."

They stepped out into a narrow alley. Crumbling stone walls bounded them on either side and ran down to an empty square. Behind them, the alley ended in a high stone wall, in the middle of which was the wooden door they'd come through. Raising his eyes above the wall, Michael could see a grove of olive trees climbing up the hill. The sky was a perfect deep blue, and the air was hot and dry and silent. Michael glanced at his sister; Emma was taking in their new surroundings and appeared unhurt. That, at least, was something.

Michael turned to the man beside them.

He was tall and thin, with unruly white hair, a rather shabby tweed suit, and a dark green tie that looked as if it had recently escaped a fire. The stem of an old pipe poked from the pocket of his jacket, and he wore a pair of bent and patched tortoiseshell glasses. He was exactly as Michael remembered.

Straightening his own glasses, Michael coughed and put out his hand.

"Thank you, sir. You saved our lives."

Dr. Stanislaus Pym took the boy's hand and shook it.

"Of course," said the wizard. "You're most welcome."

As the Screecher had crashed through the door of Miss Crumley's office, Michael had felt a hand on his shoulder and had whipped his head around, thinking that another of the *morum cadi* had snuck up behind them and the end had come. But the hand on his shoulder, like the hand on Emma's shoulder, had not belonged to a Screecher. To his complete surprise, Michael had seen the wizard, Stanislaus Pym, leaning toward them out of the wardrobe, and before Michael could utter a word, he and his sister had been yanked inside and the door had slammed shut. Michael had found himself in darkness, crushed between the side of the wardrobe and the wizard's elbow. His nostrils had been filled with the smell of Dr. Pym's tobacco and the moist, cabbagey odor of Miss Crumley's shoes. Out in the office, the Screecher was heard tossing aside chairs as it leapt toward them; then Dr. Pym had murmured, "One more turn," there had been a sharp click, and just as Michael had been certain that a sword was going to come splintering through the wardrobe wall, Dr. Pym had pushed open the door and both the Screecher and Miss Crumley's office had vanished, replaced by stone walls and blue sky and silence.

"Would you two stop shaking hands?!" Emma shouted. "What's wrong with you?"

Michael released the wizard's hand. "I was just being polite."

"Dr. Pym!" Emma's voice was high and desperate. "You have to go back! You have to find Kate! She—"

"Used the *Atlas*. I know. Tell me exactly what happened."

As quickly as they could, Michael and Emma told him about the storm, about being trapped in the tower, how the Screecher had grabbed Kate, how Kate and the creature had both disappeared. . . .

"She must've tried to take it into the past," Michael said, and he told the wizard—who, due to his abrupt departure from Cambridge Falls eight months earlier, was still in the dark regarding certain events—how the Countess had reappeared on Christmas Eve and how Kate had discovered that she could use the *Atlas* without a photograph, how she had taken the witch deep into the past and abandoned her.

"I'm sure she did the same thing with the Screecher," Michael said. "Only she didn't come back."

"So you gotta find her!" Emma cried. "Hurry!"

"Yes, of course," said the wizard. "Now, if you go straight ahead, on the other side of the square is a café. Wait for me there."

"But, Dr. Pym," Michael had to ask, "where are we?"

"Italy," came the answer.

And with that, the wizard turned and stepped toward the wooden door through which they had come. Michael was confused. Where was Miss Crumley's wardrobe? How were they suddenly in Italy? Where was Dr. Pym going? Then he saw the wizard take an ornate gold key from his pocket, slide it into the lock, step across to the other side of the wall, and shut the door behind him. There was the same distinct *click* as before. Curious, Michael walked over, listened for a moment, then opened the door.

A goat stared back at him.

"He'll find her." Emma hadn't moved, but she was hugging herself as if she might fall apart at any moment. "Dr. Pym will find her."

Michael said nothing.

Together, they walked silently down the alley. When they got to the square, Michael saw they were on the side of a hill and that the town was of no size whatsoever. A church loomed on their left. A white dog loped past. Across the square stood the café. It had a red awning and two empty tables out front.

A curtain of colored beads hung over the door, and the children passed through them into a well-lit, tile-floored room, with rough rock walls like the inside of a cave. The café was half filled with older men and women, and there was a woman with gray-black hair pulled into a bun who wore a faded green dress under a white apron. She was shorter than either Michael or Emma, and she moved about like a gnat, buzzing here and there, depositing bottles of wine and water, picking up dishes. Spotting the children, she herded them to a table, speaking in rapid Italian, and, without being asked, brought over two glasses and a bottle of fizzy lemonade.

"It'll be okay," Michael said. "It's Kate, remember?"

Emma didn't respond. Her face was tense with worry. But she reached out and took hold of Michael's hand.

The children sat there for nearly an hour, their lemonade

bubbling softly before them. Groups of men and women drifted into the café. The men were lean and hard-faced and wore ancient dark suits, white shirts, and old black hats; they looked like men who'd been outside their entire lives. The women were dark-haired and dark-eyed and had hands worn thick by work. The tiny woman in the apron bullied them all. Pushing them into chairs. Bringing them food and wine they hadn't ordered. And Michael could see that the men and women loved it; the more the tiny woman bullied, the more laughter and conversation filled the restaurant.

The place was a good place, Michael thought. A refuge. And he understood why the wizard had sent them here.

Emma leapt to her feet, and Michael turned to see Dr. Pym stepping through the curtain of beads at the door.

Michael felt his heart twist upon itself. The wizard was alone.

Dr. Pym lowered himself into a chair.

"Well, you'll be relieved to know that the *morum cadi* have quit the orphanage, and neither your Miss Crumley nor the other children were harmed."

"And?" Emma cried. "Where's Kate? You said you'd find her!"

Conversation around them stopped; the old men and women looked over.

The wizard sighed. "I did not find her. I am sorry."

Michael gripped the wooden leg of the table and took several slow, deep breaths.

"So maybe you didn't look hard enough!" Emma's voice was now the only sound in the restaurant. "Maybe she's not at the orphanage! You gotta keep looking! We'll go with you! Come on!"

She began to pull the wizard out of his chair.

"Emma." The old man's voice was quiet and calm. "Katherine has not returned to the present. Not to Baltimore or anywhere else—"

"You don't know that—"

"Yes, I do. Now please sit down. You're attracting attention."

Emma grudgingly released his arm and threw herself into her chair. The talk at the other tables resumed. The tiny woman buzzed over, set a glass of red wine before the wizard, and darted away.

"We must look at the situation logically." Dr. Pym kept his voice low. "Let us say that Katherine did indeed use the *Atlas* to travel into the past and dispose of that foul creature. Why did she not return immediately? Perhaps something or someone prevented her—"

Emma struck the table with her fist. "So we've gotta help her! That's what I'm saying! We've gotta do something!"

"She's right," Michael said. "We need to come up with a plan! We—"

"But the point you must both understand"—the wizard leaned forward—"is that if your sister is trapped in the past, then there is absolutely nothing that you or I or anyone else can do about it. She is beyond our reach. That is a fact, and you must accept it."

Michael and Emma opened their mouths to argue, but nothing came out. The hard finality of the wizard's statement, the cold, precise way it was delivered, had robbed them of speech.

"However," and with this Dr. Pym reassumed his normal, grandfatherly air, "I do not think that is what happened. Your sister is one of the most remarkable individuals I have ever met—which, considering how long I have been alive, is saying quite a bit. No matter the obstacles, if there is a way for her to return to you, she will find it."

"So . . ." Emma's eyes were welling with tears, and she'd clasped her hands to keep them from shaking. ". . . Why didn't she?"

The wizard smiled. "My dear, who's to say she hasn't?"

"You! You just said—"

"Aha!" Michael exclaimed.

Both Dr. Pym and Emma looked at him.

"You know what I'm going to say?" the wizard asked.

"Well . . . not exactly," Michael admitted. "But it just felt like . . . Sorry."

"Allow me to explain about the nature of time." The old man dipped his finger into his wineglass and dabbed a string of watery red spots across the tabletop. "You must not imagine that time is a road unspooling before us. Rather, all time—past, present, and future—already exists. Say we are here." He pointed to a dot in the middle of the line. "And your sister was here in the past; then she chose to skip over us and land here, in the future." He brought his finger down further along the line. "In that case, we just have to go forward, and we will eventually meet her."

"You mean," Michael said, "tomorrow, she'll just suddenly be there?"

"Tomorrow, the next day, the week after that—there's no telling when."

"But why would she do that?" Emma demanded. "Why wouldn't she just come back right away?"

The old man shrugged. "Who knows? We will have to ask her when we see her. Till then, we must continue with our own work. It is what she would want."

Michael saw Emma nodding. The wizard had held out a thread of hope, and she had grasped it with both hands. For his part, Michael tried hard to make himself believe that Kate was waiting somewhere in their future; he wanted to believe it, desperately. But what if Dr. Pym was wrong? What if they never saw Kate again? He saw life stretching ahead of them, a life without their sister, and the road was dark.

He took a sip of his lemonade, then set down the glass. The drink had gone flat.

Dr. Pym checked the time and suggested they order dinner. He spoke to the small woman—the signora, he called her—in Italian while Emma looked about the restaurant saying, "Get some a' that! And what that bald guy's got over there!"

It was amazing, Michael thought, the change that had come over her. Emma had embraced the wizard's theory wholeheartedly. She'd decided that Kate had jumped into the future, and they had only to keep pressing forward and they would join her. Any other possibility had been dismissed from her mind.

Nice to be young, Michael thought, and gave a weary sigh.

As the food began to arrive—pasta with sausage and peas, a salad of red and yellow tomatoes covered with hunks of soft white cheese and green strips of basil, a pizza heavy with garlic and onions and tiny fish that Emma picked off and put on her brother's plate—Michael did his best to make a show of eating, but each bite was an effort.

"Now," the wizard said, rolling up his pizza like a taco, "I want to apologize that I was never able to answer your letters. Be assured, I did receive them. However, we are together now, and I want to hear every detail of your lives since Christmas, everything you didn't tell me in your letters. I am all ears."

The children protested that he should answer their questions first, but the wizard insisted, and they finally gave in, telling him about the awfulness of the Edgar Allan Poe Home, about the awfulness of Miss Crumley, about the feral cat population that had dwindled all summer and the mystery stew the cook kept serving, about the week in July when the showers had broken and how people a block away had complained about the smell; one story led to another, and when they were finished, Michael found that his neck and shoulders were less tense and that he'd eaten two helpings of pasta and that things did not seem quite so black as before and he realized that this had been the wizard's plan all along.

"How perfectly terrible," Dr. Pym said. "Now, I'm guessing you must have a few questions for me."

"Yeah," Emma said through a mouthful of sausage. "Where've you been all this time? Where's Gabriel? Why'd you leave all of a sudden on Christmas? Who's this stupid Dire Magnus guy? And where's he keeping our parents?"

"And what're we doing here?" Michael added.

"My goodness, what a deluge. But I will answer the last question first. Oh dear." The wizard had been biting into a thickly ribbed pastry, and a large gob of cream had landed on his tie. He looked about for his napkin—it was right in front of him—and, not seeing it, wiped the cream off with his finger, and then plopped it in his mouth. "So, we are here, in the charming village of Castel del Monte, to see a man. As it happens, I was on my way here when I received a letter from your sister—"

"The one she sent today!" Michael said. "What did it say?"

"I will get to that later. But I immediately diverted my course to Baltimore and then, once I had you in hand, it just seemed easier to bring you along. As to Gabriel's whereabouts, he is on a mission for me, the same mission, one might say, that drew the two of us away so abruptly last Christmas. I prefer not to go into more detail at the moment."

"What a surprise," Emma said. "Hey, can we get another of those cream donut things? 'Cause you kinda hogged that one."

Before Dr. Pym could ask, the signora placed one in front of Emma.

"What about our parents?" Michael said. "Have you found out where they're being held?"

"No," the wizard said. "No, I'm afraid I haven't."

The mood once again became somber. None of them spoke. The silence was finally broken when a bell began tolling in the square. Dr. Pym clapped his hands.

"And that is our cue. Your other questions will have to keep."

He summoned over the small signora and spoke to her in Italian. Michael took a moment to look through his bag. There was *The Dwarf Omnibus*, King Robbie's medal proclaiming him Royal Guardian of All Dwarfish Traditions and History, his journal, pens and pencils, a pocketknife, a compass, a camera, and gum. He'd always made a point of keeping his bag fully packed for just such an emergency, and he felt a warm throb of satisfaction at seeing everything in its place.

Suddenly, there was a shattering crash, and Michael looked up and saw that the woman had dropped a large dish, spraying noodles and tomato sauce all over the tile floor. She gestured to Michael and Emma and let out a burst of Italian. She seemed to be imploring the wizard. Dr. Pym responded, and the woman crossed herself several times quickly. The entire restaurant had fallen silent.

"What's going on?" Emma whispered.

Michael shook his head; he had no idea.

"Children," Dr. Pym said, laying several bills upon the table, "we should leave."

Every eye followed them out of the restaurant. In the square, they were alone, save for the white dog from before, and even it seemed to regard them warily. The setting sun cast the world in a soft amber glow. "This way," Dr. Pym said, and he headed down the main street at a rapid pace. The village ended after only a hundred yards, and Dr. Pym turned up the hill, leading the children through a gate and into a grove of olive trees. The ground was dry and rocky and steep.

"Dr. Pym," Emma huffed, "what happened back there? What's going on?"

"I told you that we are here to see a man. What I did not say was that I have been searching for this individual for nearly a decade. Only recently did I finally track him to this village. You heard me asking the signora how to find his house."

"That's it? That's what made her drop the plate?"

"Yes, it appears that he is regarded by the locals as something of a devil. Or perhaps *the* Devil. The signora was a bit flustered."

"Is he dangerous?" Michael asked. Then he added, "Because I'm the oldest now, and I'm responsible for Emma's safety."

"Oh, please," Emma groaned.

"I wouldn't say he's dangerous," the wizard said. "At least, not very."

They hiked on, following a narrow, twisting trail. They could hear goats bleating in the distance, the bells around their necks clanking dully in the still air. Stalks of dry grass scratched at the children's ankles. The light was dying, and soon Michael could no longer see the town behind them. The trail ended at a badly maintained rock wall. Affixed to the wall was a piece of wood bearing a message scrawled in black paint.

"What's it say?" Emma asked.

The wizard bent forward to translate. "It says, 'Dear Moron'—oh my, what a beginning—'you are about to enter private property. Trespassers will be shot, hanged, beaten with clubs, shot again; their eyeballs will be pecked out by crows, their livers roasted'—dear, this is disgusting, and it goes on for quite a while. . . ." He skipped to the bottom. "'So turn around now, you blithering idiot. Sincerely, the Devil of Castel del Monte.'" Dr. Pym straightened up. "Not very inviting, is it? Well, come along."

And he climbed over the wall.

Michael thought of asking whether it might not be wiser to call ahead, but Emma was already jumping down on the other side, and he hurried to follow. They had not gone ten yards past the wall when there was a *crack*, and something zipped through the branches above their heads. Michael and Emma fell to their stomachs.

"Do you know"—Dr. Pym had stopped walking, but was otherwise standing perfectly straight—"I think he just shot at us."

"Really?" Emma said. She and Michael were flat on the ground. "You think?"

Another *crack*, and a chunk of bark flew off a nearby tree.

A voice shouted down something in Italian.

"Oh, honestly," Dr. Pym said, "this is ridiculous." He called up the hill, "Hugo! Will you please stop shooting at us? It is extremely irritating!"

There was a long moment of silence.

Then the voice demanded, this time in English, "Who is that?"

Keeping his head low, Michael peered up the slope. There was a small stone cottage just visible through the trees, but he couldn't see where the man was hidden.

"It's Stanislaus Pym, Hugo! I would like to speak with you!"

There was a harsh laugh. "Pym? You dunderhead! Couldn't you read the sign? Trespassers will be shot! Now about-face and take your doddering carcass down the mountain before I do the world a favor and put a bullet through that oatmealy mishmash you call a brain! Ha!"

"Hugo!" The wizard spoke as if to an unruly child. "Do you really think I've traveled this far just to go away? I'm coming up!"

Michael thought he could hear the man muttering angrily.

"Hugo!"

There was a bellow of rage, and then, "So come up, why don't you?! I always knew that respect for personal property was beyond your limited mental capacity!"

And there was what sounded like someone furiously kicking a tree.

Dr. Pym looked down at the children. "It's safe now."

"Are you sure?" Michael asked.

"Yeah," Emma said. "Maybe you should go first."

"It's fine. Trust me."

The children rose and brushed the dirt from their arms and legs. It was another fifty yards to the cottage, but the man didn't appear till they were ten feet from the door, when he stepped from behind an overturned cart. His appearance was in every way striking. He had a short, wide body and a wide face. His clothes looked much worn and little washed. His hair and beard were wild and black and neither had been trimmed for some time. Thick brows obscured his eyes, but the message in them was clear: this man was ready to fight the world. He held a rifle in his left hand.

"Stanislaus Pym," the man sneered. "Isn't it my lucky day? Surprised it only took you ten years to find me. You must've had help."

"You should not have disappeared, Hugo. It made things very difficult."

"And you should try not being such a great pompous carbuncle! But the world is not a perfect place."

Then he turned and pushed through the door of the cottage. Dr. Pym and Emma followed, Emma immediately pinching her nose against the smell. Michael came last, pausing just inside the door. Beside him was an old wood chest, and on the chest was a framed black-and-white photograph. In it were two men in long black robes standing before a stone building. The taller of the men was also the younger by a dozen years, and he held what looked like a rolled-up diploma. He wore wire-rimmed glasses, and his hand rested on the shoulder of the second man, a short, heavyset man with wild black hair. The black-haired man was the Devil of Castel del Monte.

Just then the real Devil of Castel del Monte appeared and slapped down the photograph.

"No snooping," he growled.

Michael stood there another few seconds, waiting for his heart to stop pounding in his chest. He had no idea why the wizard had brought them there, or who the black-haired man was. But one thing he did know: the tall young man in the photo was his father.

CHAPTER FOUR
Dr. Hugo Algernon

"Shut the door, my boy, if you would."

Michael wondered if that was such a good idea. The man's cottage smelled like a barn. And in fact, an entire half of it was covered in piles of dirty straw and appeared to have been ceded to the goats. Three of the animals idled near the back wall, eating their dinners and watching the visitors with dull expressions. The left side of the cottage seemed designated to the man's use. Besides the chest, there was a lumpy-looking mattress. An old wooden table and two chairs. A battered gas lantern. A fireplace in which a few glowing logs lay smoking. A collection of unwashed pots, pans, cups, plates, bowls. And hundreds of books. Many of the books showed signs of having been chewed on or partially eaten, perhaps by mice or the man's four-legged roommates or, Michael could almost imagine, the man himself in various fits of rage.

As Michael closed the door, the man was wrestling with a goat that was munching its way through a sheaf of papers.

"Let go, you scoundrel! I'm warning you, Stanislaus!"

It took Michael a moment to realize that the man was speaking to the goat.

"Hugo," the wizard said, smiling, "did you name this little fellow after me? I'm touched."

"Don't be," the man grunted, still engaged in a tug-of-war over the pages. "He's the stupidest goat in Italy. I wanted his name to adequately reflect the depth of his ignorance! Yours was the obvious choice— *Arrgh!*"

The goat had jerked backward, and the man lost his grip and thudded onto his rear. With a bleat of triumph, the goat clattered out the open back door and across the hill, whipping the pages this way and that.

"Ten years I've been working on that book!" the man shouted, jumping up and shaking his fist at the departing goat. "Anytime I make the least progress, one of those idiots goes and eats it. Though they're probably better judges of the material than the so-called experts." He glanced at Dr. Pym. "Present company included, of course."

"So is that what you've been up to all this time?" the wizard asked. "Writing a book? What is it about, if I may ask?"

"It's called *A History of Stupidity in the Magical World,* and needless to say, you figure prominently. I even thought of including your photo, but I didn't want to scare off potential readers. Ha!"

"I certainly have made my share of mistakes," the wizard replied.

"Listen to him! Mr. I'm-So-Reasonable! If I were you, Pym, I doubt I'd ever stop punching myself in the face!" A small kettle hung on an arm above the fire, and the man poured himself a cup of the hottest, blackest coffee Michael had ever seen. It bubbled from the kettle's mouth like boiling mud. The man said he would offer them some, but he was afraid that would give the impression he wanted them to stay. Then, without warning, he whirled about and fixed his fierce gaze on Michael.

"Do I know you?"

"No," Michael said awkwardly. "We've . . . never met."

"Hugo, these are my friends Michael and Emma. Children, this is Dr. Hugo Algernon."

"Yes, yes, yes," the man said, crashing onto a chair. "Let's just get this over with. What is it you want? Recruiting me for another of your boneheaded schemes? You may as well forget it. You hoodwinked me once, but never again!"

The wizard had pulled up the second chair, while the children had found seats on an upside-down washbasin, which, by all appearances, had never been used.

"I am here," Dr. Pym said, "for two reasons. But I must say how exasperating it has been to have to track you down—"

"No one asked you to."

The wizard sighed. "I am here to give you a warning. And to ask a question."

"A warning? From you? Ha! Let's have it!"

"Jean-Paul Letraud and Kenji Kitano are both dead."

Michael could see that the news had an effect on the man, even though he tried to act as if it didn't.

"Murdered?"

"Yes."

"When?"

"Jean-Paul I found out about on Christmas Day. Kenji was a few weeks after."

Michael looked at his sister and saw the same expression on her face that he imagined was on his. "Dr. Pym—"

"Yes, my boy, that was what called me away on Christmas. Jean-Paul and Kenji were both friends and fellow magicians. I would've told you earlier, but the signora's café did not seem the appropriate place to go into detail."

"Who was it?" Michael asked. "I mean, who killed them? Was it—"

"Who killed them?" the hairy man roared. "Who do you think killed them? The Dire Magnus! The Undying One! The—"

"Yes," Dr. Pym said, cutting him off. "Or, more specifically, his followers."

Hugo Algernon leapt up and began stalking back and forth, smashing his fists together and snarling. "This wasn't supposed to happen, Stanislaus. Do you remember? I do! I remember! I remember when you brought us all together." And he imitated, poorly, the wizard's voice, "'We must act now. We must end his power once and for all.'" He let out a harsh laugh. "That worked out well, wouldn't you say? Ha!"

"It did work," the wizard said calmly. "His power was greatly diminished."

"Oh, diminished, yes, diminished. Tell that to Jean-Paul and Kenji. I'm sure they'll agree with you. Diminished, ha!"

Dr. Pym sighed. "I did not come to argue, but merely to tell you to take precautions. He is tracking down all who once stood against him."

"What's he talking about?" Emma said. "What're you talking about?"

"My dear—"

"Emma's right." Michael tried to sit up and look as older-sibling-esque as possible. "I'm sorry, but you're always saying how now's not the time to explain stuff, and then you take us someplace and we have no idea why we're there and crazy people shoot at us—no offense, Dr. Algernon—but it's not fair! Who's the Dire Magnus? What's he want? What're you two talking about? We deserve to know what's going on!"

This was one of the longer speeches Michael had ever made, and when he finished, he was out of breath. Emma was staring at him, wide-eyed with amazement.

"Ha!" Hugo Algernon smacked the table. "The boy's got spirit! Go on and tell them, Pym! Tell them everything you've managed to learn about the Dire Magnus in thousands of years! It shouldn't take more than ten seconds!"

The old wizard frowned, but finally nodded. "Hugo is trying to be cantankerous, but he makes a fair point. Our—my—knowledge of the Dire Magnus is sadly incomplete. I believe him to be a man. And a powerful sorcerer, certainly. Beyond that, he is a mystery. His origins. His true name. I cannot tell you. What I can say is that I have been upon this earth since the first cities rose in the desert and there has always been a Dire Magnus. His power waxes and wanes. He rises and is beaten back. And since the Books were created, it has been his one goal to possess them."

"Not bad," the man said. "Twenty seconds. You knew more than I thought."

The wizard continued, "I have, over time, made attempts to confront him. The last was forty-odd years ago. I gathered together a group of magicians, wizards, witches, mages—Dr. Algernon here among them. We hunted him down. We fought him. Many of our friends fell. But we prevailed. He was destroyed."

Hugo Algernon let out another dismissive "Ha!" and threw his empty mug over his shoulder, starting a small stampede of goats out the door.

"Or so we believed." Dr. Pym rubbed at his eyes. "What we found was that death was not a prison for such as he. Even trapped in the land of the dead, his spirit continued to wield influence and power over his followers."

"And now," said Hugo Algernon, "he's settling scores."

"He is doing more than that, my friend. He is building an army." The wizard looked at the children. "You asked about Gabriel. While I have been tracking down and warning those who once helped me fight the Dire Magnus, he has been monitoring the enemy's movements. Since you last saw him, he has been in almost constant danger." Dr. Pym turned back to the man. "The enemy's strength is growing, Hugo. You can hide on this mountain and say the world is filled with fools. But a war is coming. And it will find even you."

For a moment, the fierce, bearded man seemed checked. Then his mouth curled into a sneer.

"Warning received and already forgotten. Now, what's your question? Be quick. I've got to find your namesake before he eats the rest of my book. I've come up with a new chapter while you've been talking. It's called 'Paranoid Old Fools'! Ha!"

"Very well," the wizard said. "I would like to know about the last time you saw Richard and Clare Wibberly."

Outside, the shadows had begun to lengthen, and Dr. Algernon turned on the lantern. Before setting it on the table, he held it to Emma's and Michael's faces. He stared at Michael for several long moments.

"I knew it. You're the spitting image of your father."

"Really?" Michael could feel himself grinning. "I mean . . . really?"

"I said so, didn't I? Are you deaf?"

"No—"

"You look just like him. Don't make me say it again." He looked at Emma. "The two of you twins?"

"No!" Michael said, somewhat hotly. "I'm a year older."

"Well, technically," Emma said, "we're both twelve. Technically."

Michael was about to argue when the man spoke.

"Where's the third one, Pym? There's supposed to be a third."

"Sadly, she was unable to join us tonight. But we expect to see her again soon."

"Yeah," Emma said. "Very, very soon."

The man grunted and placed the lantern on the table.

"I don't know what Pym's told you. Not much, I wager. But most of us who trafficked as magicians ended up straddling two worlds, the magical and the mundane. We had actual jobs; some idiots had families. Besides my other, call them *extracurricular* activities, I taught folklore and mythology at Yale. Your father was a grad student. And unlike most of the students, he was not a total idiot. I could tell right away he knew that magic was real. You get that in folklore departments. People have figured out the truth, but they can't come to college and study magic. So they study folklore and myth, sensing that those stories reflect how the world used to be. That was your dad.

"I was foolish back then, almost as foolish as Dr. Pudding Brain here. I thought that magic had a chance. That people like your dad could help. So I brought him along. Taught him everything I could. I remember he had an unusual affection for dwarves—"

"Dwarves?" Michael nearly jumped to his feet. "Really? I have a certain, call it *interest* in dwarves."

"He means he's in love with them," Emma said.

"Was he fond of anything in particular?" Michael asked eagerly. "Granted, there's so much to choose from. Where do you even start. . . ."

Hugo Algernon scratched at his beard. "Well, he was always

quoting this one line from old Killin Killick. Something about a great leader—"

"Lives not in his heart, but in his head!" Michael finished. "I know that quote! I was just talking about it today! Unbelievable." He clapped his hands together, smiling from ear to ear. Not only did he and his father both admire and esteem dwarves, they'd also each separately singled out the same quote. If that wasn't a sign of, well, something, then Michael didn't know what was. "Do you remember how he felt about elves? I imagine he thought they were pretty ridiculous—"

Dr. Pym coughed. "Perhaps we could stay on subject. Hugo, if you could continue?"

"Fine, fine. So in his second year, I told Richard about the Books of Beginning." Hugo Algernon looked at Dr. Pym. "How much do they know about the Books?"

"I'm sure they would be interested in anything you have to say."

"Here's what you need to remember: the Books of Beginning are three incredibly old and powerful books of magic. If you believe the stories, they could literally remake the world. Most reports start with the Books in the Egyptian city of Rhakotis, guarded by a gaggle of what had to have been the most mossy-brained magicians of all time—granted, that's just my opinion, though I'm no doubt correct. Everything's fine till one day—this is about twenty-five hundred years ago—Alexander the Great shows up, burns the city to the ground, and the Books vanish.

"So, your dad hears all this and gets a bee in his bonnet.

Why have the Books never been located? How amazing would it be if he found the Books? On and on. I told him to forget it. People had been looking for the Books for thousands of years, real magicians and wizards, and no one had ever found diddly-squat.

"Anyway, Richard took his degree, left, got married, decided the world wasn't crowded enough, and had you sardines—I mean, children. Next thing I know, Pym here's taken him up. Read some article your dad wrote. Thought he'd made this big discovery." Again mimicking the wizard, he spoke into a pretend telephone, "'Oh, cheerio, Hugo, I've found the most promising young man, tut-tut, I'm such a great galumphing booby.' He was my student first, you—"

"Just finish the story, Hugo."

The man scowled but went on. "So time passes, and one day, I'm in Buenos Aires. There was this old wizard who'd lived down there. Mad as a hatter, but an excellent archivist and a collector of rare manuscripts. He'd died, and I was going through his library. House was a wreck. Held together by dust and mouse droppings. Anyway, I'm there working when the library floor gives way. Almost broke my neck. But when I could finally look around, I saw I'd fallen into a kind of vault. Stacks of old books and documents. I spent a year going through and cataloging everything, and then . . . I find a letter. It was in an extinct Portuguese dialect. Thing was murder to translate. But I had a feeling about it. A man writing to his wife. Apparently, he was on some kind of eighteenth-century business trip. Buying pigs or llamas or something. And he writes how he'd gotten into town late and all the inns had been full and he'd had to share a room with a sick man. His roommate was feverish. All night, he raved how he and a few others had taken a magic book out of Egypt long ago and had hidden it away. He kept saying, 'I must make the map. . . . I must draw the map.'"

"And then what happened?" the wizard asked.

Hugo Algernon shrugged. "Nothing. The rest of the letter was about a pig he'd bought and how plump it was and blah, blah, blah."

"And where did this encounter take place?"

"In Malpesa."

"Ah."

"What's Malpesa?" Michael asked.

"Malpesa," the wizard replied, "is a city at the southern tip of South America, on the coast of Tierra del Fuego, the Land of Fire. It was first an Indian village, then became a colonial trading post, a stopover for ships going from the Atlantic to the Pacific. Then, when the magic world pulled away, Malpesa went with it." The old man turned back to Hugo Algernon. "So when you read this letter and realized what it meant, why did you contact Richard and not me?"

"Because, you great ninny, you're impossible to get ahold of! I thought Richard could find you! And"—he glanced at Michael and Emma and some of the energy and fury seemed to go out of him—"I knew about the children. Richard had told me who they were. That they were the children of the prophecy, the three who would finally bring the Books together and fulfill their destiny."

Michael felt his spine tighten. In Cambridge Falls, the Countess had mentioned the prophecy to Kate. Only the witch hadn't said what the Books' destiny actually was, or what it meant for the three of them.

Hugo Algernon went on. "When I got back to the States, I called him. A week or so later, Richard showed up at my house in New Haven. Clare was with him. Must've been close to midnight. I knew something was wrong. But he insisted I tell him what I'd discovered. And I did."

"When was this?"

"Christmas. Ten years ago. A day after his family had supposedly disappeared." Hugo Algernon looked at Michael and Emma. "I imagine I was the last person to see your parents."

The door behind the children had blown open, but no one moved to close it. Michael felt a cool wind against his neck. Emma was clenching his hand.

Michael reflected that he and Emma knew more about their parents' fate than ever before. But there were still so many questions. Had their parents reached this city, Malpesa? Had they found the map? Who had this sick man and his comrades been? And then there was the mystery of the book itself. Dr. Pym had taken the *Atlas* out of Egypt—Michael remembered his story of keeping it safe for a thousand years before entrusting it to the dwarves—so of the two remaining books, which one was this? What were its powers? For the thousandth time, Michael wished that Kate were with them.

The wizard rose and shut the door, then returned to the table. He said, "There's more, isn't there?"

Hugo Algernon rubbed his dirty fingers through his beard and nodded.

"I didn't find out that Richard and Clare's family had gone missing till a few days later. I tried to get in touch with you. Obviously, that was pointless."

"Tell us about it," Emma muttered.

"I talked to some of the others. Jean-Paul, for one. I didn't tell them anything. Just that I needed to talk to you about Richard and Clare. Maybe someone was listening. Maybe there was a traitor. I don't know." As the man spoke, he dug his fingernails into the wood of the table. "Must've been a week later. I get a knock at the door. I open it, not thinking anything; and there he is. Smiling." Hugo Algernon raised his head and looked at the children. "You two ever see a man coming—huge, bald, not a hair on him—run. Run, and don't ever stop running."

"It was Rourke," the wizard said.

"Yeah. It was Rourke." The man went back to digging his nails into the table.

"What happened then?"

"What happened then? You want to know how much I fought before I betrayed my friends? Oh, I fought all right. But he was too strong. And I could feel him in my head. He was laughing the whole time. I heard myself telling him that Richard and Clare had gone to Malpesa. I woke up the next morning and realized that not only had I betrayed my friends, but Rourke had broken something in me. I'd never been a great magician, we both know that, but whatever I'd had was gone. I walked out of my house. Never called anyone. Just . . . disappeared."

And Michael suddenly understood why this man had spent ten years in a lonely cottage on a mountain in Italy. He wasn't hiding from the Dire Magnus. He was hiding from what he'd done, from himself. Michael felt a strange, powerful sympathy for him.

"Then why hasn't Rourke found the book?" Dr. Pym asked. "He must have the information you gave Richard and Clare."

Hugo Algernon shook his head. "I gave them a charm that would wipe all knowledge of the book from their memories. They must've used it before they were caught. I should've taken better precautions with myself. As it was, all Rourke got from me was the name Malpesa."

"You didn't tell him about the sick man? Or the map?"

"No. I betrayed my friends, but the secret of the book, I buried deep. Even he couldn't find it."

"You shouldn't have told him anything!" Emma cried, pounding the table with her small fist. "You should've said nothing!"

The man nodded and said, "You're right, child. That's what I've been thinking about for the past ten years."

Dr. Algernon got up and walked to the fireplace. He pulled out a loose stone, then reached in and removed a folded moleskin packet.

"These are my original notes. I keep them hidden so the goats don't eat them. I always knew you'd find me sooner or later." He handed the packet to the wizard. "There may be a war coming,

Stanislaus. But I'm no good to you. The magic's left me." Then he turned to face Michael and Emma. "If you find your father, tell him I'm sorry. Tell him that Hugo Algernon's just an old fool."

Dr. Pym stepped to the door and fit his ornate gold key into the lock. He turned it four times to the right, seven to the left; there was a *click*, and he pushed the door open. Sunlight flooded the cottage. Michael and Emma found themselves looking out over a vast expanse of blue water, with the sun poised in the distance. But only the doorway was illuminated; the cottage's windows remained dark.

"This way, children."

Michael took one last look at the Devil of Castel del Monte. He sat at the table, petting a small goat that had come up to nuzzle his leg. "Dr. Algernon—" The wild-haired man lifted his head, and sunlight intended for some other place in the world revealed his eyes for the first time. They were dark brown and very sad. Michael said, "We're going to find them." And he was about to step across the threshold when the man said, quietly, "Hold a second."

Hugo Algernon went to the framed photo Michael had seen earlier and removed the backing. "Here." He pushed the photo into Michael's hands.

Michael looked down at his father, young, smiling, filled with hope. He pulled out his *Dwarf Omnibus* and slipped the photo between the pages. "Thank you."

The man nodded and turned away; Michael stepped through the door.

They were on top of a cliff. Dr. Algernon's door, now closed behind them, had become the door of a whitewashed house with red shutters. Flowers spilled from window boxes, filling the salty air with a sweet aroma. Michael looked out over the water, to where the sun hung upon the horizon. Was it sunrise or sunset?

"Dr. Pym—"

"We are in Galicia, in northwest Spain." The wizard slid the golden key into the pocket of his jacket. "This house belongs to a friend of mine. He's away, but we'll spend the night here and tomorrow head to Malpesa."

"Will Kate be there?" Emma asked. Michael could tell she was trying not to sound too hopeful, but hoping desperately all the same.

"We'll see, my dear."

And Dr. Pym placed a gentle hand on her shoulder and led her into the house.

The children sat at the kitchen table while Dr. Pym prepared glasses of warm milk and distracted them with stories of the strange things he had seen in his travels, stories that at any other time Michael would've been furiously copying into his journal. At one point, Dr. Pym switched on the light above the table, and Michael glanced out the window and saw that night had fallen; and the exhaustion of a day that had begun in Baltimore with him and Kate running before a storm settled upon him. He felt as if his head were made of stone; his arms and legs weighed thousands of pounds. However, once they'd drunk their milk and the glasses stood drying in the rack, and Emma had hugged Dr. Pym and headed up to bed, Michael found himself lingering in the kitchen.

"Yes, my boy?" Dr. Pym was packing his pipe. "What's troubling you?"

"Who was that man who hurt Dr. Algernon? Does he work for the Dire Magnus?"

"His name is Declan Rourke, and, yes, he is one of the Dire Magnus's lieutenants; indeed, his chief lieutenant, and a very dangerous and, in my opinion, unbalanced individual."

"And you think he's the one who . . . took our parents?"

Dr. Pym had his pipe going, and the sweet, almondy smell filled the kitchen.

"I'm afraid so. I think they followed Dr. Algernon's clues, and somewhere in their search, Rourke caught them." He shook his head sadly. "Richard and Clare believed that finding the Books was the only way to keep you and your sisters safe, and everything else, including their own lives, was secondary."

Michael nodded. He still made no move to go upstairs. He found he had been winding the strap of his bag around his finger and had somehow gotten it into a knot so that the tip of his finger was turning blue. He yanked it free, and the color slowly returned.

"Anything else, my boy?"

"What did that letter say? The one Kate sent you? That made you come to Baltimore?"

"She'd been having a dream. She saw an orphanage attacked by the Dire Magnus's forces. She'd recognized it as somewhere the three of you had lived. She knew it was only a matter of time before he found you. Why do you ask?"

"I just . . . She made me promise to take care of Emma. It was like she knew she wasn't going to be here. I just wondered if she'd said something."

"As a matter of fact, she did."

"What?!"

"Several months ago, she wrote to me about another dream she'd had. In it, you were holding a book she didn't recognize. Emma was with you, and the two of you were surrounded by fire."

"And Kate wasn't there?"

The wizard shook his head. Michael still made no move to leave. He began fidgeting again with his strap.

"I know the real question you want to ask."

Michael looked up.

"You want to ask about the prophecy Dr. Algernon mentioned, how it was foretold that three children will bring the Books together and fulfill their destiny. The truth is, I do not know what that destiny is."

"You could guess, though, couldn't you?"

"Perhaps. But I will not. This is what you must understand: the magic in the Books is without equal. It is the power to alter the very nature of existence, to reshape the world. Imagine that power in the hands of a being whose heart is filled only with hate and anger. With such power, the Dire Magnus would have dominion over every living creature. That is why our quest is so important. And why so much depends on you."

Michael said nothing; he felt as if his chest was being squeezed by iron bands.

"But Katherine believed in you, and so do I. Now, I foresee a demanding day ahead of us, and you need your sleep."

By the time Michael got upstairs, Emma was already in her bed and the light was off. Michael maneuvered by moonlight, doing his best to be quiet.

Emma spoke to him from the darkness.

"Michael?"

"Yes?"

"Do you really think Kate's waiting for us in the future?"

Michael took a deep breath and wondered what Kate would want him to say.

"Yes," he lied, "I do."

"Me too."

Michael kicked off his shoes and got into bed. He set his bag on the floor. The window was open, and he could hear the far-off sound of the sea hitting the rocks.

"Michael?"

"Yes?"

"Don't leave me, okay?"

"I won't."

Soon afterward, Michael knew that his sister was asleep. But exhausted as he was, he lay there, long into the night, watching the moon move across the water, thinking about their parents and how they had disappeared, thinking about Kate lost somewhere in time, thinking, again and again, how it was now all up to him.

Kate, he thought, where are you?

CHAPTER FIVE
Rafe

"Nah, look, she moved; she ain't dead."

"Poke her again."

Kate felt something jab her in the ribs. She stirred and tried to push it away.

"See? Told you she ain't dead!"

"Too bad. We'd a' gotten five dollars for her if she was dead."

"How five dollars?"

"Rafe says you can sell dead bodies to the doctor college. They give you five dollars each one."

"What they want dead bodies for?"

"So's they can cut 'em open and look at their guts and all."

"Five dollars, huh?"

"Yeah. Poke her again."

The voices belonged to children, boys. Kate thought it best to speak up before they got any ideas.

"I'm . . . not dead."

She forced her eyes open and pushed herself into a sitting position. Her head, indeed her whole body, was throbbing. She felt as if she'd run a marathon, gotten in a fight, and then been systematically pounded on for several hours. Even her teeth ached. She took in her surroundings. She was lying on a wooden floor, and the room about her was cold and small and the only light was what filtered through a pair of filthy windows. Two boys were leaning over her. She guessed they were about ten. Their faces and hands were streaked with dirt. Their clothes had been patched, torn, and then patched again. They both wore cloth caps. One of them held a stick.

"I'm not dead," Kate repeated.

"Nah," said the one, not bothering to hide his disappointment, "I guess you ain't."

"Where am I?"

"You're on the floor."

"No, I mean, where is this?"

"What're you talking about? You're in the Bowery."

The whites of the boy's eyes stood out against the dirtiness of his face.

"The Bowery." The name was vaguely familiar, but she couldn't place it. "Where is that?"

"She means what city," said the boy with the stick.

"Come off it," the other said, finally smiling, forgetting the five dollars he'd have gotten for Kate's corpse. "You don't know what city? You're in New York."

"New York? But how—" And then she remembered.

She remembered being with Michael and Emma in Miss Crumley's office, and the storm outside, and the Screecher breaking through the tower window and seizing her arm, and she remembered how she had called upon the *Atlas* for the first time in months, and her terror as the magic had swept through her.

She remembered opening her eyes and finding herself on a beach under a blazing sun as three wooden ships with tall white sails approached across a sea of brilliant, shimmering blue. She remembered the pain in her arm telling her that the Screecher had not let go. And Kate remembered how, without thinking, she had called upon the magic a second time, and a second time it had flowed through her, and a moment later, she and the creature were struggling atop a stone wall. It had been night; there'd been fire and smoke and shouting, a city in flames, and still the creature had gripped her arm. And Kate remembered how frantic she'd been, knowing that her plan wasn't working, knowing that she was getting weaker. And she'd called on the magic a third time, thinking, Please, help me, and suddenly she'd been standing in a muddy field under a sky of gray. There had been more screaming, and another sound, like insects whizzing past her face, and still the creature held on. And Kate remembered the explosion and the feeling of being lifted into the air. . . .

And then she remembered nothing.

And then she remembered waking up in the mud, and men with guns running past, their mouths open and screaming, though all she could hear was the ringing in her ears, and she remembered seeing the Screecher sprawled ten yards away and the *Atlas* between them, and how the creature had begun crawling toward the book, and she remembered knowing that her life depended on getting there first, and knowing also that the creature was closer. And she remembered the second explosion, the one that had knocked the monster away, and how, with one final effort, she had reached out and laid her hand upon the book.

Kate lurched to her feet.

"Where is it?"

"Where's what?"

"My book! I had a book! A green book!"

The floor was covered with piles of dusty rags, dented cans, yellowed scraps of newspaper, rotted-out burlap sacks; Kate tore through it all, tossing things left and right so that the two boys were forced back against the door.

"What've you done with it? Where is it?"

"We didn't take no book!" said the boy with the stick.

"Yeah, what'd we want a book for?" said the other, as if having or wanting a book was the silliest idea in the world.

An awful thought occurred to Kate.

"How . . . long have I been here?"

"Dunno."

"When did you find me? It's important!"

"Couple hours ago. You were just lying here. I went to get Jake." He nodded at the boy with the stick. "Figured if you were dead, we could get the wheelbarrow, take you down to the doctor college. We coulda used five dollars."

Kate couldn't breathe. She pushed past the two boys and through the wooden door. Pale sunlight blinded her, and she threw up an arm. She looked about, blinking. She was on a rooftop; a maze of low buildings stretched out in all directions. The room she'd woken in was a kind of shed. The air was bitingly cold. She could see her breath before her. Ice and old snow crunched beneath her feet. Dressed for summer, Kate could only hug her arms tight to her body.

She stepped to the edge of the roof and looked down. The building was just six stories high, and she could make out huge snowdrifts funneling people along sidewalks. In the street, horses were pulling carts, undisturbed by the presence of cars and buses. Kate listened for engines, horns, the squeal of tires; but the only sounds were of people and carts and horseshoes. She scanned the horizon. There was not a tall building in sight.

Her heart began to beat faster, and a memory came to her. Michael had been trapped in the past, held prisoner by the Countess, and she and Emma had gone back to rescue him. They'd been in the past scarcely half an hour when the *Atlas* had faded and vanished before their eyes. Kate remembered the witch explaining how the *Atlas* belonging to that time had exerted its dominance, that two copies of the book could coexist for a brief period, but eventually, one would vanish.

The boy said that he'd found her two hours ago. The book was long gone.

A hand grabbed her arm and she whirled about, thinking the Screecher had somehow followed her. It was one of the boys.

"You gotta be careful. You're gonna fall."

Kate stepped back from the edge. "What's the date?"

"December something."

"I mean, what year is it?"

"You kidding?"

"Just tell me."

"It's 1899," the other said. "How don't you know that?"

Kate said nothing. She just looked out at the white rooftops of the city. She was cold, and alone, and she was trapped in the year 1899. How was she ever going to get home?

The boys—their names were Jake and Beetles (no explanation)—said that seeing as things hadn't turned out as they'd hoped and she appeared to be more or less alive, she had to come and see Rafe. Kate told them that she didn't know who Rafe was and she had no intention of going to see him. The only thing that mattered—she thought this, but didn't say it—was finding a way back to her brother and sister.

"Where're the stairs?"

"You can't just go off," Beetles said. "Anyway, you'll freeze."

The boy had a point. While he and his partner each had on two jackets, multiple shirts, and heavy-looking wool trousers (every article patched and raggedy, but no less warm for that), Kate wore just an old pair of sandals and a sleeveless summer dress. She was already shaking. She was also, she noticed, covered in dried mud.

"Fine. Where"—her teeth had begun to chatter—"where can I get a coat?"

"Over on Bowery."

"I thought I was in the Bowery!"

"I mean the street. Come on!"

The boys led her to the fire escape, a rickety, rusting skeleton flimsily attached to the side of the building, which they raced down pell-mell, setting up a great rattling and shaking. Kate hurried after them, certain that at any moment the whole contraption was going to break free of its moorings and plunge into the alley. A ladder at the bottom stopped nine feet off the ground, and the boys dangled from the last rung and dropped, landing catlike on their hands and feet. Kate did her best to follow suit, but found herself hanging in midair, unwilling to let go.

"Come on!" the boys yelled. "It ain't far! Come on!"

She grunted in pain as her feet struck the frozen stones and a shudder passed through her ankles. She stood, the heels of her hands stinging.

"Finally," Jake said. "I thought you were gonna set up house there or something."

"Maybe open a shop, huh?" said Beetles.

"Yeah. The Hanging-at-the-End-of-the-Ladder-Too-Scared-to-Let-Go Shop!"

"You're hilarious," Kate said. "Just show me where to get a coat."

They led her down the alley and across the street that Kate had seen from the roof of the building. Her sandaled feet sank deep into the drifts, and hard crusts of snow scratched her bare legs. She tried not to notice the stares she got, a girl in a thin dress in the middle of winter, and she followed her two guides down another alley and out into a street that was wider than the first and lined end to end with stalls. Throngs of darkly clad men and women milled between the ramshackle booths as vendors stood about, extolling the qualities of their goods in one language after another.

"This here's Bowery," said Beetles. "You can get a coat here."

"I don't—I don't have any money."

Now that they'd stopped moving, Kate was trembling badly.

"You got anything you can trade?" Jake asked. "What about that locket?"

Kate's hand went to her throat, her numb fingers fumbling at the gold locket. Her mother had given her the locket the night their family had been separated.

"I . . . I can't. . . ."

"What else you got?"

But Kate had nothing else. Her mother's locket was the only valuable thing she owned. And she was freezing, literally freezing to death. She could ask for help from the people walking past, but that would require explanations: who she was, how she had come to be here. . . .

"The chain's gold. I can trade the chain. But I'm keeping the locket."

The boys took her to a mute old man who examined the chain, nodded, and gave Kate a shabby, moth-eaten coat and a wool hat. She pulled them both on, grateful, and her shaking began to subside.

"All right," Jake said. "We helped you. Now you gotta come see Rafe."

Again, Kate refused.

"Rafe ain't gonna like it," Beetles said.

"I really don't care what Rafe likes."

And she turned away down the line of stalls. She was still shivering slightly, the cold being very cold and her new coat and hat very thin and ragged; but she had held on to her mother's locket and she was not going to freeze to death. That was all that mattered. So what if she couldn't feel her toes?

Your problem now, she told herself, is getting home.

Her copy of the *Atlas* had disappeared because another copy already existed in this time. Kate knew where that copy was—far to the north, in the mountains surrounding Cambridge Falls, it was locked in a vault beneath the old dwarf city—and her first thought, back on the roof when she'd realized her situation, had been to make her way north and retrieve the book. But she'd quickly abandoned that plan. The copy in the vault had to be there for her and Michael to discover in the future. It felt strange to be protecting events that were still a hundred years off, events that in her mind had already taken place; but such were the ironies of time travel. And truth be told, Kate was relieved that she wouldn't be swimming through the long underground tunnel that led to the vault. The last time she'd done it, she'd watched a dwarf get pulled down by the creature that lived in the depths, and she was not at all eager to go back.

Her second idea was, on the surface, much simpler. Find Dr. Pym and have him send her home. The Countess had helped Kate travel through time without the *Atlas*; the witch had tapped into the magic inside her, the power of the *Atlas* that was, even now, coursing through her veins. Kate was certain that Dr. Pym could do the same. But how to go about finding him? Could the dwarves help? Michael had said that a dwarf might live for hundreds of years. Was it possible that Robbie McLaur was alive? Surely he would be able to contact the wizard. Once again, it seemed that Kate's only hope lay in going to Cambridge Falls. But it was a daunting journey. She would need to take the train to Westport (provided that trains in this time ran to Westport). Find passage across Lake Champlain. Then there was the long road into the mountains. And she would need money to buy tickets and food and, as soon as possible, shoes and socks and a sweater and . . .

She willed herself not to panic. One step at a time. She could do this.

She sensed the boys coming up beside her, and glanced over to see them each juggling a blackened, smoking potato. They passed their prizes from hand to hand, blowing on them until they were cool enough to crack open, an act the pair performed with relish, inhaling as the released steam rose into their faces.

"You want some?" asked the boy named Jake.

Before she could answer, he'd ripped his in half and handed it over. The skin of the potato was black and flaky, but the inside was soft and smeared with a greasy, buttery fat, and as she ate it, Kate felt herself warmed, and she was grateful to the boy for sharing. She felt no ill will toward them for hoping to sell her corpse. They were clearly very poor, and in 1899, five dollars was no doubt a fortune.

As the trio threaded their way through the crowded market, Kate found herself wondering who the boys were. Did they have families? Unlikely. Their clothes were too hodgepodge, their faces too dirty. Perhaps they lived in an orphanage? Also unlikely. Kate knew what orphanage children looked like. Even the rebellious ones had an anxiousness that these boys lacked. So where did they live? Who protected them?

They reached an intersection. A bone-thin, dark-haired man stood in the midst of a small crowd, talking loudly in a language Kate didn't understand. He had a long black beard, no shirt, and in his left hand, he held a flaming torch. With a cry, the man ran the torch over his pale, sunken chest, down his other arm, over his head, and suddenly the whole upper half of his body, including his long beard, was engulfed in flame.

Kate was about to scream, to call for water, when the small group of spectators began clapping their mittened hands. And she saw that the man's skin was neither burning nor blackening; indeed, he appeared to be grinning. What was going on?

Then she heard:

"Dragon eggs! Real dragon eggs! Raise your own dragon!"

Coming toward her was a red-faced, frazzle-haired woman whose hands and forearms were marked with burn scars. The woman carried a basket lined with old hay in which were nestled three enormous eggs. The eggs were dark green and leathery, each one the size of a grapefruit, and they were all smoking ominously.

"Dragon eggs!" the woman called, continuing down the street. "Three weeks from hatching! Makes a wonderful companion!"

Kate turned to the boys, who were licking butter off their fingers and seemed totally unfazed.

"Did you see that?"

"See what?" asked Jake.

"What do you mean, what? That man's on fire! People are clapping! And that woman's selling those . . . eggs!"

The boy shrugged. "That's Yarkov. He's always setting himself on fire."

"And I bet those ain't real dragon eggs," Beetles said. "You'd probably end up with a chicken or something."

Kate was so stunned by their reactions that she involuntarily took a step back and was jostled sharply.

"Oi! Watch it, you nit!"

She looked around and saw a stocky, bearded figure whom she immediately recognized as a dwarf. He had a dead goose draped over each shoulder, and the birds' long necks hung limply down his back. Grumbling about tourists, the dwarf marched away, the goose heads bobbing at his heels.

Kate managed to say, "That's a dwarf."

"Course it's a dwarf," said Beetles, who was now cleaning his teeth with a match. "What else would it be?"

"But—" Kate stammered. "—But—"

And then she understood, remembering the day that she and Emma had sat with Abraham beside his fire in the mansion in Cambridge Falls and the old caretaker had told them how the magic world had once been a part of the normal world, but then the magic world had pulled away and hidden itself. According to Abraham, the division had happened on the last day of December in 1899. That meant—

"It's all still here," Kate said. "Magic is still here."

"Not here." Beetles jerked his head in the direction the dwarf had taken. "The magic quarter's that way."

"Show me."

A minute later, Kate was standing at the end of a block of tenements. The muddy street was crammed with makeshift stalls, vendors were hawking products, shoppers were bundled up and hurrying against the cold. For being the magic quarter, Kate thought it all looked very normal. Then she noticed that one of the tenements, a reddish building with a wide front stoop, kept switching places with the building to its right, the result being that it was slowly making its way up the street. And she saw that another building shivered each time the wind blew, and that the windows of another—this made Kate very uneasy—kept winking at her.

And besides the average-looking men and women going about their shopping, Kate saw dwarves moving through the crowd, smoking their long pipes and attracting no notice whatsoever. And there were other creatures, smaller than dwarves and beardless, who wore furry caps and stood arguing in tight groups, poking one another with their tiny fingers. Kate watched them in amazement till a woman passed by carrying a basket and drew her attention. The woman was sweet-faced and grandmotherly, and Kate was about to smile at her when she saw that the woman's basket was alive and squirming with snakes.

"Come on," said Jake and Beetles, and they each took an arm and led her forward.

The first stall sold wigs of fairy hair in different colors: gold and silver, pure snowy white, a rather arresting pink. The next stall promised to remove curses. The one after that let you buy curses (boils, baldness, pursued by cats . . .). There were three or four stalls occupied by fortune-tellers, one of whom was a girl of Kate's age who watched her closely as she went by. There was a stall that sold toads, tended by a man who looked like a toad himself and called out his wares in a deep, reverberating croak. There was a large tent where four shirtless and sweating dwarves hammered away at anvils with a rhythmic clinking and banging while another dwarf worked the bellows of a fire so hot that Kate actually unbuttoned her jacket. There was a tent devoted to eggs: not just dragon eggs, but also unicorn eggs, griffin eggs, manticore eggs, and eggs of animals that Kate had never heard of. There was a stall whose entrance was covered by a tarp, with a dense green smoke escaping from under the canvas, the tendrils crawling across the slush and cobblestones. Kate followed the boys' lead and stepped carefully past. Another tent was stocked with thousands of stoppered glass bottles, and the boys informed her that this was where you bought glamours. A glamour, they told her, was a potion that let you change your appearance, and many of the more eye-stopping magical folk used them when they went among normal humans. As Kate and the boys passed by, a tall, thin man with green, scaly skin like a fish downed the contents of a clear glass vial and was instantly transformed into a short, pudgy man with brown hair. And there was a stall that was stacked high with wooden boxes and had a sign declaring THINGS THAT BITE. When they'd passed the stall for the third time without having doubled back, the boys told her that it was a trick some vendors used, making their stalls appear again and again. And there were tents where men and women in dark cloaks who had strange markings on their faces and hands were huddled and muttering over boiling black cauldrons that smelled of dead fish, burning hair, and sickness. Kate kept well clear of these.

As they'd walked, the street had veered and become even darker and narrower; Beetles now plucked at her sleeve.

"We should go back."

"Why? There's more—"

"Here on out is Imp territory. It ain't safe."

"Who're the Imps?" Kate asked.

"The Imps is the Imps. The gang what controls this part a' the Bowery. They only been here a few months, but they're bad, real bad."

"Real, real bad," said Jake.

"We should go back and find Rafe."

"Yeah, no foolin' anymore; Rafe's gonna want to talk to you."

Kate didn't respond. A plan had begun forming in her mind. Couldn't any wizard or witch send her through time? Maybe she didn't need Dr. Pym. Maybe she didn't have to go all the way to Cambridge Falls. Her eyes fell on a woman in a dark green shawl who sat before a covered booth. She had brown hair that was streaked with gray, and there was a softness in her eyes that appealed to Kate. She pulled free of the boys and walked over.

"Excuse me?"

The woman looked up. "Yes?"

"I'm sorry," Kate said haltingly. ". . . Are you . . . a witch?"

"I am. Do you need help?"

"Yes. Please."

"Well, come in. Let me see what I can do."

The woman stood and opened the canvas flap. Kate hesitated, wondering if she was being rash. But the thought was fleeting. Cambridge Falls was a long and difficult journey, and this woman was right here.

The woman smiled, as if guessing Kate's thoughts.

"I promise, child, I don't bite."

Nodding, Kate stepped into the stall. She glanced back and saw Jake and Beetles gesturing for her to come away. Then the witch dropped the flap and shut them out.

"First things first, you want tea. You look half frozen. Have a seat; there's a chair behind you."

To Kate's surprise, the inside of the booth was warm and cozy. Three or four overlapping rugs shielded them from the cobblestones. A squat black stove, its pipe snaking up through the roof, heated the stall nicely. There was another armchair opposite the one Kate occupied, and beside that, a wooden cabinet from which the woman was taking a small earthenware jar. She opened the jar, extracted a handful of green-black leaves, and stuffed them into a pot that was bubbling on the stove. The smell of peppermint filled the air.

"Lovely," the woman said. "Always reminds me of Christmas."

"I don't have any money," Kate said. "I don't know how I'll pay you—"

The woman gave a dismissive wave. "Worry about that later. What seems to be the problem? Is it a boy? I'm quite famous for my love potions."

"No, it's not a boy."

"Trouble with your parents? You wish they'd be more under-standing? Move your feet closer to the stove."

Kate obeyed; her toes had begun to thaw, and they ached as the feeling returned.

"It's . . . not my parents."

"Perhaps a beauty charm. Though I don't think you could be much prettier." She handed Kate a steaming mug of tea. "Drink up now."

"I need to go to the future."

The woman stopped and looked at her, making no attempt to hide her surprise.

"That's not a request I get every day. And why would you want that?"

"It's . . . where I'm from. I came here by accident."

The woman sat in the other armchair. The booth was small enough that she and Kate were knee to knee. Her eyes were deep blue and gentle.

"My dear, I think you'd better tell me what happened."

Kate dropped her gaze to the untouched tea. "It's compli-cated. I can't . . . tell you everything. But the magic that brought me here, some of it's still in me. You can use it to send me home. Someone did it before. She . . ."

"What's wrong, child?"

The stall was becoming uncomfortably hot. Kate felt herself sweating.

"Nothing. I'm fine. Can you help me?"

"Well, I won't pretend I'm the greatest witch in the world.

But there's certainly magic in you. I sensed it the moment you walked in."

"So you'll send me back?"

Kate hated how desperate she sounded. And the fact was, something was wrong. Her vision had begun to blur. The woman's face swam before her.

"Are you sure you're feeling well? Let me have that before you drop it."

The mug was taken from her hand. Kate started to rise. She needed to get out. She needed cold air to clear her head.

"Where are you going, child?"

"I just . . . I need . . ."

And then she pitched forward into darkness.

When she woke, she heard voices and, for a moment, thought she was back in the rooftop shed and that the voices belonged to Jake and Beetles. But these weren't boys' voices. They were harsh and guttural, and spoke as if the very act of making words was foreign and unnatural. Then she heard the witch's voice.

"You're not cheating me out of this one. She's special."

Kate opened her eyes. She was lying on the ground, her cheek resting on one of the rugs. There was a cloud inside her head. The witch had drugged her. Something in the tea fumes. How long had she been unconscious? Past the iron legs of the stove, she made out two pairs of muddy boots.

"We never paid no hundred dollars. You know that."

The voice sounded like a wild animal that had been taught to speak. Every word was a growl. Kate had to get away. Praying that no one was watching, she began to inch toward the door.

"I'm telling you," the witch said, "this one has magic in her. Deep magic. More powerful than any I've ever seen. He'll want her. Believe me; he'll want her."

"Seventy dollars."

"A hundred. And if he thinks she's not worth it, I'll return the money."

"People are saying crazy things now," snapped the harsh voice. "Everyone's trying to get what they can before the Separation."

"This is nothing like that. A hundred dollars is fair."

"Fine. But if he ain't happy, we'll be back."

Kate knew she was out of time; she would have to make a dash. She tried to push herself up, but her arms gave way. She was too weak. Too weak to run, too weak to fight. Then leathery, sharp-nailed hands were grasping her under the shoulders and heaving her to her feet. Kate saw the witch counting a wad of money.

"Please . . ."

The witch smiled, her eyes as gentle as ever. "You should've just asked for a love potion, child."

Kate was dragged out the back of the tent and onto a crowded sidewalk. To her dismay, the cold air did nothing to clear the fog in her head, and she struggled to catch the attention of the people walking by.

"Please . . . help me. . . ."

"Quiet," growled one of her captors. "No one cares."

And so it seemed. For as they yanked her stumbling along the sidewalk, passing eyes would glance up, see what was happening, and quickly turn away. Kate could hardly blame them. She'd now had a chance to see her kidnappers. In some respects, they looked like short, thick-bodied men, dressed in dark suits and overcoats, their round hats pulled low. But these were not men. Their skin was like the hide of an animal, rough and hard and dimpled. Their nails were thick and sharp. Stiff whiskers shot straight from their cheeks, while their lower jaws jutted up and out, displaying a pair of short yellow tusks. No, not men. So what were they? And what did they plan to do with her?

"Where're you . . . taking me?"

"To the boss. Now shut it, or we'll rip your tongue out."

They jerked her down a narrow alley. It was dark and empty, and the sounds of the street soon faded away. Kate didn't know when she'd started sobbing. She was just suddenly aware that she was shaking and that it had nothing to do with the cold. What was going to happen? To her? To Michael and Emma? To their parents? Why had she been so stupid! Why hadn't she just gone to Cambridge Falls and found Dr. Pym! She'd doomed them all!

And to make matters even worse, the witch's poison had returned. A deadness was spreading through Kate's arms and legs. She stopped walking, but her captors simply dragged her on, her feet scraping over the cobblestones. She knew she could not stay conscious much longer. She had no strength left to fight.

Then came the sound of something moving through the air. There was a hard *thunk*, and the creature on Kate's left grunted and fell. Released, Kate tumbled to the ground. She turned to see the other creature spinning, growling, a knife already in its hand. Too late, the creature sensed the cord that had looped around its neck, and as a figure leapt down from above, the cord snapped tight and the creature was yanked to its toes. The cord, Kate saw, had been strung through the bottom of the fire escape, and the figure now took his end and wrapped it around a pipe protruding from the building's wall. Kate's captor was left dancing on tiptoe, clawing at the noose about its neck.

The figure was a boy. He looked to be about Kate's age, or perhaps a year older. He had unkempt black hair, pale skin, and a nose that had been broken at least once. He was dressed lightly for the cold, but was not shivering. Kate watched as he went to the fallen creature and wrenched a knife out of its back. He cleaned the blade on the creature's coat and slipped it into a sheath at the back of his trousers. Then the boy gave the snarling creature at the end of the cord a kick that sent it dancing across the alley. Finally, he looked at Kate, who had not moved from where she lay on the ground. Stunned as she had been by his sudden appearance, the boy—judging from the way he stopped and stared—was even more stunned by her.

He said, ". . . It's you."

Kate didn't know what to say. She had never seen this boy before.

He pulled her to her feet.

"We need to move. There'll be more Imps coming. Can you walk?"

"Who . . . are you?"

"My name's Rafe."

The name echoed in the dark cloud of her mind.

"The boys . . ."

"Yeah. They got to me."

"But . . . how do you . . . know me?"

They were hurrying down the street; Kate was leaning against him. She could feel herself slipping. And, as the darkness closed in, she heard:

"Doesn't matter. You shouldn't have come. . . ."

CHAPTER SIX
Malpesa

"Get back!"

"Shouldn't we run—"

"No."

"But—"

"It will think you're food."

That was good enough for Michael, and he pressed himself into the alcove, wedging his shoulder tight against Emma's. He could hear the slow *thud . . . thud . . . thud* of the creature's footsteps coming down the alley, and at each impact, Michael saw dust shake loose from the stone columns of the archway. His confidence wavered.

"Are you sure—"

"Quiet," Emma hissed.

"Indeed," said the wizard.

Before they'd left the cliff-top house in Spain, Dr. Pym had warned the children about what to expect in Malpesa. "Remember," he'd told them, "Malpesa is a city in which normal, nonmagical humans live side by side with dwarves, elves, merfolk, witches and wizards, partially housebroken trolls—"

"Trolls?" Michael had exclaimed, trying not to sound too panicked. "But don't trolls . . . eat kids?"

"I suppose," the wizard had said, "that trolls are somewhat partial to children. But really, the odds of our meeting a troll are so astronomically low, I shouldn't have mentioned it. Banish it from your thoughts!"

Astronomically low, Michael thought as the ground shook and the creature came into view. Right.

The troll was the size of an adult elephant, with the same saggy gray skin and shambling gait, but with none of an elephant's innate intelligence. Indeed, Michael had never seen any creature that projected an air of such perfect stupidity. The troll was busy cleaning one of its enormous ears with a garden hoe, scraping out great boulders of earwax, crusts of greenish bread, a cracked teapot, a bewildered-looking seagull. . . .

"We're lucky," Dr. Pym said when the creature had lumbered past. "At least it was wearing clothes."

Much to the children's frustration, they had spent all day at the house on the coast of Spain. Dr. Pym had told them that Malpesa was infested with the Dire Magnus's spies and they could not risk entering the city till nightfall. The children had argued that they didn't care about the danger, they wanted to find Kate and rescue their parents. "Be that as it may," the wizard had said,

"I have other reasons for waiting till dark." He had refused to explain further; and in the end, Michael and Emma had spent the day listlessly exploring the cliffs and nearby beach as the sun made its sluggish way across the sky.

The wizard had disappeared in the afternoon, returning after dark laden with heavy pants and shirts, sweaters, coats, wool socks, and boots that fit surprisingly well. "It's still winter in South America," he'd said. "We have to dress appropriately."

Then, making use of his golden key once more—and after a final warning that the children must do exactly as he said while in Malpesa—Dr. Pym had led them through the kitchen door and into another land.

More or less immediately, they'd encountered the troll.

As the creature's footsteps faded away, the wizard bid them follow and turned down a narrow alley.

Michael hesitated. . . .

The sun had gone down, but there was still enough light to see, and what he saw was an old colonial town of stone streets and three- and four-story houses with red tile roofs and wide ground-floor arcades. Half a dozen spires and towers rose above the nest of buildings. To Michael's left, the street ran down to a harbor, where a score of fishing boats lay berthed. With their black nets strung up and drying, the ships looked both spooky and elegant, like a gathering of widows. Next to the boats was a pair of small floatplanes, bobbing on the tide. Beyond that stretched the blue-black table of the sea. Looking the other way, Michael saw that the town was walled in by mountains, snowy and massive, their peaks hidden among the clouds.

He was charmed: elegant old buildings, a perfect setting, and best of all, you could walk out your front door and be face to face with a wizard! Or a dwarf!

Michael had already forgotten his terror at the troll's appearance.

I was born too late, he thought, and allowed himself a philosophical sigh.

"Michael!" Dr. Pym's voice echoed down the alley. "Please don't linger!"

The wizard led them along a series of twisting streets. There were patches of ice among the paving stones, and they passed restaurants and stores—grocery stores, clothing stores, a shuttered flower shop—that might've been found in any city in the world, and next door to those were taverns with signs announcing DWARFISH ALE ON TAP and shops that sold charms for seafarers: protections against drowning, fair-weather spells, a potion that let you speak to whales. They saw men and women, bundled up and going about their shopping, and they saw groups of dwarves, dressed in thick, dark coats and woolen hats with long tassels, marching past with clay pipes sticking from their bearded mouths.

They crossed many canals, or rather they crossed the bridges that spanned the canals, so many bridges and so many canals that the city seemed almost more water than land. Most of the canals were only a dozen feet wide, but at one point, the street opened up and the children found themselves at the edge of a wide canal lined with stately columned houses, many of which had seen better days. In the gathering dusk, lights reflected off the dark water, and men called to each other from their narrow, black-hulled boats, their voices echoing as they passed beneath the stone bridges.

"It's like Venice," the wizard said, "without the tourists."

"But with trolls," Emma grumbled.

"Well, given the choice, I'll take the trolls."

"Dr. Pym," Michael said, "can't you tell us where we're going?"

"You'll see soon enough, my boy."

And he started off again with his quick, long-legged stride.

The children knew they were here to search for the map mentioned in Hugo Algernon's letter, the same map their parents had gone searching for ten years before; and it was likewise apparent that Dr. Pym had a theory about where to look, but so far, the wizard had not been forthcoming with details.

"If I tell you where we're going," he'd said—this was still back at the house in Spain—"you'll only start worrying."

As if saying that, Michael reflected, wasn't enough to make a person start worrying.

They pressed on through the maze-like streets, over bridge after bridge, and as they walked, Michael stole a glance at Emma. At breakfast that morning, he'd tried to get her to acknowledge his new authority as oldest sibling, wanting to be clear on the matter before, as he put it, they were "out in the field" and their survival depended on her following his orders "without question."

"But we're both twelve," she'd said.

"Yes, technically. But only for a few more days. I'm basically thirteen."

"So till then we're equal."

"But Kate put me in charge, remember? In Miss Crumley's office, she said, 'Look after Emma.'"

"That's probably because she saw you first. If she'd seen me, she probably would've said, 'Emma, look after Michael! He really needs it!'"

"I seriously doubt that."

"Well, don't worry." And Emma had patted him on the arm. "I'll look after you anyway."

Then she'd gone to throw rocks into the sea, and that was that.

"Here we are," said the wizard.

They had emerged from yet another alley and were standing on a stone embankment, looking out over a seemingly endless stretch of dark water. Michael felt as if they'd arrived at a kind of border: behind them was Malpesa, with its lights and noise; before them, this great emptiness, and no sound save the soft lapping of the sea against stone.

"We have a few minutes," Dr. Pym said. "The bridge will not appear until night has well and truly fallen."

"What bridge?" Michael asked.

"You'll see, my boy. Now, as this may be our last quiet moment of the evening, there is something I need to give you."

From an inside pocket, the wizard produced an object the size and shape of a marble and made of milky blue-gray glass. A thin wire looped about it and attached to a rawhide band, as if the marble was to be worn as a necklace.

"This arrived two weeks ago at the house in Cambridge Falls.

There was no note, but the envelope was addressed to 'The Eldest Wibberly.'"

"Who sent it?" Emma asked.

"That, my dear, is the question. Who knew that you three had been at Cambridge Falls? Of course, there's the Dire Magnus and his followers. But such stratagems are not his style. Another possibility, and it is only a possibility, is—"

"Our parents," Michael said. Due to the strange twists and turns of time travel, the children's adventure in Cambridge Falls had taken place before they'd actually been born, and subsequently, Dr. Pym had told their parents about what was going to happen. "You really think it's from them?"

"I do not know. That is part of what is troubling me."

"What's the other part?"

"That I don't know what the blasted thing is! Still, I've been unable to detect any sort of curse or malignancy, and I believe the time has come to turn it over to you."

Emma immediately reached out her hand, only to have the wizard stop her.

"My dear, it was addressed to the eldest Wibberly, and in the present circumstances, I think it should go to Michael."

Emma huffed, but Michael was pleased.

Finally, he thought.

He took the orb by its rawhide strap. "What do I do with it?"

"We could smash it," Emma suggested.

To Michael's surprise, the wizard nodded. "You'd be surprised how many magical objects give up their secrets when bashed to bits. Unfortunately, that might also destroy it, and if it is from your parents, I would hate to lose the message. Either way, the decision is yours."

Michael sensed them watching him. The glass marble felt light, almost hollow.

"Kate's the real oldest," he said finally. "I'll keep it till she comes back."

He knew it was strange that his first decision as oldest sibling was to pass the authority back to Kate; but saying that he believed his sister would return felt good, like an act of faith, and Michael smiled as he slipped the marble over his head.

"Excellent," the wizard said. "Now I think it is dark enough."

And, turning his back on the city, Dr. Pym took out a coin and threw it into the water. There was a shimmering in the air, and a bridge appeared, arcing away from the embankment. It was made of black granite and guarded by two forbidding stone sentries. The figures were roughly carved, armed with heavy swords, and swathed in long robes and hoods that obscured their faces and hands.

"Over this bridge," the wizard said, "lies an island. For a thousand years, it is where the citizens of Malpesa, magical and non-magical alike, have buried their dead. It is where I hope to find what we are searching for. Come. There is no time to waste."

And he led them past the sentries and out upon the bridge.

It seemed to Michael that the air grew colder with each step, as if they were moving into some deeper current, and as they crossed the top of the bridge's arc, Michael saw the silhouette of an island emerge from the darkness, and the salty tang of the sea became mixed with another smell, the odor of old soil and the cut-up ends of things, of death and decay. At the far side of the bridge, Michael and Emma followed the wizard past two more stone sentries and onto the island of the dead.

Dr. Pym raised his hand. "A moment to get my bearings . . ."

The children hovered behind him, hardly daring to breathe. Standing where he was, Michael had no sense of the island's true size. The tombs and mausoleums—some of which were a dozen feet high and crowned with snowcapped stone figures—crowded in upon one another, leaving only narrow gaps through which to pass. Michael's impression was of an ancient, overgrown forest, dark, and silently watching.

As they waited, Michael's hand drifted to his bag, nervously checking the contents—journal, pens, pencils, pocketknife, compass, camera, King Robbie's badge, *Dwarf Omnibus*, gum. Assured that everything was in place, he brought his hand to his chest, where he felt the hard nub of the glass marble hanging from his neck. Already it felt like a part of him.

A cloud moved, and the moon cast down a pale, unearthly light, which reflected off the patches of snow.

"This way," the wizard said. "Stay close." And he started off through the thicket of tombs.

It was all Michael and Emma could do to keep up. Dr. Pym moved at his usual brisk pace, following a zigzag path that only he could see. And as the group pushed forward, the tombs pressed in and the way became darker and narrower still. Michael worried that he or Emma would trip and the wizard wouldn't even notice, but just continue on, leaving them lost and alone in the warren of gravestones.

"Dr. Pym," he had to ask once more, "what're we doing here?"

"And can't you walk a little slower?" Emma said. "Your legs are, like, a hundred times longer than mine."

"My apologies. And I suppose it is time to explain why I brought you to this ghoulish place. You remember, of course, the letter that Dr. Algernon found? The pig merchant's story of coming to Malpesa and meeting the man with a fever, the one who ranted that he and others had taken a great, magical book out of Egypt long ago?"

"Yeah, and he wanted to make a map," Michael said, hurrying past a tomb that was emitting a low, strangled gurgle. "The sick guy, I mean."

"Exactly so, my boy. What we don't know is what happened afterward. Did the sick man die? Did he succeed in making his map? The story requires us to use our imaginations." He paused and read the inscription on a tombstone, then moved off in another direction. "Now, if the sick man recovered and left Malpesa, then he and his map are lost to us. There are a million directions he might've taken, a million fates he could've met. But let us suppose that the sick man was very sick indeed. Let us suppose he perished in Malpesa. If so, this island is where he would have been buried."

"Wait, so you think the map got buried with him?" Emma said. "Also, you're still walking too fast."

"That is my theory. And I suspect it was your parents' theory as well."

"Okay," Michael said, "but we still don't know his name. We can't just go around digging up graves till we find him!"

"Yeah," Emma said. "That would take forever."

"And it would be wrong," Michael said.

"Yeah," Emma said, with little conviction. "That too."

Michael was peeved that Dr. Pym hadn't run his plan past him earlier. Michael could've saved them a lot of time by pointing out the glaringly obvious flaws, like trying to find the grave of some nameless man who might or might not have died hundreds of years before! Certainly, as the oldest sibling, he had a right to approve all—

"I believe this is the grave," said Dr. Pym.

"What?" Michael said.

"I believe this is the tomb we are searching for."

The wizard was standing before a rectangular stone box. It was roughly seven feet long, three feet wide, rose four feet off the ground, and seemed to Michael no different from any of the scores of tombs they'd already passed.

"That was easy," Emma said.

"But," Michael said, "how do you know?"

"Different areas of this island were developed at different times. The pig merchant's letter was dated in the last quarter of the eighteenth century. That would place our deceased sort of here-ish." The wizard waved his arm in a half circle. "I thought we'd have to search a bit, but it appears we got lucky."

"But how do you know this is *his* grave?" Michael demanded. "We still don't know his name."

"My boy," the wizard said, "we don't need to know his name. We have this."

He gestured for them to approach the tomb. There, chiseled into the center of the stone lid, visible through a glaze of ice, were three interlocking circles. Michael later sketched the symbol into his journal—

"What is it?" Emma asked.

"It is a thing I have not seen for more than two thousand years," replied the wizard. As he spoke, he reached out and traced the rings with a finger. "Long ago, before Alexander the Great attacked the city of Rhakotis and caused the Books of Beginning to be scattered and lost, the Books were kept beneath a tower in the center of that city. The magicians who had created the books established the Order of Guardians, fierce warriors who had pledged to protect them with their lives."

"Wait, I remember!" Michael exclaimed. "The Countess told us about them!"

The wizard nodded. "And as you know, when the city was overrun, I myself fled with the *Atlas*, which I later entrusted to the dwarves of Cambridge Falls."

Michael nodded, signaling his approval of the wizard's choice.

"It has always been my suspicion that the Order escaped with at least one of the books. But though I have searched unceasingly all this time, I have found no sign of either the missing two books or the Order. That is, until now. This"—he laid his hand flat upon the tomb, almost obscuring the rings—"is their symbol."

Michael's heart was pounding with excitement. He'd decided

he would excuse the wizard's lapse in oldest-sibling protocol this one time.

"If Dr. Algernon's letter is to be trusted," Dr. Pym went on, "and this is the tomb of that same feverish man, then we may assume that the Order did indeed rescue one of the books. The questions now are: Did our fellow make a map? And if so, is the map still here, or did your parents take it? There is only one way to find out."

"You mean," Michael said, "we have to open the tomb?"

"I am afraid so."

"That dead guy," Emma said, "he's not gonna be a zombie or anything, is he?"

"I think the chances are very low."

"You said that about meeting a troll. And guess what, we—"

"My dear, he is not a zombie. I promise."

The wizard told the children to go to one end of the tomb, while he positioned himself at the other.

"Remember, lift with your legs."

"Dr. Pym," Michael said, "this is solid stone. It must weigh a thousand pounds."

"Michael's kinda weak," Emma said. "I'll do most of the lifting."

Michael was about to argue, but the wizard cut him off.

"I have a feeling it is not as heavy as it looks. Ready? One . . . two . . . *three!*"

To Michael's surprise, the stone lid came off easily.

"That's it," the wizard said. "Watch your fingers and toes."

They leaned it against the side of the tomb.

Emma looked at Michael. "Don't bother thanking me or any-thing."

"Oh please, Dr. Pym obviously—"

"Well, that is interesting."

Dr. Pym was peering into the tomb. The children joined him.

"*Ahhhh!*" Emma shrieked, and fell back.

The entire bottom of the stone box was one dark, squirming mass. Michael could make no sense of what he was seeing; it was almost like—

"Rats!"

There were dozens of them. Perhaps hundreds. Wriggling and crawling all over each other. Long, naked tails whipping this way and that. Their gray-brown bodies writhing atop each other, their eyes glittering black and jewel-like.

"Those're rats!" Michael said again.

"That they are."

"Don't just stand there!" Emma cried. "Do something! Zap them or something!"

"And why would I do that, my dear?"

"Why? What do you mean, why? They're rats!"

Emma's whole body was rigid, and there was a look of pure, undisguised panic on her face. It occurred to Michael that his sis-ter was afraid. But that was ridiculous. He'd never known Emma to be afraid of anything, even things a person should be afraid of, like giant hairy spiders. Once, a wildlife expert had brought a bunch of snakes and lizards and spiders to their school for a demonstration. Halfway through, an enormous yellow-and-black tarantula had gotten free. There'd been a stampede of screaming children. But Emma, sitting in the front row, had calmly picked up the spider and plopped it back in its glass cage.

"Tell me," the wizard said, "do you notice anything odd about these rats?"

"Uh . . ." Emma's voice was not at all steady. "They're still alive and you're not doing anything about it?"

But Michael thought for a second, then said: "They're quiet."

"Exactly so," the wizard replied. "This many rodents should be creating a terrible racket. There is more here than meets the eye."

Emma muttered, "I'm gonna throw up."

The wizard stepped to a scraggly tree that was growing between two mausoleums and broke off a long, dry limb. Michael watched as the wizard then poked the stick into the swirling gray mass. To Michael's surprise, it went right through.

"An illusion. Designed to discourage intruders. There are no rats. Indeed, I seem to feel a sort of shaft."

Emma took a half step closer. "So . . . they're not real?"

"Not at all. Now, one of you should come below with me while the other stays here and watches the way back to Malpesa. Just in case we were seen."

"You mean climb down into the rat hole?" Emma asked. "You—"

"I'll do it," Michael said quickly. "Emma can stay up here."

"Very good," the wizard said. Then he took the branch he was holding and broke it into thirds. He handed one of the sticks to Emma.

"Rub this on any surface, and it will burst into flame. But only do so if you're coming below. Otherwise, you'll make yourself too visible." The wizard looked at Michael. "I'll go first."

He draped his long legs over the side of the stone coffin. Michael and Emma watched with horrified fascination as his foot went into the swarming tide. For a moment, the creatures seemed to swirl around it, then his foot disappeared, and then his legs, and his chest, and finally, his white head vanished into the nest of rats.

The children were alone. Michael turned to Emma.

"Are you warm enough?"

"Uh-huh."

"Don't stand on top of a mausoleum. Silhouettes are really visible in the dark."

"Okay."

"And sound will carry a long way; so I'm afraid no singing or whistling to keep yourself company."

"Got it."

"Oh, and don't stare too long at any one thing. Look at something, look away, then look back. It's an old sentry's trick."

"Michael . . ."

"Yeah?"

"I'll be fine. You be careful too." She gave him a hug. "I love you."

She released him, and Michael stood there awkwardly, unsure of what to say.

"Go ahead," Emma said finally. "Dr. Pym's waiting."

Michael nodded, then climbed up the side of the tomb, took a deep breath, and lowered himself down.

CHAPTER SEVEN
And Three Will Become One

"Take this."

The wizard handed Michael a burning torch. They were in a large cavern directly below the grave. Michael had found it unnerving, submerging himself in the squirming pool of rats, and though he'd known it was an illusion, he'd shut his mouth and eyes tight as he'd gone under. But he hadn't been bitten, and a moment later, he'd found himself in a shaft that burrowed downward from the tomb. An iron ladder was affixed to the rock wall. The wizard had called up to him, and Michael had seen the red glow of the wizard's torch thirty yards below.

"So," Dr. Pym said, "we must decide which way to go."

The cavern was unlike the caves and tunnels that Michael and his sisters had explored near Cambridge Falls. Both the ceiling and the floor were studded with stalactites and stalagmites, so the effect was like being in the mouth of a great, many-fanged beast. And there was water everywhere, dripping from the ceiling in a constant *thip . . . thip . . . thip,* running in rivulets down the walls, collecting in pools upon the floor. And there was the air itself, which was so moist and thick with minerals that every breath tasted like a dose of medicine.

As to where they should go, Michael could see two choices, two tunnels that faced one another across the cavern.

"Now, I would wager that tunnel," the wizard pointed to their left, "runs back to Malpesa. While this fellow," he gestured to the right, "seems to continue on beneath the cemetery. What do you think?"

Michael had no idea. Part of his mind was still back in the graveyard. He hoped that Emma had listened to his advice. He hated leaving her alone.

He tried to make himself focus.

"Well—"

"Or we could go that way!"

Dr. Pym pointed to the far side of the cavern. At first, Michael saw only rocks and the play of shadows. But then, looking closer, he perceived that one of the shadows was in fact a narrow fissure, a sort of crack in the cavern wall.

The wizard smiled. "Lucky we're both slim, eh?"

They had to scoot through the crease sideways, and the jagged edges of the rock wall ripped at Michael's jacket and the legs of his pants; once, he banged his knee and had to bite his tongue to keep from crying out. Finally, the crevice widened, and Michael and Dr. Pym could walk normally. But the way was still dark, and the only sounds were their footsteps and the soft flutter of the torches. Michael hung close to the wizard's heels and began to ask questions. Mostly, he wanted to hear the wizard's voice.

"So, that letter Dr. Algernon found was from two hundred years ago?"

"Yes, give or take."

"And the man with the fever, the one who was in the Order, said he and the others had taken the book out of Egypt; and that happened more than two thousand years ago."

"That's right. Oh, Michael, my boy—"

"Yes, sir?"

"Please don't set fire to my suit. It's my only one."

"Sorry." Michael slowed and put another few inches between his torch and Dr. Pym's back. "So wouldn't he, the sick guy, have had to be really, really old?"

Michael heard Dr. Pym chuckle; the sound seemed to bounce from wall to wall.

"Indeed he would. Which raises an even more interesting question. There are two remaining Books of Beginning. Each has unique powers. Tell me, have you given any thought as to what those powers might be?"

Michael had. He and Emma had debated the subject end-lessly since their return to Baltimore—Kate had refused to join in, saying, "The Books'll be what they'll be; I don't want to think about them till I have to." But all of his and Emma's theories about the Books' possible powers—the power to fly, the power to become superstrong, the power to talk to insects (Michael had once seen a documentary that said there were more than a trillion insects on earth and how if they all worked together, they could take over the planet), the power of endless ice cream (one of Emma's favorites, which Michael had maintained was not actually a power), the power to talk to people a long way off (another of Michael's, though whenever he'd mentioned it, Emma had always said, "Yeah, that's called a telephone")—suddenly seemed either too small or just plain silly.

"Yeah, but nothing good."

"Allow me to give you a hint," the wizard said. "You correctly pointed out that the man in the pig merchant's letter would have been thousands of years old. And yet, the members of the Order were men with normal life spans. How do you explain this fellow living as long as he did?"

"You mean . . . that was the book?"

"Just so. Now, what name would you give such a book? Remember, the Books deal with the very nature of existence, and the *Atlas* is the Book of Time. Think big, my boy."

There was only one answer. "I guess . . . the Book of Life?"

"Exactly. Or as it's also known, the *Chronicle*. And granting long life is only one of its powers. So this fellow in the letter, he and the other members of the Order, they hide the *Chronicle* in a secret place, and as long as they are close to it, they live on, century after century. Then this man comes to Malpesa, perhaps leaving the book with his comrades, and once separated from its power, he grows sick and dies. As to why he would embark on such a journey, well, that is another question."

They walked on; but Michael had one more thing to ask.

"Dr. Pym . . ."

"Yes?"

"So the last book, the third one, is it . . . well . . ."

The wizard stopped and faced him.

"Yes," the old man said, "the last is the Book of Death. But that is not a matter to concern us now." He seemed to study the boy, the torchlight reflecting off the old man's glasses and making it appear as if small flames danced in his eyes. "Hugo was right. You do look so like your father."

And again, despite all that had happened, despite all that was still happening, Michael felt a warm glow spread out from his chest and down to the tips of his fingers. He did not even try to suppress it.

He said, very quietly, ". . . Cool."

"Yes," the wizard said. "It is cool."

Ten yards further on, they found the inscription.

On a section of the tunnel wall that had been sanded smooth, someone had chiseled the same symbol—the three interlocking circles—that had been on the tomb. Below that, likewise carved deep into the stone, was what Michael took for writing, though the language was one he did not recognize. In some ways, it reminded him of Chinese or Japanese, in that the characters were ornate and heavily structured, but there were no breaks between them; everything seemed to flow together, and Michael couldn't tell if you read it forward, backward, top to bottom, or bottom to top.

He thought it was very beautiful.

"Amazing." Dr. Pym held his torch close to the rock wall and gripped Michael's shoulder. "So many years I've been searching. We are close, we are very close."

"What does it say?" Michael asked. "Can you read it?"

"I can. It is the ancient language in which the Books of Beginning are written. Here is the oath of the Order of Guardians." He pointed to the script just below the symbol and read aloud, his voice reverberating off the walls, "'Bear witness all that I, nameless, do pledge my breath, my strength, my very life, to this sacred task. None shall harm that which I have vowed to protect. So I swear till death frees me of my bond.'"

Michael decided that it was a very good oath. Granted, if a dwarf had written it, there would've been more mentions of bashing in an enemy's helmet and of promises hardened in the forges of eternity, but Michael knew you couldn't hold everyone to a dwarfish standard.

"And this part," Dr. Pym continued, tapping his finger on the lower portion of text. "'I have failed in my mission. What I leave, I leave in hopes the Keeper may one day arrive. Choose rightly, and you may never die. Choose wrongly, and you will join me. . . . And Three will become One.'"

"What does it mean?" Michael asked.

"Three becoming One is a reference to the Books of Beginning. According to legend, one day the Books will be brought together, three working as one to fulfill their destiny. But the part that interests me is where he writes 'What I leave, I leave in hopes the Keeper may one day arrive.' That implies that our mysterious friend has indeed left some sort of map to find the *Chronicle*. We may yet be in luck."

"Wait, what's that?" Michael pointed to a line of very small writing at the bottom of the inscription. He thought it looked like a different language.

The wizard leaned forward, and suddenly let out a loud, echoing laugh.

"What?" Michael demanded. "What does it say?"

"'Tunnel and tomb constructed by Osborne and Sons, Dwarf Contractors, Malpesa.'" The wizard was still laughing. "I'd wondered how our sick fellow had burrowed down from that grave. He hired dwarves to do the digging for him."

"And he would've trusted them to keep his secret?" Michael asked, and immediately felt guilty for having said it.

"Oh, I doubt he conveyed the true nature of his secret, but in essence, yes. He would have trusted them. Dwarf builders are known for their discretion. There's not a safe or vault in the magical world that wasn't built by a dwarf. I'm surprised you don't know that."

"Well," Michael said defensively, "you can't expect one person to know everything about dwarves. There's so much. You could learn everything about elves in a good twenty minutes. But dwarves—"

"Yes, yes. Come along."

And they set off once more.

As they walked, Michael thought about the Keeper mentioned in the inscription, and his mind went back to what Dr.

Pym had told him the night before, that Kate had dreamed of him holding a strange book. Could that book have been the *Chronicle*? But then if he got the Book of Life, did that mean Emma got the Book of Death?

She's not going to be happy about that, Michael thought.

"Oh dear."

Michael stopped beside the wizard. Before them, the tunnel came to an abrupt end where a sloping mound of dirt and rocks stretched to the ceiling.

"A cave-in," Dr. Pym said. "It looks quite recent. This may take some time to deal with— My boy, what're you doing?"

Michael was clambering up the rocky slope. He'd spotted a small hole or tunnel near the ceiling. Once level with the opening, he balanced himself between a large boulder and the wall and reached his torch into the tunnel's mouth.

"It goes through," he said, still breathless from his climb. "It's only ten or twelve feet. I think I can fit."

"No. Absolutely not."

"Dr. Pym, the longer we're down here, the longer Emma's in the graveyard by herself. Just let me go take a look. Please."

"Michael—"

"If Kate was here, you'd let her go. You know you would."

The wizard sighed. "Very well. But you are only to look and report back, you understand?"

Michael said he did, and immediately stripped out of his thick coat. Then, with the torch held before him, he wriggled into the tunnel. It was smaller than he'd thought. He had to crawl on his belly, using his forearms and elbows to drag himself along. Soon, he had scrapes on his arms and elbows, on his shoulders, chin, legs, the top of his head. And then he got stuck. He twisted this way and that, but it was no good. He told himself not to panic, that he was nearly at the end. Gripping with his hands while bracing one foot against a rock, he heaved himself forward with all his strength. It was a ferocious effort, so much so that he pitched himself completely out of the tunnel and landed hard on a rocky floor.

He was up in an instant, scrambling about for his dropped torch. He could hear the wizard's voice echoing through the tunnel:

"Michael, say something! What was that noise? Are you hurt?"

Michael opened his mouth but no words came. His torch was illuminating a small chamber. There was a wooden table, there was a chair, and there was the thing that sat in the chair, staring at him.

Emma had climbed onto the roof of a large mausoleum, and from her perch, she had views both down into the rat tomb (where she was very consciously not looking) and out over the uneven skyline of the graveyard. The bridge to Malpesa had vanished. Everything was silent and dark and still.

To pass the time, and as a way of not thinking about the squirming pool of rats—fake or not, she didn't trust them—Emma had started imagining that Kate had come back from the past and was sitting beside her. She had only to turn her head and Kate would be there, smiling, ready to take Emma in her arms. The more she imagined it, the more real the vision became, till Emma started to think that Kate actually *was* there and only waiting for her younger sister to notice her presence.

Don't look, she told herself. She's not there; don't look.

Emma looked. She was alone.

Turning back, she had to wipe her hand across her eyes, as the lights of Malpesa had begun to blur and shimmer in the distance. She wrapped her arms around her knees and began to rock back and forth.

I want Kate back, she thought. I want Kate back I want Kate back I want Kate back. . . .

The night was cold and dark, and nothing moved in the graveyard.

What were Michael and the wizard doing?

She glanced up. The lights in the distance were still blurry, and Emma rubbed at her eyes. She looked again, and the lights were moving. She started to stand, then remembered Michael's warning and crouched low, peering through the darkness.

The bridge to Malpesa had reappeared, and a line of torches was marching across it, coming toward the cemetery.

Snatching up the stick the wizard had given her, Emma rushed to the edge of the roof. She had to warn Dr. Pym. But then, slipping to the ground, Emma heard a voice close by, echoing through the tombstones.

"They're here! Spread out! Find them!"

With horror, Emma realized that there was another group

already in the graveyard. She'd let them slip by while she'd been thinking about Kate! She cursed herself. Dr. Pym had trusted her to do one thing, and she'd let him down!

She could hear the stomping of boots, and the same voice spoke again; it had an accent she didn't recognize.

"Find the children! You hear me? I want the children!"

Crouched beside the mausoleum, she could see torches flickering between the gravestones. She had to cross ten yards of open space to get to the tomb. She would be completely exposed, but there was no other way. Gathering herself, Emma bolted across, climbed up the side of the tomb, and froze—

Below her, the sea of rats roiled and squirmed. Panic seized hold of her.

She could hear the stamping of boots coming closer. . . .

Do it, she commanded. Now!

And she lowered herself down, praying she didn't throw up.

The figure in the chair was a skeleton. It—or he (Michael was fairly sure it had been a man)—wore the rotted remains of an ancient tunic and sat behind the wooden table, positioned so as to face anyone who entered the chamber. The skeleton's hands rested on the table, the right one curled about the hilt of a naked sword. Hanging from one of the joints of its left hand was a gold ring bearing the now-familiar symbol of three interlocking circles.

It seemed to Michael that the skeleton was watching him.

"Michael!" The wizard's voice was insistent. "Answer me! Are you hurt? Are you in danger?"

"I'm . . . I'm fine! Just give me a second!"

Michael took a tentative step closer. The skeleton didn't move.

Okay, Michael thought, let's stay calm and see what we have here.

The table had clearly been prepared for visitors. There were three jars, arranged in a line, and an old metal goblet. The goblet was on Michael's, not the skeleton's, side of the table. Michael glanced again at the skeleton. It still hadn't moved.

He recalled the message on the wall.

What I leave, I leave in hopes the Keeper may one day arrive. Choose rightly, and you may never die. Choose wrongly, and you will join me. . . .

It was a puzzle! You had to drink from one of the jars.

Michael rubbed his hands together. Things were looking up. He loved puzzles, riddles, anything you could work through logically.

"You sly fellow," he said to the skeleton. He really was feeling much more comfortable. He turned to tell Dr. Pym what he'd found—

Then stopped.

No doubt the wizard could solve the puzzle in an instant. But perhaps this was an opportunity. He was the oldest now; he'd been given Kate's role. Only Michael was aware that no one really saw him that way. This was his chance to prove himself. He imagined climbing out of the tunnel, and Dr. Pym saying, "What did you find out? What do I need to do?" and as he casually dusted himself off, Michael would reply, "Save your spells, Doctor. I solved the puzzle. Good old-fashioned logic." Even Emma would be impressed.

"Michael, what's going on in there?"

"Just one more minute!"

He would have to be quick.

Choose wrongly, and you will join me. . . .

That was pretty self-explanatory. Drink from the wrong jar, and you become a skeleton yourself.

Choose rightly, and you may never die. . . .

This man, when he'd been a man, had lived for thousands of years thanks to the Book of Life. Indeed, the whole thing was perfectly clear. Two jars were poison. One would guide him to the *Chronicle*. He only had to make the right choice.

He started with the jar on his left. It was a reddish-brown clay jug, bell-shaped and stoppered with a cork. Michael pulled out the cork and sniffed. He jerked back in revulsion. It was as if someone had filled the jug with sludge from the bottom of a swamp and mixed in kerosene, vinegar, and something that smelled like wet dog. Michael stuffed the cork back into the jug and stepped to the right.

The middle container was a slender, ruby-colored bottle half filled with dark liquid. Michael removed the cork, leaned forward, and—gingerly this time—sniffed. He sniffed again. He hadn't imagined it. Whatever was in the bottle smelled like root beer.

He moved on to the last container.

It was a small metal flask the size of a bottle of perfume. The cap was held in place by a lever shaped like a tiny claw, and when Michael pressed a button, the cap popped up. He brought the flask to his nose. He smelled nothing. He held it closer and inhaled more deeply. Still nothing. He released the button and returned the flask to the table.

"Michael"—the wizard's voice was now more annoyed than worried—"I insist you tell me what is going on."

"There's no map! There's a table with three jars! Oh, and there's a skeleton! But he's just sitting there."

Michael looked at the skeleton. He hadn't moved, had he? Michael tried to remember if the skeleton's head had been in that exact position.

"Michael, I forbid you to touch anything! In fact, come back right now! Do you hear me?"

"I'm just . . . tying my shoe."

"Well, for goodness— Oh, hold on a second, my boy!"

Michael thought he could hear another voice, further off, his sister's, and the wizard was calling to her. He wondered if something had happened in the graveyard. Michael sensed that his time was running out.

Choose rightly, and you may never die. . . .

Choose wrongly, and you will join me. . . .

The clay jar certainly smelled like poison, but maybe that was the point. When designing a puzzle, you always put the solution where it's least expected. In which case, the swampy, wet-dog-smelling concoction was Michael's best bet.

Or was that a little too obvious? Wouldn't the skeleton man have assumed that Michael or whoever would automatically go for the most disgusting alternative? Wouldn't it be far more clever to have the least poisonous-seeming option not actually be poison? In that case, Michael should choose the ruby-colored bottle and its promise of root beer.

Except . . . there was still the metal flask to consider. That smelled like nothing at all. How did that figure into the equation? And, come to think of it, was he making a mistake in not looking at the containers themselves: a clay jug, a glass bottle, a metal flask? Was there some meaning there? Or perhaps the clue was in their respective placements on the table?

What I really need, Michael thought, are lab rats. I could feed each of them one of the potions and see who survives.

Michael glanced about, but the chamber was depressingly rat-free.

Admit it, he thought, you have no idea which is the right potion.

Very quietly, he murmured, "Eenie . . . meenie . . . miney—"

He stopped, too embarrassed to continue.

Choose, Michael told himself. You just have to choose. Do it. Now.

He uncorked the clay jug and tilted it into the goblet. His hands shook and he had to steady the jug against his body. Slowly, almost reluctantly, a foul greenish-yellow sludge slithered into the bowl of the goblet. Michael stared. How was he supposed to drink this? He'd need a spoon. Or a fork.

As Michael raised the goblet to his lips, he had to pinch his nose to keep from gagging. He could actually see the goop crawling toward his mouth. He knew he was being stupid. If only he'd had more time, he could've worked it out. Perhaps found some rats in another cave. He was glad that Kate couldn't see him, or Dr. Pym, or his dad, or even G. G. Greenleaf, author of *The Dwarf Omnibus*—

Michael abruptly lowered the cup, the goop a hairbreadth away from touching his lips.

Setting down the goblet, Michael pulled the *Omnibus* from his bag. He knew the chapter he was looking for and opened directly to it. He read: " 'Puzzles have long been a key part of every magical quest, and no surprise, dwarves have always excelled at them!' "

Michael felt relief washing over him. Good old G. G. Greenleaf!

The key to solving any puzzle is to place yourself in the mind of the puzzle maker. What were his intentions with the puzzle? Whom did he want to solve it? Whom to fail? Always go back to the directions; someone wrote them for a reason. Also, if nothing else works, try smashing the puzzle with your ax. It's frequently effective.

Michael closed the *Omnibus* and looked at the skeleton. The man had been one of the last Guardians of the book; he'd wanted to protect it. Therefore, he'd wanted most people to fail the test. But if someone just randomly chose a potion, he had a one-in-three chance of succeeding. Michael thought that seemed too high. The Guardian would not want one in three to succeed, but *the* one. The Keeper.

Michael was suddenly sure that none of the potions was the right answer, and that if he'd drunk the foul-smelling sludge, he would now be dead.

"*Michael!*"

Emma's voice yanked him to the tunnel. He could see the flickering of torchlight at the far end.

"What is it? What's wrong?"

"You gotta get outta there!" She was desperate. "They're coming! Lots of them!"

"Who? What're you—"

"Screechers! I saw them! Hurry!"

"But we still don't know where the next book is! I can—"

"Michael"—it was the wizard speaking—"we'll find the book some other way! Come back now! That is an order!"

But Michael was already turning back to the table. He was certain that if he didn't get the answer now, didn't discover the location of the *Chronicle*, then they would never find the book. And everything depended on that. Which meant everything depended on him. He opened the *Omnibus* and read the passage again. One phrase caught his eye: "Always go back to the directions; someone wrote them for a reason. . . ."

The directions, Michael thought:

Choose rightly, and you may never die. . . .

Choose wrongly, and you will join me. . . .

And Three will become One.

Michael felt a shiver of excitement.

And Three will become One. . . .

Dr. Pym had said it referred to the three Books of Beginning, and perhaps it did. But perhaps it also referred to something else.

The green-yellow sludge was now half solid in the bottom of the goblet. Michael yanked the cork from the red bottle and splashed in the root-beer-smelling liquid; there was a hissing and bubbling, and the concoction turned black and, if possible, smelled even worse than before; but Michael was already upending the tiny flask, shaking out a few clear drops. The effect was immediate. The hissing and bubbling stopped, and the liquid in the goblet turned the color of pure silver.

"Michael, this is your last warn—"

"I'm drinking from all three jars!"

He wanted them to know what was happening. In case he was wrong.

Then, unable to resist the dramatic gesture, he raised the goblet toward the skeleton. Unfortunately, he couldn't think of anything suitably offhand and cavalier to say as a toast. Finally, he just muttered, "Well, here goes . . . ," and drank.

It was as if he'd poured ice water directly into his heart. The goblet clattered to the floor as Michael dropped to his knees. The cold was spreading through his body, and he could feel himself beginning to shake. Was it possible he'd been wrong? But he'd been so sure! He tried calling to his sister, but his voice failed him. He could feel his lungs freezing, ice forming in the chambers of his heart; his vision went dark; he bent forward, his forehead pressed against the rocky floor; a pounding shook his entire body. What a strange way to die, Michael thought. The pounding came again, and again. Then Michael's vision cleared, and he realized that the pounding was the beating of his heart, and he felt life and warmth moving through him, and he took a deep, deep breath, and once again he could hear Emma calling his name, crying, begging him to please, please come back. . . .

"I'm coming!" he shouted, getting to his feet. "I'm okay!"

And he was better than okay, much better than okay, for he knew where the *Chronicle* was hidden.

What happened afterward was a blur.

He scrambled through the tunnel. Hands pulled at him. Emma hugged him, told him he was an idiot, and Dr. Pym shouted to come away, there was no time. . . .

And then running. Back through the crease, reaching the cavern underneath the tomb, hearing the Screechers so close above them, the wizard yelling for the children to follow him, plunging into the tunnel that led toward Malpesa . . .

And running again, as fast as they could.

They had to get to the port; there was something waiting for them; plans had already been made; something would take them away. "I had a feeling"—the wizard's voice was coming in quick huffs—"that we might need to leave Malpesa in a hurry."

And as they ran, the awful screams echoed down the tunnel, enveloping them, making everything inside the children small and cold and weak, and it was all they could do to run on, faster and faster.

Abruptly, the tunnel spilled out into a wide underground canal, through which a dark river flowed, and they splashed into the water, which was ice-cold and slimy and reached to their knees. As they struggled forward, the lights of their torches showed the mouth of another tunnel, paved in brick, on the far wall, and Michael knew they'd arrived at the sewers of Malpesa. Then the chilling cries erupted behind them, and he turned to see dark shapes leaping from the tunnel they'd just quit.

"Run!" the wizard cried. "Don't stop! Run! Leave them to me!"

Michael took two steps and realized that Emma hadn't moved. He seized her by the arm and dragged her forward, stumbling through the black water.

"It's not real!" he shouted. "The screams can't hurt you!"

"I—I know!" she shouted back. "Stop yelling in my ear!"

Glancing over his shoulder, Michael saw Dr. Pym standing to meet the Screechers; only the wizard wasn't facing the monsters, he was looking up the canal, into the darkness. Michael and Emma reached the far side, and Michael pushed Emma up the embankment. Then he turned again and saw Dr. Pym wading toward him, a dozen Screechers in pursuit and more pouring like rats out of the other tunnel, and he became aware of a roaring, and then a great wall of water rushed down out of the darkness, filling the tunnel, and the wizard heaved him into the sewer as the wave struck the Screechers and carried them away in a tumble of dark water.

The next thing Michael knew, they'd reached a ladder; Emma went up first, and he followed hard on her heels. They climbed out of a well beside an old church, and the city was so quiet, so still, and then the wizard was climbing out and Emma was asking if Dr. Pym had caused that flood, but before the old man could speak, they heard a fast, stamping *thud-thud-thud*, the ground shook, and the lumbering shape of a troll rounded the corner, swinging an enormous, metal-studded club, and charged toward them.

It was like fleeing before an earthquake; the ground trembled so that it was hard to find footing. The wizard led them down a narrow alley where the troll could not follow, and Michael heard it bellowing in rage, bashing the walls with its club. And then they were running along a crooked, boat-lined canal, and they heard the cry of a Screecher, and then another, and another, closing in from all sides, and Dr. Pym seemed to be rearranging the map of the city as they ran, causing bridges to vanish behind them, forcing buildings to smash together and bar their enemies' way; but at every turn, three or four *morum cadi* would appear, rushing toward them, swords drawn and shrieking.

"The port," Dr. Pym kept saying, "we must reach the port."

Then they rounded the corner to the main canal and found a dozen Screechers guarding the bridge, and there was a man standing before them. He was the largest man Michael had ever seen. He wore a long, dark overcoat and black leather gloves, and his bald head shone in the lamplight. The very sight of him filled Michael with fear, and he felt Emma grab at his arm.

"Doctor!" The man held his hands out wide as if in welcome. "We've been waiting for you! Now, enough of this running about. We're going to wake the neighbors."

"You can't have them, Rourke!" The wizard had moved in front of the children. "Not while I'm alive."

"Well, you see, Doctor." And the man smiled. "I'm actually okay with that."

The Screechers charged forward, but Dr. Pym blew on his torch and a wall of flame sprang up in the middle of the street. Then, as if conducting an orchestra, the wizard threw up his arms, and a ball of fire shot into the night sky, turning in a great circle above the city.

"Dr. Pym!" Emma cried. "What're we going to do?"

"If we cannot reach the port"—the wizard's face was grim, and he had to shout over the noise of the fire—"then the port must come to us. This way!"

They sprinted to a decrepit four-story building that clung to the edge of the canal, and Dr. Pym pushed through a rotted door into the dark, musty interior and herded them up a wide staircase.

"To the roof! Hurry!"

As they climbed upward, Michael heard the door being torn from its hinges. His legs were burning and trembling with fatigue. At the top floor, a ladder led up through the rotten rafters, and the wizard urged them up, up, up, and then they were all three standing on a slanting, half-ruined tile roof, looking out over the city and the dark water of the canal, and the wizard sent another ring of fire, like a flare, into the sky, so that it hung there, burning above them.

"Who . . . ," Michael panted, ". . . was that man?"

"Rourke," the wizard said. "The right hand of our enemy. I have to gather myself. They will be on us in moments, and we need time. Time above all else."

Bells had begun to clang across the city, and Michael could

see lights going on in windows as voices called to one another in fear and alarm, and then the Screechers began to gain the roof. Some of them came up the ladder, but others scaled the outside of the building, clambering over the edge of the roof.

"Back!" the wizard commanded the children. "Get back!"

Michael and Emma retreated, but the tiles were loose and slippery, and one gave way under Michael's feet, and he slipped and nearly slid off the edge.

There were Screechers everywhere now, and Dr. Pym sent a crescent of flame toward the creatures, the dry rags of their uniforms catching fire in an instant, and many of them fell flaming off the roof; and then the whole building shook, and Michael could hear enraged bellowing from below, and he peered over the side and saw a pair of trolls hammering at the building like lumberjacks attempting to fell an enormous tree. Meanwhile, Emma was hurling broken bits of tile as fast as she could snatch them up, and there was nowhere to go, nowhere to run. . . .

Then Dr. Pym was grabbing Michael's arms and leaning close. The fire that was raging on the roof held the Screechers at bay.

"Michael, listen to me! You must find the *Chronicle*! It all depends on you! You saw where it is hidden? You can find it?"

"Y-yes."

"The Dire Magnus must not have it! Promise me. Promise me!"

"I . . . promise."

"You will be its Keeper! Katherine foresaw this! You understand? Do you understand?"

Michael nodded, but he felt panic grip him, and he suddenly

knew that he wasn't ready. Why had he pretended he was? He tried to say this, but his throat was dry and the words wouldn't come.

Emma was shouting, pointing down the canal.

The wizard turned. "Thank goodness, he saw my signal."

Michael could hear it now, an engine, growing louder. And he saw a floatplane skimming along the canal, its pontoons cutting large Vs in the still water. It was passing under a bridge and would be even with them in seconds.

"Once you land in the water—listen to me, Michael—once you land in the water, hold to your sister tightly. They will only have one chance to pick you up."

"You—you're coming too," he managed.

"No. Someone must stay. Rourke knows about the grave. We cannot risk him learning the location of the *Chronicle*. I am the only one who can slow him down. I can buy you time you need."

"But I—"

"I know what you're afraid of. Trust Emma. Trust yourself. You have a good heart. Let it guide you."

"But you can't—"

"He is coming. Go now."

And Michael could see the bald man stepping up onto the roof.

"Now you have to jump! Go!"

He pushed Michael toward Emma. Michael seized his sister's hand.

"We have to jump!"

"What about Dr. Pym?"

"He's not coming!"

Before she could argue, Michael clenched her hand tighter and—remembering to take off his glasses and slip them in his bag—took three running steps and Emma had no choice but to jump.

They fell and fell and fell. Hitting the water was like striking concrete. Emma's hand was ripped from his as Michael plunged deep underwater. He struggled upward with all his might, and as he broke the surface, he saw the propeller of the plane bearing down. Emma was a few feet away, looking bewildered and scared, and he swam to her, wrapping his arms tightly around her, and, at the last moment, the plane swerved, the propeller missing them, and Michael felt himself seized by iron hands, and he and Emma were lifted from the water and into the plane. Emma cried out, and Michael, still sprawled on the floor and struggling to breathe, saw her hugging Gabriel, Gabriel, who had pulled them in and who was now shouting to the pilot, and the plane was rising into the air, clearing a bridge by inches, and they climbed higher and banked, and Michael scrambled to put on his glasses and, through the open door, he saw on the roof two distant shapes, facing one another and outlined against the flames. Then the building teetered and collapsed, crumbling into the canal, and the plane, still rising, banked again, and Malpesa vanished behind them, and there was no sound save the engine and the rushing of the wind, and nothing to see but the darkness of the night sky, and Emma was hugging Michael and crying, "Oh, Michael, Dr. Pym . . . he . . . oh, Michael . . ."

CHAPTER EIGHT
The Savages

"I say, Master Jake . . ."

"Yes, Master Beetles?"

"I do believe she's finally waking up."

Kate opened her eyes. She was once again lying on the floor, and, once again, two sets of eyes were fixed upon her. But the room she found herself in was a different one, and the two boys were not leaning over and inspecting her for signs of life; they regarded her from a pair of rickety wooden chairs, their feet propped up on crates and pushed close to a battered iron stove. Both boys were smoking pipes.

"How long have I been asleep?" Kate raised herself to a sitting position.

The one named Beetles removed his pipe and seemed to consider the question thoughtfully.

"How long would you say she's been asleep, Master Jake? Five hours?"

"Oh, I'd venture six hours, Master Beetles."

"Six? That many?"

"At the very least. I half suspected she was going to open a shop—"

"All right," Kate said.

"Is that so?" Beetles grinned. "What sort of shop, Master Jake?"

"Why, one a' those Sleepin'-on-the-Floor-All-Day-Gettin'-Nothing-Done sorts a' shops, Master Beetles."

Kate shook her head as the boys collapsed into laughter, Beetles making a great show of doffing his cap and bowing, evidently in deference to his friend's wit. She took a moment to look around.

Pale winter light forced its way through a single dirt- and frost-scrummed window, illuminating a small, unremarkable room. There was little to behold apart from the stove, the overturned crates now serving as footstools, and the chairs the boys were sitting on. The room's one notable aspect was that the walls and floor were constructed from large blocks of gray stone. Only the ceiling beams were wood.

Kate saw she had been laid on a folded blanket, and that another blanket had been placed over her bare feet. The gesture seemed oddly considerate. She was still wearing the wool overcoat she'd gotten in the Bowery, the one she'd acquired by trading the chain from her mother's locket, and her hand now went into her pocket, seeking out and closing over the locket's familiar egg-like shape. She would have to find a new chain soon. She missed the weight of the locket around her neck, being able to reach up at any time and know it was there. She thought about the magic bazaar, and the witch who'd drugged her, and the two creatures who'd tried to carry her off. She thought about how she'd been saved by that other boy, Rafe, and she saw him again, leaping down from above—he'd known her, recognized her. But how was that possible? Who was he?

She glanced at Jake and Beetles. They were having a smoke-ring competition, though every time one blew a ring, the other would conveniently cough or leap up crying that something had bitten his backside, and in the process destroy his friend's ring, until Kate realized that disrupting the other person's smoke ring was the game.

They were having such a good time she couldn't help but smile.

"You do know," she said finally, "that smoking's bad for you?"

The boys found this frankly hilarious.

"Listen to her, smoking's bad!" guffawed Beetles. "Everyone knows a pipe's about the best thing you can do for your body."

"Best medicine in the world!" Jake agreed, and blew another ring.

"Smoking ain't good for you! Har-har!"

"And look who's telling us what's good," Jake said. "Didn't we tell her not to go to that witch?"

"We did," Beetles replied. "We told her and she done it anyway."

"Fine," Kate said. "Next time I'll listen to you."

"Good," said Beetles. "'Cause we ain't always gonna find Rafe in time to save you, right?"

"So, Rafe—is he the one who brought me here?"

"Yeah," Beetles said. "You were passed out. He had to carry you the whole way."

Kate thought about the blanket placed over her feet and wondered if that same fierce boy from the alley had been the one to do that.

"Where is he?"

"Well, well, well, ain't this a nice change, Master Jake?" Beetles grinned broadly. "Suddenly, someone wants to see ol' Rafe."

"Sure. She's in love with him, ain't she?"

Kate felt a rush of heat across her face and was glad for the gloom and smoke.

"I want to thank him for saving my life."

And, she thought, ask him how he knows me.

"He's a busy man, Rafe is," Beetles said. "He told us to make sure you don't go running off."

"Though that ain't likely now's you want to marry him," Jake said.

"Nope. Not likely at all."

"You should open a shop. The I-Wanna-Marry-Rafe-and-Have-a-Hundred-Babies Shop."

Kate could sense when she was being baited and let the remark pass.

"So where am I?"

"You're in the hideout, course!"

"What hideout?"

"What hideout?" Jake repeated. "Ours! The hideout a' the most ruthless, most best gang in New York!"

"Best gang anywhere!" Beetles said.

"Yeah, best gang anywhere, that's us! The Savages!"

The hideout—Kate had been laid in a back room—turned out to be an old, abandoned church. It must have been, at one time, a magnificent structure, for, on stepping into the long main hall, Kate was struck by the scale of the thing. Stone columns rose eighty feet to a vaulted ceiling. Many of the stained-glass windows had been broken and covered with boards, but those that remained filtered in green and red and yellow and blue light, in complex and beautiful patterns. There were lines of cots up and down the stone floor, and sheets hung up to cordon off areas, and Kate's impression was that it looked like the dormitory of a large orphanage.

She saw perhaps twenty children, girls and boys, most around the age of Jake and Beetles. And as she and her two guides walked between the lines of cots, it struck Kate that the other children, despite being neither especially clean nor well dressed, all looked fed and happy. In their lives of going from orphanage to orphanage, Kate and her brother and sister had learned to read the mood of a place almost instantly. Was it happy, sad, desperate? Were the children or adults vicious or generous?

She knew right away that this was a good place.

In the center of the church, a group of girls and boys stood at a large table sorting through a pile of objects—watches, silk handkerchiefs, rings, necklaces, earrings, small ornamental boxes, fur coats and wraps—while a boy with a ledger carefully wrote down what the other children called out.

"What is all that?" Kate asked.

"They're doing the day's take," replied Beetles.

"What do you mean, the day's take?"

"What was brought in by all the different teams. That's a pretty good haul, that is."

Kate realized what they were saying, what the huge pile of loot was—

"Wait, you're—*thieves!*"

"That's right," Beetles said, proudly hooking his thumbs into his suspenders. "Best thieves in New York City."

"Or Brooklyn," Jake said.

"Or there," Beetles said. "Though we never precisely been there."

Kate knew that it was unreasonable of her to be angry with the children, but she couldn't help herself. "So that's your gang? You're a gang of thieves?"

"Yep," they said happily. "Everything we learned, Rafe taught us."

"He's the best, Rafe is," Jake said.

"The very best," Beetles affirmed.

"Great," Kate said, biting her tongue, "that's just great."

After agreeing that it was indeed great, Jake and Beetles asked where to find Rafe and were told he was in the teaching room.

"What's he teaching?" Kate asked. "How to pick pockets? How to break into houses?"

But the boys only laughed and led her away. The room was

down a hallway at the back of the church, was well lit, and had a wood floor and a large fireplace. When Kate and her companions entered, the boy called Rafe, the one who'd saved her in the alley, was stoking up the fire so that it blazed and crackled furiously. A dozen children, all of them younger than Jake and Beetles, sat on the floor, facing him. A thin-shouldered, nervous-looking girl stood at Rafe's elbow.

There was an unlit candle, Kate saw, positioned close to the fire.

"You ready?" Rafe asked the girl.

She nodded, though she was clearly scared. None of the other children spoke or moved.

"What's going on?" Kate whispered.

Beetles shushed her. "Watch."

Rafe placed his hand on the girl's shoulder. "Go on then." And the girl reached out her small, trembling hand into the fire—

"No!"

Kate ran forward and yanked the girl back. She'd been fast enough: the girl wasn't burned, and Kate hugged the startled child to her, as if afraid the boy might try and steal her away.

"What're you doing?" she cried.

Rafe looked at her without expression.

"Heya, Rafe!" said Beetles brightly. He and Jake stood at the door. "We watched her just like you said."

"She didn't run off 'cause she's in love with you," Jake said.

"Obviously," Kate said, "that's not true."

"Yeah." The dark-haired boy turned to the children. "We'll finish later." The children, including the small girl, who had squirmed out of Kate's arms, hurried from the room. Rafe set the poker against the hearth. "The boss wants to talk to you."

"Answer me—what were you doing to her?"

"Teaching her. Trying to."

"What? How to get burned?"

The boy looked at her for a long second. Then he bent over and calmly placed his own hand directly into the fire. Kate gasped, but to her amazement, the boy's hand didn't burn. The skin remained unmarred. Then he reached out his other hand and touched the wick of the candle. It burst into flame.

The boy took his hand from the fire and touched Kate's wrist. His skin was cool.

"I wouldn't have let her get burned."

He blew out the candle.

"Now come on, the boss is waiting."

He led her to the bell tower, at the base of which a large iron bell lay on its side, its shell cracked open and the stone floor beneath it smashed to rubble. A wooden staircase curled upward along the wall.

Kate said, "Wait—"

The boy stopped on the second step.

"I don't understand—are you . . . a wizard?"

The boy laughed. "Wizards read books. Know all sorts a' spells. I'm no wizard."

"But that thing you did—with the fire—"

"Just something I can do."

"So the others, the children, are they—"

"Every kid here has magic. It's why they're here. We teach 'em to use it, is all."

He started to turn, but Kate stopped him once more.

"I wanted . . . to thank you. For saving me in the alley. From those things."

"The Imps."

"Yes."

"Jake and Beetles were gonna try and save you themselves. I only did what I did to stop them."

He stood there, his hand resting on the wooden banister, and Kate searched his face for some sign of recognition, some sign that, in whatever way, he knew her.

But there was none.

Kate felt self-conscious and drew her coat more tightly around herself. She didn't understand what was happening, who this boy was, who these children were, but she told herself that it didn't matter. What mattered was getting to Cambridge Falls, locating Dr. Pym, and finding her way back to Michael and Emma.

"Look, I appreciate what you did—"

"You said that."

"But I have someplace I need to go. It's a long way, so the sooner I get started, the better."

"Where is it?"

"Up north."

"How're you gonna get there?"

Kate shifted nervously. "I don't know. I'll take the train."

"You got money for a ticket?"

"No, but—"

"You probably got no money for food either, huh?"

Kate said nothing.

"It's gonna be dark soon and a lot colder. Even with that coat, you're not dressed right. How're you gonna stay warm?"

"I don't know, but—"

"Seems to me you don't know much. 'Cept how to go out and freeze to death as quick as possible."

Kate opened her mouth to argue, but the boy said, "You need to come see the boss," and started up the tower. A few moments later, an annoyed Kate followed.

The tower was tall, and neither spoke as they climbed. At different spots along the way, the stairs had been smashed, and boards hung splintered and loose and some were missing altogether. The gaps had to be leapt across, and when she jumped, Kate sensed both the gulf yawning below her and the boy above, watchful, ready to catch her if she slipped. She made sure not to. She had no intention of thanking him again.

The higher they went, the colder the air became, and the more the wind blew through cracks in the walls. Kate felt lightheaded and hollow. She'd had nothing to eat since the potato she'd shared with Jake. And before that? What had been her last real meal?

At the top of the tower, dozens of pigeons were strung along the belfry ropes and cooing softly, their feathers ruffled against the cold. There was a large, uneven hole in the middle of the ceiling, and Kate could see a wedge of gray winter sky.

A ladder slanted up through a trapdoor.

"Wait—"

The boy turned, his foot on the first rung. "What now?"

He was looking at her, and Kate felt a sudden trembling in her chest. The feeling wasn't new. She'd felt it in the room downstairs when she'd stood next to him and he'd placed his hand in the fire. But now, with the two of them alone in the tower and him looking directly at her, the feeling was stronger, and it confused her even more.

"In the alley. You acted like you knew me. How is that possible?"

The boy seemed to study her face. It was like being stared at by a wild animal; there was something so fierce in him. Kate willed herself to hold his gaze.

"I was wrong," Rafe said. "You just look like someone I know." He headed up the ladder, and Kate stood there, taking long, slow breaths, till the boy called down:

"You coming?"

She climbed up through the trapdoor and, a moment later, was standing in the open air. The top of the belfry was a large, rectangular space, crowned by a peaked dome that was supported by columns running around the edge of the tower. Standing there was like being in a house with a roof but no walls. Three enormous iron bells, identical to the one at the base of the tower, hung above her, and she saw the space for the missing bell, like a smile where a tooth has been knocked out.

It was bitterly cold, but Kate hugged herself and looked out to the right, up the long avenues, to the open expanse of the park, winter-dead and white in the distance. She looked the other way, taking in the maze of buildings and streets that made up downtown. Glancing behind her, she saw that the church was perched beside a wide gray river, and that there was ice creeping in at the edges of the water.

Then Kate turned and looked across the belfry.

Twenty yards away, a woman sat at a desk, writing. She was hard at work, and the desk was covered with stacks of weighted-down papers that fluttered in the wind like a fleet of tiny sails. She seemed completely untroubled by the cold or the wind, and remained focused on her task.

Kate supposed her to be in her early fifties. She had gray hair cropped short like a man's, and she wore a high-necked, long-sleeved black dress and had a black shawl wrapped around her shoulders. Her posture was stiff and unbending. Kate couldn't see her right hand, but the woman's left hand, the one holding the pen, displayed no rings or jewelry of any kind. Nor did she wear a necklace, a cameo, or earrings. Kate had the sense of a person of pure will, as if the woman's own internal fire not only warmed her, up here in the cold and the wind, but had burned away everything about her that was not essential.

Kate felt a weight settle on her shoulders. The boy had placed a long, heavy coat over her own.

"That coat a' yours ain't worth much. This here is bear."

The coat had thick black fur and was very warm and very heavy. The boy tugged it forward so that it hung on her like a cloak. He made a point, it seemed, of not meeting her eyes. Kate thought of the blanket that had been put over her feet while she'd slept, and she knew that that also had been him.

"Come on."

He turned and headed across the belfry, skirting the hole in the center, and Kate followed, her bearskin coat trailing on the floor.

Rafe stopped her a foot from the desk, and they stood there, waiting for the woman to notice them. Finally, she set down her pen and looked up.

"So"—the woman's voice was like someone striking flint—"you're the girl who's causing so much fuss."

She stood and came around the desk. She was not tall, only an inch or two taller than Kate, but the way she held herself, as if she had iron fillings in her bones, made her seem much taller. She had sharp gray eyes, and the skin of her face was lined and weathered, suggesting she had spent much of her life outside. Kate could imagine her on the deck of a ship, or on the Great Plains of the West, as if the woman required those wide-open spaces to exercise the full extent of her will. The gray eyes studied Kate, and while the gaze was not unkind, there was no mercy or softness in it.

"What's your name, girl?"

"Kate—Katherine."

"I am Henrietta Burke."

She held out her left hand, and it was then Kate saw that the woman's right hand, which she'd thought was tucked inside the shawl, was missing. The arm stopped at the elbow, and the sleeve was sewn over the stump. Kate already had her own right hand extended, and she awkwardly switched to her left. The woman gave Kate's hand a quick, hard clench. It was like shaking hands with an eagle.

"You observe I lost my right hand. Ten years ago, it was cut off by a pack of fools and degenerates in St. Louis. They accused me of doing witchcraft. Which, of course, I was. And they somehow thought that taking my right hand would stop me. They soon learned the error of their ways. It was tedious, learning to write and perform spells with my left hand, but one can do anything if one sets one's mind to it."

"Yes, ma'am." Kate wasn't sure what else to say.

"Forgive our meeting up here. But I find the cold sharpens my thoughts. Is it true you're from the future?"

Kate was taken aback. "How—"

"I know because it is my business to discover what people are saying. And I would ask you to answer my questions quickly and to the point. I have little time and less patience. So I'll ask again, do you come from the future?"

"Yes."

"And you wish to go back there?"

"Yes."

"But you need the help of a powerful witch or wizard. It was for this reason that you went to that witch in the bazaar who sold you to the Imps, is that correct?"

"Yes. Can you—"

"Send you back? No. Though I am an adequate witch in most respects, what you require is beyond me. Bring down Scruggs."

This last was said to the boy, and Rafe went to the edge of the belfry, took hold of a rope, and quickly climbed up and out of sight. A moment later, Kate heard his footsteps moving over the rooftop.

"Scruggs," Henrietta Burke poured herself a cup of coffee

from a pot on the desk, "was once a formidable wizard. But he overreached and cast a spell that broke him in two. Still, he has power. He placed a concealment over this church. The police and the Imps could walk right past and never see us. Now he spends his days talking to birds."

More footsteps above, and the boy reappeared, sliding down the rope. There was something fastened to his back. Kate saw that it was an old, bony-limbed, grizzle-haired man, wrapped in a tattered brown cloak. Once Rafe's feet were safely on the floor, the old man unwrapped his legs from around the boy's middle and his hands from Rafe's neck and, taking no notice of Kate or Henrietta Burke, settled himself into a chair beside the desk and began to chew his nails.

"Scruggs," the woman said, "this is the girl. Can you help her do what we talked about?"

Scruggs, Kate thought, looked like he needed help himself. The skin of his face was slack and gray. Both eyes were bloodshot. His hands were twisted and swollen. His long, scraggly hair was greasy and windblown. He needed help, she thought, or maybe a bath.

The old man stared at Kate and grunted, still gnawing on a fingernail.

"She has the power. She's fighting it; but I can pull it out."

"Thank you, Scruggs." Henrietta Burke turned back to Kate. "Do you know what tomorrow night is, child?"

"The . . . Separation?" Kate managed to recall the word used by the creatures who had bought her from the witch.

"Yes. On New Year's Eve, the magical world will go into

hiding. It is an event that has been decades in the planning. Can you imagine the scale of such a thing?" As she spoke, the woman walked to the edge of the belfry and looked out over the city. "A spell had to be devised to alter the memories of every non-magical human on the planet. Large swaths of land had to be made invisible. Agreement had to be obtained from each magical community that its members would abide by the Separation and not reveal themselves to those on the outside. Foolishly, there are some who yet oppose it, but even they have been brought to heel. The Separation is key to our survival." She turned back to Kate. "I mention all that only to say that until the Separation is accomplished, I will require Scruggs's full attention and powers. The next day or so are sure to be perilous. After that, he will send you home. Can you wait that long? If not, you are free to go."

Kate was about to thank her and say no. She had no intention of entrusting herself to Scruggs, despite anything the woman might say about his abilities—the old man had just discovered a bowl of soup on the desk and was trying to eat it with his fingers—but she paused. What, then, was her plan? To reach Cambridge Falls and contact Dr. Pym, but how? The boy had been right. She had no money; she was still wearing her summer sandals. How was she going to pay for the train ticket, food, warmer clothes?

"And what do I have to do for you?"

The woman smiled, if it could be called a smile: the narrow line of her mouth became an eighth of an inch wider. "So you've learned that nothing in this world is free. Good. I'm glad that young girls of the future are not complete fools."

"I won't steal anything—"

The woman laughed; it was like a dry clap. "And yet you have the luxury of scruples! The truth is, I don't know what the price will be. I will ask it when the time comes, and you can choose to pay it or not. Is that acceptable?"

Kate glanced over to where the boy, Rafe, still stood at the edge of the roof. She had not looked at him for several minutes. When she looked at him now, he quickly turned away. But in that moment, Kate saw in his face the recognition she'd been searching for. He'd lied; he did know her.

"I need an answer."

Still looking at the boy, Kate said, "Yes."

Mrs. Burke instructed Rafe to find Kate warmer, less noticeable clothes, and to get her something to eat and a place to sleep. Tomorrow, she said, they would talk more. When Kate and the boy reached the main hall of the church, Rafe called over a girl who was perhaps a year or two younger than Emma.

"She needs clothes," he told the girl. "Boy's clothes. The Imps're looking for her. The more hidden she is, the better." As the girl was leading Kate away, he called after them, "And a cap for her hair!"

"I know, I'm not stupid!" the girl yelled back. "He acts like I'm stupid."

The girl brought Kate to a room piled high with well-worn clothes. She literally dove into the mound of clothes and began flinging out wool pants and shirts, socks and sweaters, all of which Kate had to catch as they flew toward her.

"Just try on stuff till something fits," the girl said.

The girl was the same one whose hand Kate had pulled from the fire. Kate wondered if the girl remembered and thought about asking, but she had a feeling the girl would say of course she remembered, and then accuse Kate of thinking she was stupid.

And, for a moment, Kate was reminded so vividly of Emma, and how much she missed her sister, that her whole body clenched into one great sob of sadness.

"You all right?" The girl was holding up a pair of pants that Kate and four or five other people could've all fit into at once. "You look like you're gonna cry. Don't worry. We'll find you stuff."

Kate wiped at her eyes and tried to smile. "I know. Thanks."

Eventually—after rejecting what was too big, too small, too holey, too smelly, and anything that had been home to an animal—Kate stood dressed in a pair of thick wool pants, a wool shirt over a softer cotton shirt, a short canvas jacket to go under the coat she'd bought in the Bowery and had become attached to, and a pair of heavy wool socks. The girl, who seemed never to stop moving, was kneeling at her feet and jamming on a succession of boots, tossing the unwanted pairs over her shoulder into a large, disorderly pile.

"Perfect!" the girl announced.

Kate saw that the boots didn't match; but as they both fit and the heels were more or less the same height, she let it go.

"You just need a cap!"

The girl went back to digging in the pile.

"So that boy, Rafe. Who is he?" Kate asked.

"Rafe? He's the best!"

"Yeah, I've heard. Besides that."

"He's the one brought me here." Only the girl's legs were visible as she plowed through the pile of clothes. "My parents both died from the consumption. Then I was working at this factory downtown. Awful place. There were a bunch a' us girls. The owner kept us locked up, sewing day and night. Beat us. Fed us like dogs."

"But"—Kate was shocked—"they can't do that! There're laws!"

"Laws? Ha! When you're a kid and you got magic in you, the normal humans grab you quick and put you to work. No one cares. The stuff we make is special, see. The shoes or cabinets or whatever. They got magic in them. Like the clothes we sewed made folks look prettier or taller or not as fat. Then the owner'd sell 'em for lots a' money. Give money to the cops. No one cares."

"Why didn't you escape?"

"Don't be stupid," the girl said in exactly the way Emma might've. "Just 'cause you can do some magic don't mean you can shoot lightning outta your nose." She returned with a handful of cloth hats. "Anyway, Rafe found us. He gave that man, a grown man, a terrible whipping. He told us, 'You can go your own way, or you can come with me. You'll have to work, but there'll be no beatin' and you can leave when you want.' He done that to every kid here. Saved 'em. Same way Miss B saved him when he was a kid. You heard that story?"

Kate shook her head, and the girl lowered her voice ominously.

"Don't say I told you, but Rafe killed a man. He was only six years old, and he stabbed this man right through the heart." The girl, with a good degree of relish and an *uuuugggghhh* sound, pan-tomimed stabbing Kate in the heart. "Right, so then this mob a' humans was hunting him down. Miss B got in front a' them. They could see right away she was a witch, and she said she'd turn the first man who touched Rafe into a pig. Then she done it to one fella just to prove she could. That's when the Savages got started. With Rafe. And he found the rest a' us."

The girl took one of the caps and tried to yank it over Kate's head.

"I think it's too small," Kate said.

But even as she said it, the hat seemed to expand so that it became a perfect fit. The girl threw the others away.

"Great!"

Then Kate glanced down and saw that her boots, which a moment ago had looked nothing like each other, now matched. And her clothes, which had been sort of roughly her size, now looked as if they had been tailored for her. Was this how the children's magic worked? It leaked into the things they touched or made?

"Let's get supper." The girl smiled brightly. "'Fore it's all gone. Oh, my name's Abigail. 'Case you were wondering."

And she skipped out of the room.

Kate stood there, her mind spinning. Who were these children she had fallen among? And who was this boy? At six, he'd killed a man. Then he'd set about saving other children? None of it made sense.

And—this troubled Kate most of all—how did he know her?

At that moment, the boy was a dozen blocks to the south, hurrying down a street that would soon disappear from every map of New York. Night had fallen. Large white snowflakes drifted out of the darkness. The boy turned in at a shabby tenement, climbing down a set of stairs to knock three times at the basement apartment.

An old woman—a crone—shawl pulled tight over her bony shoulders, opened the door. Rafe passed a few coins into the mottled hand, and the woman stepped back to let him pass. The boy moved quickly through the dim rooms. The air smelled of boiled radishes, sweat, and tobacco. Men and women sat on the floor or against the wall and whispered in languages from lands far away.

He stopped at a door at the back of the apartment. Wavering candlelight shone under the sill. He raised his hand to knock, then a voice said:

"Come in."

He stepped into a small room lit by a single candle. A dark-haired, dark-eyed girl no more than fourteen sat at a table, an empty chair opposite her. Besides the candle, the table held a shallow clay bowl, a knife, and several small jars.

The boy reached into his pocket and pulled out a folded piece of cloth. He opened it, displaying a single blond hair, and handed it to the girl.

He said, "I want to know who she is."

The boy sat, watching as the girl filled the clay bowl with water, sprinkled in oil, then singed the hair on the flame and dropped it in the bowl. The liquid turned cloudy. She watched the surface for a few seconds. Finally, she looked up, and her eyes cleared.

"She has come from the future."

"Why? What's she doing here? What's she want?"

"She wants to go home. But in coming here, she has changed things."

"What do you mean?"

The girl stared at him for a long moment. "You've seen her before."

It was not a question. The boy nodded. "I saw her in a dream."

The girl held out a hand, and the boy reached up and pulled out one of his own hairs. She singed the hair and dropped it in the bowl. It was a long time before she looked up.

"You are being hunted."

"By who? The Imps? I killed one of theirs today—"

"That is not why they are hunting you. You are the reason they are here. The reason they have come to this country. To find you."

"What're you talking about?"

"You have something they need. Something their master wants. Had it not been for her, they would have found you today. Your path would have crossed with the giant's. But the girl's coming changed the course of events."

"Changed them how? Would I have been killed?"

"No, you would have joined them."

The boy laughed. "Me, join the Imps? You're crazy."

He started to rise, but the girl said, "The giant would have offered you power. Power to protect your friends. Power to punish your enemies. He would have promised you the answers you crave. You could not have resisted."

The boy sat back down. "So what happens now?"

"That is not clear. The girl is the key. Through her, you will understand your destiny. But you know that already. Your dream has told you."

When the boy spoke again, his voice was strangely quiet. "And the rest of my dream, what about it? Will it come true?"

The girl nodded. "Yes. She will show you who you are. And then she will die."

CHAPTER NINE
Ice

As they pulled away from Malpesa, it was pandemonium inside the aircraft—Emma crying that they had to go back for Dr. Pym, clutching now at Gabriel, now at Michael, yelling at the pilot to turn the stupid plane around, both children soaking wet and starting to shiver from being plunged into the ice-cold water of the canal. In the midst of this, Gabriel quietly took charge: wrapping the children in blankets, giving them clothes to change into—the pilot had packed extra shirts and pants; luckily, he was a small man, though not so small that his clothes weren't comically large on the children—and soon Michael and Emma were dry and dressed, their shaking had stopped, and Emma seemed to have accepted that the stupid plane was not going back for Dr. Pym; they were going on.

Gabriel checked them both for injuries, taking time to dress

Michael's various cuts and scrapes. With the man kneeling before him, Michael studied their friend. So much about him was the same: the old scar ridged along his cheek, the unreadable, granite-colored eyes. But Michael also noticed the streaks of gray in Gabriel's black hair, and the lines on his face, and it occurred to him that unlike Dr. Pym, Gabriel was just a man, and it had been fifteen years since their adventure in Cambridge Falls. He still looked almost impossibly strong and powerful. But—and perhaps it was just the lines around his eyes or the gray in his hair— Michael sensed a new slowness, not in movement but in manner.

"How are you?"

Michael shrugged. There was no way to answer the question. Too much had happened. Also, he felt silly in the enormous clothes.

Gabriel said, "You will see the wizard again."

"And Kate?"

"Her too."

"How do you know that?"

"Because I know them."

Michael had told Gabriel what had happened on the rooftop, how the wizard had stayed behind to prevent Rourke from following them, or at least to slow the man down, and how he, Michael, was charged with finding the *Chronicle*. Not surprisingly, he'd mentioned nothing about how he'd nearly broken down and pleaded with the wizard that he wasn't ready for the task being given him. Ashamed, Michael was already burying the memory in a deep, dark place where he'd never have to look at it again.

The plane didn't have seats, just benches that folded down,

and the children were sitting side by side, wrapped in blankets, with their backs to the wall. Emma had taken one of Gabriel's hands and was holding it in her lap, half for comfort and half, it seemed, to ensure that her friend did not disappear.

"Tell me," Gabriel said, "what did you learn about the book?"

Taking a deep breath, Michael told them—for Emma had not yet heard the story—about crawling into the chamber with the skeleton, how he'd realized the inscription in the tunnel was a riddle, how he'd drunk from all three jars and had suddenly known where the *Chronicle* was hidden—

"That's what you were doing in there?" Emma punched him in the arm. "That was so—*stupid!* Don't ever do anything like that ever again, you hear me? Ever!"

"Okay."

"You'd better not." And she hit him again for good measure.

Michael rubbed his arm and, despite himself, smiled.

"What do you mean, you know where the book is hidden?" Gabriel asked. "You had a vision?"

"Not exactly. It was like I remembered where it was. Like I'd been the one to hide it. That probably sounds crazy."

"Yes," Emma said.

"No," Gabriel said. "Such a thing is common in the magical world. The dead man somehow placed his memories into those potions, and they were transferred to you."

"But I see it all in pieces," Michael said. "And I can't point to anything on a map."

"Be that as it may, the pilot needs a heading. Where should I tell him to go?"

Without thinking, Michael said, "South. Tell him to go south."

"There is nothing south of Malpesa."

"Yes, there is," Michael said. "There's one thing."

And Gabriel looked at him, nodded, and crept forward to tell the pilot.

Michael burrowed down inside his blanket, letting himself feel the buffeting and rocking of the plane. Gabriel returned and said that they had enough gas to reach an outpost on the Ronne Ice Shelf on the coast of Antarctica. Once there, they could refuel, get clothes for the children, and plot the rest of their course. The journey to the outpost would take most of the night.

"Your sister is right to sleep."

And Michael glanced over and saw that Emma's head was on his shoulder and her eyes were closed. When Michael turned back, Gabriel was studying his face, and he knew that the man was gauging his strength for what lay ahead.

"I'll be okay," Michael said. "I'm just tired."

But his voice sounded so feeble that even he didn't believe it.

Gabriel put his hand on Michael's arm. It was a strangely gentle and eloquent gesture. Then Gabriel went forward to the cockpit, and Michael rested his head against the humming wall of the airplane as Emma shifted about. He glanced out the window, but all was dark. They were headed south, to the bottom of the world. He closed his eyes. It was a long time before he drifted off to sleep.

• • •

Michael dreamed of snow. He dreamed of fields and valleys, plains and mountains, all covered in snow and stretching to the horizon. He was flying over it, floating. He was alone, but not afraid. . . .

A pair of giants crouched in the distance. He flew between them, passing through the teeth of a dragon. . . .

Then he was in a long tunnel. A red glow throbbed all about him. The heat was incredible. His skin crackled like dry paper. Each breath burned his lungs. Suddenly, he was standing beside a bubbling lake, and the heat was much, much worse. He stared at the fiery surface—

"Michael! Michael! Wake up!"

Emma was shaking him. He opened his eyes and had no idea where he was. Then he recognized the interior of the plane, saw Gabriel moving about, getting their things together, and he remembered.

"Are you all right?" Emma asked. "You were making noise."

"What did I say?"

"Not so much words. More like *mmmrrrraaaaggghhhhh*."

"Oh."

"Get ready. Gabriel says we're landing soon. And Michael . . ."

"What?"

"He says we might see penguins!"

Michael rubbed his eyes and looked out the window. In the dim predawn, ghostly white cliffs rose up before them. Michael watched as an enormous ice shelf cleaved off the cliff and collapsed, almost gently, into the sea. Then the plane passed over the wall of ice, and there was nothing but whiteness below them and before them.

I brought us here, Michael thought. Whatever happens is my fault.

He set about pulling on his boots.

"There! Look! Don't scare him!"

The penguin waddled toward them, flat wings held out wide to balance its wobbly, bowling-pin body. The penguin came to just past their knees, and its webbed feet went *thop-thop-thop . . . thop-thop-thop* on the hard-packed ice and snow. Michael and Emma stood perfectly still as the bird maneuvered by them and disappeared around a building.

"That's the best thing I ever saw," Emma said. "Ever."

It was nine in the morning, and the sun had yet to rise. The temperature was only ten degrees below freezing, which was apparently quite warm. The plane, whose pontoons doubled as skis, had landed on a runway of compacted snow beside the outpost. The outpost itself seemed like something you might find on the moon: nine or ten low metal buildings, domed roofs studded with antennas, half-buried tunnels snaking here and there.

It looked like a space station, Michael thought, or a giant hamster run.

Gabriel had made the children wait in the plane till he returned with new cold-weather gear and their own clothes, which he'd run through the dryer at the outpost laundry. It was fortunate that Dr. Pym had given them warm clothes before going to Malpesa since the outpost store did not cater to children. Gabriel had simply bought the smallest sizes he could find, and Michael and Emma both got long underwear, heavy parkas with fur-lined hoods, insulated snow pants to go over their normal pants, thickly padded mittens, liners to go inside the mittens, face masks, hats, goggles, and shell-like boots that fit over their old boots. "Like boots for our boots," Emma said. "Cool." Michael's parka and pants just about fit him, but Gabriel had to cut some length off the sleeves of Emma's parka and the bottoms of her pants, the edges of which he then sealed with heavy tape. When both children were finally dressed, Michael felt as if he were embarking on an undersea expedition or a journey into deep space. Emma looked at him and giggled.

"You look like Mr. Sausage."

"So? You're dressed the same."

Then she tried to punch him, lost her balance, and fell over.

Even dressed as they were, when they stepped out of the plane, Michael's breath was ripped away by the cold. It was a kind of cold that the children had never experienced, and they stood there, taking short breaths, getting used to the cramped feeling in their lungs. It was then they saw the penguin, whom Emma immediately named Derek, and this put them in a good mood as they headed to the outpost café to join Gabriel for breakfast.

The windows of the metal hut were steamed with heat, and the floor was a steel grating through which the snow that people tramped inside could melt away. There were a dozen tables, perhaps half of them full. Gabriel and the small pilot sat in the corner. Gabriel got the children trays and plates and let them place their orders—scrambled eggs, pancakes, bacon, toast, hash browns—with the man at the grill. As Michael pressed the button to fill his hot chocolate, he noticed the stares he and Emma were getting. Gabriel had told them that the outpost was a way station for scientists, oil workers, explorers, and traders from all over Antarctica, but that children here were rare.

"We'll leave as soon as we've eaten and the plane is refueled. The fewer questions asked, the better."

At the table, Gabriel and the pilot had laid out a large map of Antarctica.

"Now," Gabriel said to Michael, "as long as the weather holds, Gustavo will fly us wherever we want. But you must tell us where to go."

"It's not easy," Michael said. "It's all in pieces in my mind. But the next thing we're looking for should be a pair of mountains. They're really tall and thin. There're other mountains around them, but they're the biggest. And they're right next to each other. Does that make sense?"

As Gabriel spoke to the pilot in Spanish, Michael saw that Emma had already eaten both of her pancakes and was half finished with her eggs. He knew he'd better hurry or she'd start in on *his* breakfast. The pilot was saying something to Gabriel and pointing to a spot on the map. Michael could see a shaded area, which he knew indicated mountains.

"He says," Gabriel interpreted, "you mean the Horns. A pair of mountains at the head of the Victoria Range. It is perhaps two hours' flying from here. What do we do when we get there?"

"There should be a cave between the two mountains," Michael said as he chewed through three pieces of bacon. "And there're these rock formations in front of the cave that make it look like a mouth with huge teeth. The dead man called it the Dragon's Mouth. He must've called it that in his own language, but somehow I know that's the name."

Gabriel spoke to the pilot, and the pilot replied and shook his head.

"He knows of no such cave, but that means nothing. What then?"

"Then," Michael said, fending off Emma's fork, which was stabbing at one of his pancakes, "there's, like, a gap in the memory. I told you it was all in pieces. But on the other side of the cave, we should find a volcano. That's where the *Chronicle* is hidden."

Again, Gabriel spoke to the man. Again, the man said something and shook his head. Then the pilot rolled up his map and walked out.

"He says," Gabriel told the children, "that there is no volcano in that region, and that this would be a thing he knows since he has flown all over this area. But he will fly us to the base of the Horns, and we will see if we can find the cave. We must hope the weather holds."

"There is a volcano," Michael said, surprised at his own stubbornness. "I know there is."

Gabriel nodded. "I believe you. But I am worried about this cave. These memories you inherited are more than two hundred years old. In that time, there could have been landslides. Earthquakes. The cave could be hidden or collapsed. Either way, we shall see. Now eat. The sun will soon be up."

"I'm getting seconds," Emma said. "Since Mr. Sausage here won't share." And she picked up her syrup-smeared plate and carried it to the grill.

Soon, they were in the air. The sun had finally risen over the horizon, and as they flew, Emma kept jumping from one side of the plane to the other, pressing her face against the windows. The night before, she'd been too tired and upset to appreciate her first-ever plane ride. Today, she was fed and rested. Though really, Michael knew, the change in her mood was due to Gabriel. After breakfast, in the tunnel-like corridor outside the café, Michael had heard him whisper, "I won't leave you again," and Emma had leapt up and thrown her arms around his neck. Since then, she had been more and more her old self, and now, with the sun shining in the distance and a beautiful, strange land passing below, she was clearly enjoying the moment.

He was not quite so carefree.

The certainty he'd felt in the café had given way to doubt. What if the pilot was right and there was no volcano? Or there was, but the Guardian was sending them into a trap? Michael only had a few of the dead man's memories; he didn't truly know the man's mind. He could be leading Emma and Gabriel to their deaths! He wanted to mention this to Gabriel, to let the man assuage his fears, but he was terrified of appearing less than completely confident. He couldn't come across as weak.

"Michael!" Emma cried. "Come quick!"

He joined her at the side of the plane.

"Look!" She pointed to the ground far below. "It's Derek!"

Michael could just make out a small, dark shape moving across the white expanse.

"Are you sure that's him?"

"Oh, that's definitely Derek. I'd recognize him anywhere." She pressed her forehead against the window, peering down. "I wonder where he's going."

Michael felt a hand on his shoulder. It was Gabriel, and he motioned them to the cockpit. Michael and Emma crowded in behind the pilot, who grinned and pointed through the window.

Emma let out a low gasp.

Directly before them was a range of enormous mountains, white peaks rising from a white plain. The mountains were wide-waisted and packed in tight, one against the other, but two peaks stood out. They were the furthest forward, and the tallest and the thinnest; there was no mistaking them.

The Horns, Michael thought.

He experienced a moment of intense déjà vu. For though he was seeing them for the first time, he knew the mountains from the dead man's memory. Michael found it unsettling, as if his sense of who he was—the things he knew, the things he remembered, the things that made him him—had begun to blur at the edges.

"These are the mountains?" Gabriel asked.

"Yes." His voice was barely audible over the whine of the engine.

The pilot then spoke to Gabriel, who nodded and turned to the children.

"We will be there in twenty minutes. He will land a few miles from the base of the Horns. From there, we will go on foot. It is time to get ready."

Michael's hand shook as he tried to zip up the front of his parka, and he turned so no one would notice. Soon, both children were muffled in parkas, hats, face masks, goggles, mittens; all that remained were the hard outer boots that Gabriel had bought at the outpost. The children were too stiffly dressed to bend over, so Gabriel had them lie on the floor while he stuffed their old boots into the new ones and snapped them shut. Then he checked to make sure all their gear was zipped and cinched properly.

Michael could scarcely move, and he wondered how in the world they were supposed to hike for three miles.

The plane bumped and rocked as they glided lower. Clinging to a strap on the wall, Michael watched as Gabriel went over the contents of a large pack, double-checking that he had food, water, an emergency shelter, ropes, an ice ax, and other necessary gear. He also, Michael saw, strapped a slender, three-foot-long, canvas-wrapped object to the pack. Michael knew it was Gabriel's falchion, the machete-like weapon the children had seen him use while fighting in Cambridge Falls. It reminded Michael—as if he needed reminding—that they had no idea what lay ahead.

The plane skipped across the ground, and Michael and Emma lost their grips on the wall straps and flew forward, crashing into the bulkhead, though their many layers kept them from getting hurt. Twice more the plane struck the ground and rebounded into the air, for while the snow was hard, it undulated like a frozen sea. Finally, the plane settled, wobbled unevenly for a hundred yards, and came to a halt.

Michael looked at his sister.

"Are you okay?"

"I'm hot," Emma grumbled. "I wish they'd open the door."

"I meant—"

"I know what you meant. I'm just hot."

Gabriel checked their clothing one last time.

"We have four more hours of daylight. If we find this cave, the Dragon's Mouth, we will continue on. Failing that, we will either return to the plane or camp if we can find shelter. Gustavo will wait till midnight, then fly back to the outpost. He will come here every day for three days and wait for us during daylight hours. Are you ready?"

Michael saw that Gabriel was looking at him, waiting for an answer, and it crossed his mind to say, "You know, now that I've had time to sit with it, I think we should scuttle the whole thing." But he knew that wasn't what Gabriel was asking. Their way led onward, not back; and in asking if he was ready, Gabriel was merely letting Michael make the decision to begin.

Michael reached up to straighten his glasses, realized he was wearing goggles, and straightened them instead.

"Yes. Let's go."

Gabriel opened the door, and it was as if all the cold air in the world swept into the plane. Gabriel carried his pack out first, then helped Emma to the ground. Michael saw the pilot, Gustavo, watching them with a worried expression.

"Thank you for the ride," Michael said, his voice muffled by the mask. "We'll see you soon. I hope."

And he followed Emma out into the cold.

The ground had a hard, icy crust, which allowed them to walk without snowshoes. The Horns loomed above them, outlined against a blue sky, their crooked peaks bending in toward each other. Gabriel led, with Emma in the middle and Michael bringing up the rear. Looking back, Michael could see the pale disk of the sun hanging above the rim of the earth. More than ever, he felt like a voyager on some distant planet.

With the extra weight of the clothes and the boots, walking was hard work, and Michael's legs soon grew heavy. His watch was buried under multiple layers, and the only landmarks he had to gauge their progress by were the mountains before them (which seemed to grow no closer) and the plane behind them (which, somewhat distressingly, became smaller and smaller).

They had been walking, Michael guessed, for half an hour when Gabriel stopped and turned, staring past the children.

"What is it?" Michael could see nothing except the plane, tiny and dark, in the distance.

"I am not sure."

Gabriel knelt and took a rope and set of metal clips from his pack. He ran the rope between the clips, and fastened the clips to his, Michael's, and Emma's jackets, linking them together.

"What's this for?" Emma asked.

"Safety."

They kept walking. The ground rose. Michael was cold now, even though it seemed impossible that a person could be cold while wearing so many layers. To distract himself, he thought about the library in the house in Cambridge Falls, and how much he wished he was sitting beside the fire with a cup of hot chocolate and *The Dwarf Omnibus* open in his lap, watching the snow fall outside. Maybe eating a grilled cheese.

And he was thinking this, and thinking how much nicer it was to read about adventures than to actually have them, when he noticed how faint his shadow had become. All the time they'd been walking, his shadow had stretched before him, sharp and black against the white ground, but now it was barely visible. He turned and saw that the sun had disappeared. But that made no sense. There were still several hours of daylight left. Then he realized that he could no longer see the plane either. He began to have an uneasy feeling in his stomach.

"Gabriel—"

That was all he managed before the storm hit. It was like a wave, crashing over him, knocking him into Emma. Sprawled upon the snow, the children were blown helplessly forward. Michael scrambled for something to cling to, but his hands found no purchase. He saw the two of them being blown, like leaves before a hurricane, to the other side of Antarctica. Then—with a jerk—they stopped. Gabriel had dug his boots into the ice, planted his ax, and wrapped his arm around the rope tying them all together. Like a fisherman reeling in his catch, he drew the children toward him, angling his back to take the brunt of the wind. Michael and Emma huddled into the small eddy of his body. The howling filled their ears. Visibility was an arm's length or less.

A whiteout, Michael thought, having read the word somewhere. We're in a whiteout.

Emma yelled something, but her words were swept away.

Gabriel leaned forward, shouting over the wind.

"I will set up our shelter! It is useless trying to return to the plane! We would become lost! We must wait out the storm!"

"But we're so close!" Michael shouted. "If we get to the cave, we'll be safe!"

"We'll never find it! Even the mountains have disappeared!"

"I can find it!"

The words surprised Michael. He hadn't thought them, or planned on saying them, but he knew that what he'd said was true. All the time they'd been walking, some invisible force had been pulling him forward. He was only fully aware of it now that they'd stopped; but he knew that if he let himself be led, he would find the cave.

"What's going on?" Emma turned from Michael to Gabriel. "I can't hear anything!"

Gabriel was staring at him, his eyes hidden behind dark, frost-covered goggles.

"Are you sure? It is a risk!"

He means we could all die, Michael thought. Become hopelessly lost. Stumble into a crevasse. Setting up camp was the only sensible, practical thing to do.

He looked at Emma, swiveling her head between him and Gabriel, saying, "Huh? What'd you say?! It's so loud! Huh?!" It wasn't fair. Michael would risk his own life willingly; why did he also have to risk his sister's? Or Gabriel's?

"You must decide!" Gabriel shouted.

Michael closed his eyes. The tug was still there, like an invisible hook attached to his chest. He knew it was the *Chronicle*.

"Yes! I can find it!"

"Find what?" Emma shouted. "What're you two talking about?"

Gabriel didn't answer, but set about switching the rope so that Michael was leading.

"We'll follow you!"

He handed Michael his ice ax, and Michael stood and started off through the storm. He had to brace himself at every step to keep from being blown over, and it was incredibly tiring, walking forward while pushing back with all his strength. With the gusting of the wind, there were brief moments when things would clear and Michael could see ten or even fifteen feet ahead. But most times, he waved his hand before his face and saw nothing.

Please, he kept thinking, please don't let me be wrong.

But he could feel the *Chronicle* out there, calling to him, more and more strongly with each step. He found himself thinking of a field trip that he and his sisters and a bunch of other kids had taken to a farm a few years before. They'd been out in the middle of nowhere, and the driver of the van, a sulky teenager, had scoured the radio for any station that, as he put it, "didn't play banjo music." Finally, he'd found one. It had been scratchy and faint at first, but as they drove on, and presumably got nearer to the source, the signal had become more and more clear.

Michael felt that way now, as if he'd finally gotten close enough to hear the music.

"Michael!"

Emma had shouted in his ear, and was grabbing his shoulder and pointing.

Michael looked up—he'd been staring at the ground, focusing on not leading everyone into a chasm—and there, ten feet away, just visible through the whirling snow, past three pillars covered in snow and ice, pillars that tapered as they rose to give a very credible impression of fangs, was the dark, gaping maw of a cave.

Moments later, they were inside the cave, stamping their feet, beating the caked-up snow and ice from their bodies, brushing the crystals off their fur-lined hoods, as the storm raged outside. Gabriel clapped Michael on the shoulder.

"Well done."

Michael tried to shrug, but the gesture was lost inside the enormous parka.

"Oh, you know, it was no big deal."

"Yeah," Emma said, "you're probably right."

"Well," Michael said, irked, "it was kind of a big deal."

Then Emma laughed and clapped her mittens together (or tried to—she couldn't quite make her hands meet while wearing the parka) and told Michael that of course it was a big deal and if

King Robbie were there he'd probably give Michael a dozen more dwarf medals.

"Ha-ha," Michael said. Though he couldn't help thinking a medal wouldn't be uncalled for.

"Are you still cold?" Emma asked. "You're shaking."

In fact, Michael was trembling, but it had nothing to do with the cold. In trusting his instinct, he should have been filled with confidence. But the opposite had happened. He didn't understand *how* it had worked, *how* he'd succeeded. He felt out of control, and the feeling scared him. He'd gotten very lucky, and he mustn't count on it happening again.

"I just need to start moving."

"Then let us." Gabriel had taken three flashlights from his pack, and he handed one to each of the children. "You're the leader. Lead."

Michael looked at Emma, who shrugged and said, "Just don't get us killed."

And with that, Michael turned, and they set off into the cave.

The cave was different from all the other caves and tunnels the children had explored in one major respect: it was covered in ice. Floor, ceiling, and walls were glazed in a hard blue-white shell. Luckily, the new boots Gabriel had bought them had rough soles that gripped the slick surface. Still, they proceeded slowly, and their flashlights kept reflecting back at them, making the children's hearts beat faster as they imagined beasts with glowing eyes peering at them from the darkness.

Soon, the sound of the storm had faded, and the tunnel opened into a vast cavern, and they walked along a narrow track that hugged the wall. They shone their lights into the abyss, illuminating a lake of black ice, and Michael peered down and saw things with claws and teeth and wings held in a frozen sleep. The tunnel resumed on the far side of the lake, and the ice on the walls began to give way to bare rock till there were only patches of ice here and there, and then finally none at all. Michael found himself pulling down his mask, pushing back his hood, unzipping his jacket.

Then he snapped off his flashlight.

"Michael . . . ," Emma whispered.

"I know."

The end of the tunnel was before them, and light poured through it. Not the dim, grayish haze of a snowstorm, but sunlight, golden, warm, bright sunlight.

Only that wasn't possible. Michael knew that wasn't possible. And then . . .

"Michael, can you hear . . ."

"Yes."

It was the sound of a bird singing.

CHAPTER TEN
The End of the World

"Did you know—"

"No."

"None of this . . ."

"No."

"Because it's . . . wow."

Yes, Michael thought. Wow.

They had come out of the tunnel and were high above an enormous, crescent-shaped valley. From where they stood, sheer rock walls dropped down nearly a mile to the valley floor, while snowcapped mountains rose above them, encircling the valley in an unbroken ring. Michael guessed it was at least a mile to the other side. To both the left and the right, the valley curved away and out of sight. The sky was a pure, crystalline blue, and the air was warm and still. Far below, the valley floor looked to be covered in a dark canopy of green.

Michael thought of taking a Polaroid, then decided a photo wouldn't do the view justice.

"But we're at the South Pole!" Emma said. "There should be penguins! And snow! And—and polar bears!"

"Polar bears are at the North Pole."

"You know what I mean! This is—"

"It's the *Chronicle*," Michael said. "Thousands of years ago, I bet this was just like the rest of Antarctica. Then the Order brought the *Chronicle* here and everything changed."

They were silent, staring down at the impossibly lush valley. Then Gabriel said:

"There."

He was pointing to the right. Past the bend of the valley, just visible over the shoulder of a mountain, a thin trail of black smoke rose into the air.

"The volcano," Michael whispered.

"Amazing," Emma marveled. "You were actually right."

"You don't have to act so surprised," Michael said.

"But I am," Emma said. "I'm really surprised."

Quickly, for they were already hot and sweating, the trio removed their cold-weather gear—their parkas, heavy boots, insulated pants, long underwear, goggles, mittens, and hats—and Gabriel stowed everything inside the cave for their return journey. Michael was surprised to find the gray-blue marble hanging from a strap around his neck and realized that in the excitement of the last twenty-four hours, he'd forgotten all about it. Obviously, now was not the time to ponder who had sent it or what its purpose might be, but as he tucked the glass orb back inside his shirt, Michael promised himself he would try to figure it out the moment he got the chance.

The tunnel had given onto a promontory, from which a set of nearly vertical stairs, cut into the face of the cliff, wound down to the valley floor. Gabriel took the safety rope and clipped it to the children's belts.

"We'll get to the bottom," he said. "Then make for the volcano."

The stairs were more like a ladder than a staircase, with every step nearly two feet high. Only once did Michael peer over the side to check their progress, and he found it was a straight drop to the bottom. After that, he kept his attention on each individual step. The further they descended, the warmer and more humid it became. Michael's glasses kept slipping down his nose, and his T-shirt stuck to his back. Birdcalls echoed through the valley, and soon they could hear the sound of running water.

They stopped halfway down, and Gabriel gave them bread, hard sausage, and dried fruit from his pack. Michael was checking his watch, thinking that the sun should've set and yet it was still light, when they heard something that was not a bird. The cry came from the direction of the volcano. It was harsh and savage and silenced everything in the valley.

"What was that?" Emma whispered.

Gabriel shook his head. "I do not know."

Neither did Michael. But he did know that whatever had made the sound was very, very big.

They finished their meal in silence and resumed the descent. Thirty minutes later, they reached the canopy of trees. From above, Michael had expected to find a tropical jungle, but the valley floor was covered by a forest of enormous redwoods. He recognized the trees from photos and movies, but these were taller and larger than any he had ever seen. Indeed, the valley floor turned out to be much lower than they had thought, for even after reaching the canopy, they kept climbing down and down and down.

"Can you believe," Emma said when they were finally at the bottom, "we have to go back up that?"

The light had now begun to fade, and it was darker still under the canopy.

"I know you're tired," Gabriel said. "But we should push on. I would like to camp closer to the volcano so we can arrive there tomorrow morning."

Michael nodded, Emma groaned, and they kept walking, no one mentioning that the creature's cry had come from the direction of the volcano. Michael felt as if they were walking through a forest of sleeping giants. Even Gabriel stared up in awe at the massive red-brown trunks. But the going was slow, as the forest floor was covered in a thick bed of ferns, and Gabriel had to use his falchion to bushwhack a path.

Little else moved in the forest. The birds kept to the canopy, and the only other wildlife were shiny black beetles that scuttled up the sides of the great trees and, with a furious whirring and clicking, abruptly took flight, weaving away between the trunks. The beetles were the size of turtles, and after Michael was struck in the back of the head and literally knocked off his feet, the children learned to duck when they heard one coming.

Still, Michael thought, fingering the sore spot behind his ear, if this is all there is, birds and beetles, why do I feel like we're being watched?

As they hiked, the sound of rushing water grew louder, and eventually they came to a river, perhaps forty yards across, running clear and swift down the center of the canyon. They were hot from the walk, and Gabriel let them lie on their stomachs and dip their faces in the stream. The water was ice-cold, and they drank until their teeth ached.

Refreshed, the small party continued on, following the bank of the river until it was too dark to see and both children were dragging their feet and Emma had said for the fifteenth time, "This looks like a good place to stop." Gabriel made camp on a large rock that gave views both upstream and downstream, and he brought out food—more bread, sausage, and dried fruit—and said they would not risk a fire. Michael wondered if Gabriel also felt they were being watched; if the man did, he said nothing. After they had eaten, Gabriel cut fronds from nearby ferns and made a thick, soft bed on the rock, and Emma lay down and was asleep in a moment.

"Sleep," Gabriel told Michael. "I'll stand watch."

Michael fully intended to tell Gabriel to wake him in a few hours and let him stand his turn, but exhausted and aching in every part of his body, and lulled by the murmur of the river, Michael lay down beside his sister and slept.

Michael dreamed.

Again, he was in the long, dark tunnel, walking toward the red glow.

Again, he stood before the lake of fire, staring into the surface as his eyes burned and the heat stifled his breath.

He knew the *Chronicle* was somewhere nearby. But where?

And then, strangely, he heard music. It seemed to be all around him. The heat lessened. He could breathe without pain. A weight lifted from his shoulders. He felt as light as air, as if he could float up into the sky and sail away. . . .

A hand on his shoulder jostled him awake.

It was still dark; Gabriel was leaning over him, a finger to his lips telling Michael to remain silent. There was music drifting out of the forest, and Michael recognized it as the music from his dream. He sat up; indeed, he might have leapt up had Gabriel's hand not rested on his shoulder.

"I heard—"

"Yes, it began a minute ago. I am going to investigate. Stay with your sister." Gabriel rose, then paused. "You will stay with her."

There was a question in his voice.

"Of course, yes, I'll stay with her."

The man stared at him. Michael couldn't help himself.

"Just the music . . . it's so . . . beautiful."

"Try not to listen."

"Okay."

Gabriel kept staring at him. Michael realized he was humming. He stopped.

Gabriel said, "I will be back soon." And, unsheathing his falchion, he slipped noiselessly into the trees.

Michael glanced at his sister. Emma was smiling in her sleep. Michael had never seen Emma smile in her sleep. Usually, she slept with her hands clenched into fists as if she were fighting battles in her dreams. He wondered if she could hear the music. It really was so beautiful—

No! Gabriel had told him not to listen!

Taking off his glasses, Michael lay down on the rock and splashed ice-cold water on his face. He was instantly wide-awake.

That's better, he thought.

Then he realized the reason it was better was because he could hear the music more clearly. He stood, water dripping from his face, and looked about the starlit darkness. Everything around him—the air, the water, the earth, the rocks—all seemed to be responding to the song. But Gabriel had said not to listen! Well, Michael thought, Gabriel was a wonderful fellow and knew about a great many useful things, but music was obviously not one of them. There could be nothing dangerous about such a song. It was a song about the air and the water, about the trees and the birds, about those giant beetles that flew without looking where they were going; it was a song about life. And it was asking you to join it—to dance. Michael began swaying back and forth, his right hand ghost-conducting in the air. And I love dancing, Michael thought, even though he'd never danced once in his entire life and had always taken great pains to avoid it.

He shook Emma awake.

She moaned and kept her eyes shut. ". . . Stop it."

"Emma, wake up!"

"But I was dreaming and there was . . ."

She fell silent. Michael saw she'd heard the music.

"It's real. . . ."

"I know!" Michael was bursting with happiness. He'd had the most wonderful idea. He'd told Gabriel he wouldn't leave Emma, but what if he brought her along to search for the music? "Come on! We've gotta find it!"

And he seized Emma by the hand and dragged her into the forest. The music was coming from further along in the direction of the volcano. Strangely, the ferns that had fought their passage all day now seemed to give way before the children, bending back to open a path.

"Where's—Gabriel?" Emma panted.

"He went to look for the music!"

"You think we'll find him?"

"Maybe. If not, we can look for him while we're dancing!"

"Yay!" cried Emma, who generally disliked dancing at least as much as Michael did. "And then Gabriel can dance with us!"

"Ha! He's probably there dancing already!" Michael laughed.

And then, quite suddenly, they arrived.

It was a large, circular clearing, ringed by great trees. The ferns stopped at the edge of the clearing, and the ground beyond was covered by low, thick grass. Across the clearing, Michael could see figures with torches emerging from the trees. They were too far away to see well, but Michael knew that they were the ones making the music. And it was then he realized that the music was singing, that voices were making those beautiful sounds.

Emma let out a small cry and leapt forward, but Michael yanked her back.

"What're you doing? We—"

"I just had an awful thought." They were crouched beside one of the trees at the edge of the clearing. Michael tried to sound as grave as possible. He needed Emma to understand the seriousness of what he was about to say. "What if we're not wearing the right clothes? I don't want to look stupid."

Emma stared at him, then nodded. "That's really good thinking."

"I know," Michael said. And he cursed himself for not making Gabriel carry a set of fancier clothes in his pack. He should've known something like this would happen.

The figures were moving toward the center of the clearing, and as they drew closer, the torches shone on their faces. The children stared in wonder.

"Michael . . . are those . . . ?"

"Yes."

"Really? I mean, really and truly?"

"Yes." His voice was dry as a stone, but he managed to say, "Those are elves."

There were perhaps forty of them. Some were carrying torches, others had lanterns. All of them were singing, and while not exactly dancing, the very way they walked, even their small-est gesture, was more graceful than any dance. And every one of them—Michael's heart sank as he realized this—was dressed incredibly well.

What Michael thought of as the girl elves wore long white-and-cream dresses of frilly material, while the boy elves wore white trousers and shirts, along with pink-and-white-, blue-and-white-, or green-and-white-striped jackets. The boy elves wore stiff-brimmed straw hats. The girl elves twirled parasols on their dainty shoulders. A few of the elves carried wooden tennis rackets.

Michael recognized the clothes as the fashions of a hundred years ago, and the logical part of his brain, which was still func-tioning, albeit at a very low level, reminded him that it had been a hundred years ago that the magical world had gone into hiding. The elves, it seemed, had simply kept up the trends of that time.

And right they were, Michael thought. They looked mar-velous.

"Their clothes are so beautiful!" Emma was on the verge of tears. "We'll never find clothes like that!"

"Shhh," Michael said. "I want to hear."

For the elves had all gathered in the center of the clearing, and they abruptly shifted from the ethereal, wordless song that Michael and Emma had heard in their dreams to a new song, one with a jaunty, let's-all-go-boating sort of tune.

And this time, Michael could make out the words:

> Oh, she has to eat, she has to eat,
> She'd better watch her figure.

Her shape is long and slender,
Her nails, they cut like ice.
Her eyes still shine like diamonds,
And yet her stomach rumbles on.
Oh, she has to eat, she has to eat,
She'd better watch her figure. . . .

"What're they singing about?" Emma asked.

"I don't know," Michael said. "It's a lovely song, though. Don't you think?"

"It is," Emma said. "Very lovely."

And it occurred to Emma that she didn't use the word *lovely* half as often as she should and she would definitely correct that. It was a lovely word, *lovely*.

"Lovely, lovely, lovely, lovely . . ."

"What're you doing?" Michael whispered.

"Just saying the word *lovely*," Emma whispered back.

"Oh," Michael said, wondering why he hadn't thought of that. "Right."

And as they watched the elves and listened to the song, they both murmured, "Lovely, lovely, lovely, lovely, lovely, lovely, lovely . . ."

Some of the elves were doing cartwheels around the clearing, a few played leapfrog, and one was riding around on one of those old-fashioned bicycles with a giant front wheel and a tiny back wheel. Several of the elves had opened wicker picnic baskets and were handing out beverages and food, mostly cake. Two of the elves had begun to set up what looked to Michael like a dunking booth. The whole scene was strangely familiar, and Michael realized where he'd seen such things before: in old movies, when people would have town fairs, with bobbing for apples and pie-eating contests and something involving a greased pig. Just as their clothes were stuck in the past, so too were the elves' traditions. Michael was charmed.

"Lovely," he murmured. "Lovely."

And the song went on:

> Her arms are just so shapely,
> Her waist is slim and fine.
> Her nose knows no equal (ha-ha!)
> And her teeth, her teeth, oh let them always
>   shine.
> Oh, she has to eat, she has to eat,
> She'd better watch her figure. . . .

"Did you know there were elves here?" Emma whispered.

"No. It's a really nice surprise, though," Michael said.

"It sure is. How's my hair look?"

This was the first time in her life that Emma had asked this question.

Michael looked at her. She had not showered since the previous day, when they'd stayed at the cottage in Spain, and since then they'd climbed through a tomb, run through a sewer, jumped into a canal, hiked through a blizzard—which involved the wearing of hats and hoods and much sweating—and slept on a bed of ferns.

"Honestly?"

"Yes."

"It looks like a bum's hair. I'm sorry. But you have bum hair."

"It's okay," Emma said. "You have bum hair too."

"Look what they've got!" Michael exclaimed.

"Oh, lucky!"

The elves had set up a long wooden vanity with four stations, each one facing a mirror and outfitted with a full complement of brushes, combs, tweezers, clippers, various ointments, tonics, and powders, and the children were filled with such desire for those brushes and tonics and powders that they very nearly rushed into the clearing, and indeed might have had not the vanity's chairs been instantly filled by girl and boy elves fixing their hair, powdering their cheeks, plucking invisible hairs, though several of them, Michael noticed, just sat gazing at themselves in the mirrors, exclaiming, "You look wonderful! You really do! You look wonderful!"

"We can't go out there like this," Michael said. "I've got scissors on my knife. We'll just cut off all our hair! No hair's better than bum hair, right?"

"Wait," Emma said, "I've got a better idea!"

She ran a few feet into the forest and returned with an armful of fern fronds.

"We're going to make fancy hats! Then no one will see our bum hair!"

Michael could scarcely believe what amazing ideas Emma was having tonight. First saying *lovely* over and over, and now the fancy-hats idea.

They set to work, using Michael's pocketknife to cut the fronds into five- and six-inch pieces, but they soon hit an obstacle, realizing they had no way of actually attaching the fronds. Then Michael got the idea of scooping up handfuls of moist, mud-like earth from the bases of the trees and using it to coat their heads.

"It'll be like glue! The fronds will just stick to it!"

Emma was so pleased that she told Michael he was her favorite brother.

"I'm your *only* brother," Michael said.

"I know! Isn't it great? Now hurry up! I bet they're gonna start dancing any second!"

Not wasting any time, the children smeared the mud from just above their eyebrows, over the tops of their heads, all the way down to the base of their necks. Gooey helmets in place, they seized fistfuls of fern fronds and began slapping them, more or less willy-nilly, to any free patch of mud. In a few moments, Michael and Emma had more than two dozen floppy green fronds sticking out in all directions from the top, sides, front, and back of their heads.

"How do I look?" Michael asked his sister.

"You look great! How do I look?"

"You look amazing! You should wear that hat all the time! Even when we're not dancing!"

"I was just thinking that!" Emma said, supremely pleased.

"Are you ready?" Michael said.

"Am I?! Let's go!"

"Hold on!" Michael pulled the blue-gray orb from inside his

shirt so that it lay on his chest like a sort of decorative necklace. He had never been one for jewelry before, but he thought the glass marble gave him a certain flair. He saw Emma's eyes go wide.

"Oh, I want one!"

"I'll let you borrow it later. Come on!"

And the children were about to plunge into the clearing when the song changed:

> We've brought you something special
> To remind you what you were.
> For deep below that nasty hide
> There's a princess hiding still.
> Please come back, oh please come back,
> We really, really miss you.
> Please come back, oh please come back,
> Change your gold band for this one. . . .

And the children saw four elves emerge from the trees, carrying something on a litter: an object draped in black cloth. The crowd sang louder and louder, and the elves all joined hands so they were dancing around the litter in a large, skipping circle.

Sensing that something momentous—and potentially wonderful—was about to happen, the children hesitated at the edge of the trees.

The four elves carried their burden to the center of the clearing and set it down. It was not easy to make out what was happening, what with the wavering torchlight and the elves moving around and around and blocking the view. Then two of the elves whipped away the black cloth, and Michael had a glimpse of something ghostly and white, and there was a flash of gold. The pitch and frenzy of the celebration increased tenfold, the singing filled the entire canyon, the dancing elves whirled about faster and faster, and Michael thought that if he didn't go and dance right that very instant, he would never be happy again.

"Michael!" Emma cried. "We have to—"

"I know, I know!"

And, with a quick fluffing to ensure their leafy headpieces appeared to best effect, the children jumped up. But they were destined never to join the dance, for just at that moment, a cry tore through the valley. It was the same savage, chilling, terrible shriek they had heard while descending the rocky staircase that afternoon. In an instant, the singing stopped, the torches went out, and the whole party of elves, along with the dunking booth, the wooden vanity, the picnic baskets, and the giant bicycle with the two different-sized wheels, vanished.

It was dark and silent and the children stood alone in their fern-frond helmets at the border of the trees.

Michael felt a heaviness enter his body. He no longer wanted to sing and dance. Indeed, he remembered he hated dancing. And what did he have on his head? He glanced at Emma, visible in the starlight, and saw a mass of mud and ferns matted into a tangled nest upon her head. A few of the fronds had begun an oozy slide down the side of her face.

"Do I have a bunch of leaves and gunk stuck in my hair?" Emma asked.

"Yeah," Michael said, hoping that what he felt moving over his ear wasn't a bug. "Do I?"

"Yeah."

Wordlessly, the two children pulled off the fronds, wiping away, as much as was possible, the half-solid mud caking their hair. Neither asked the other how he or she looked.

"Where'd all the elves go?" Emma said.

Michael shrugged; he was far too irritated to care. He'd always known that elves were lazy and vain, but it turned out they also sang songs that made you want to dress up and rub mud all over your head and—and—

They were just children, he thought. Just silly, stupid children!

Looking out into the clearing, Michael saw that the elves had left behind the ghostly object they'd unloaded from the litter. Suddenly, he had to know what it was.

"Wait here."

"What? Michael, no—"

Emma tried to grab him, but Michael was already running in a low crouch across the clearing. Just as he reached the object, another harsh cry echoed down the valley. It was closer than the last. Whatever was making that noise was on the move.

But even so, for a long moment, he simply stood there and stared. The object was the figure of an elf girl carved in clear ice. She looked to be about Michael's age, and her crystalline hair tumbled down her back and she had been carved smiling and laughing. Even though Michael's elf annoyance was at an all-time high, he had to admit that the elf girl was the most beautiful creature he had ever seen. He reached out and ran a finger along the elf girl's arm and felt the coldness and slickness of ice starting to melt. A thin gold band, almost like a crown, had been placed on her head. Very carefully, Michael lifted it off. The ice girl was so lifelike that Michael half expected her to protest. She didn't, of course, and Michael, glancing down at the circlet, saw it was actually dozens of fine gold bands all woven together.

But what did it all mean? And who was she?

Michael was woken out of his reverie by another of the awful shrieks. It was closer than ever. The thing was coming, and coming quickly.

"Michael!"

Emma was running toward him across the clearing. Without thinking, he slipped the golden circlet into his bag, and he had just started to yell at Emma to go back when there was a shout and Michael turned and saw Gabriel charging out of the trees from the other direction.

"Get down!" the man shouted. "Down!"

Then there was another cry, this time from almost directly overheard, and before Michael could look up, he was pushed roughly to the ground.

"Stay down!" Gabriel commanded.

Emma was still calling her brother's name, and Michael, flat on his stomach, heard the sound of wing beats, and, looking past Gabriel, he watched as the monster swooped down out of the night sky and plucked his sister into the air.

"Hey, wake up! Come on, wake up!"

The small girl named Abigail, the one who'd helped her find clothes, was leaning over Kate and shaking her.

"I'm awake," Kate said groggily.

All around her, throughout the old church, the day was starting. Children were making their beds, lighting fires in stoves, sweeping the stone floor. The air was so cold that Kate could see her breath before her.

"Guess what just happened?" Abigail said.

"It started snowing?" Kate yawned. She reached under her pillow, where she'd placed her mother's locket the night before, and slipped it into her pocket.

"No. Well, yeah. It's been snowing all night. But not that. Rafe was just here," the girl was barely able to control her excitement, "and he said seeing as tonight's New Year's Eve and the big Separation and all, Miss Burke wants to have a party!"

"Oh?" Kate glanced around; the boy Rafe was nowhere to be seen.

"Last time we had a party, Scruggs did fireworks. This one, he made a goblin appear. Lots a' kids got scared and screamed. Not me. Well, maybe me a little. If he does that again, I'm not gonna scream. Put your boots on, let's go get breakfast. Wow, you move slow in the morning! Is that 'cause you're so old?"

Breakfast was served at two long tables in the basement. The fare was scrambled eggs, potatoes, and thick slices of fried bread. The head cook was a thirteen-year-old girl, who was assisted by an army of younger children, all of whom seemed to take their jobs very seriously. The talk at the tables was about the party that night, and what life was going to be like after the Separation.

"So if the magic world is invisible," asked a small boy whose hair stuck out in all directions, "does that mean we're gonna be invisible too?"

"No, dummy!" replied Abigail. "Just, like, certain streets and stuff are gonna be invisible!"

"And are people really gonna forget there're such things as wizards and dragons?" asked a girl further down the table.

"They ain't gonna forget! They're just not gonna think they're real!"

"So if I'm invisible—" asked the small boy again.

"You ain't gonna be invisible!" Abigail insisted.

"Maybe his brain's gonna be invisible!" shouted another boy.

"Yeah, it's invisible already!" added a third.

"Is not!" said the small boy, though he looked somewhat concerned and even reached up to touch his head.

Kate listened, but didn't join in. She was thinking about how she'd woken in the middle of the night to find the church silent and dark and Abigail, having snuck into her bed, curled up against her. Kate had put her arm around the girl, as she'd put her arm around Emma countless times, and she had been about to drift back to sleep when she'd noticed a shadow moving among the children. She'd realized it was Rafe, whom she had not seen since her interview with Henrietta Burke in the tower. He was going from bed to bed, touching a shoulder or a head, whispering to this or that child, letting them know he was there.

Suddenly, there was a great banging of pots and pans, and Kate looked up from her reverie to see Jake and Beetles standing on a bench and calling for attention. Over the shouts of the other children, the two boys announced that they were on a special mission from Rafe, a mission—they took care to point out—that Rafe had not felt comfortable entrusting to the intelligence of anyone else (this occasioned much groaning and cries of "Yeah, yeah, go on!" and "You mean he couldn't find anyone else stupid enough to do it!" and a few lobbed pieces of bread, which Beetles expertly caught and stuffed in his mouth).

"—and we are here," Beetles mumbled through the bread, "to read out the various duties that you scrubs will have to accomplish to get ready for the party!"

This was greeted by cheers, at which both boys bowed, followed by more thrown bread and cries of "Read it! Go on! Read it!" And they proceeded to read a list of names and chores and who was responsible for what.

"And you gotta do it double-quick!" Beetles said, swallowing the last of his bread.

"Yeah," Jake said, "so if any a' you were thinking of sitting here and opening a shop—"

After breakfast, Kate went upstairs to get her coat—she'd promised to help Abigail with her errands—and she'd turned down the long hall that led to the main body of the church when something lunged out of the shadows and grabbed her arm.

"Why are you here?" demanded a raspy voice.

It was the old magician, Scruggs. He was wrapped in his tattered brown cloak and was still wild-eyed and unwashed. Kate sensed that he'd been waiting for her.

"I'm going to get my coat—"

"No! Here!" His grip, already tight on her arm, became even tighter. "Why did you make the *Atlas* bring you here?"

Kate felt a chill that had nothing to do with the cold. "You know?"

The old man grinned. "That you're the Keeper of the *Atlas*? Of course I know. It's written on your face. At least for those with eyes to see. You're here for the boy, aren't you?"

"I . . . don't know what you're talking about. What boy?"

He shook her arm, hissing, "You're here for the boy! You're here for Rafe!"

"What? No! I came here by accident! I just want to get home!"

She tried to twist free her arm, but the man was too strong.

"You're telling the truth." He seemed almost surprised. "So it wasn't you at all. It was the *Atlas*." And he murmured, "Deep, very deep . . ."

"What're you talking about?" Kate demanded.

The man leaned closer. "You think it was chance you came here? To this time! To this place! It wasn't you, yes! I see that. It was the *Atlas*! It has plans! Him, I've known about for years! Tried to tell Henrietta. She wouldn't listen! But now you arrive. Things are finally becoming clear, yes. And of course it would happen now, with the Separation upon us."

"What're you talking about? Who is Rafe?"

"Tell me." The old man leaned even closer. "Are you here to save us, or to destroy us?"

Mastering her voice, Kate said, "I just want to go home."

The sound of a violin drifted down the hall. Kate went rigid.

"What is it, girl? Don't like the music?"

Kate didn't respond. The last time she'd heard a violin had been aboard the Countess's boat, when it had heralded the arrival of the Dire Magnus. But that song had been manic, feverish, otherworldly. This tune was nothing like that. It was a slow, mournful song, and very real. It was coming from a room at the end of the hall.

The old man gave a snort. "We'll see what happens, won't we? We'll see, we'll see. . . ."

He released her arm and shuffled off down the hall. Kate

waited there a moment longer, the music moving through her, unsettling her. Then she turned and hurried away.

Outside, it was still snowing. More than a foot had fallen during the night, though most of the snow had been tramped down and pushed to the edges of the sidewalk. Kate's breath plumed before her, and she burrowed her hands deep into the pockets of her coat. Abigail did not seem bothered by the cold. She carried four or five empty canvas bags over her arm and was repeating aloud the things they had to get.

They had just started off when there were cries of "Hey! Wait!" and Jake and Beetles came huffing up.

"We're coming with you!" Beetles said.

"Did Rafe tell you to watch me?" Kate asked, sounding as annoyed as she felt.

The boys looked at each other, then at her. "No."

"Uh-huh, you two are terrible liars."

"Well," Beetles said, "maybe he did and maybe he didn't. But we ain't gonna tell. Not even if you torture us."

"Yeah," Jake said. "You can chop off our heads, cook 'em, eat 'em; we still won't tell you!"

"That's right!" said his friend. "Ha!"

"Oh, come on," Kate said.

It turned out to be fun having the boys along, and the four of them spent the morning going around the city from store to store, taking care of the items on Abigail's list. Their first stop was a cheese shop, where Abigail bought two medium-sized blocks of cheese, ignoring the boys' pleas to buy the massive wheel of cheese in the window, which was larger than any of them and would've had to be rolled back to the church like a wagon wheel.

"Boys," Abigail muttered to Kate. "That's why I keep the money."

After that, they went to the pasty shop and ordered five dozen pasties of different sorts—ham and cheese, potato and herbs, cheese and potato and mushroom—and, after a great deal of begging, with Jake and Beetles finally agreeing to do all of Abigail's chores for a week, she bought them each a sausage and onion and cheese pasty. "I would've gotten them pasties anyway," Abigail confessed to Kate as they walked through the falling snow eating their hot turnovers, with the boys before them each extolling the virtues of his own pasty while peering into the other's and pronouncing with great regret that his friend had been tricked and his pasty was filled with chopped-up rat butts. And they went to a chocolate shop, and the smell of the cooking chocolate made the air seem itself like a delicacy, and Abigail bought five pounds of chocolate to use for cocoa. The owner was a jovial fat man who gave the children steaming mugs of hot chocolate, and they sat on oak barrels in the front of his store, watching the snow fall past the window, the men and women hurrying by with their bundles and packages, the horse-drawn carriages clopping along the street, tossing up clumps of grayish-white slush. And they went to a pie shop, where Abigail placed an excitingly long and complicated order, which they would return for later that afternoon, and then it was on to a shop that sold varieties of cider, and the boys bemoaned the fact that they hadn't been given the job of going to the sweetshop or the fireworks shop, as everyone knew they were the two best.

"Pshaw!" Abigail sniffed. "You be glad you got what you got by coming with us! Left to yourselves, you'd've been peeling potatoes all day."

By noon, Abigail's bags were stuffed to bursting and divided among them, and the boys were complaining that their feet hurt and they were hungry, and Abigail said they had one more stop, down in Chinatown, and they would get lunch there, and as she said it, the boys looked at her, exclaiming, "Wait, you're getting firework makings for Scruggs, ain't you?" And Abigail smiled and said, "Rafe gave me special orders 'fore I left," and the boys whooped and led the way.

As they came into Chinatown, they found the streets packed with noodle stands inside canvas lean-tos, small vendors selling massive, twisted roots of various colors, jars with dried and blackened leaves, one vendor who seemed to be selling nothing but teeth, ranging from the impossibly tiny to a yellow canine as large as Kate's arm. Men and women bustled past in padded jackets, the men with long, tightly braided pigtails hanging down their backs. Everywhere Kate looked there was something interesting to see, and she wished Michael and Emma were there with her.

"Hey!" Beetles shouted. "There's Rafe! Hey, Rafe!"

Kate saw the older boy at the edge of a vendor's stall twenty yards away. He seemed like he'd been caught out and was even then contemplating slipping away. But then he changed his mind and turned to face them.

"What you doing here, Rafe?" Jake asked. "You getting stuff for the party?"

And Kate thought, He was waiting here, for me.

"We came down to get fireworks like you told me," Abigail said. "But we were gonna get lunch first 'cause these two're belly-aching."

"Were not!" Jake said.

"Yeah," Beetles said. "We were worried about you fainting, is all."

Abigail just laughed. "Ha!"

"Go to Fung's around the corner," Rafe said. "It's the best place in Chinatown."

"Yeah, sure," Beetles said. "Fung's. We know that place. Got a green door."

"A red door," Rafe said.

"Oh yeah," Beetles said. "They musta changed it."

Then Rafe, looking at Kate, said, "You all go on. She'll catch up."

The children hurried away and Kate and the boy were left standing there. She saw snowflakes were melting on his hair and shoulders, and there were dark circles under his eyes. She wondered how much he'd slept the night before, or if he'd slept.

"Those're the clothes Abigail gave you?" he asked.

Kate looked down, feeling suddenly self-conscious in her shabby wool pants and old boots, the patched shirts and jackets.

"Yes. What's wrong with them?"

"Nothing. I should've looked at you before you left the church. Where's your cap?"

Kate pulled it out of her pocket.

"I didn't need it. My head wasn't cold—"

"It ain't just to keep you warm. Put it on."

Kate twisted up her hair and pulled the cloth cap low over her eyes. The boy reached toward her face, and she flinched back.

"Hold still."

He tucked a couple of loose strands of blond hair into her cap, and she felt his fingers brush the tops of her ears.

"All right, lemme see your hands."

She held them out, and he took them, turning them over. She saw how clean and white her hands were compared to his. There was a small coal fire burning in front of the stand they'd stopped beside, and he bent and gathered soot and ash from the fire and rubbed the warm black powder over her palms and fingers and the backs of her hands. Then he reached up—Kate held still this time, though to her annoyance the trembling in her chest had returned—and brushed his fingers over her cheeks and forehead. She stared at his face as he did so, the deep-set green eyes, the slightly crooked nose, and she noticed how carefully he avoided her gaze. She had the strange sense that he was as nervous as she. He stepped back, clapping off the excess soot on the legs of his pants.

"There. You could walk past an Imp now, and he wouldn't know you."

"Thank you," Kate said, her voice fainter than she would've liked.

"So what's this then?"

It took Kate a moment to understand what he was holding;

and by the time she realized that he had her mother's locket, that he must've taken it from her pocket while he'd been checking her wardrobe, Rafe had snapped it open and was looking at the decade-old picture of her and Michael and Emma.

"Give that back!"

Kate snatched the locket from his hand and clutched it tight in her fist.

"I wasn't going to steal it," the boy said. "But you should get a chain instead a' keeping it in your pocket. You'll lose it that way."

"I had a chain," Kate said angrily. "I traded it for this coat."

"Yeah? Well, if it was gold like that locket, you got robbed."

"And you would know all about robbing someone, wouldn't you?"

Her face was hot, the nervousness gone.

"So who are they? In the picture?"

Kate stared at him, weighing whether or not to respond. "My brother and sister," she said finally. "The picture's ten years old. They're the reason I need to get back."

"What about your parents? Where're they?"

Kate said nothing, and the boy seemed to understand. They stood in silence for several seconds, then Kate said:

"So is that it? I'm hungry."

She started to walk away, but Rafe placed a hand on her arm. "I'll show you the place."

He turned down a narrow street and led her to a flight of stairs, at the top of which was a red door marked with a symbol Kate couldn't read.

"That's it there."

Kate started up the stairs, not intending to say goodbye, when the boy said:

"I shouldn't have taken your locket. I'm sorry."

Kate stopped. She was two steps above him. She knew for certain then that he had come to Chinatown to find her and that he was indeed sorry. She thought again of her encounter with Scruggs that morning and heard herself say:

"Why don't you come in?"

He shook his head. "I ain't hungry."

"But you haven't eaten, have you? I mean . . . I hear this is the best place in Chinatown."

He looked at her a moment longer, then nodded and stepped up past her and opened the door. A pair of rugs hung from the ceiling a couple feet inside the restaurant, providing a buffer against the cold, and Rafe waited there till Kate had closed the door behind her. For a moment, the two of them were standing close and facing each other in the small space, then Rafe pushed through the rugs, and they stepped into the restaurant.

It was loud, crowded, and smoky, and the air was heavy with the smell of cooking oil, onions, and ginger. There were long tables with benches, all of which were full, and there was a counter at the back for more diners, and behind the counter at least a dozen cooks were taking orders and shouting while passing bowl after steaming bowl out into the waiting hands of the crowd. There were several groups of dwarves scattered among the tables, but most of the diners were Chinese men, all of whom, it seemed to Kate, were speaking at once, and everyone was packed in so tight and close that Kate felt herself retreating from the press of bodies.

"There they are," Rafe said, pointing to where Jake and Beetles and Abigail were stuffed together at a table and waving.

"There's no room," Kate said.

"We'll sit at the bar."

And he took her hand and led her through the throng and found space at the counter. They were crammed in tight, shoulders, elbows, and hips pressed against the diners on either side and against each other. There was a short wall separating the counter from the cooks' area, and Kate watched a young Chinese man dice an onion with such blurring speed that she was sure several fingers would end up in someone's soup.

Rafe spoke to the cook and, a moment later, two steaming bowls of honey-colored noodles landed before them. The noodles were served in a milky broth, and she could see, but not identify, various vegetables and herbs floating among hunks of egg and chicken. Rafe handed her a set of chopsticks, and she watched how the boy balanced his own between his fingers and the crook of his thumb. He saw her staring.

"They don't have these where you're from?"

"We have chopsticks. I've just never used them. Especially not with soup."

He grinned; it was the first time he'd truly smiled at her.

"It kinda involves a lot of slurping."

He demonstrated, shoveling a wad of noodles into his mouth and then sort of vacuuming up the tail ends. The noise it made was tremendous, and only covered by the fact that everyone around them was doing the exact same thing.

"I guess manners are a modern invention," Kate said with a smile.

"Try it."

Realizing that she was starving, and that she hadn't eaten anything since her pasty with Abigail hours before, Kate applied herself to the bowl. The noodles were thick and squishy, and it took her four tries to get one that didn't immediately slip out of the chopsticks, and even then she bent close to the bowl, fearful that if she brought the noodle higher, she would lose it. The noodle slapped the side of her cheek as she slurped it up.

"Well?"

She turned to him, a stunned look on her face. "That's amazing."

"Told you." And he grinned again.

For a while, Kate forgot everything but her noodles and was slurping away as loudly as anyone in the restaurant. When she glanced over and saw Rafe lifting his bowl and drinking the broth, she did the same, and after that, she got braver and began lifting the noodles high, sometimes with a piece of egg or chicken, and lowering the whole delicious mess into her mouth; and as crowded and loud and smoky as the restaurant was, and though she was constantly being bumped and jostled, or feeling cold air against her neck when someone pushed through the rugs by the door, somehow it was all wonderful. It was as if Kate had managed to leave outside everything she carried with her on a daily basis, her thoughts of her parents, the need to find them, her constant worry about her brother and sister. Sitting there, wedged at the counter, she was, however briefly, just a girl in a strange, exciting place with a boy her own age.

"So you're really from the future?"

"Yes."

"And the Separation, it works? People forget that magic is real?"

Kate nodded. "Everyone thinks—I used to think—it's just from fairy tales."

The boy idly stirred the remains of his soup with his chopsticks. "Well, maybe Miss B's right then. Though I still don't see why we should be the ones hiding."

Kate stared at him. An uneasy feeling began to stir inside her.

"Not all normal humans hate magical people. You can't judge everyone that way."

The boy turned on her. The intensity in his green eyes was like nothing Kate had ever seen. It required effort not to look away.

"Course they hate us. What do you think happened to Miss B's arm? Who you think did that?"

"But it doesn't make sense. You're human too! You're no different. Just, you can do magic."

The boy laughed, but there was no humor in it. "You don't think that's enough? They hate us 'cause we can do things they can't. Makes 'em jealous and afraid." The boy began flexing one of the chopsticks between his fingers. "There've been riots in other cities. Mobs burning down magic quarters, chasing folk out, killing them. That's the whole point a' the Separation, a way to protect ourselves. Then, even if we're still living among 'em, they won't know it. I guess it's the right thing." The chopstick snapped, and he laid the pieces down.

Neither spoke for a moment, then Kate said:

"Was that you playing the violin this morning?"

The boy looked at her.

"I was in the hall," she said. "I couldn't help but hear."

Rafe nodded. "It was something my mother taught me. From her old village. She always had me play it to her, said it reminded her of home."

"Oh. Is she—"

"She's dead."

"I'm sorry."

They were both silent again, which seemed fine, as the restaurant was so loud around them.

"Hey, you guys done yet?" Beetles and Jake were behind them.

"Abigail's outside already," Jake said. "She says we gotta hurry and get the rest of the stuff. She's kinda bossy."

"I'll be right there," Kate said.

The boys hurried out through the crowd. Kate looked at Rafe.

"Thank you for lunch."

Rafe nodded and then, abruptly, as if he'd made up his mind and feared that if he hesitated he might not follow through, he reached into his jacket and pulled out a small, fat purse.

"Here. Take it."

Kate glanced at the purse, then at him. The boy wasn't looking at her.

"What is it?"

"Money. Enough to get you to that place up north. Or wher-ever."

"I don't understand. Miss Burke said it would be a few days."

"This has got nothing to do with Miss B."

"I don't understand—"

"There's nothing to understand." The boy was keeping his voice low, but he was getting frustrated and when he looked at her Kate saw something like desperation in his eyes. "I'm telling you to go. I'm asking you."

"But why're you doing this now? Now, all of a sudden?"

"I got my reasons. Just take it. All right?"

He grabbed her hand and curled her fingers around the purse. Kate felt utterly confused. On some level, she sensed that the boy was trying to protect her; but she also knew there was much he wasn't saying.

"And you won't tell me why?"

"I can't—"

"Or how you know me? Because I know you do. There's no point in lying."

The boy said nothing. Kate pulled her hand away from his. She felt the heaviness of the purse, the shapes of the coins under the old leather. She could go up to Cambridge Falls, find a way back home, be reunited with her brother and sister; but then she would never learn the boy's secret. And she thought of what Scruggs had said, that the *Atlas* had brought her here for a reason. Was it possible that this boy was the reason? If so, who was he?

She set the purse on the bar.

"Then I'm staying."

And she walked out.

Abigail and the boys were in high spirits after lunch. They went to the firework maker, picked up Scruggs's order, and then headed back toward the church, laden with their purchases. Kate glanced behind them several times, but could not see Rafe following. She felt deeply confused.

And then something happened that confused things even more.

They were walking down a narrow cross street, and as they passed a small house, they saw a dwarf couple—it was the first time Kate had ever seen a female dwarf; mostly, she looked just like a male dwarf without the beard—carrying out furniture to load into a donkey cart.

"See that," Jake said. "They're getting out before the Separation. Probably going to one a' them big places upstate. What they calling them? Reserves?"

"Once the Separation happens," Beetles explained to Kate, "there're gonna be a few streets downtown that're only for magic folk. Normal humans won't even know they're there. But dwarves and gnomes and stuff, all them that can't pass for human, or that can't afford glamours to disguise themselves, lots a' them are getting outta the city for good."

Suddenly, something struck the dwarf in the head, exploding all over his face and shoulders. It was a snowball, Kate realized, and then another struck the dwarf's wife, hitting her square in the back. A few more snowballs smashed against the cart. Kate saw three surly-looking teenagers across the street, packing snowballs and jeering.

"Go on!"

"Get outta here!"

"We don't want you!"

They threw another volley of snowballs, striking both dwarves and knocking a small figurine off the pile of goods in the cart. The figurine hit the curb and shattered. Kate started forward, furious, not sure what she was going to do, certain only that she was going to do something, when Abigail grabbed her arm and pulled her back.

"Let me go! Don't you see what they're doing?"

"Better not make trouble," Abigail said quietly. "Rafe says we're supposed to keep clear when things turn bad. They're okay. See?"

Leaving the pieces of the figurine on the sidewalk, the dwarf and his wife had climbed into their cart and were driving down the street, pursued by the taunts and snowballs of the teenagers.

"Come on," Abigail said, and pulled Kate away.

Kate was deeply troubled by the incident. So was everything Rafe had told her true? The teenagers seemed to hate the dwarves for no reason but that they were different. She felt sick to her stomach.

"So it's really always like this?"

Abigail laughed. "That ain't nothing."

"It's worse?"

"Worse? You heard what happened to Rafe's ma?"

"What're you talking about? She's dead."

"Yeah, and how'd she die? Some human without a drop a' magic in him killed her."

"What?" Kate stopped in her tracks.

"No one talks about it, but we all know. Why you think Rafe hates them so much? And he's gonna be real powerful someday. I heard Scruggs telling Miss B—"

Kate grabbed the girl's arm and wrenched her around. "What did you hear? Tell me."

Abigail seemed surprised at Kate's vehemence. "Nothing, really. Just I'd gone up to the belfry—they didn't know I was there, see—and I heard 'em talking about Rafe."

"And what did Scruggs say? Please, Abigail, this is important."

"Just what I told you, that Rafe is gonna be a real powerful wizard. Why?"

Kate had no answer. All she had was her deep conviction that Rafe was connected to her, and not just to her but to Michael and Emma, to the search for the Books. But how? And was he their friend or enemy? She needed to know.

Just then there was a pounding of feet, and they turned to see Beetles and Jake running toward them, red-faced and grinning.

"We gotta go!" Beetles said.

"Why?" Kate said. "What happened?"

"Remember how we weren't supposed to do nothing?" Jake said. "Well, we didn't do that."

"We threw some snowballs," Beetles explained. "We didn't think they'd be magic or nothing, but after we threw 'em, the snowballs started changing colors on their own and getting all goopy and—"

"There they are!"

The cry had come from down the block, and Kate turned and saw the three thuggish teenagers, led by a tall, angry, pinch-faced youth who looked to be covered in a greenish sludge, sprinting toward them.

"Get the freaks!"

"Run!" Kate cried.

The children needed no encouragement. They bolted down the street, the teenagers hard behind them, howling with fury.

"Can't you—do something?" Kate panted. "Some—magic?"

"You gotta be calm to do magic," Beetles said. "It don't work if you're scared." And he added, "Not that I'm scared!"

"Me neither!" Jake said.

Kate's mind was racing; she knew they couldn't outrun the teenagers. But then she saw, past the end of the block, an avenue crowded with pedestrians, carriages, carts. On a packed street, there would be places to hide. That would work, she knew, as long as someone led their pursuers away.

"Listen, when we turn the corner, you three are going to hide. I'll make them follow me."

"Uh-uh!" Jake said. "Rafe said we're supposed to watch out for you!"

"Stupid!" Beetles said. "You're not supposed to tell her that!"

"There's no time to argue! You look after Abigail. I'll meet you back at the church!"

"I don't need anyone lookin'—" Abigail began, but they were already rounding the corner, and Kate spied a set of steps leading to a basement below a grocer's. She pushed the children toward it.

"There! Go now!"

Jake and Beetles grabbed Abigail and dragged her down the stairs and out of sight. Kate leapt into the midst of traffic. She heard cursing and the neighing of horses, the sound of reins being snapped tight, but she plowed ahead, her feet sliding in the slush, looking neither left nor right, till she reached the far sidewalk. Once there, she turned. The three teenagers had reached the corner and were searching for their quarry.

"Hey! Here I am! Come catch me!" she taunted.

Shouting with rage, they charged after her.

That's right, Kate thought, come on.

Then she turned and ran for her life.

But she hadn't gone more than thirty yards when she realized the boys were going to catch her. They were too big, too fast, and too angry. She could hear the pounding of their footsteps growing louder and louder. Then she spotted the ladder of a fire escape hanging down. She thought if she could climb up and pull the ladder after her, she could get away. Kate put on a final burst of speed and, five yards from the ladder, crashed into a man stepping out of a shop.

It was like colliding with a brick wall. Her head snapped back, and her entire body seemed to rebound and slam against the sidewalk. She was dizzy and her vision blurred. Her hat had fallen off, and she had to push back her hair to make out the man standing above her, a mountain of a man in a long fur jacket and fur hat. He hadn't moved.

"You all right there, lass? You should be looking where you're going. Running pell-mell like that through the streets."

She heard the boys skidding to a halt behind her. She looked back, still too unsteady to get to her feet, and saw the tall, pinch-faced boy, backed on either side by his thuggish friends, pointing his finger at the man in the fur coat.

"Get away from her! She's ours!"

Kate knew she had to run, but she also knew if she stood now, she'd just fall over.

"And what would you be wanting with a sweet, innocent girl like this?" the man asked. "Sure, she's done nothing wrong. Face of an angel, she has."

"She's a freak! She—"

And Kate, who was still looking at the boys, watched as their expressions changed. Something they'd seen had given them pause.

"What's that you're saying about freaks?" the man asked.

The tall boy looked angrier than ever.

"You'll get yours too one day! All a' you!"

"Begone," the man said, "before I find myself losing patience."

The tall boy spat on the ground, then they all three sulked off. Feeling steadier, Kate slowly stood and turned to thank the man. She froze. He was flanked on either side by bowler-hatted Imps, their small eyes fixed upon her.

"It's her," one of the creatures said. "I remember."

"Sure, isn't it herself," the man purred. "Can't I see it written on her face?" He placed a large hand on Kate's arm. "Would you mind coming with us for a wee bit? There's someone who would very much like to speak with you. Oh, but where're me manners?" He removed his fur hat, revealing the great bald stone of his head. "The name is Rourke."

CHAPTER TWELVE
To the Fortress

Twice, Gabriel lifted Michael to his feet, and twice, the boy's knees buckled and he crumpled to the ground.

"If you fall again," Gabriel said, pulling him up once more, "I will have to leave you here."

"That—thing took Emma!"

"I know."

"But it took her!"

"Yes, and I cannot both pursue it and carry you; so either stand or you will be left behind."

They were in the clearing. Emma and the creature had disappeared moments before. In the starlight, Michael could see the thick vein of Gabriel's scar pulsing on the side of his jaw. Michael knew that Gabriel was restraining himself from going after Emma alone. He knew he needed to pull himself together.

Gabriel released his shoulders, and Michael swayed, but kept his balance.

"That thing," Michael said. "Did you see—"

"Yes."

"And was it a—I mean, was it actually—"

"Yes."

It seemed that neither man nor boy wanted to name the creature aloud; but for Michael, it was enough that Gabriel had seen what he had—the great, leathery, bat-like wings, the long serpent's body, the jagged line of spines ridged along the creature's back, the enormous talons that had snatched Emma off the ground. . . .

He hadn't imagined it; his sister had been taken by a dragon.

"But"—and, for a second, he felt so weak and lost that he was sure he would topple over and be left there by Gabriel—"what're we gonna do?"

"We will find your sister and kill the beast that took her."

"But what if—what if she's already—"

Gabriel lunged, seizing a handful of Michael's shirt. His face was cloaked in shadow, his voice a growl.

"She is alive. She is alive, and we will find her. Now—come!"

And he sprinted away across the clearing, with Michael staggering along behind.

Michael lost track of time. Half an hour. An hour. Gabriel kept disappearing into the darkness, leaving Michael to carve his own path through the thicket of ferns that blanketed the forest floor. Again and again, just when Michael was convinced that Gabriel had finally abandoned him, the man would appear from behind a tree, hissing, "This way! Faster!" and Michael would push himself on as the ferns beat at his arms and face and the same refrain played over and over in his head:

You lost Kate, and now you lost Emma. . . .

You lost Kate, and now you lost Emma. . . .

You lost Emma. . . .

You lost Emma. . . .

Then, abruptly, the trees and ferns ended, and Michael stepped out onto a rocky plain and found Gabriel waiting. Free of the weight of the forest, Michael felt the immense openness of the night sky, and he took a deep, relieved breath.

"There. You see?"

Gabriel was pointing up the valley to where the volcano rose from the plain, a quarter of a mile distant. It had not occurred to Michael what direction they were heading in, and he stared now in wonder. The volcano took up almost the entire width of the plain, a perfect pyramid rising nearly to the height of the canyon walls. Looking up, Michael could see an ominous red glow emanating from the cone.

Unbidden, the memories he'd acquired in Malpesa came surging up, and he had again the feeling of déjà vu. The *Chronicle* was close.

"You see it?" Gabriel asked.

Michael realized that Gabriel was pointing to a spot about a third of the way up the volcano's slope, where a light flickered in the dark. Squinting, Michael could just discern the outline of a large structure. The dead man's memories filled in the rest.

"It's the Order's fortress," he said. "This is where they brought the book."

"What I care about," Gabriel said, "is finding your sister."

And they set off once more.

The lower slope of the volcano was a jumble of giant black rocks, and Michael had to clamber upward on all fours as Gabriel strode ahead. Soon, the boulders gave way to small rocks and scree, and for every two steps, Michael slid back one. Still, he kept on. By now, the fortress was in sharp relief, and Michael could make out thirty-foot-high walls of black stone, ramparts and battlements where a defender might take position. He could see nothing of the buildings inside the walls save a lone tower that rose into the sky, at the crown of which a fire blazed forth.

It was an impressive, imposing structure, but Michael couldn't help but question the wisdom of building on the side of a volcano.

"I mean," he muttered, panting his way up the slope, "they do blow up after all."

Gabriel was standing before the fortress gates, a pair of heavy wooden doors the height of the walls, and Michael arrived trembling and out of breath.

"Sorry. I'm . . . actually in excellent shape. Must be the altitude—"

"Look."

Gabriel gestured to the three interlocking circles carved into the door. The fortress, the whole valley, was still and silent.

Michael whispered, "Do you . . . think they know we're here?"

Gabriel picked up a large rock and hammered—*thud*—*thud*—*thud*—*thud*—till the doors swung open. He dropped the rock.

"Yes."

With Gabriel leading, they passed into a courtyard of packed earth. Michael waited, and when no arrows came whistling out of the dark, he relaxed and allowed himself a quick survey. The fortress had been built on a flattened plot a hundred feet wide and perhaps twice that in depth. The central courtyard—where he and Gabriel stood—was dominated by a two-story stone building with long, narrow windows. The high, flame-topped tower rose from the building's back corner. A wooden skeleton of ladders and catwalks clung to the inside of the fortress walls, providing access to the battlements. Other than that, Michael saw a few ramshackle structures—a small pen for livestock, a blacksmith's forge, several storerooms—and all were dark and empty.

Gabriel unsheathed his falchion. "Stay behind me."

Michael didn't argue.

Gabriel kicked open the door of the stone building, and they stepped into a large, high-ceilinged room. Thick-bodied columns ran the length of the chamber, while an eerie red glow, rising from a gap in the floor, pushed back the darkness. The building was a keep, Michael realized, a place to retreat to should the fortress be breached.

They advanced slowly to the gap in the center of the floor. It was perhaps fifteen feet square, and there were a dozen steps leading down to a heavy iron gate, past which Michael could make out the mouth of a tunnel. The red glow was coming from deep in the volcano, and the heat rose up and stung Michael's eyes. Still, he could feel himself being pulled forward by an invisible force.

"The *Chronicle* is down there," he said quietly.

"Then it is not alone."

Michael glanced at him, questioning.

"That gate locks from the outside," Gabriel said. "It is not meant to keep us out; it is to keep something in."

He nodded upward, and Michael found himself looking through a large, jagged hole in the keep's ceiling. The hole was directly over the mouth of the tunnel, and Michael imagined that something very big—something, say, dragon-sized—had come roaring out and blasted through the roof of the keep.

Except that the gate over the tunnel was down and locked, which meant the dragon had returned home. Michael thought of the creature he'd glimpsed in the clearing, the huge, razor-sharp talons, fangs the length of his arm. . . .

"I guess," he said, trying to sound gruff and ready and not completely, bone-shakingly terrified, "we should go down there, huh?"

"Yes."

Michael nodded. And suddenly he knew that scared or not, if going into the tunnel was the way to save Emma, he would do it. Though he wondered if he should take a moment to stretch.

"But first," Gabriel said, "we will search the tower."

"What? Why?"

"The dragon did not close that gate. I want to know who did."

He headed for a doorway in the far corner, through which a set of stairs could be seen climbing upward. Michael hurried after him, and for a few moments, the chamber was still. Then a shadow separated from one of the columns, and a cloaked figure drew a sword and followed.

"Emma!"

Michael ran forward and threw his arms around his sister.

He and Gabriel had reached the top of the tower. Climbing the last flight of stairs, Michael had looked up and seen the night sky still brimming with stars, the looming, snowcapped mountains, the red and smoking cone of the volcano; he'd seen a fire burning in a brazier on the tower wall; he'd been nervous, not knowing who or what might be waiting in ambush; then he saw Gabriel stiffen in surprise, and he turned and there was his own sister, alive and unharmed.

"Oh, Emma!" He hugged her as if he would never let her go ever again. "I was so worried! Gabriel too! We were both really, really worried!"

Gabriel said his name, but Michael ignored it.

"Emma," he said, holding her arms and stepping away. Now that she was safely back, he felt the need to be the stern older brother. "I know you've been through an ordeal, but I did ask you to stay out of that clearing. I think there's a lesson here, don't you? Perhaps you should pay more attention when I tell you things?"

"Michael . . ."

"Just a moment, Gabriel. Emma, do you hear me?"

"No, I do not think she does."

"What? What're you—?" Then Michael finally realized that the whole time he'd been hugging her, Emma hadn't once groaned or tried to push him away or made a joke about why didn't he go hug a dwarf.

"Something has frozen her," Gabriel said.

For a moment, Michael stared at his motionless sister. Her arms were stiff at her sides and her eyes unblinking; the curled tip of a fern was stuck in her mud-caked hair. As he reached over and plucked it out, he felt the coldness of her skin.

Then he said faintly, hopelessly, "Can you fix her?"

Gabriel shook his head.

"What about Dr. Pym?"

Gabriel hesitated only a fraction of a second, but Michael understood. They had left the wizard fighting for his life in Malpesa. Who could say when they would see him again?

"Never mind," he said. "I know—"

Without warning, Gabriel spun around, his falchion hissing through the air; there was a loud metallic *clang*, and Michael turned to see a cloaked, sword-wielding man stagger back.

The man had almond-colored skin, long, unkempt black hair, and a wild black beard. He was shorter than Gabriel and very thin. His clothes were ragged and patched and looked to have been salvaged from a dozen different sources, giving him the appearance of a down-on-his-luck harlequin. Michael's eyes went to the man's tunic, where, stitched into the fabric, were three faded, interlocking circles.

Gabriel took a step forward, more to shield Michael than to attack, but the man dropped his sword, threw up his hands, and fell to his knees, crying, "I yield! Don't kill me! Don't kill poor Bert!" and promptly burst into tears.

"He's not what I expected," Michael said.

"He has likely been here a long time," Gabriel said. "Perhaps alone. Solitude can have a terrible effect on the mind."

That much, Michael thought, was obvious.

The man had finally stopped whimpering and seemed to believe, at least for the time being, that Gabriel and Michael were not going to murder him. He was sitting on the short wall that encircled the tower and consoling himself by munching on a fat black beetle he'd taken from a pocket of his cloak.

"I just expected someone . . . cleaner. And not named Bert."

"Do you want to question him or shall I?" Gabriel asked.

That was clearly the next step. Finding out who the man was. Was he indeed a member of the Order? Was he alone here or were there others? Was the dragon locked safely inside the volcano? Was it guarding the *Chronicle*? What was the dragon's connection to the man? Why had it left Emma atop this tower? And, most importantly, what exactly had happened to her and could it be reversed?

Michael looked at his sister. Her mouth was slightly open, as if she'd been on the point of speaking; her eyes were narrowed, and there was a wrinkle of fury on her brow. Michael saw that her hands, down at her sides, were clenched into fists. He knew the signs and was not surprised: his sister had been fighting when she'd been frozen.

"I will." Emma was his sister, his responsibility.

"Very well. I will be here if you need me. But be quick." Gabriel gave him a meaningful look. "Sooner or later, the dragon will return."

Michael conceded that Gabriel had a point. He stepped forward.

"Right. I want to ask you a few questions."

The man had been picking at his teeth with one of the beetle's legs, but now he sat up, running a hand down his beard, and put on an eager-to-please smile. He was crazy, Michael thought, but he appeared to be nice-crazy, and not I'll-kill-you-I'll-kill-you crazy.

"Happy to talk. Love having visitors. Bert hasn't had any in, well, ever." He spoke in choppy, heavily accented English. "Oh, Bert's very sorry about the whole"—he mimed hacking at them with an imaginary sword. "He thought you were elves."

"Yes, well, that's certainly understandable," Michael said. "No one wants elves sneaking about." As he spoke, Michael was mentally reviewing passages from *The Dwarf Omnibus* about the art of interrogation (the *Omnibus*, as Michael had often reflected, really did touch on everything). He remembered that G. G. Greenleaf suggested first establishing rapport with your subject. He also said that when the subject's guard was down, the interrogator should "whack him in the head with a club. He won't see that coming! Ha!" Michael wasn't planning anything quite so violent, but considering how skittish the man was, building rapport seemed like a good initial step. With that in mind, Michael tried to make his tone as chummy as possible. "So tell me, friend, you're one of the Order of Guardians, aren't you?"

The man shook his head. "No, no! Bert's not one of the Order—"

"But you've got the symbol on your—"

"Bert's not one of the Order! He's all of the Order! He's the last there is! Beginning, middle, and end!" He thumped his chest proudly.

Michael thought of the silent, deserted fortress and decided the man was telling the truth.

"What happened to the others?"

"Gone," the man said quickly, in a way that told Michael there was more to the story. "Bert's been alone for a very, very, very, very long time." And he popped another beetle in his mouth.

"But you're not completely alone. I mean, there's a dragon here."

The man jerked forward, his voice dropping to a whisper. "You've seen the dragon?"

"Yes. In the forest." Then, as if it were the most casual thing in the world, Michael asked, "Just out of curiosity, where is the dragon now?"

The man raised a finger to his lips and pointed toward the volcano, whispering, ". . . Sleeping . . . best not to wake."

Michael was taking note of the things he would return to later: the dragon, what had happened to the man's comrades. . . . He decided it was time to come to the key issue.

"What can you tell me about my sister?"

The man's eyes widened. "That's your sister? Oh. Oh no. . . ."

"What do you mean, oh no? What's happened to her?"

"Well, she's frozen, isn't she? Thought that much was fairly obvious."

"I can see that!" Michael felt his let's-be-friends mask slip for a second. "But what froze her in the first place? Dragons don't freeze people. It's not in any of the literature."

The man began nervously braiding his beard. "Hmm, well, Bert didn't know she was your sister. Dragon just dumped her in Bert's lap! She was very loud. Lots of threats. About how a certain fellow was going to cut off Bert's head! Shouting, shouting, shouting. All these years alone, Bert isn't used to so much yelling. And she kicked Bert in the shin—hard! Bert will have a bruise tomorrow!"

He began rolling up the cuff on his pants.

"Stop that. What did you do?"

"Do? Oh, nothing . . . much. . . ."

Michael gave his best glower. He was honestly rethinking whacking the man in the head. The deranged Guardian seemed to get the message. He reached into one of the pockets of his cloak and drew forth a folded patch of cloth.

"Bert used to be quite the hand at potions. They taught us magic, the wizards did. Long ago." He unwrapped the cloth and displayed a scorched needle. He began murmuring, like someone repeating a recipe, "Two parts dragon's blood. Three parts deathshade. Ground-up sloth tongue, not too fine. Water from an untouched stream. Add salt. Heat. Then one quick prick"—he made a jabbing motion with the needle—"and silence."

"You drugged her?"

The man nodded, then reached into another pocket. "Beetle?"

"I don't want a beetle! Is she"—Michael had to swallow before he could find his voice—"is she alive?"

"Oh yes, yes. Still alive. But the life has been stopped within her. Like a frozen river. Quite a powerful little potion. One prick." He jabbed the air with the needle again.

"So how do we fix her?! She's my sister! I'm supposed to be looking out for her."

All of Michael's relaxed, rapport-building demeanor was gone. He wanted to grab the man by the beard and shake him.

"Can't."

"Can't what? Can't tell us? Because my friend here—"

"Can't fix her. No antidote. At least, none Bert has. But she doesn't look that bad. And you could put her somewhere nice. She would really brighten up a room."

"My sister is not a piece of furniture!"

"Of course, of course," agreed the man, "but she's not going to be much good for conversation anymore, you do realize that, don't you?"

"I'm going to cut off his head," Gabriel growled.

The man's bottom lip began trembling, and he let out a low moan.

"Oh, stop it!" Michael snapped. "You're supposed to be the last of an ancient order of warriors. Have some dignity."

As the man pulled his cloak over his head in an effort to hide, Michael took a moment to regroup. This wasn't going well.

There seemed to be no quick way of restoring Emma, and the more time that passed, the more likely it was that the dragon would wake up, and then what? As much faith as Michael had in Gabriel's strength, a dragon was, after all, a dragon. And he still didn't understand the relationship between the Guardian and the dragon. Was the man the creature's master? It didn't appear so. But clearly there was something between them, or the dragon would have killed the man long ago.

Michael found that he was unconsciously rubbing the blue-gray orb that hung around his neck. Could the glass marble possibly help? Should he just smash it, as Emma had suggested? What if it had been sent by their enemies? With Emma frozen, smashing the orb seemed too much of a risk. Michael slipped it back inside his shirt.

Plan B, Michael thought. We leave now. Before the dragon wakes up. Gabriel carries Emma back to the plane. We find Dr. Pym—assuming he's still alive—and he fixes Emma. Then we all come back for the *Chronicle*.

Reviving Emma had to come first.

But Michael also knew they couldn't leave without hearing the deranged Guardian's story. There was no telling what might help them when they returned for the *Chronicle*.

"I want you to tell us everything. How you came here. What happened to the other Guardians. Where the dragon came from. Start at the beginning. But be quick."

"And if you lie to us," Gabriel said, "I will most certainly chop off your head."

• • •

They had not moved from atop the tower, and as the man spoke, Michael glanced now and then at Emma. Part of him kept expecting her to start laughing and announce that she had been playing a practical joke and wasn't frozen at all.

But she stayed just as she was.

Don't worry, he promised silently. I won't leave you like this.

"Four thousand years ago," the man began, "when the world was a very different place than today—much dustier, for starters— there was a council of big-brain wizards in the city of Rhakotis on the coast of the Mediterranean Sea."

To Michael's great annoyance, the man seemed unable to tell the story without indulging in any number of digressions, on topics as diverse as the varieties of edible fruits, the intelligence of camels, the stupidity of birds, and his own astonishing amiability. Along with all this, he made repeated offers for Michael and Gabriel to share his supply of beetles, offers that Michael and Gabriel always declined while pressing him to get to the point. . . .

"And these big-brain wizards decided it would be a wonderful idea to write down their greatest, most terrible, most secret secrets, the ones that concerned the very making of the world. In the end, they created three books." The man held up two fingers. "One dealt with time. One with life. And one with death. And they were locked away in separate vaults below the city—which really was a lovely city."

There followed a disquisition on the many charms of Rhakotis, till a growl from Gabriel prompted him to continue.

"Then the big-brains in their braininess created an Order

of Guardians who were sworn to protect the Books with their lives. There were only ten Guardians at any one time, but they were versed in both magical and nonmagical combat and were supported by the power of the wizards." He scratched his beard. "Time passed. The big brains grew soft and were perhaps not quite so big as they once had been. This is where Bert enters the story. He was a young Guardian. Bright-eyed. Zealous. Amiable, oh my—"

"Skip that part," Michael said.

"And then everything changed." The man leapt up and began pacing back and forth, waving his arms about violently. Michael and Gabriel moved in front of Emma so the man didn't strike her by accident. "It was a beautiful day, the sun was shining, Bert was atop the watchtower—out of nowhere, a thousand ships materialized off the coast. Fire filled the sky. Dragons appeared in the east of the city. Sand trolls attacked from the south. It was Alexander, the boy conqueror, and the big brains were doomed. Alexander was too strong. Had too many dark wizards in his army. It was up to Bert and his brothers to get the Books out of the city. But by the time they reached the vaults, only the *Chronicle* remained. The other two books were already gone."

The man's mind seemed to drift off. He stood, stroking his beard and murmuring, "Not Bert's fault, did his best, can't fault old Bert . . . ," until Michael called him back.

"In the end, only four Guardians escaped the city. The rest died in the fighting. The survivors fled south, to the bottom of the world. There were elves living here, in the ice and snow. At first, Bert liked them. He should've known better."

"Why?" Michael asked. "What'd the elves do?"

The man didn't answer; he was caught up in his story.

"Bert and the others tapped into the power of the book. The valley became lush. They gained long life. They hid the *Chronicle* anew and built this fortress. More time passed. Century upon century. They had a scrying bowl that showed the outside world. So many changes. But though they searched and searched, they saw no traces of the two missing books." The bearded, wild-eyed man faced them, grinning. "But they learned of the prophecy. The Keepers of the Books would appear. They would bring the Books together once again. Bert convinced the others it was their duty to guard the *Chronicle* until its Keeper arrived. Then . . . then . . ."

His energy abruptly ran out. He slumped onto the tower wall. Michael and Gabriel had to wait several moments for him to continue.

"Men are not meant to live for thousands of years. The minds of the strongest become dry and brittle. One of Bert's brothers decided that he was the *Chronicle*'s Keeper, and Bert and the others were keeping it from him. Brother slew brother! O murder! O treachery! The blood! Terrible! Terrible!" He covered his face with his beard and spoke through the matted hair. "Bert's false brother was finally slain, but then only Bert and one other remained. Not enough to defend the *Chronicle*. Bert's last brother ventured forth, in an attempt to find the true Keeper. Poor, brave soul! Poor Bert, all alone!" And the man began bawling once more.

Michael glanced at Gabriel. They were thinking the same thing. The other Guardian, the one who had left, had to have been the skeleton that Michael and Dr. Pym had discovered in Malpesa.

"So where'd the dragon come from?" Michael asked. "And what did the elves do that you don't trust them? And would you please stop crying?"

The man dropped his beard and laughed, slapping his knees in joy. "Yes! Yes! The elves! It was when Bert was alone that the elves showed their true colors. Tried to steal the book! But they didn't know that Bert and his brothers had brought a dragon's egg from Rhakotis! Bert hatched it in the heat of the volcano! Bonded it to the *Chronicle*. When the elves marched on the fortress, well . . ."

"Ho, ho, ho," Michael chuckled. "I'll bet they weren't expecting that!"

Then he saw Gabriel scowling and dropped the smile.

"And that"—the man clapped his hands, apparently pleased with himself—"is that! Now"—he leaned forward, peering at Michael—"tell Bert the truth. Have you come for the book?"

"Well . . . yes—"

"Ha! Knew it! But the real question, the big question . . ."

The man came closer, his breath rasping through his beard. He placed a trembling hand on Michael's shoulder.

". . . Are you the Keeper? The one Bert has been waiting and waiting for?"

Past the dirt and matted hair, the man's face was unlined.

Only his eyes betrayed his age. They were eyes that had lived with one single purpose for nearly three thousand years; they were asking: Is it over? Is it finally over?

They were the saddest eyes Michael had ever seen.

"Are you the Keeper?"

It should have been a simple question to answer. Michael had been told he was the *Chronicle*'s Keeper by Dr. Pym. And then he'd felt the book calling to him through the snowstorm. Still, saying it, acknowledging it, was somehow different.

But there was no hiding from the eyes.

He said, in a whisper, "Yes. I am."

The madman nodded and took his hand from Michael's shoulder. "I suppose we'll soon see, won't we?"

"Wh-what do you mean?"

"You want to restore your sister, yes? The screaming shin kicker?"

"Of course—"

"And you've seen the forest. That was once ice and snow. What do you think called it to life? The *Chronicle*! It will revive your sister! Awaken the life sleeping within her! It is the only way."

"Then let us waste no more time," Gabriel said, and started for the stairs. "We know it is in the volcano."

"No!" The man jumped to block him. "The dragon will kill you!"

"But don't you control the dragon?" Michael demanded. "You said you hatched it from an egg!"

"No, no, no! The dragon doesn't obey Bert! The dragon

serves the *Chronicle*! Bert is suffered to live because Bert serves the same purpose. However"—once again, he leaned close to Michael—"the *Chronicle* is hidden in the volcano, yes, and the dragon will kill any who enter. Even Bert. But the true Keeper can pass unharmed." He gripped Michael's shoulder. "To save your sister, you must go into the volcano and face the dragon—alone."

Not surprisingly, Gabriel wanted to go in Michael's place. He said that the Guardian's warnings were meaningless.

"Why should we take the word of a madman who eats beetles as candy?"

"Says him," muttered the Guardian. "He hasn't tried them."

"At the very least, we should go together."

They were still atop the tower. Emma was still frozen. Only the sky had changed, softening from inky black to a deep, dark blue. Michael held firm.

"We can't both go. What if we're killed? There'd be no one to look after Emma. And if you went alone and got killed, I couldn't carry her out of here. I have to go, and you have to stay. That's all there is to it."

"And if the dragon doesn't obey you?" Gabriel said. "What then?"

He means, Michael thought, what if I'm killed.

"Then you take Emma to Dr. Pym."

"Let us go and find the wizard now, and return when your sister is well. There is no need to take such a risk as this."

Michael shook his head. They had no way of knowing what had happened in Malpesa after they'd left. What if Dr. Pym had only slowed Rourke down? The bald man could already be on the trail of the *Chronicle*. Michael had been willing to risk abandoning the book when there was no other way of saving Emma. But now getting the book also seemed to be the surest, fastest way of waking up his sister. It was a chance they had to take. Even if it meant Michael going into the volcano alone.

And after all, he'd figured out the potions in Malpesa—he could do this!

In the end, Michael won, as he was right, and Gabriel knew it.

Gabriel knelt and pulled a knife from his belt. He said it had been a gift from Robbie McLaur, the king of the dwarves near Cambridge Falls. The blade was a foot long and surprisingly light and would cut through bone as easily as paper. It would also, both Michael and Gabriel knew, be useless against a dragon. Still, Michael thanked him and tucked it into his own belt. He felt better for having dwarf steel at his side.

"We have a saying among my people." Gabriel laid a heavy hand upon his shoulder. ". . . A man can die only once."

Michael wondered if this was supposed to be encouraging.

"I guess that's . . . good to know."

"You remember that first morning in my cabin? After I saved you from the wolves?"

"Yes."

"You had betrayed your sisters to the Countess in hopes that she would help you find your parents. Do you remember?"

Michael stared at the ground. Did he remember? The memory haunted him. It was the single worst thing he'd ever done. By his own weakness and stupidity, he'd nearly lost what was most important to him—the love of his sisters. He couldn't think of it without pain, and yet, in the eight months since Cambridge Falls, Michael had replayed what he'd done over and over, hating and cursing himself, and ending always with the promise that he'd never let Kate and Emma down again, no matter what.

"Look at me."

Michael raised his eyes to Gabriel's.

"Each day, by our actions, we decide who we are. You are no longer that boy. Your sisters are fortunate to have you as a brother. And it is an honor for me to call you a friend."

Michael's throat was too thick to speak. He could only nod his thanks. Then, wiping his eyes, Michael hugged his sister, crushing her thin arms against her sides, whispering, "I'll be back soon," and turned and followed the last Guardian down the stairs.

In the large ground-floor chamber, Michael stared at the mouth of the tunnel while the Guardian turned a crank fixed to one of the columns. A chain clanked, and the iron gate began to rise.

"She'll know you're coming."

"She? The dragon's a girl?"

"Oh, yes. Now, you'll be safe as long as you're the true Keeper. She serves the book, and the book serves the Keeper."

"Okay."

"If you're not the true Keeper, she'll most likely eat you."

"Okay."

"She might roast you first."

"Okay."

"Or just gobble you up."

"I got it."

The gate was up. Michael stood there, feeling the heat wash over him.

"Don't close the gate," he said, and started down the stairs.

It was just as in his dream.

The long tunnel . . .

The red glow in the distance . . .

The brutal, throat-scorching heat . . .

The difference being this was no dream, and Michael knew what lay ahead.

The tunnel had turned a few yards past the gate and now ran straight on and down. The porous black rock was warm to the touch, and there was a sulfury sourness to the air. At first, Michael kept his feet moving with thoughts of Emma, frozen atop the tower; but with each step, the pull of the *Chronicle* became stronger, and soon it alone was drawing him on. Then the tunnel began to climb, and there was a new smell, one Michael had never encountered, and he could think only that it was the stench of dragon.

Knowing he was close, Michael knelt down and, with trembling hands, pulled out *The Dwarf Omnibus*. There were several passages where G. G. Greenleaf had written about dragons, and Michael quickly found the relevant sections:

Dragons are notable for their lust for gold—not a bad quality taken in moderation! . . . Dragons are immune to fire, obviously. . . . All dragons are terrifically vain; indeed, as to who is more vain, a dragon or an elf, I would not want to be the one to decide (hint: an elf!). . . . A dragon should never be engaged in conversation, as they are inveterate liars and tricksters, though if you're actually talking to a dragon, you're pretty much toast anyway. . . . Never, ever call a dragon a worm, no matter how much they're asking for it!

Michael snapped the book shut. He did not feel any better. He was about to rise when his thumb felt the stiff edge of the photo that Hugo Algernon had given him. He pulled it out, and there was his father, smiling up at him from deep in the past. Michael felt a hard knot of sadness in his chest. Would he ever actually meet his father? Would the day ever come when they would sit down, as Michael had often imagined, and talk about their love of all things dwarfish? When his father would tell Michael how proud he was of him? Crouching there in the reeking, sweltering cave, yards from a dragon's lair, Michael thought that day seemed very, very far away.

Michael slipped the photo into the book and then, on a whim, flipped through and opened to a different page:

In the spring of that year, the goblin hordes marched into dwarfish lands, burning and pillaging everything in their path. King Killin Killick raised an army and rode out to meet the monsters. A young squire, riding alongside the king, asked what was the secret to his long and successful reign. King Killick replied, "A great leader lives not in his heart, but in his head."

It was the quote that Hugo Algernon had said his father loved. It was the quote that Michael loved and tried to live by. He read on:

"Emotions cloud the issue," the king explained. "The one who can see most clearly will always triumph." Unfortunately, the day was fine, and Killick had chosen to ride without his helmet, and just then a goblin leapt from a tree and split his noble head in two. But let us take comfort that though the goblins routed the army, razed the countryside, and renamed Killick's capital Goblin-Town (showing, thereby, their typical goblin flair with names), the great king's words live on and are a lesson to us all.

Michael closed the book and stood, feeling fortified. He slid the *Omnibus* into his bag, making room for it beside the gold circlet he'd taken from the sculpture of the elf girl. He adjusted his glasses. It's time, he told himself.

Twenty-seven nervous steps later, he entered the cavern.

Gabriel stood atop the tower. He had cleaned the mud from Emma's cheeks and the last bits of fern from her hair. He couldn't stop wondering if he'd done the right thing in letting Michael go into the volcano alone. Would the wizard have approved? After all this time, had he made a mistake when it mattered most?

Fifteen years earlier, Gabriel had almost died while fighting in Cambridge Falls. King Robbie McLaur's dwarves had found him and saved his life. Later, while he'd been recuperating in his village, the wizard Stanislaus Pym had come to see him. He'd told Gabriel about the Dire Magnus and his hunger for the Books of Beginning and what it meant for the children.

"The enemy knows the children will lead him to the Books. He will hunt them."

It had been autumn, the air cool and crisp, and Gabriel had just begun walking without crutches. The wizard had gone on:

"Our only hope lies in finding the Books first. I will do all I can, but I need someone strong at my side. Someone who cares about the children."

Gabriel had been about to answer that he could depend on him, but the wizard had laid a hand on his arm.

"Understand what I'm asking. A war has begun. It will go on for years to come, and I will need you every day of that time. For all your strength, you are a man, with a man's span of years. This is the time you would find a wife, start a family. Know what you would be giving up."

Standing there, in the forest above his village, Gabriel had thought of the life that could be his. Then he'd thought of Kate, Michael, and Emma, especially of Emma, who had touched his heart in a way he'd never thought possible.

"You are sure that finding the Books will keep the children safe?"

"Yes."

"Then I am yours to command."

He had never once regretted his decision. His only fear had been that he would somehow fail in his duty. And it was with that in mind that he turned to go down into the volcano, to seek out Michael and help however he could, when a crushing blow struck him across the back of the head.

The cavern was roughly circular in shape, perhaps fifty feet across, with a ceiling that rose into darkness, and a large pool of lava that occupied most of the cavern floor. A narrow ring of black rock ran around the base of the walls. On the far side of the pool, Michael could make out the mouth of another tunnel. There was no dragon to be seen.

Michael stepped to the edge of the pool, his eyes watering from the heat and fumes. He stared down at the bubbling surface and thought:

You've gotta be kidding.

The book's pull was stronger than ever, and the source was, without question, within the pool of lava. The Order had put the book in a pool of lava! He almost couldn't believe it. Indeed, he wouldn't have believed it if the force pulling at him hadn't been so strong. And he had to admit, it made a crazy sort of sense. Assuming the lava didn't damage the book—which had to be the case—the Guardians must've planned for the molten rock to serve as a final line of defense.

Great, Michael thought. But how am I supposed to get it out?

He started looking around for a long stick.

"Hello, Rabbit."

Michael stumbled backward, tripping, skinning the heel of his hand on the rocky floor. A deep, feline chuckle echoed around the cavern walls.

"My, what a clumsy little rabbit you are."

Michael jerked his gaze upward. He had an idea where the voice was coming from, and he could just make out a large silhouette against the darker rock of the ceiling. The dragon was hanging upside down like a bat.

"St-stay where you are! Don't come down here!"

"The rabbit comes into my home and starts giving me orders? Where did you learn your manners? Also, you have a very funny nose. I can see it from here."

This last was, undoubtedly, a strange thing for a dragon to say, but Michael was scrambling to his feet and didn't notice. He'd had time now to take several deep breaths and remind himself that the dragon had to obey his commands. And as his initial panic subsided, a phrase of G. G. Greenleaf's came back to him: *Dragons are immune to fire.* In a flash, Michael realized how he was going to get the *Chronicle*—the dragon was going to get it for him.

Good old G.G., Michael thought, always there when you need him.

"You're right," he said, softening his tone. "I'm sorry. You just surprised me, was all. I should introduce myself . . . my name is Michael P—Wibberly."

"Puh-Wibberly? What an odd name."

"No, just Wibberly. No *P*."

"Well, Michael Just-Wibberly. It's a pleasure to make your acquaintance. I don't get many visitors."

"Really?" Michael said. "It's their loss."

He was gaining more confidence with each second and, indeed, felt that he was carrying himself remarkably well. Look at me, he thought, just standing here talking to a dragon. He decided that after he got the *Chronicle*, he would have the dragon pose for a picture with him. He glanced around for a rock on which he could prop the Polaroid.

"Thank you, Michael Just-Wibberly. I want you to know that I'm going to remember how polite you were after I've eaten you."

Michael said, ". . . Excuse me?"

"I said, I'm going to remember how polite you were after I've eaten you. That is the plan, you know."

Don't panic, Michael told himself. It doesn't know you're the Keeper.

"I'm afraid"—he was trying to maintain his confident tone—"you can't eat me."

"Aren't you the cutest rabbit? But you're wrong. I can and I will and I must. I don't really have much choice in the matter."

Michael heard the sound of iron-hard nails scraping on rock, the metallic slithering of scales. The great lizard was uncoiling itself from the ceiling. Michael felt suddenly, incredibly small. The idea arced across his mind that perhaps Gabriel had followed him into the tunnel and would now leap out to protect him.

Don't be silly, he thought. You're alone. Gabriel wanted to come, and you told him not to. Your own fault for being such a top-notch debater. Just stay focused.

"Listen, dragon"—it was time to adopt a sterner tone, such as one might use with a willful puppy—"there'll be no eating me, you hear? You can't! So just put that out of your head! I'm the Keeper!"

"The what?"

"The Keeper! I'm the Keeper of the *Chronicle*! That's why I'm here! You're supposed to get it for me!"

"Really?" The dragon seemed genuinely surprised.

"Yes! I need it to help my sister!"

"That was your sister I snatched from the clearing? I thought I noticed a family resemblance, though she seems to have escaped the tragedy of your nose. Now, do you prefer to be eaten raw or should I roast you a little first?"

"But you have to do what I say! The man—the Guardian—he said so!"

Laughter rolled about the cavern.

"That man and his lies! Let me ask you something, Rabbit. Did he tell you what happened to the other members of the Order? Did he say why he's alone here? With only me for company?"

Michael's neck was starting to get sore from staring upward.

"That's neither here nor there!" he said irritably. "Just hop down and get me the *Chronicle*; then we'll take a quick picture—"

"Did he tell you how he became convinced the *Chronicle* was his, and then murdered two of his comrades in the dead of night?"

Michael didn't move. Despite the cavern's overpowering heat, he felt a chill settle upon him.

"That's . . . not what happened."

"Oh, it is, I assure you. Only one of his comrades managed to escape, and my master has long feared that he will return with allies to claim the book. That, of course, is where I come in. To help him defend his blood-drenched prize."

"No, that's—no! One of the other Guardians went crazy! And you're here to protect the *Chronicle* from the elves! That's why he hatched you. The Order, they brought an egg all the way from Rhakotis! He told us!"

Michael commanded himself to remain firm and not fall for the dragon's tricks. Though it didn't help that the creature's laughter was filling the cavern.

"Protect the book from the elves? Why would the elves want some silly old book? And he didn't hatch me from any egg, I'll tell you that." The dragon became strangely somber. "But you are right; the elves will not trouble him. Would you like to know why?"

"I'm not interested in more of your lies."

The dragon murmured, "Those bad manners again," but went on, as if Michael had asked to hear the story.

"You see, Rabbit, after killing and driving off his comrades, my master was not in his right mind. He saw enemies everywhere. And the elves were close by and strong. He convinced himself that they coveted his treasure. So one day, he surprised the elf princess in the forest—it is her kingdom at the far end of the valley. He tricked her, placed a curse upon her, and has kept her captive ever since. You will not see her, but she is here. The elves do not dare attack."

"And they didn't even . . . want the book?"

"No. So my foolish master is safe from an enemy that was not an enemy and his treasure is safe from a people who never wanted it. Is that not madness? And now he's tricked you into coming here. Poor, doomed Rabbit."

"You're lying. That's what dragons do. They lie."

"Well, let's do a little test, shall we? Give me an order, and let's see if I have to obey it. This will be fun."

Michael was beginning not to like this very much. He wanted to get the book and be done. He decided he would forgo the photo.

"I'm waiting, Rabbit. Give me an order."

"Go . . . go get me the *Chronicle*."

"Hmm, no."

"I said"—Michael was trying, and failing, to keep the panic from his voice—"go—get—the—*Chronicle*!"

"I heard you the first time, Rabbit. No need to shout."

"So go get it!"

"You go get it."

"Stop it!"

"Stop what? Stop going to get the *Chronicle*? Or stop talking?"

"Stop talking!"

The dragon laughed. "You're very cute when you're angry."

Michael was trembling all over. His fists were clenched tight, and his eyes burned with tears of frustration. It couldn't be true; it just couldn't. . . .

"But why would . . . why—"

"Why would he lie? Why send you down here? From what I gather—I can't read his thoughts exactly, but I do feel what he's feeling, we're connected, you see—he's nervous about a companion of yours, some big, strapping fellow, and wanted to put you both at your ease. So he had you meet Bert."

"But . . . he's Bert . . . isn't he?"

Michael could see the shadowy form of the dragon moving across the ceiling. The creature was even larger than he remembered.

"Yes. And no. He's also Xanbertis, murderer and oath breaker. And he wants me to kill you. So I'll ask again—and please stop looking toward the tunnel, you're not going anywhere—do you prefer to be eaten alive or roasted? I say roasted. Less to clean up after."

Michael heard a growl that he was almost sure came from the creature's belly.

"Li-listen," he stammered, "don't do anything rash. . . ."

As he spoke, Michael's hand was rummaging in his bag,

searching for anything that might convince the dragon not to eat him. His fingers fumbled with his pocketknife, compass, camera, *The Dwarf Omnibus*, the badge proclaiming him Royal Guardian of All Dwarfish Traditions and History—all useless, all worthless.

"If you're being held here against your will, I have a friend who's a very powerful wizard. . . ."

Running was pointless; the dragon would catch him in an instant. But there had to be something, anything—

"Wait! I'll give you this!"

Michael's hand had closed around the golden circlet he'd taken from the sculpture of the elf girl. It wasn't much; indeed, it was very little with which to bargain for his life; but it was all he had—and G. G. Greenleaf had said that dragons suffered from gold lust and G. G. Greenleaf had never been wrong.

Even so, Michael was unprepared for what happened next.

The moment the crown cleared his bag, the dragon gave a roar so fierce, it was like a wind striking Michael's body. He saw a blur of gold fly toward him, a flash of fangs and claws. Michael turned away in terror. Without thinking—and this was the action that no doubt saved his life—he held the golden circlet out over the pool of lava.

"I'll drop it!"

The dragon landed a foot behind him, the impact shuddering through the rock. Michael could feel the creature's breath, like the hot blast of a furnace, crinkling the hair at the back of his neck. Up close, the dragon smelled of burnt metal and sulfur and something else that Michael couldn't place, almost like . . . perfume?

For a long moment, neither boy nor dragon moved or spoke.

"So drop it," the dragon said finally. "I don't care."

"Yes, you do!" Everything about Michael—his hand, his legs, his voice—was shaking terribly. "The lava will melt it in a second! I'll drop it, and you'll never get it!"

"Do that," the dragon said, "and I'll kill you."

"Aren't you going to kill me anyway?"

"True. But since you have to die, at least give me the crown. Don't be a poor loser."

Michael's arm was already growing tired. He looked down and saw one great talon only inches from his right foot. To Michael's surprise, there was a gold band, almost like a bracelet, clasped tight around the dragon's foreleg. Was that why it wanted the circlet so badly? So it would have a matching set? G. G. Greenleaf was right; dragons were certainly vain creatures.

"Come now, Rabbit. Give me the crown, and I promise to make the roasting very quick and even."

"Wait! I want to see the *Chronicle*! I've come a long way. If I'm going to die, I want to see it at least once. You have to give me that!"

"And then you'll give me the circlet?"

"Yes."

"You swear?"

"Yes."

"What will you swear on? What's most important to you?"

"My sisters," Michael said without hesitation. "I'll swear on them."

"Then, Rabbit, we have a deal."

Michael heard the rasp of talons pushing off rock, and he turned to see the dragon launch itself into the air. For an instant, it hung above the pool, its golden scales reflecting the red glow from the lava, leathery wings outspread, armored tail whipping this way and that, and Michael gasped, for the creature was, despite all its fearsomeness, stunningly beautiful. Then the dragon dove and disappeared, seal-like, into the bubbling lake.

Michael dropped the circlet onto the rocky floor and ran.

He ran as he had never run before and never would again. Indeed, in that strip of tunnel between the dragon's lair and the fortress, Michael Wibberly, who had never won a single race in school, who was always picked last for every team (and then only if the other team accepted some handicap, like having a turtle play first base), for that brief stretch, was the fastest boy in the world.

For all the good it did him.

Rounding the last corner, he stopped dead in his tracks, staring in horror. The gate over the mouth of the tunnel was closed.

Michael threw himself against the bars. "Gabriel! Gabriel!"

A pair of boots hurried down the steps into view.

"What're you still doing alive?"

Michael felt all his strength desert him. The Guardian stood on the other side of the gate. In every way but one, the man looked exactly as he had when Michael had first seen him atop the tower—the same mismatched rags, the same wild hair and beard. The single difference was that Michael could discern not a trace of madness in his face; there was only a gleeful, greedy triumph.

The man brandished a wooden club.

"That friend of yours had a very thick skull. I had to give him three hard taps before he finally stayed down. Now, where is that dragon—"

Just then there was a shriek of fury from deep inside the mountain.

The Guardian smiled at Michael, and chuckled, "Uhhhhhh-oh . . ."

"Let me out! Please! Let me out! She'll kill me! You—"

The man's hand shot through the gate, seizing Michael's shirt.

"Boy, the *Chronicle* is mine! I've guarded it for nearly three thousand years. For its sake, I've taken the blood of those I loved most in the world! Neither you nor any other will ever have it! You understand? *Never!*" He leaned closer, staring into Michael's terrified face. "I always wondered who my old comrade would send against me. I've imagined wizards, warrior elves, troops of armored dwarves marching here to steal my treasure! And after all this time, he sends a pair of children! You were his great champions!"

The man began cackling, and Michael found himself revising downward his opinion of the man's sanity. He could hear the dragon's footsteps thundering closer.

"You know something?" Michael said. "You're an idiot."

The man stopped laughing. "What—"

That was all he managed before Gabriel—who had been creeping silently up behind the man—cracked him across the head with the butt of his falchion.

And then Michael was shouting, his words a panicked jumble of "dragon" and "gate" and "hurry" and "hurry, please," and Gabriel was staggering up the stairs, turning so that Michael saw the blood covering the side of his face and head, and there was a crackling in the tunnel, the sound of air catching fire, and the gate began to lift slowly, slowly, and Michael was crawling under it, yanking free the strap of his bag as it caught on one of the spikes, feeling the ground beneath him start to tremble; and then he was through, scrambling over the body of the Guardian, shouting, "Close it! Close it!" and sprinting up the stairs as an echoing roar told him the dragon had rounded the last corner.

To Michael's surprise, the creature did not crash into the gate. It did not rend and tear the metal in a fury to reach him. Michael lay on the stone floor of the chamber, gasping for air, his heart racing, listening to the sound of the dragon breathing just inside the mouth of the tunnel.

And then, the dragon laughed.

"Rabbit, you really are making things very difficult! If you weren't so cute, I'd almost be angry. I suppose you know this gate is enchanted. Otherwise, I'd have torn it apart long ago."

"Of course," Michael panted. He'd known no such thing.

"Unfortunately, even though my master is unconscious, his order to kill you still holds. And you don't really think that after two hundred years I haven't found another way out of the volcano, do you?"

Michael was up instantly. He could hear the dragon racing back down the tunnel.

"Gabriel, we—"

But Gabriel was unconscious on the floor, the wounds he'd received from the Guardian having taken their toll. After checking to make sure that his friend was breathing, Michael raced for the tower stairs. He had no plan. All he knew was that he had to get to Emma. As he climbed, he cursed himself for going into the volcano. He'd been stupid! Arrogant! It was Cambridge Falls all over! He'd thought he was smarter than everyone else, but he wasn't, and now his sister would pay the price! The fact that he would die as well never entered Michael's mind. He only knew that he had let down Emma, and let down Kate—again.

As Michael emerged from the stairs into the open air, he saw Emma, exactly as he'd left her, motionless and staring into space. There was a shriek from above, and Michael spun about and saw the dragon, red streams of lava dripping from its wings, erupt from the mouth of the volcano. The dragon turned, a creature of fire, burning against the blue-black sky, and, with an eerie, graceful slowness, dropped down the side of the mountain. Michael seized Emma in his arms and struggled with her stiff body to the stairs, managing only a few awkward steps before he tripped and the two of them rolled in a tangle to the landing below. Michael's nose was bleeding, his whole body was bruised and banged, and he was kneeling over Emma, repeating, "I'm sorry, I'm so sorry," as the top of the tower was suddenly ripped away. Michael looked up and saw the dragon banking in the air to come back for another pass. He threw himself across his sister, but the dragon didn't ram the tower; it hovered there, using its great tail as a mace to knock away the remaining stones. In moments, the stairway was open to the sky, and Michael felt the dragon settle upon the wall.

Something landed beside his feet.

"There, Rabbit. I promised you a look at the *Chronicle*, and I keep my promises."

Michael leapt up, putting himself between the dragon and Emma, and drew the knife Gabriel had given him. Though it was crouched on all fours, the dragon still towered above him, all armored muscle and claw and fang. Michael was nothing next to it. Not even a rabbit. But he stood his ground, even as his legs shook beneath him.

The dragon regarded him through narrow eyes the color of blood.

"I really don't want to eat you, Rabbit. In another life, I think we could have been friends. But I can't disobey the will of my master."

"I'm not—" Michael stammered, "I'm not afraid of you."

"Yes, you are. But you're trying not to be, and that's what matters. Because of that, I'll give you one free tickle with your needle before killing you. Come closer."

Michael took one trembling step forward. He could feel the heat coming off the creature's body. The dragon was right; he was scared. But also angry. It shouldn't be ending this way: he and Emma separated from Kate. Emma not able to fight for herself. Him all alone.

"You don't know anything!" he shouted, tears now streaming down his cheeks. "You don't know anything about us! Me and my sisters, why we're doing this! You're just—you're just a stupid worm!"

"That's it, Rabbit. Let your anger flow. Your death will be so quick you won't even know it. Strike."

The dragon's breath was steaming Michael's glasses. But as he raised the knife above his head, he saw, once again, the golden bracelet around the dragon's foreleg. It stopped him. If the bracelet was gold, shouldn't it have melted in the lava? Unless, Michael thought, the bracelet was enchanted in some way. Just as the iron gate had been enchanted. Suddenly, the song the elves had sung in the clearing came back to him:

> For deep below that nasty hide
> There's a princess hiding still. . . .
> Please come back, oh please come back,
> Change your gold band for this one.

The dragon had said that a curse had been put on the elf princess. . . .

And the Guardian had said the dragon was a girl. . . .

But was it possible? Was it actually possible?

"Strike, Rabbit! Now! Strike!"

There was no more time to think. Michael swung down with all his might. He felt the knife cut neatly through the golden band and into the dragon's leg. The dragon shrieked in rage and reared up, claws raking the sky. Michael closed his eyes and waited for the talons to rip through him.

I was wrong. I'm dead. Emma's dead. I've killed us both.

And he was aware of an enormous, crushing sadness, greater

than any fear of death, because he knew that he had failed his sisters.

Then he heard a sound like a moan, and something struck the landing. Michael opened his eyes. The dragon was gone. In its place, a golden-haired elf girl, the living, breathing image of the sculpture in the clearing, lay amid the ruins of the tower. A severed bracelet was beside her. And beside that, a glowing red book.

Well, Michael thought, look at that.

And then he collapsed.

CHAPTER FOURTEEN
The Hothouse

"*Separation*. That's their word for it. *Surrender* is more like it. Cowardly. Base. We are lions fleeing before rats. Nature revolts at the very idea. Cigar?"

Rourke produced a leather case from inside his fur coat and flipped open the top, displaying four cigars lined up like missiles. The carriage was rumbling along the cobblestone streets, and Rourke, sitting across from Kate, had stretched out his great legs so that his feet rested on the seat beside her. He seemed a man very much at his ease.

"No, thank you," Kate managed.

"Well, sick to my stomach it makes me, and that's no lie."

Rourke bit off the end of his cigar and spat the nub out the window with such force that it knocked off the hat of a passerby.

He chuckled and lit a match with his thumb. Soon, sweet cigar smoke filled the carriage.

"I'm not denying that something had to be done. How the nonmagical vermin have been multiplying, the abuse and oppression of our kind. But nature teaches the rule of the strong. Let me tell you a story. Do you know Ireland at all?"

Kate gave a small shake of her head.

"My home, it is. And a beautiful and tragic place. I grew up in an orphanage outside Dublin run by the Sisters of Sweet and Enduring Charity. Never knew my parents. Though I was told that my mother was half giant, which is not difficult to believe, given the eye-boggling size of me. As it was, I was regarded as a freak. A thing not wholly human. And treated accordingly."

Kate said nothing. She was only half listening. She was searching through her pockets. It had to be there. She couldn't have lost it. . . .

"By the tender age of nine, I was larger than any man in Dublin, and was sold by the good sisters to a fella who owned a quarry. He chained my leg to a spike and I spent twelve hours a day hammering big stones into smaller stones. But I wasn't yet finished growing, was I? Got bigger and stronger every day. Finally, my own master came to fear me. Indeed, so great was his fear, he plotted to kill me. Luckily, I discovered his sanguinary intentions, broke free, and, with the very hammer he gave me, smashed that empty head of his to pieces. Ah, a great day that was, dark and bloody and beautiful."

He smiled at the memory and exhaled a cloud of smoke.

"Sure, I was caught easy. Too stupid to run. And sentenced

to hang as soon as rope could be found strong enough to hold me. But the night before the sentence was to be carried out, I'm sitting alone in me cell, and suddenly I'm not alone. He's there with me." The man leaned forward eagerly. "And what did he say? 'Declan Rourke, you are not human. Their laws cannot condemn you. If I free you, will you serve me faithfully?' And how did I respond? 'Brother,' says I, 'if you get me out of here, I'll clean the mud from your boots.' And didn't he take me away and make me the man I am? Opened my eyes. Gave me power. A great, great man. And now, lass"—the bald giant smiled, leaning back—"you're about to meet him."

The carriage passed through a pair of iron gates and into the courtyard of a large four-story mansion set in the middle of a block of mansions. An Imp stepped forward and opened the door. Rourke peered at Kate through the smoke.

"You all right, lass? You do look awful pale."

"I . . . lost something," Kate said. "It was in my pocket."

"And what was it? I'll send an Imp back to search for it. Must've fallen out when we collided."

Kate imagined one of the Imps picking up her mother's locket, touching it. She realized she'd rather never see it again.

"It's not important."

"In that case"—he gestured with his cigar—"my master awaits."

"We're not blaming you."

"You should!" Abigail cried, pointing a finger at the two boys. "Ain't they the ones that threw those snowballs? Hadn't been for that, those kids never would've chased us and the Imps never would've gotten her! It's their fault!"

Beetles and Jake were both uncharacteristically quiet. They stood, side by side, twisting their caps in their hands. They were gathered in the belfry atop the church, arrayed in a line before Henrietta Burke's desk. Rafe stood to the side. The old magician Scruggs, wrapped as always in his shabby brown cloak, sat against one of the pillars. The sun was low in the sky, a dull smudge visible through the clouds. It would soon be dark.

"And it was definitely Rourke who took her?" Henrietta Burke asked.

"It was him," Beetles said quietly. "There ain't no mistaking him. They put her in a carriage and took her to their mansion uptown. We followed 'em. Ran the whole twenty blocks behind the carriage."

"Yeah, you're a coupla real heroes," Abigail sneered.

"Enough," Henrietta Burke said. "You children can go."

Abigail, Jake, and Beetles headed toward the trapdoor. The boys paused at the top of the ladder and looked back at Rafe.

"We didn't mean nothing to happen," Jake said. "We liked her."

"Yeah," Beetles said. "We're real, real sorry."

Rafe nodded. He was clenching something in his right hand. As soon as the boys were gone, he turned to Henrietta Burke.

"I'm going to get her."

The woman shook her head. "She was never our responsibility, and now that is doubly so."

"Didn't you hear? She got caught trying to protect them! We owe—"

"Our duty is to those here! All day there have been reports of human mobs attacking magical folk. The humans sense that something is happening. I need you here. The Separation is only hours away. The girl is on her own."

"No."

Henrietta Burke had already gone back to her papers, but now she looked up sharply. Even Scruggs, who had been chewing his fingernails, took notice.

"Excuse me?"

Rafe stepped close to the desk; his voice, his whole body, was trembling with emotion. "Scruggs's spell keeps the church hidden. You don't need me. You just don't want me going there. Ever since the Imps showed up, you've tried to keep me clear of them. Why?"

"Because there is nothing to be gained by feuding—"

"That ain't it. I know Rourke's looking for me—"

"How do you know that?"

"It ain't important. Tell me what he wants!"

Henrietta Burke stared at him. Her face gave away nothing. Finally, she said, "It is not Rourke who hunts you. He is merely the right hand. It is his master. A being whose power is beyond any of us."

"Whoever he is, if he needs something from me, I can bargain. I can get him to give up the girl—"

"He will never give up the girl. And if you enter that mansion, you will not emerge from it." Then her gray eyes appeared to soften. "I know you want to save her. But you cannot sacrifice yourself."

"What aren't you telling me?" The boy struck the desk. *"What do they want from me?"*

Henrietta Burke glanced at Scruggs, looked back at the boy, and shook her head.

Rafe stepped away. "Fine. But I'm going to get her."

"Why? What is it between you and this girl? Why would you risk so much?"

For a moment, Rafe was silent. He was no longer trembling. He opened his hand and glanced at the golden locket Beetles had given him. The boys had picked it up from the sidewalk after Kate had been taken. He said, "You have your secrets. I have mine."

He'd started to turn when Scruggs spoke.

"Wait." The old magician shuffled to his feet. "There is a way to save her and still escape. You just have to enter without being seen. . . ."

Kate had expected to be taken to the Dire Magnus immediately. But after entering the mansion with Rourke, she found herself engulfed in a flurry of activity. Imps in their shirtsleeves were moving about furniture, carrying crates of champagne, iced platters of salmon and oysters, large bouquets of flowers; there were small, wizen-faced creatures—gnomes, Kate learned—polishing floors, cleaning windows, spitting on and wiping down anything brass.

"We're having a bit of a do tonight," Rourke said as he led

Kate up a wide set of stairs. "You certainly picked the right time to drop in."

Still gripping her arm, he led her through a pair of double doors and into a ballroom. Kate had only ever been in one ballroom, the one in the mansion in Cambridge Falls, and this one dwarfed the other. The floor was a shining expanse of blond wood. To the right, French doors gave onto a balcony that looked out over the street. To Kate's left, a wall of mirrors reflected the snowy scene outdoors. Red-cushioned chairs were being placed along the walls by a crew of Imps, while in the center of the room, an enormous crystal chandelier, with twisting, briar-like arms, had been lowered till it hung a foot off the floor, and three gnomes were using long metal tongs to fix white candles into dozens of holders.

Rourke stopped Kate beside the chandelier.

"Mistress Gnome."

One of the tiny creatures turned. She was three feet tall, with a face wrinkled like an old apple; she wore a gray dress that went to her toes, and she had a faded red kerchief covering her head.

"This young lady is here for an audience with our master. Clean her up a bit, won't you? There's a dear."

The little creature set down her tongs, snapped at a female gnome who was polishing the floor, and seized two of Kate's fingers in her small, rough hand.

"I'll be seeing you very soon," Rourke said.

The gnome led Kate out of the ballroom and down a dark-walled, portrait-lined hallway, with the second gnome trailing behind. Kate thought that this was her chance to get away—she was, after all, nearly twice the size of the gnomes—and when they reached a stairway and the gnome matron had started up, Kate tried to jerk away her hand, intending to bolt down the stairs to freedom.

"Ahhhh!"

Kate fell to her knees as the gnome bent her fingers to the point of breaking. The second gnome thudded into her back with both feet, so that Kate was slammed flat onto her face. The first gnome kept bending and twisting her fingers while the other jumped up and down on her back, cackling gleefully. The red-kerchiefed gnome peered into Kate's face.

"Now, Missus Big-Shoes," she said in a high, squeaking voice, "are we going to have any more kerfuffle from you?"

"No," Kate cried as the other gnome dug her doll-like fingers into Kate's hair and yanked.

"Ah, but big-shoes is all liars, ain't they?" And the wrinkle-faced gnome gave Kate's nose a painful wrench.

"No! I'm not lying! I promise!"

"Hmph," said the tiny creature, releasing Kate's fingers and nose and nodding to the other, who let go of Kate's hair and leapt off her back. The lead gnome started up the stairs, and Kate, her fingers, scalp, nose, and back aching, followed obediently.

She was bathed in a tub of scalding water. Her skin was scrubbed raw. Her hair washed. Her chewed-up nails filed down evenly. One of the gnomes raked a hard-toothed comb through her hair, pulling at the tangles with such fury that Kate was sure that by the time they finished, her scalp would be bald and bleeding. They yanked her into undergarments, like a dress, and then into a long-sleeved, high-collared ivory dress that had intricate lacework across the breast. And finally, one of the gnomes buckled Kate's feet into a pair of leather boots with dozens of hooks, while the other tugged her hair this way and that in a complex braid.

It was then the door opened, and Rourke entered.

"Ah now, I knew there was a young lady hiding under all that dirt."

The red-kerchiefed gnome jerked Kate to her feet and dragged her before a mirror. Kate hardly recognized the girl staring back at her. In the old-fashioned, high-necked dress, she looked like a girl from a book or a movie. There were pink blushes on her cheeks. Her dark blond hair shone, and it had been pulled up and braided in a way that showed angles of her face that Kate had never known existed. She looked down at her nails and saw that they had been trimmed and filed so that the evidence of her constant worried chewing was nowhere to be seen.

"Yes," said Rourke, "you're ready to meet him."

He led her up another set of stairs. Unlike the rest of the mansion, this floor was quiet and still. She and the man walked along a dimly lit hallway, the wooden floor moaning under Rourke's weight, and Kate glanced out the window and saw that it was growing dark. Evening was falling, and it was snowing again.

And then, halfway down the hall, she heard the sound of a violin.

Kate stumbled, the heels of her boots folding beneath her.

"Steady there," Rourke said, and lifted her by the elbow.

This was not Rafe's song, the mournful, gray-toned winter song he'd played that morning. This was the song that Kate had heard on the Countess's boat, the one that was somehow both manic and haunting. It was the song that would play as the world burned. The Dire Magnus was near.

An Imp stood at the end of the hall, and as Kate and the bald man approached, the creature opened a door. Unobstructed, the music poured forth, and Rourke placed a hand in the small of her back and she was propelled forward, as if she were dinner chucked into an animal's cage, and she heard the door slam shut behind her.

Kate staggered to a stop. The violin was silent. She was standing on a narrow gravel path and seemed to be surrounded by jungle. All about her were oily, fat-leafed plants, tall, spiny-stalked palm trees, fan-fronded ferns, plants with orange and red and yellow and purple flowers clustered in tight profusion. The air was warm and humid. Kate glanced up and saw the glass dome of the greenhouse. The heat had steamed the panes, obscuring the world outside.

The gravel path wound away, and a voice spoke from deep in the jungle:

"Come here, child."

Kate shuddered; she knew that voice. It was the voice of the being that had possessed the Countess; it was cold, and ancient, and savage.

"I am not accustomed to asking twice."

Very slowly, Kate stepped forward, her new boots crunching the gravel. She held her breath, tensing for her first sight of the speaker. Then, as she came around the bend, the jungle opened, revealing a gravel cul-de-sac at the end of the greenhouse, and there, surrounded on all sides by a tropical forest, an old man sat in a wooden wheelchair, a blanket across his lap.

He was the oldest person Kate had ever seen, almost more skeleton than man. His flesh seemed to have been sucked away, and his body had begun to collapse upon itself, though his head and hands were both strangely, grotesquely large. His skin was loose and scabbed and had a rotten greenish tint. He looked like something that had crawled its way out of a grave. He raised his lumpy head, and Kate saw that the old man's eyes were clouded with cataracts. He flicked two fingers, and a chair appeared across from him.

"Sit."

When Kate didn't move, there was a hiss, and she felt herself pulled forward and forced into the chair.

"Better."

Oddly, his voice was still the voice she remembered from the Countess's boat, full of energy and fire. But could this gnarled, shrunken creature really be the Dire Magnus? Kate had built the Dire Magnus up in her mind as a force of almost unimaginable power and malevolence, not this shattered wreck with milky eyes.

The old man grinned, displaying a mouthful of yellowed and broken teeth.

"You are wondering how this wasted thing before you could be the Dire Magnus? How could he lay claim to such power? Inspire such loyalty and terror? One might ask how a young girl, little more than a child, could contain within herself the ability to reshape time. One must not be misled by appearances. Power is power. While an outward appearance"—he flicked his fingers again—"is quickly changed."

A mirror appeared in the air, and Kate saw, staring back at her, a silver-haired crone whose face was so wrinkled that her skin seemed to be melting from her bones. Gasping, Kate raised her hands and saw her knuckles were swollen, her nails thick and clawlike. Before she could cry out, the old man waved his hand again, and Kate looked in the mirror and saw her face returned to normal.

"Do not place your trust in appearances, child."

Kate's heart was pounding as the old man chuckled wetly. She tried to force herself to remain calm. Even if he really was the Dire Magnus, he couldn't know anything about her. It was a century before they would meet on the boat in Cambridge Falls. She just had to stay quiet. She could get out of this.

The old man cocked his head, as if hearing some far-off tune.

"We've met before, haven't we? Or not yet. In the future."

Kate said nothing. Was the man reading her thoughts?

The old sorcerer went on speaking.

"The Keeper of the *Atlas*. Of course, I knew the moment you arrived in the city. I couldn't say exactly where you were, but I felt your presence. And how auspicious that you should be here this night of all nights. Tell me, child, do you know why tonight is so important?"

"The . . . Separation," Kate said, relieved to be talking of something where she could give nothing away. "The magic world is disappearing at midnight."

"Yes. We are going into hiding. Ceding the world to the non-magical for no reason but that they hate us for our power and outnumber us ten thousand to one."

Kate didn't know how to respond and so said nothing.

"They say, those who wish us to retreat, that the age when magic ruled the world is long past. That Separation, retreat, hiding like scared children, is our only hope for survival. In part, I agree." The man's wheelchair crawled closer. "It is pointless to live on equal terms with those not touched with magic. We are not equal and never will be. But magic can rule the world once more. All that is required is will and power. I have the will. And soon, very soon, I shall have the power."

Kate had been thinking only of protecting herself, giving away as little as possible. Now, suddenly, she was beginning to understand.

"I foresaw this all long ago. I saw that magic would fade. That our kind would be swallowed by the rising sea of humanity. I tried to make others listen. But magician fought magician. Elf fought dwarf fought goblin fought dragon. None would face the true enemy. And the power we needed was there. It had even been gathered together into one place, as if waiting for me to take it."

"The Books of Beginning," Kate whispered.

"Exactly so. But the wizards of Rhakotis, for all their learning, were fools. They had written the Books merely to have the world know that they had written them, never to actually use them. Still," the old man wagged his monstrous head, "the council was powerful. For centuries, they were too strong to attack. But my day finally arrived, and I helped the warlord Alexander to conquer the city."

"You partnered with a lowly human," Kate said, unable to resist the jab. "I thought you hated them."

The Dire Magnus shrugged. "War makes for unlikely bedfellows, and I killed him soon after."

"But you didn't get the Books, did you?" Kate said.

The old man moved his white eyes toward her, and Kate felt an invisible weight settle upon her chest. The man's face showed no emotion. The weight became greater. Kate was determined not to scream or ask for mercy, but the weight pressed harder and harder and finally, while she still had breath, she cried, "Stop! Please!" The weight lifted, and she gasped quietly.

"You are right, child," he said, continuing as if nothing had happened. "The Books had vanished by the time I arrived at the vaults of Rhakotis. For twenty-five hundred years, I searched for them. And all the while, humans grew stronger, and the magical world grew weaker. Now, what is the great solution? We will hide. Only I have not given up. I will yet find the Books, and humanity will tremble. Your coming is only the first sign. Tell me, where are the other two books?"

"I don't know."

He laughed. "I don't think you're being entirely honest."

He crooked one gnarled finger, and Kate felt the magic rise inside her. She tried to push it down, but the man was too powerful. The greenhouse vanished, and Kate was somewhere else entirely. And then—Kate barely stopped herself from crying out his name—she saw Michael. Fire swirled about him. He clutched a book with a red leather cover. She knew she wasn't really there, that Michael couldn't see her. Then, just as quickly, Kate was back in the greenhouse. She felt the magic settling inside her.

"You see, child, you do know. That was the *Chronicle*, the Book of Life. And holding it . . . your brother?"

Kate gripped the arms of her chair and said nothing.

"We will look into this later. We have other, even more pressing matters." His wheelchair crept forward another inch, and the man brought his giant head close. "For the Separation is not the true reason why tonight is significant. Tonight is significant"— and again he showed his jagged yellow grin—"because I am going to die."

"What?"

It was all Kate could manage to say. She was vaguely aware of a large red snake slithering through the jungle to her right. The old sorcerer chuckled.

"You're surprised? Perhaps you thought the Dire Magnus was immortal? But death is the sea to which all water flows. Elves might live for thousands of years. Dwarves a few hundred. Wizards and witches are too close to humans. We might survive a century or two. After that, if we wish to continue living, we must resort to more . . . forceful measures. As you see me here, I am three hundred and forty-one years old, and tonight, finally, I will die."

"But . . . I don't understand. I met you . . . in the future. . . ."

"You met me, yes. And yet you met another. What happens when a king dies? A new king rises to take his place, taking on all the titles and powers of the old, wrapping himself in the dead man's office. The Dire Magnus is one man, but also many men.

"I am the ninth Dire Magnus. I was chosen as a young boy. I had no knowledge of who I was, what my destiny would be. I was called. And when I awoke to myself, I took on not just the title of the Dire Magnus, but also the powers and memories of the eight who preceded me. Just as when I die tonight, I will also be reborn, as I pass on my power and memories to my successor. He will carry us all forward. He will be the greatest of us. The most powerful. He will also be the last. It will fall to him, the duty of turning the world back as it is meant to be. And he will not fail."

Kate shook her head; the heat in the room was making her thickheaded.

"There's . . . another? Another Dire Magnus?" Even as she asked the question, a terrible thought occurred to her, and she felt a stab of dread. "Who is he?"

"A boy. It is always a boy. He is ignorant of his power. Ignorant of his destiny. But there is power in him even now. Others will feel it. . . ."

Kate couldn't breathe; the heat and moisture in the room were choking her. She wanted to rip away the collar of her dress. It wasn't possible. It couldn't be possible!

The old sorcerer went on speaking:

"It has taken years to track him to this city. And still some magic cloaks him from my view. Rourke has hunted the boy the length and breadth of the island, yet he continues to elude us. No doubt, whoever is hiding him thinks they are protecting him." He waved his hand, brushing the matter aside. "It matters not. The boy will come to me tonight. He will be drawn here. He cannot escape his fate. He will come, and the chain will not be broken."

Kate felt herself gripping the arms of her chair as if she might tumble forward.

"What . . . what's his name?"

The ancient creature smiled, and Kate sensed that he had been waiting for this moment.

"You ask that, child, but you have already met him. His presence is all around you. I felt it the moment you entered." The old man's milky eyes cleared, and Kate stared in horror, for they burned the same shade of emerald green she had seen that morning as Rafe had brushed soot over her cheeks.

"He will come," the old man hissed. "He will come, and the Dire Magnus will live again."

Kate was aware of the Imp entering the greenhouse and lifting her out of the chair. She heard the old Dire Magnus say, "Take her to a room and watch her. She will be my guest at tonight's ceremony." She felt the cold air as she entered the hallway. At the head of the stairs, she heard Rourke's brogue, "Here now, I'll take the lass," and she was passed from the Imp to the huge man, and then she heard shouting coming up the stairs, and she was pulled out of her daze, for the voice that was shouting below was Rourke's, and yet Rourke was standing beside her, and the Imp seemed to notice the strangeness as well, and then, without warning, Rourke kicked the Imp hard in the chest so that he flew crashing out of the window. Then there were boots pounding up the stairs, and Kate saw a shimmer in the air in front of Rourke, and suddenly, standing beside her was not Rourke at all, but Rafe.

"So much for that," the boy said. "You feel like running?"

Michael woke, saw blue sky above him, and, for one perfect moment, had no idea where he was.

Then a face appeared, upside down, leaning in very close to his own.

"How do you see out of these? They make everything so fuzzy!"

Instantly, Michael was on his feet. He took in the blurred outlines of the forested valley, the snow-covered mountains, the volcano, the ruined tower. . . .

Okay, he thought as his heart galloped in his chest, okay, I know where I am.

Then his hand went to his throat and he felt the bump of the glass marble, still hanging from the rawhide strip about his neck. Reassured, Michael reached up to adjust his glasses and realized he wasn't wearing glasses, that they were being worn by the figure in whose lap his head had been resting just moments before.

"You don't really need these awful things, do you?" The elf girl had taken off his glasses and was holding them as one might hold a particularly slimy piece of seaweed. "You look so much better without them. Except for your nose. Were you in an accident?"

"What? No."

"Or cursed by a wizard?"

"No—"

"So you were born with that nose? I suppose after we're married I'll just make a point of not looking at your face too often so that it doesn't frighten me."

Michael was still groggy from sleep and struggling to get his bearings—not to mention that what the elf girl had said was so utterly horrifying—and he had no idea how to respond. He simply said, "Can I please have—" then cut himself off. "Wait—where's Emma? Where's my sister? And where's the *Chronicle?*"

"Your overly large friend carried her downstairs. And he took that annoying book with him. As if I ever want to see it again— oh la!"

"Gabriel? He's okay?"

"Perfectly fine. Shall I throw these away then? We're agreed?" She dangled the glasses off the side of the tower.

"No! I need them! Please."

"Oh, very well." The elf girl skipped over and handed Michael his glasses. "To the rest of the world, you may be terrifying to behold, but to me you will always be the most handsome man alive. Provided, of course, I periodically look away from your face." She curtsied. "Princess Wilamena, at your service."

"You're . . . a princess?"

"Well, of course! Why do you think I wanted my crown back so badly?" She touched the gold circlet now around her brow. "Don't you think it becomes me?"

"What? Oh, uh, sure. Lots."

With his glasses on, Michael could finally see the elf girl clearly. She was a perfect living duplicate of the ice sculpture. Her hair, he decided, was the color of morning sunlight. Her eyes were bluer than a cloudless summer sky. Her nose—

Bluer than a cloudless summer sky? Michael thought. What's wrong with me? She's got blond hair and blue eyes; that's it.

But even then, Michael heard himself comparing her voice to birdsong, the whiteness of her skin to new snowfall—

Stop it, he told himself. You're being duped by some elf magic, is all.

"Oh, wonderful." The elf girl clapped her hands. "You've already fallen in love with me!"

"I have not—"

"Don't be silly! You should see the ridiculous look upon your face! By the way, have you noticed the way my hair moves?"

"Listen," Michael said with as much sternness as he could muster, "I need to know you're not going to turn back into a dragon. You're not, are you?"

At this, the elf princess grew somber and reached down to pick up the severed gold bracelet from where it lay amid the rubble. Michael saw that the bracelet had shrunk down to person size, but even so, it looked large and bulky in the elf maiden's delicate hands. Wilamena ran her fingers over the cut made by Michael's knife.

"It was almost two hundred years ago when I came upon Xanbertis in the forest. He offered me this bracelet as a symbol of the friendship between the Order and my people. I had no knowledge then of the atrocities he'd committed. So I accepted the gift, and became his slave. Two centuries of darkness and fire. A prisoner in my own horrible body. But no more. The dragon is dead and I am saved—all because of you!"

She gazed up at him with tearful, adoring eyes.

And Michael thought, Poor thing, she's had a rough time of it.

Then he thought, Her hair really does move all by itself. . . .

The elf princess clapped her hands in delight.

"Oh, you *are* in love with me!"

"What—no, I just—"

"Yes, you are! My own rabbit!"

"Please, don't call me Rabbit."

"Bunny!"

And she leapt forward and kissed him on the cheek, causing Michael to stumble back.

"Don't do that either! I'm serious."

He could feel his cheeks burning and a tingling where she'd kissed him.

"True," she said. "There'll be plenty of time for kissing later. Oh yes indeed!"

Enough of this elf nonsense, Michael thought.

"I want to see my sister. Now."

They found Emma in the Guardian's quarters, a low-roofed building tucked along the back wall of the fortress. The furnishings were spare—a wooden chest, a cot, a stool, a table—but considering the Guardian's own fairly filthy appearance, the room was surprisingly clean and tidy. Gabriel had laid Emma on the cot and covered her with several blankets, and when Michael and the elf princess entered, he was sitting beside her, holding her small, lifeless hand in both of his. Michael had the impression that Gabriel had been sitting like that, without moving, for hours.

Gabriel, whose head was wrapped in a bandage, rose and embraced him.

"I am very proud of you."

"Oh, well . . . you know . . ." Michael was suddenly tongue-tied. ". . . It's no big . . . well, you know . . ."

Then Michael tried to return Gabriel's knife, but the man refused to take it.

"You have earned it. King Robbie would agree."

Michael thanked him and slid the knife back into his belt.

The red leather book was on the table beside the cot. Michael had felt its pull the moment he'd entered the room, and his hands itched to hold it. But as he took Gabriel's place on the stool, he gave all of his attention to Emma. Save for the fact that she was lying down and covered with blankets, she appeared exactly as she had the night before. Her eyes stared out at nothing. There was the same crease of anger on her brow. Her mouth was still slightly open. Michael picked up the clenched hand that rested on the outside of the blanket. It was as cold as a stone.

It's okay, he said silently. I'm here now.

And only then, finally, did he turn to the book.

It was both smaller and fatter than the *Atlas*. In size and shape, it reminded him of *The Dwarf Omnibus*, a book Michael considered to have near-perfect proportions. As Michael had predicted, the *Chronicle* showed no signs of having been submerged in a pool of lava; indeed, it was in far better shape than the *Omnibus*, whose black leather binding was scarred and worn with age. Michael did find, however, that a design had been carved into the leather cover. He couldn't say what it was for sure, but the network of ripples and whorls made him think of tongues of flame. For a moment, Michael wondered about the significance, then filed the question away and turned his attention to the most intriguing, and unusual, aspect of the book.

Two metal hooks, fixed along the edge of the back cover, were clutching what looked like an old-fashioned pen. It was four and a half inches long, smooth and slim, and it tapered to a point at one end. It appeared to be made of bone.

"What is this?"

"That's the stylus." Princess Wilamena was standing behind him; and even with his back to her, Michael was frustratingly aware of her presence, and of the fact that her hair smelled of springtime and honey and—

Focus, he told himself.

"What do I do with it?"

"You silly, that's how you get the *Chronicle* to work! You write in the name of whomever you wish the *Chronicle* to fix upon, and voilà! The thing is done! Is that helpful?"

"Yes," Michael said. "Actually, it is. Thank you."

"Is it worth a kiss perhaps?"

Michael ignored that. He snapped the stylus out of the brackets. It was very light; it felt almost hollow.

"And now I just write Emma's name in the book? Seems so easy."

The elf girl laughed. "Do you even know what the *Chronicle* is, you rabbit you?"

"I told you—"

"Hush! You're about to learn something. The *Chronicle* is a record—you could even say *the* record—of all living things. Any creature that walks or talks or breathes or sings or laughs or cries or runs or blows bubbles—I do like blowing bubbles!—is listed in its pages. And the list is constantly changing as the lives around us bud and wither. By writing someone's name in the book, you add them to the scrolls of the quick."

"But Emma's already alive; she's just frozen—"

"As I was about to explain, the *Chronicle* is, first and foremost, a record; but the stylus allows you to focus the power of the book—the power of life itself—upon a specific being, either to call them into existence, or—and think now of your dear, sweet sister—to heal them. But all *you* have to do is write the name down with your little rabbit hand." And then Michael heard her whisper to Gabriel, "He doesn't like me to call him Rabbit, but I do it anyway because he's such an adorable rabbit. Don't you agree?"

Gabriel gave a noncommittal grunt.

Michael opened the book. He was not surprised to find the pages blank, although, unlike the *Atlas*, whose pages were smooth and white, these were rough and marked with tiny splinters of wood. Michael flipped through to the middle and flattened the book on his knee. He paused. He had the sense that this was one of the shining moments of his life. To get here, he'd triumphed over great odds and great danger. He imagined Dr. Pym learning of what he'd done, or Kate, or King Robbie, or even, one day, his father. As Michael set the tip of the stylus to the page, a smile creased the edges of his habitually serious face and, with a confident stroke, he wrote his sister's name.

Nothing happened.

"Um, Rabbit . . ."

"What?" Michael said irritably.

"You will need ink. The letters won't just magically appear."

"Well, you could have told me that. Does the Guardian have any—"

"Oh, you don't use normal ink." The elf princess came forward and took his thumb in one hand and the stylus in the other. Michael was about to ask what she was doing—even as he marveled at the rose-petal softness of her skin—when she jabbed the sharp point of the stylus into his thumb.

"Oww!"

"Don't be a baby bunny. Here, you see?" And she dipped the stylus into the drop of blood welling on the pad of his thumb. "Not only does it function as ink, but the blood also forges the connection between you and the book. A bit gruesome, but very effective. Now wake up your poor sister, we'll all go outside, and I'll let you braid my hair!"

Michael said nothing about this last suggestion (though a small voice in his head thought it sounded wonderful), but took a deep breath, gave one final glance at his sister's motionless face, and touched the stylus to the page.

He jerked upright. It was as if he had jammed a fork into an outlet; an electric current was coursing up the stylus, along his arm, and out through his entire body.

"What's happening?" he heard Gabriel demand. "Is he in danger?"

"No, he's linked to the *Chronicle*," the elf princess whispered. "Watch."

It seemed to Michael as if all of his nerve endings, from the tips of his fingers, to his earlobes, down to the bottoms of his feet, were humming. After the initial shock, the feeling was not painful, or even unpleasant, and as Michael began to relax, he realized that his senses had become almost supernaturally keen. He saw flecks of gold he'd never noticed in Emma's eyes; he smelled the faint oatmealy odor of the soap they used at the orphanage in Baltimore; he even heard, though this seemed impossible, the soft, fluttery beating of her heart. . . .

He began to write, and the letters smoked and bubbled as he laid them down, as if he were somehow soldering his sister's name into the pages of the book; and then Emma lurched upward, shouting, "You'd better not—" She stopped and looked about, saying, "Huh? How did—" and a loud and joyful chaos broke loose all around her. Gabriel swept her up in his arms, Wilamena clapped and kissed Emma, declaring that she was so happy that they were to be sisters, and Emma said, "Huh? Who are you? Where's that dragon?" and in the midst of this, only Michael was silent, sitting there on the stool, his hands trembling as he closed the book, his face bled white with fear.

"So there I was in the clearing, and this big, stupid dragon—" Emma glanced at Wilamena. "Sorry."

"Oh la!" The elf princess waved her hand. "It's nothing. We're family, after all. Or we soon will be."

"Huh?"

"Skip it," Michael said.

"Well, then we flew over the forest," Emma went on, "which was actually kind of cool, and landed on the tower, and that hairy, smelly guy jabbed me with a needle, and next thing I knew, I was here."

Here being the Guardian's quarters, where they were all still gathered. Emma had just been told, partially by Michael, but mostly by Gabriel and Wilamena, everything that had transpired since she'd been frozen: how Michael and Gabriel had tracked her to the fortress, how Michael had gone into the volcano alone, how the Guardian had tried to murder them, how Michael had figured out that the dragon was really the elf princess, how he'd managed both to lift the curse and retrieve the *Chronicle*. . . .

"The rabbit was quite extraordinarily brave," Wilamena had said.

"What rabbit? There's a rabbit?"

"She means me," Michael had said glumly.

"He was willing to lay down his life for you. Imagine a little rabbit like that standing up to a dragon with only a puny dwarfish knife."

Michael had felt everyone staring at him, and he'd quickly asked Emma to tell her story. When she was done, Gabriel announced it was time to think about leaving.

"It is a long journey back to the plane, and we will be hard-pressed to arrive before nightfall. Still, we cannot walk on empty stomachs. How much food is kept in the fortress?"

"Oh, quite a bit," the elf princess said. "I can show you."

Sensing his chance to escape, Michael said that while she and Gabriel did that, he was going to try and wash the mud out of his hair, and he hurried out the door.

Michael went directly to the keep. Slivers of light stretched across the floor of the chamber. The Guardian sat lashed to a column, his hands tied behind him, his chin resting on his chest. Michael stopped a few feet away. He was trembling; he had kept himself together ever since Emma had woken up, knowing he could come here.

"I need you"—he tried to keep his voice from shaking—"I need you to tell me how to use the *Chronicle*. Princess Wilamena tried to tell me, but . . . she must've missed something or not known it. I need to know what I'm doing wrong. You know, I know you do!"

Slowly, the man lifted his head off his chest and looked at Michael. Amazingly, he seemed even more ragged and wretched than before. His eyes were bloodshot, his hair was matted with dried blood, and his tunic was ripped open at the shoulder.

But upon seeing Michael, he smiled. "So you used the *Chronicle* to bring back your sister. What happened, boy? I want to hear all the details."

"Just . . . tell me how to use it. I have to know. Please."

"You don't want to say, fine. I will. For a moment, you were connected to your sister. Her heart became yours. Anything she's ever felt, you felt. And I'm guessing that you didn't like it, did you?"

His tone was gleeful, and what he described was exactly what Michael had experienced. He had felt the power of the book rising and rising, but he'd been entranced, enchanted, and by the time he'd finally realized what was happening, it'd been too late. Like a swimmer who finds himself in a strong current and can only watch the shore recede, Michael had been carried out to sea.

Or rather, he'd been carried toward Emma. Just as the Guardian had said, her entire life had opened before him. Not just her life, but her heart. He'd understood what it had been like growing up as the youngest sibling, with no memories at all of their parents, no memories of a life that didn't involve moving from orphanage to orphanage, no family but him and Kate. He'd understood, at a level he never had before, that he and Kate were Emma's entire world, that Emma, the bravest person he knew, was completely governed by fear, the fear that she would somehow, someway, lose her brother and sister and then be utterly alone. And Michael had felt how, when he'd betrayed her and Kate to the Countess, the slender foundations of her world had been destroyed. And he'd understood how much it had cost her to forgive him, to trust him again, but how that sense of certainty she'd once felt, knowing that her brother and sister would always be there, had never returned.

"Just tell me," he said, wiping the tears from his face, "what I'm doing wrong."

"What you're doing wrong? The only thing you're doing wrong, boy, is imagining that you're the Keeper." The man leaned forward, furious now, straining against his bonds. "The *Chronicle* forms a connection between you and whoever's name appears in the book. That person's life, however awful, however terrible, however painful, becomes your life. What they feel, you feel. That is the way it is."

"But—that's not fair!" Michael cried, knowing he sounded like a child, but not able to stop himself. "The *Atlas* just takes you through time. Why can't—"

The man laughed. "It is the Book of Life! And life is pain! The true Keeper must be able to bear the pain of the world. Is your heart that strong, boy? I don't think so. You can scarcely carry your own pain, much less anyone else's. The moment I saw you, I said, This boy hides from life. He's doing everything to run away from pain. But there's no running away from the book." The Guardian spat, and the look on his face was pure scorn. "You wanted the *Chronicle*—it's yours. But you're not the Keeper!"

Michael found a barrel of water along the side of the keep and dunked his head, again and again, scrubbing at the hardened bits of mud still stuck to his hair and scalp. When his hair was as clean as it was going to get, he dried his face on his shirt and leaned against the barrel, taking long, slow, deep breaths.

"Michael?"

Quickly slipping on his glasses, Michael turned about. It was Emma.

"I was looking all around for you. . . ."

"Sorry," he said, "I—"

"Are you mad at me?"

"What?"

"I just thought you might be mad at me. You know, for not listening to you last night and getting caught—"

"Of course not. No. How could you think that?"

Water dripped from his hair onto the lenses of his glasses, but Michael saw Emma clearly, with her muddy hair and dirt-streaked face; she looked small and uncertain.

"Only, you didn't seem all that glad to see me, and then you just kind of ran away . . . and . . . I can't believe the things you did." Her eyes were shining with tears. "You fought a dragon for me, and I didn't say it before, 'cause it's none of that elf girl's business, but I'll never, ever forget what you did, never, and if you're mad—"

"Emma, I'm not mad at you. I just . . ." And he knew he had to say something, so he chose something that at least was true: "I was scared. I'm sorry."

Emma let out a sob of relief and rushed at him, seizing him in a fierce clench. "I'm sorry too. I should've listened to you." They stood like that for several seconds, and Michael, who'd just barely succeeded in stitching himself together, thought he might break apart all over again. Be strong, he told himself, you have to be strong.

Finally, Emma stepped away, wiping her eyes with the back of her hand.

"Hey, wait for me, okay?"

Moving past him, she went up on tiptoe and leaned over to dunk her head in the now-cloudy water in the barrel. It was mid-morning, and the sun was bright and warm. Michael could feel his own hair drying. Already he was telling himself that he would never use the *Chronicle* again. It was enough that they'd kept it from the Dire Magnus.

When Emma was finished, she shook her head, spraying water in all directions.

"Hey, Michael?"

"Yeah?"

"Can I see the book?"

Michael only hesitated a second, then went to his bag and pulled the *Chronicle* from where it was nestled beside *The Dwarf Omnibus*. He stood there quietly as Emma flipped through the pages.

"Where's my name? I thought you wrote my name."

"It disappeared."

"And you really used your own blood as ink?"

"Yes."

"Gross. And this is the pen thing?"

"The stylus."

"Huh."

Emma ran her hand over the rippled design on the cover and handed the book back. Without looking at it, Michael slid the

Chronicle into his bag and slipped the bag over his shoulder, feeling its weight settle against his hip. He let out the breath he'd been holding.

"So is it yours? Like how the *Atlas* is Kate's?"

"I guess so."

"That must mean the next one's mine. I hope I don't have to write in it with my own blood. I mean, no offense, but *bluuh*."

Michael thought about telling her that the next book was the Book of Death, then decided that that information could probably wait.

"Michael, honest, are you sure you're okay?"

He looked at Emma, her damp hair sticking up all over her head, and thought, She's alive; whatever the cost, it was worth it.

He said, "I'm fine."

And he managed something like a real smile.

"Can I ask one more question?"

"Sure."

Then Michael saw a familiar, mischievous sparkle in Emma's eyes and he braced himself for what was coming:

"Is Princess What's-Her-Name your girlfriend now?"

"No," Michael said firmly. "Absolutely not."

Emma grinned. "You sure about that? 'Cause—"

"Of course I'm not his girlfriend!"

They both turned and saw the elf princess standing beside the corner of the keep, hands on her hips, glaring imperiously at Emma.

"Oh la! We are *much* more serious than that!"

"Gotcha," Emma said, smiling broadly at her brother.

"Now," Wilamena went on, "I come with two messages. First, breakfast is ready. Second, there is black smoke in the valley. Apparently someone named Rourke has found you." She clapped her hands. "So, I hope you're both hungry."

CHAPTER SIXTEEN
For Auld Lang Syne

There was no time to talk, no time for Kate to ask Rafe how he had found her, how he'd disguised himself as Rourke. No time, for that matter, to ask why he'd come for her. After the glamour that had cast him as the giant, bald Irishman faded, and shouts and the thudding of boots sounded up from below, Rafe grabbed her hand and they raced up the stairs, through a door, and out onto the cold of the roof.

The night air swept away the last of Kate's grogginess, and it was then, looking out at the untouched snow, with Rafe's hand still tight around hers, that she had a single moment of hesitation.

"What?" Rafe demanded. "What is it?"

What could she tell him? That she had just learned that the Dire Magnus, her enemy, was not one man, but many? That the new Dire Magnus was to be chosen that night, and he, the very boy now rescuing her, was next in line?

"We have to go!"

And she let herself be pulled away.

As they came to the short wall that bounded the edge of the Imps' mansion, Kate saw that the roof of the next house was a full story lower. She started to balk, but Rafe placed his hand around her waist and leapt. They fell and fell, landing in a thick cushion of snow, and Rafe was up instantly, pulling Kate to her feet, and they were off and running once again. The snow was high and heavy, and it was awkward for Kate in her new boots and dress, but Rafe kept urging her on, vaulting the short walls that separated the houses, weaving between the chimneys and the snow-banked summer gardens; they were halfway down the block when Kate glanced back and saw the figures of four Imps charging after them.

"They're—"

"I know!" Rafe said. "Keep running."

Kate could see the end of the block ahead, and past that the wide gap of the avenue. The wet snow dragged at her legs and dress, and she could hear the stamping footsteps of the Imps closing in from behind.

"There!" Rafe shouted.

Kate looked to where he was pointing, ahead and to the left, and she saw the long, dark snake of the elevated train. The tracks ran along the avenue, just below the tops of the houses. The train would be even with them in seconds, and Kate realized then what Rafe meant to do. But it was impossible; there was no way—

"Hurry!" Rafe yelled.

The first snowcapped train cars were already rattling past.

"We can't! It's going too fast! We—"

"Just jump!"

Then they were at the end of the block; there was nowhere else to go; she could hear the rasping of an Imp at her shoulder, and, holding Rafe's hand, she jumped.

It was further than she'd thought. At least seven feet between the edge of the building and the train. For a moment, they hung in the air; Kate could see the train moving below them, and she feared they would land in one of the gaps between the cars and fall down and be crushed. Instead, they hit dead center on the roof of a car; but the second they hit, her feet slipped on the snow, the boy's hand was ripped from hers, she landed hard on her hip, her momentum carrying her forward, and before Kate knew what was happening, she was sliding over the side of the train. Scrambling, she caught herself on a railing, so that she hung off the train, forty feet in the air, as it tore down the avenue.

She heard another heavy *thump* further down the train and knew that at least one Imp had also made the jump. She told herself she had to do something, pull herself up, break through a window, anything except hang there, but just then the train jerked around a corner, one of Kate's hands slipped, and she swung out wide, dangling now by just four fingers, and she saw the street below her, the carriages, the horses, the people, and then the train straightened and she swung back, slamming against the side of the car. She glanced up to see Rafe and the Imp struggling atop the train, and then the train twisted again, she was losing her grip, finger by finger, and one of the bodies, she couldn't tell which, went flying past her, and the next thing she knew someone had grabbed her wrist and was pulling her up.

"Are you okay?" Rafe asked. "Are you hurt?"

Kate shook her head. She was still stunned, still trying to understand. They were alone on top of the train. Rafe was kneeling before her, his hands on her arms.

"Scruggs gave me a glamour to sneak into the house. That's why I looked like Rourke. But I hadn't quite planned out the whole getting-away part."

Kate began shaking and couldn't stop.

"Why . . . why did you come back for me?" Her hair had come loose and blew around her face, and she had to shout to be heard over the sound of the train. "Why would you do that?"

Snow swirled past them. Buildings raced by. The boy looked at her, the lights in passing windows sweeping across his face. He took off his jacket and slipped it around her shoulders.

"I'll tell you," he said. "First let's get somewhere safe."

Kate and the boy rode the train all the way downtown, getting off at a stop near the Bowery. Rafe didn't want to go back to the church. Not right away, he said. Just in case the Imps were following them somehow. Kate didn't argue, but by the time they got off, her hands were frozen into claws, and her forehead and ears ached from the cold.

They had not spoken during the trip. It had been too difficult to make themselves heard over the constant rattling and the metal-on-metal shriek of the brakes every time the train turned a corner or came into a station. And besides, Kate had had no idea what to say. For now that the immediate danger was past, she couldn't stop thinking about what she'd learned from the Dire Magnus and what it meant about Rafe. Was Rafe her enemy? How much did he know? And what was she supposed to do? Scruggs had said that the *Atlas* had brought her here for a reason; so what was it? She felt confused and wished she could shut off her mind; but each time she looked at Rafe and met his eyes, she was reminded of how the Dire Magnus's milky eyes had glowed green at that last moment, and her thoughts began spinning all over again.

As they came down the steps from the platform, Rafe said, "You'll need a longer jacket. That's dress ain't exactly subtle."

The clothing stalls were mostly closed or closing, it being New Year's Eve, but Rafe managed to buy a long wool coat that stretched nearly to Kate's knees, covering the white dress, as well as keeping her warm.

Being in the Bowery, Kate felt an odd sense of coming full circle. This was where she'd arrived two days before, and now she was back, and with Rafe. She had the sense that things were nearing their end, but she still didn't know what she was supposed to be doing.

As they walked along, Kate noticed, as she hadn't that first morning with Jake and Beetles, that nearly every other storefront was a saloon or a theater or a dance hall. Loud laughter and music spilled out onto the street, and there were signs in the windows saying CELEBRATE THE END OF THE CENTURY! And men and women staggered by with their arms around each other, singing.

Rafe stopped in the middle of the street and looked around.

"In a couple hours, none of them will remember that such a thing as magic was ever real. Doesn't seem right somehow. After all they've done to us."

Kate shivered and pulled her coat closer. The boy looked at her.

"You had anything to eat since lunch? You gotta be hungry."

He started to turn, but she took his arm.

"The reason you came for me, it's because you know me, right? The same way you recognized me that first day. How—"

"Don't worry, I'm gonna tell you. I promise."

There was a girl going between saloons with a tray filled with ears of hot sweet corn stuck onto tiny spears, and Rafe got one for each of them, which they ate as they walked through the maze of streets, making way for weaving bands of revelers. The corn was even better than the potato Kate had had with the boys that first day, and when she was finished, Rafe bought them a cup of steaming cider to share. They huddled near the cider man's cart, sipping the strong, spicy drink and passing the cup back and forth.

"Did you meet him?"

Kate looked at Rafe, but the boy had his face over the steaming mug. She knew who he meant but asked anyway. "Who?"

"The man who runs the Imps."

Kate's own voice sounded hollow to her ears. "Yes. I met him."

"What's his name?"

"I—I don't know. They call him . . . the Dire Magnus."

"Did he say anything about me?"

It seemed to Kate that the noise from the saloons and the-aters had died away, and all she could hear was the furious pounding of her heart.

"He never mentioned your name."

That, at least, wasn't a lie. But again, Kate felt like things were spinning out of her control, and beyond her understanding.

The boy nodded. "So you want to hear how I know you?"

"Yes."

"Come on then. I have to show you something."

They turned down the next street and passed through a dense warren of alleys, and Kate noticed more dwarves and a few gnomes, and men and women in cloaks, and she realized they had entered the magic quarter. Then, on a narrow, nearly light-less street, Rafe led her down an alley next to a three-story tene-ment, and, stopping under the fire escape, leapt and grabbed hold of the ladder, pulling it down, along with a great cascade of snow, most of which landed on his head. Kate laughed; she couldn't help it.

"Yeah," the boy said, smiling, "should've expected that."

He shook himself like a dog, the snow flying off him, though for a time afterward his dark hair was streaked with white, like an old man's. They climbed to the roof, and he led her to the side of the building that faced the street. He brushed the snow from the ledge so they could lean against the wall. The music and laughter from the saloons and dance halls sounded faint and far away. Rafe gestured.

"See that building across the way? The window three stories up on the left. Watch; the light should go on in a minute."

Kate waited. It was cold on the roof, and she could feel the boy's shoulder pressed against her own.

"There," he said quietly. And Kate felt that he'd been holding his breath and only now let it out. She saw that the window was indeed illuminated, and an old woman was shuffling about a small apartment.

"That's where my mother and I lived. She moved us in a week after we landed in New York. I was just a baby. My dad had died; that was why we came here. She made her living as a scryer."

"What's a scryer?" Kate asked. Her hands were balled deep in the pockets of her coat, and she had turned her head to look at him. Only the boy's eyes reflected the lights from the street; his face was in shadow. He kept his gaze fixed upon the window.

"It's someone who can see things that ain't there. She'd take a bowl a' water, pour in some oil, and then she could see whatever she wanted to, no matter how far away. And people would pay her to show 'em things. Sometimes, it'd be when they'd lost something valuable, like a ring or a watch or something. More often, it'd be people who'd just come to New York, wanting to see the ones they'd left behind, their mothers and fathers and brothers and sisters. Sometimes parents looking at children. Watching 'em grow up in my ma's bowl. She did it for everyone. Magic and normal folk alike. They all loved her for it. Our apartment was only one room. I used to be there, behind the blanket that hid my bed, and I would watch 'em, men and women, crying, hugging her. She never asked for much money. Just enough for us to live."

"Who lives there now?"

"No one. I pay the rent myself. The old woman lives below. She comes up every night and turns on the light."

And you come up here and watch, Kate thought, and imagine your mother's still alive.

Then he said again, quietly, "Everyone loved her."

And Kate knew he was talking about himself.

They were both silent. Kate could sense that the boy was gearing up for what he had to tell her and that there was no need to press. He began speaking again with no warning.

"So one night this man comes to our apartment. He said he wanted to see his wife, and I remember he threw down all this money. He was drunk and calling his wife names. 'Show 'er to me! She's hiding! Show 'er to me!'

"I was there behind the blanket separating my bed from the apartment, and I watched my mother get out her bowl and pour the oil in it and light the candle. And she told the man she'd need something from the woman, like a lock of hair or something that had belonged to her. And the man laughed and he reached into his pocket and he threw down a silver ring. It was a wedding ring, I could tell. I saw my mother take it and she was real still, you know, real quiet. And she put the ring into the bowl and I could see her whispering and concentrating real hard, and the man was breathing loud and heavy. And he started asking, 'What do you see? Where is she? Where's she hiding?' And my mother said nothing for a long time, then she looked up from the bowl and she said, 'Did you do that to her?' And the man, he started cursing her, saying she was magic scum, and it was none of her business and if she didn't want the same done to her and worse she'd tell him where the woman was, and my ma just took the bowl a' water and splashed it on the floor and told him to get the hell out."

The boy paused, his gaze still fixed on the lit window across the street.

"He knocked her down to the floor. I ran out and was screaming at the man and hitting him, and I could hear my ma yelling at me to get back, and the man hit me and my head banged the wall and it all went black. When I woke up, the room was quiet, and I was on the floor and my ma was lying beside me on the floor and she was dead."

Kate stared at the boy, hardly able to believe what he was saying, that this had happened, her heart breaking for him. Rafe went on; he hadn't finished his story.

"They buried my ma in pauper's field. I got back from the funeral and there were people who wanted to put me in a home. But I hid. See, I knew who the man was. He owned a butcher's a few blocks over. No one had arrested him or nothing. They were all normal humans, him, the cops. So that night after the funeral, I snuck in his shop, and when he come in the next morning, I took one a' his own knives and stabbed him through the heart. People seen me do it and come after me. That was when Miss B saved me."

He fell silent, and the city seemed quiet around them.

"Thing is, my ma always told me I had a destiny. She said, 'When you get older, you'll have to choose.' She always said that. 'You'll have to choose.' Then she died, and years later, I had this dream. I saw this person. I didn't know what it meant, so I went to this witch. She's young, but real powerful. She can see things. She told me that the person in my dream would show me who I was, what my destiny was."

He looked at Kate.

"It was you in my dream. That was how I recognized you."

Their faces were only inches apart. Kate couldn't move.

"But she told me," the boy went on, "that after I find out the truth, you'll die. That's why you've gotta leave. Promise me. Promise me that tomorrow you'll leave. You'll go up north or wherever, but you'll get away from me. Promise."

And then he reached into his pocket and pulled out something and Kate saw that it was her mother's locket, and not only that, it was strung on a golden chain, and it was her mother's gold chain, and she realized he must've gotten it that afternoon, tracked down the man who'd sold her the coat, and she felt a tightness in her heart as he reached around her neck and fastened the clasp.

"There, now you got everything. You have to go."

They climbed down the fire escape and began walking through the streets. Kate assumed they were heading to the church, but she didn't ask. She found her hand in his, but if she had taken his hand or if he had taken hers, she couldn't say.

Neither spoke. It had begun snowing once again.

Three blocks from his mother's apartment, the party from a dance hall suddenly flowed out into the street, the revelers and musicians streaming around the boy and girl, and, as the band struck up, fifty people began dancing all around them.

Rafe turned toward her. Kate had never danced with a boy before and wasn't sure what to do. But without a word, Rafe put one hand around her waist and took her free hand in his own and guided her, in a slow spinning circle, around the snowy street. She felt his fingers wind through hers, and soon she rested her head on his shoulder. She imagined she could feel his heart beating against her chest.

Kate wished she could reach inside herself and call up the magic to stop time.

I could live here, she thought, in this moment.

The song finally came to an end. The band began playing another, but Kate and Rafe stayed as they were, in the midst of the turning men and women. At some point, Kate tasted salt and realized she was crying.

Rafe stepped back. "What is it? What's wrong?"

She stared at him. He had the eyes of her enemy, but he wasn't her enemy. He couldn't be!

"It's about him, isn't it? The Dire Magnus? Tell me. Please. Whatever it is you're afraid of, it doesn't have to happen. We can change it."

Kate nodded. She had to tell him. He deserved to know. And maybe, just maybe—

"Rafe!"

A small shape was pushing through the crowd of dancers. It was Beetles; his face was flushed and terrified.

"You gotta come! You gotta come now! They're burning the church!"

CHAPTER SEVENTEEN
The Hostage

The smoke rose in a thick column from somewhere past the curve of the valley. There were no sounds to be heard. Even the birds had fallen silent. Michael stood with his sister and Gabriel atop the half-demolished tower.

"How do we even know it's him?" Emma asked. "Maybe someone just, you know, forgot to put out their campfire?"

Gabriel said nothing, but continued staring down the valley.

"Here I am!"

They all turned as Wilamena appeared at the top of the stairs. She was flushed from running up the tower, her cheeks like two pink peaches—

Stop it, Michael told himself.

The elf princess was carrying a large, shallow clay bowl and a small jar, and she had a waterskin slung over her shoulder. She knelt on the landing and set the clay bowl carefully before her.

"This is Xanbertis's scrying bowl; it will allow us to see what is transpiring in the valley."

She poured out an inch or so of water from the skin, then unstoppered the small jar and dribbled a crescent of oil across the surface.

"Gather close."

Gabriel and the children knelt around the bowl. Michael felt Wilamena slip her hand into his, and he thought about protesting, then let the matter go.

Almost immediately, an image began to appear in the bowl. It was both clear and strangely fluid. Michael likened it to watching television at the bottom of a pool.

Emma let out a gasp. "Screechers! I never seen so many!"

They were looking at a scene taking place in the forest: a score of black-clad creatures, carrying swords and crossbows, were moving quickly through the gloom of the great trees. It was a fearsome sight—and all the worse, Michael reflected, as the Screechers were not alone.

"What is that thing?"

With his free hand, Michael pointed to one of the thick-bodied figures marching beside the *morum cadi*. The creature had leathery-looking skin and carried a barbed mace. Short yellow tusks jabbed upward from its jaw.

"An Imp," Gabriel said. "A foot soldier of the Dire Magnus. I have had dealings with them before."

"That means he killed a whole bunch of 'em," Emma said.

Michael ignored this, saying, "When did they get here? They must've been climbing into the valley all night."

Gabriel said, "Show us where the smoke is coming from."

Wilamena dribbled in more oil; the image before them dissolved, and a new one rose to take its place. At first, they could only make out a large, pale blob. Then the picture snapped into focus, and Emma cried out and leapt to her feet.

"That's him!" She pointed down at the bald man whose head now filled the bowl. "That's the guy Dr. Pym stayed behind to fight!"

"So it is Rourke," Gabriel said, and there was a note of finality in his voice, as if some chance or hope had been extinguished. "Can we see more?"

The elf princess moved her hand over the bowl, and it was like a camera pulling back; the image widened, revealing Rourke standing in the same clearing that Emma had been taken from the night before. And behind him, where the elves had placed the sculpture of Wilamena, they saw that an archway had been fashioned out of newly cut trees. It was perhaps fifteen feet high and ten feet wide, and flames coursed along the wooden struts, sending up a spiral of black smoke.

"Look," Michael said, "do you see . . ."

Imps and Screechers, in twos and threes, were stepping out of the flaming archway and into the clearing. But the strange thing—what had drawn Michael's and now drew the others' attention—was that the creatures were not passing through from one side to the other; rather, they seemed simply to materialize beneath the crossbeam, as if appearing out of thin air.

"Rourke has created a portal," Gabriel said. "He must have

come through the mountains with a small band, then he made this gateway to transport the rest of his army."

"Well, so he's got an army," Emma said. "So what? We'll just . . ." She looked at Gabriel. "What're we gonna do?"

Gabriel turned to Wilamena. "How many ways are there out of this valley?"

"Only one. The tunnel through the mountains."

In other words, Michael thought, they were trapped, with Rourke's army between them and the only avenue of escape.

Gabriel asked the princess what help they could expect from the elves, but Wilamena couldn't say.

"At dawn, I lit a signal fire to tell them that my curse had been lifted. They will come; but to reach us, they will have to pass these creatures."

Emma had knelt back down, and Michael felt her take his right hand. He closed his eyes and imagined it was Kate, and not Wilamena, holding his left hand, and that both his sisters were with him.

We'll get through this, he thought. I'll get us through this. I have to.

"If Rourke is here," Gabriel said, and Michael opened his eyes to see the man staring out at the black column of smoke, "then Dr. Pym cannot be far behind. We have to hope that he or the elves arrive in time to aid us."

"But there must be something we can do," Michael said. "I mean . . . isn't there?"

Gabriel looked at him. "Yes. You can eat your breakfast."

• • •

Despite arguing that they had no appetites, a few minutes later, Michael and Emma were in the small building along the fortress wall that served as a kitchen, wolfing down bowls of stew. "Whatever happens today," Gabriel had said, "you will need all your strength." And once they had begun to eat, which they did standing beside the fire where Gabriel had made the stew, the children had found that they were famished. Not counting the sausage and dried fruit and bread from the day before, Michael and Emma had not had a proper meal since the outpost café on the coast of Antarctica, and already that felt like a lifetime ago. Moreover, the stew was delicious, as Gabriel had found the fortress storerooms chock-full of fresh vegetables, all grown to gigantic sizes in the magically fertile soil of the valley.

As Michael and Emma bolted down their stew—Gabriel had gone to look over the fortifications and see what, if anything, could be done—Michael thought about the Guardian. When he and Emma had passed through the keep, the man had not looked up; but Michael had heard the Guardian's words echoing in his head, "You're not the Keeper! You're not the Keeper!"

Emma abruptly lowered her bowl, and what sounded like the war cry of a great prehistoric toad erupted from her throat, filling the entire room. The children looked at each other; Emma seemed nearly as taken aback as Michael.

"Sorry."

"Uh-huh."

"But wow, huh?"

Then they heard "Darling Rabbit and his sister! Come quickly!" and they dropped their bowls and ran.

Arriving in the main courtyard of the fortress, they found forty elves, lined up in neat rows, all kneeling before the princess. Gabriel stood beside Wilamena. The first thing Michael and Emma noticed about the elves—besides the fact that they were each and every one astonishingly good-looking—was that they were not dressed like the old-fashioned dandies the children had seen in the clearing the night before. These elves looked like elves out of a fairy tale. Soft leather boots. Medieval tunics. Vests of silver rings. Hooded capes of green and brown. They all had swords at their sides and held smooth wooden bows, while quivers bristling with arrows were slung across their backs.

One elf was out in front of the others. He had dark, shoulder-length hair, very pale skin, and the bluest eyes that Michael and Emma had ever seen. Indeed, his eyes were so blue that they made the children reevaluate their whole notion of blue, as if everything they had ever called blue before would now require some new name, like not-blue, or almost-blue, or nothing-remotely-approaching-blue.

"And my father is well?" asked Wilamena.

"Save missing you," replied the blue-eyed elf.

"Tell me, Captain, what is the state of his hair?"

"Not as lustrous since your captivity, but I'm sure it will regain its natural fullness and bounce once you are home."

"The poor dear. Let us hope so."

The elf princess turned to Michael and Emma. Her smile, Michael had to admit, was radiant, and for once he did not try to smother his thoughts.

"I told you my people would come. This is Captain Anton, the head of my father's guard. Captain, tell your troops to rise."

The blue-eyed elf gave the command, and the rows of elves sprang to their feet.

Wilamena placed her hand on Michael's shoulder. "This is the fearless knight who lifted the curse. I owe my life and freedom to him."

The elf captain bowed to Michael. "You have returned the sun to our skies. Thanks to you, we no longer live in darkness, Sir—"

"Rabbit," said the elf princess.

"Actually," Michael said, "my name—"

"Three cheers for Sir Rabbit!" cried the captain.

"Oh, forget it," Michael grumbled.

And he stood there as forty elves—with Emma gleefully chiming in—hurrahed the brave Sir Rabbit.

There then followed a brief interlude where members of the elfish troop would raise their hands and ask permission to speak, Wilamena would grant it, and the elf soldier would compliment some facet of the princess's beauty.

"Your eyes are luminous! They shine like the Andromeda in the coldness of space! Compared to them, diamonds are as lumps of coal!"

"Your chin is a perfect round nub connoting both firmness of purpose and compassionate pliability. Also, I like your dimple!"

"I have composed an ode to the curve of your foot! 'O Sublime Foot—'"

Finally, Gabriel broke in, asking what the elf captain had seen of Rourke and his army of monsters in the valley.

As much as it was possible, the elf's face became grim.

"Very little. We came along the far side of the river, as there was a foul air seeping from the clearing. This man—Rourke—who is he? What does he want?"

"He wants these children," Gabriel said. "And he wants the book that the Guardian was defending."

Then Wilamena spoke, and in her voice Michael heard a new, distinctly regal tone:

"Just as the rabbit saved my life, now we have a chance to save his and his sister's. We must be thankful for this opportunity."

The elf captain bowed. "We are with you and Sir Rabbit to the death, Princess."

Gabriel asked if they could expect reinforcements.

The captain shook his head. "We ourselves did not come expecting war, but merely to escort the princess home. And the rest of our colony will be busy preparing for Princess Wilamena's party. If we lit a signal fire, I doubt any would see it."

"Light one anyway," Gabriel said. "A chance of help is better than none at all. In the meantime, we must do what we can."

Michael and Emma were given the task of evaluating the fortress water supply. A search through the storerooms and of the various rain catches revealed four large barrels of water, though one of them, Michael admitted, had a good deal of mud floating in it.

When he and Emma returned to the courtyard to give their

report, they found the siege preparations well under way. Elf soldiers were repairing damaged areas of the ramparts; other elves were using their knives to fashion arrows, bundles of which were being stationed at intervals along the walls; another team of elves was buttressing the main doors with thick wooden beams; even the forge had been lit, and an elf was hammering away at the anvil. Not surprisingly, all the elves were singing, though once Michael heard the words, he decided that he didn't much care for the song:

> Oh, such a day for fighting;
> It may just be our last.
> The demon hordes are on their way,
> Tra-la-la-la-la-la.
> We'll fight for our princess,
> And for her rabbit dear. . . .

"I wrote it myself!" Wilamena said, skipping toward them. "When I couldn't think of anything, I just had them say *tra-la-la*. There's an entire verse about your nose and how generous I am to overlook it."

"Great," Michael said.

"Why aren't they dressed like the elves we saw last night?" Emma asked. "All old-fashioned-y?"

"Oh, you're so funny! You can't expect a body to dress the same way every day of the week! We're not dwarves!"

"Listen—" Michael said, having just about reached his limit.

But at that moment, there was a deep rumble, and the earth

shook beneath their feet. Michael and Emma grabbed at one another, and Gabriel, who'd been overseeing the work on the main doors, rushed to their side.

"Is that . . . ," Michael said, ". . . is that Rourke?"

"No," Gabriel said, "that was something else."

They all turned; a fat black cloud was billowing up from the cone of the volcano.

"That's not good, is it?" Emma said.

"You think it's because we took the *Chronicle* out of the lava?" Michael asked. "Like somehow it was keeping the volcano stable?"

"If so, there is nothing we can do," Gabriel replied. "Come."

He led them to a ladder, and the children and Wilamena climbed up behind him to where Captain Anton stood on the battlements, staring down at the distant tree line.

"They are massing just inside the forest," said the captain.

Michael marveled at the elf's eyesight. To him, the trees were little more than a large, dark smudge.

Gabriel said, "It will not be long now."

The singing died away as the elves stopped work and took up their positions. Soon, all was quiet save for the steady *clink-clink-clink* from the forge. Michael glanced left and right at the elves stationed along the walls. They all stared calmly down the slope, bows in hand, full quivers upon their backs. He suddenly felt very small and mean for his years of relentless elf bashing. Yes, they could be silly, and yes, they spent a great deal of time thinking about their hair, but Michael knew beyond a shadow of a doubt that every elf within the fortress would die to defend him and his sister, and, before the day was over, many of them probably would.

"There," Anton said.

Michael turned his gaze back down the slope and saw what was coming.

He tried to swallow, but his throat was filled with sawdust.

"There's kind of a lot of them, huh?" Emma said.

"Yeah," Michael croaked, ". . . kind of."

Rourke's army was pouring out of the forest in a great black tide. There seemed to be no end to it. The creatures just kept coming and coming. Michael tried to count them, but there were too many; and still more continued to stream from the trees. Soon, the entire plain, from the base of the volcano to the edge of the forest, was one dark, teeming, murderous mass.

He thought, We're doomed.

And he said out loud, "We'll . . . be okay."

And as Michael was beginning to think there really would be no end, that Screechers and Imps would still be charging from the trees as the front lines swarmed over the fortress walls, the last of Rourke's army finally emerged.

"Trolls," the elf captain said, spitting out the word like it was poison.

Three massive, gray-skinned creatures had burst awkwardly onto the plain and were moving forward in a sort of lumbering jog, swinging clubs that were half the size of the trees themselves.

"Perfect," Emma said. "'Cause it wasn't, like, bad before."

Then, as the first rank scrambled up the boulders at the base of the volcano, the shrieking began. There were hundreds of

morum cadi among the host, and the cries rose in a dreadful cho-
rus, the din echoing off the canyon walls and doubling back, join-
ing new shrieks and growing even louder. The air trembled, and
it seemed to Michael that his heart and lungs were being crushed
out of him. . . .

Then he heard Emma whispering, "It's not real . . . it can't
hurt me . . . it's not real . . . ," and he murmured along with her;
the pain eased, and he could breathe again.

There was a flash beside him; Gabriel had unsheathed his falchion and was holding it at the ready. The elf captain spoke a
single word, and every elf along the walls had an arrow notched
to his bowstring.

The black horde surged up the slope, close enough now that
Michael could see the jagged swords of the Screechers, the sea of
glowing yellow eyes. . . .

"Both of you," Gabriel said, "go—"

But before he could order them away, the horde abruptly
stopped, fifty yards from the fortress. They filled the entire slope,
pulsing like some vast, terrible beast. The shrieking continued.
Michael's gaze traveled over the Screechers' ragged uniforms and
decaying green bodies, the small, hateful eyes of the Imps. . . .

Why didn't they attack?

Why didn't the elf captain order his troops to shoot?

Everyone, defenders and attackers alike, appeared to be waiting; but for what?

The answer came as a lone figure was spotted advancing
across the plain. Even at a distance, Michael could see Rourke's
bald head gleaming in the sun. A path opened in the center of

the host, and Rourke ascended the volcano in long, sure strides. As he came closer, Michael saw that the man was wearing a uniform of some kind; it looked like an old cavalry uniform: high leather boots, breeches flared out wide, a khaki shirt with braids upon the shoulder. In one hand, he held a short riding crop.

Reaching the front of the army, Rourke halted and held up the whip.

The shrieking stopped.

"A good day to those within!"

It was Gabriel who answered. "You are not welcome here! Leave now! We will give you this one chance!"

The bald man laughed. "Will you then? That is kind indeed!" He shaded his eyes with his hand. "Do I spy wee Michael and Emma hiding among all those pesky elves? My, my! What a chase you've led us on! Whyever did you leave Malpesa so quickly? I so had wanted to make your acquaintance!"

The man had an easy, lilting accent that Michael couldn't quite place.

"And I could've introduced you to a friend of mine!"

Rourke turned, and Michael saw that another figure was making its way across the plain. This figure had none of Rourke's brisk forward momentum, but came on slowly, steadily. It was a man, Michael perceived, of normal size, walking with his head down, as if unsure of his footing. Then, as he picked his way past the large boulders at the foot of the volcano, the man looked up, the sun reflected off his glasses, and Michael felt a hand reach into his chest and seize his heart.

He let out a gasp and had to steady himself against the fortress wall.

"Michael?" Emma asked. "What is it? Who is that?"

"That's . . . that's . . ."

But the word died in his throat.

By then, the man was beside Rourke. He wore faded jeans and an old button-down shirt. He had a short beard and reddish-brown hair that was badly in need of a trim. He was visibly thin; his clothes hung loosely on his frame. He looked very tired.

Michael felt Emma stiffen; she knew.

Still, he had to say it, at least once:

"That's . . . Dad."

Rourke placed his giant's hand on their father's shoulder. "I'm thinking you've guessed the identity of my friend here. I would only like to point out that he hasn't been harmed in the least. Fit as a fiddle, aren't you, Richard? Go on and tell the kiddies."

The children's father hesitated, as if he were reluctant to be a part of what was happening.

"Speak up, my lad." And there was an edge of menace in Rourke's voice. "Don't keep us in suspense. I'm sure Michael and Emma have been worried sick."

Their father finally raised his head. Michael watched his eyes scan the walls and then fix on him and Emma. Seeing them, he seemed to sag slightly.

"I haven't been harmed! Neither of us have! Your mother and I are both well! I'm . . . so sorry about this!"

Their father's voice was dry and ragged, but Michael could

feel it, like an old key fitting in a long-forgotten lock, opening something deep inside him.

"Sorry?" Rourke exclaimed. "What on earth is there to be sorry about? You're delivering welcome news! Now, kiddies, don't imagine that we've minded having your ma and pa as guests. Become like family, they have. Of course, like family, you do sometimes want to bash their heads in!" He laughed and slapped the children's father on the back. "Anyway, to business. Can't keep everyone waiting. Don't want your elf mates late for the hairdresser. Here is the deal I'm prepared to offer, and I think you'll find it a very fair one: wee Michael and Emma will turn themselves and the *Chronicle* over to me, or I kill dear old Richard on the spot where he stands! Any questions? Grand. You have two minutes to decide!"

So that's it, Michael thought. This is how it ends.

Over the years, Michael had imagined meeting their father—indeed, meeting both their parents—many, many times. And he'd always imagined it the same way. There would be all the necessary hugging and kissing and crying, which Michael and his dad would both generously put up with; then, after his sisters and their mother went off to do girl stuff (Michael wasn't sure what that was, but thought it probably involved more hugging and kissing and crying), he would hand his dad *The Dwarf Omnibus*, saying that he had kept it safe for him, and his dad would say something like "But it's yours!" and Michael would reply, "Don't need it. Got it memorized," and after his father had made suitable sounds of being impressed, the two of them would sit down and talk about dwarves all evening (the scene always took place in the evening). The one time Michael had shared this with Emma, she'd told him it was hands down the weirdest thing she'd ever heard and that dwarves were not nearly as great as he thought they were. But Emma hadn't understood that it had nothing to do with dwarves. The point was that his father would've seen who Michael was and he would've liked him. He would've been happy to have spent an evening in his son's company. That was it. That was all Michael wanted. And they could've talked about dwarves or earthquakes or dragonflies or nothing at all.

But that was never going to happen. Not now.

"Someone shoot that bald guy!" Emma was shouting at Gabriel and the elf captain. "He's just standing there! What're you waiting for?"

"They can't," Michael said. "The Screechers would kill Dad."

"But—"

"Your brother is right. Your father would never make it to the fortress." Gabriel knelt, bringing his face level with the children's. "I will only say this: were it up to me, I would never have you pass into the enemy's power. But this is your decision, and a terrible one to have to make. Whatever you choose, I will not stand in your way."

Michael looked at his sister. "What do you think?"

Emma was biting her lower lip and glancing feverishly from Michael to Gabriel and back to Michael. "I don't . . . I don't know. . . . Whatever you think."

So it was up to him. Just as, he reflected, it would've been Kate's decision if she were here. Not surprisingly, Michael found himself remembering King Killick's words: *A great leader lives not in his heart, but in his head.* Michael believed that; he knew his father believed that; he also knew that the Dire Magnus absolutely could not gain control of the *Chronicle.* If that happened, all was lost.

The logical course of action was clear.

There was only one problem; Michael couldn't let his father die.

I'll trade myself and the *Chronicle,* he thought. But not Emma.

"Time's up!" Rourke shouted.

Michael felt Gabriel's hand upon his shoulder and he raised his gaze to the man's eyes. He apologized silently, and Gabriel nodded.

Then Gabriel said, "Do this for me. Ask to talk to your father. The more we can delay, the better. The wizard may yet come."

"Yeah," Emma said eagerly, "that's a great idea! Go out there and talk and talk, long as you can! Be real boring! You can totally do that!"

Michael had made his decision and now he wanted it over. But he said he would do what they asked, knowing that if it didn't work, he was ready. He looked down the slope. His father's glasses were two bright disks in the sun.

"I . . . want to talk to him first!"

Rourke shrugged. "Very well. Only fair you get to inspect the goods."

Emma hugged him. "Just talk to Dad. Don't do anything else. Promise?"

Michael promised without looking her in the eye. Then he

turned, feeling the soft brush of Wilamena's hand touching his, and followed the elf captain down the ladder and over to the fortress's main doors.

There Captain Anton stopped him, speaking in a low voice:

"You give the sign, and my archers will have twenty arrows in that bald giant before he can blink. If your father knows to run, perhaps you can both make it back alive. We will cover you the best we can."

"What should the sign be?"

"You could scratch the back of your head?"

"Okay. But . . . what if I just need to scratch my head normally?"

The elf looked at him. "Resist."

"Oh, okay."

Then the captain gave a signal, the heavy bolts were pulled back, the extra beams removed, and the fortress doors swung open. The elf clapped Michael on the arm.

"Go well, Sir Rabbit."

A moment later, Michael had passed through the gates and was outside the walls, and there was nothing between him and the horde of monsters. He had never felt so exposed. Michael focused on his father's face and began walking, his right hand pressing his bag to his hip, feeling the bulge of the *Chronicle* alongside the familiar shape of *The Dwarf Omnibus*. In the whole valley, there was only the sound of Michael's boots upon the rocks.

He stopped ten yards from Rourke and his father. The slope here was relatively flat, and Michael had to gaze up into his dad's face. He looked much older than in the photo with Hugo Algernon, much older and much more tired. The beard too was new. Though Michael thought he looked less like someone who had a beard and more like someone without the time or means to shave. Up close, he was even thinner.

His dad smiled sadly. "I'm so sorry, Michael."

"It's not your fault."

"Are you okay? Are you hurt at all?"

Michael shook his head. "I'm fine."

"And Emma?"

"She's okay. She's back there."

"But Kate's not with you?"

"No. It's . . . a long story."

Rourke chuckled. "True enough, lad. But you'll be seeing your lovely sister before long. Oh yes indeed."

Michael sensed that the man knew something about Kate and was taunting him. But Michael wouldn't take the bait. He thought about what the elf captain had said and wondered if he and his dad could actually make it to the fortress.

"So you know," Rourke said, as if reading his mind, "if those shifty elves try anything, I have a dozen *morum cadi* with crossbows who will kill your father before he takes a step."

Well, Michael thought, so much for that.

"Where's Mom?"

"They won't let me say. But she's fine. She sends her love. And she says that whatever you decide, we'll understand. I am happy to see you. Even like this."

Michael nodded and said, quietly, "Me too."

They were both silent for a moment.

"I tried." Michael could hear his voice breaking. "I did my best."

"I know you did," his father said. "It's okay."

"And Kate's not here!" It was all spilling out as the walls that Michael had built up came tumbling down. "I had to be the leader! I had to make all the decisions! I tried to do what you would've done! Like King Killick says!" He paused, overcome, not wanting to cry in front of Rourke. Finally, when he had composed himself, he looked back up. There was confusion on his father's face. "You know, what King Killick says about leadership . . ."

He stopped, thinking his father would continue. But instead he saw his father, for one flickering moment, glance at Rourke.

"I'm sorry, Michael. A lot's happened in the past ten years; I don't think I remember."

"Yes, you do!" And it was suddenly vitally important that his father did remember. "Dr. Algernon said it was your favorite quote. King Killick said, 'A great leader lives not in his heart, but in his head.' Don't you remember? You have to remember!"

"Oh, of course," his father said, smiling. "I always did like that quotation. And it's very true."

And then, without even really understanding what he was doing, Michael said, "Killick was an old king . . . of the elves."

His father's smile never wavered. "Yes, I remember now. The elves have a great deal of wisdom. Thank you for reminding me of that."

"Well," Rourke cut in, "this has been a delightful reunion. But we're not here to natter away the day. You and your sister come along and you have my solemn promise that neither you nor your parents will be harmed. Refuse, and I'll put Richard and every elf in that fortress to the sword, and you will still leave with us. Understand?"

Michael's mind was spinning. His father hadn't remembered the quotation. Then he'd acted like he had! And he'd thought that Killick had been an elf! Had he just forgotten?

"Boy, you're severely testing my patience."

"Okay. But I . . . I have to explain it to my sister. I'll bring her out."

He needed to get away; he needed space and time to think about what had happened. He started to turn.

"Wait."

Rourke had his knife to their father's throat.

"You want to bring out wee Emma yourself, fine. Leave the *Chronicle*."

Michael could feel the tension in the fortress, the hunger coursing through the Screechers and Imps. It seemed as if all their lives were poised on the edge of Rourke's blade. He reached into his bag and felt for the hard leather cover he knew so well.

"Let my dad hold it, though. Just till Emma and I get back."

Rourke smiled. "Of course."

Michael stepped forward and handed his father the book.

"There's . . . a curse on it. Keep it closed."

He watched as his father ran his hand over the cover.

"I thought it was red."

"The Order hid it in the lava, so the leather got burned. I'll be right back."

He started up the slope toward the fortress. He had to force himself to go slowly. His heart hammered; his nerves were raw and jangly. He stumbled on loose rocks. Halfway to the gate, he glanced over his shoulder. Rourke was watching him, and the moment their eyes met—perhaps the bald man saw something or perhaps he was already suspicious—Rourke snatched away the book that Michael had given his father. Michael didn't wait for him to open it and look inside; he was already sprinting forward.

"*Stop him!*" Rourke shouted. "*Stop the boy!*"

The cries of Screechers tore the air. Michael was twenty yards from the gate when he tripped, sprawling full out upon the rocks. He was up in an instant, but the delay had cost him. He could hear the Screechers closing in. Then the elf captain was running out of the fortress, bow outstretched, his hand a blur as he fired a volley of arrows that whistled past Michael's head and shoulders, finding their marks with an accordion-like *thik-thik-thik-thik*. The elf grabbed him by the arm, shouting, "Run!" and pulled him on. Then they were through the gate, Michael heard the huge doors slam shut, and he fell to his knees, panting.

"Michael?! What happened?! Are you all right?" It was Emma, clutching at his arm. "You gave him the book! And what about Dad?! He's still out there!"

Michael forced himself to stand. "That's not . . . that's not Dad. . . ."

"What do you mean?"

"He forgot this quotation, the one he's supposed to love, and . . . and he thought King Killick was an elf . . . and I gave him *The Dwarf Omnibus* and he thought it was the *Chronicle*. That's not him!"

Michael could see that Emma didn't understand, but there was no more time to explain. Out beyond the walls, Rourke was shouting his name. Quickly, with Emma and the elf captain following, Michael climbed up to the battlements.

Wilamena rushed toward him as he stepped off the ladder. "Oh, Rabbit—"

"Not now," Michael said.

He ran to the wall. Gabriel was already there, staring down the slope. Below them, Rourke had a knife at the throat of the man Michael no longer believed to be his father. *The Dwarf Omnibus* lay upon the ground.

"Lad! I'm giving you one last chance."

Michael turned toward Emma. "Listen, I know you don't trust me—"

"What?! What're you talking about?"

"I mean, not the way you used to! And I understand! But you have to trust me now! That's not our dad!"

Emma stared at him, and, even without the power of the *Chronicle*, Michael saw the pain of his betrayal still so fresh inside her. It was awful to see it, awful to know that he was responsible. But he didn't look away. He knew what it was he was asking.

"You're sure?" she said. "Like, one hundred percent sure?"

Was he that sure? Was it even possible? Even with all the evidence—forgetting the quotation, mistaking Killick for an elf, not recognizing *The Dwarf Omnibus*—with all that, there was still room for doubt. There was no way to be one hundred percent sure.

But Michael knew, in his gut and in his heart, that that man was not their father.

"Yes. I'm sure."

"Okay," she said. "I trust you."

Michael turned to the elf captain. "Shoot him."

"The bald man? With pleasure." He notched an arrow and drew it back.

"No," Michael said. "The man pretending to be our dad."

Emma, the captain, Gabriel, and Wilamena all stared at him.

"You are certain of this?" Gabriel asked.

"Yes." He took Emma's hand, felt how it trembled. "That's not our dad."

Emma's eyes darted nervously from Michael to Gabriel. She was scared, but she was with him. She nodded.

"Boy—"

There was a soft *twang*, and then the shaft of an arrow was protruding from the chest of the man beside Rourke. The mountainside fell silent.

"Michael . . ." Emma gripped his arm.

"Wait."

The man slumped to his knees and fell forward onto the black rocks.

Michael stayed absolutely still. He didn't blink; he didn't breathe. . . .

Then Rourke began to laugh, a deep, rolling laugh that echoed all through the canyon. With his boot, he flipped the man over. Their father had disappeared. In his place lay a short, sandy-haired man with an arrow in his chest.

"He was wearing a glamour!" Wilamena cried. "Rabbit, you're a genius!"

She seized him and kissed his cheek.

"My dad would never mistake *The Dwarf Omnibus*," Michael said, trying not to show his relief. "Or think that King Killick was an elf. Ridiculous." Then he looked at Emma and squeezed her hand. "Thanks for trusting me."

Emma said nothing, but hugged him tightly.

"Well, lad," Rourke shouted, "I guess we'll do this the old-fashioned way." He turned to his horde. "Bring me the children! Kill the rest!"

And so the battle began.

CHAPTER EIGHTEEN
Henrietta Burke's Last Wish

"What do you mean? Who's burning the church? The Imps?"

Kate, Rafe, and Beetles were standing in the middle of the street as the revelers continued to spin and dance about them. Rafe had grabbed Beetles by his jacket.

"Ain't the Imps!" Beetles cried, his eyes wild. "It's humans! There're mobs all over the city! Going after anything to do with magic!"

"But the church is hidden!" Kate said. "It's supposed to be invisible!"

The boy shook his head. "Not no more."

Rafe said, "What happened to Scruggs?"

"He was with you, right? Went to the Imp mansion?"

"But he didn't come in! After he gave me the glamour, he stayed in the street."

"Yeah, well, coming back to the church, he run into a mob going after these two witches. Scruggs stopped 'em, but someone threw a brick or a rock or something and clopped him smack on the head. He's dead, Scruggs is."

"Scruggs is dead?" Kate was stunned.

"Sure. Them two witches brought 'im back to the church, told us what happened. I was there when they brought 'im in. He said, 'I'm thirsty.' Then fell down dead as dead. Second later—*bang*—the church was there for everyone to see. People on the street started shouting and pointing. Wasn't a half hour later the mob came. They had torches and guns—"

"And they knew," Rafe said, "they knew there were kids inside?"

"Sure they knew," Beetles said. "Miss B told 'em. They didn't care. They just started burning the church!"

Rafe charged through the crowd, disappearing down the darkened street. Beetles took off after him, and it was all Kate could do to keep up. The long coat hampered her legs, and the boots the gnomes had given her kept slipping on the snow and ice. It was quickly apparent that Beetles was telling the truth: on street after street, they passed gangs of men—sometimes bands of three or four, sometimes a dozen—moving through the city with torches and burning anything that hinted of magic. Kate wondered how she and Rafe hadn't seen or heard the mobs before, but then perhaps they had, only from a distance, the shouting and the torches were easily mistaken for celebration. It seemed to Kate as if a madness had taken hold of the city, as if people could sense the coming change and knew this was their last chance to vent their rage before the magic world disappeared.

"What time is it?" she shouted to Beetles as the two of them raced through the streets.

"Past eleven! Got less than an hour till the Separation!"

"Where's everyone else? Where's Jake and Abigail?"

"Dunno. The mob was all round the church, and Miss B told me to go find Rafe. She thought he mighta taken you down there. What were you two doing?"

Kate didn't respond. By then, she could see the flames against the night sky and hear the shouting, and when they came around the last corner, Kate was stopped dead by the sight before her. The church was completely engulfed in flames, the snow melted for a dozen yards all around it. A crowd had gathered in the street; many people waved torches and appeared to be cheering on the fire. She didn't see Rafe.

"Over here!"

Beetles was sprinting toward an alley across the street from the church. She followed him, and there, huddled between the buildings, were Abigail and twenty other small children. Their faces were streaked with soot, and their eyes were large and filled with fear. Abigail immediately threw herself into Kate's arms.

"You're okay?" Kate asked, hugging the girl tightly. "You're all okay?"

Abigail nodded and wiped at her eyes, tears smearing the ash on her cheeks. "Miss B sent us out the side door. Whole place was on fire, but she went back in, said there were others she had to get out. She's still in there!"

"What about Jake?" Beetles demanded. "You see Jake get out all right?"

The girl shook her head.

"He'll be okay," Kate told him. "He'll get out."

Even as they were talking, another group of children came running into the alley. They were covered in soot and terrified. They said they had been trapped inside the church, but that Rafe had broken through the door and led them outside. Kate could see Beetles looking around frantically; he seemed on the verge of tears.

"Where's Jake? Somebody musta seen Jake? Who seen him get out?"

The children all shook their heads.

"I seen him in the church," one girl said. "I thought he was coming with us. I don't know where he is."

Without another word, Beetles sprinted off toward the church.

Kate looked at Abigail. "Is there somewhere safe you can go?"

Abigail nodded. "The Bowery Theater. Down near the magic quarter. The manager's a friend of Miss B's."

"Go there then," Kate said. "You're in charge. You can do this."

Watching Abigail push out her jaw and square her shoulders, Kate was reminded again of Emma. The young girl turned to face the other children.

"Right! Everybody find someone else to hold hands with! We're going downtown."

The children moved about, finding buddies.

"What about you?" Abigail asked Kate.

"I'm going after Beetles."

And she turned and ran toward the fire.

The church stood at the corner of First Avenue and a narrow cross street, and the mob was massed along the avenue. There were men and boys, and they held torches and knives and clubs. They were all shouting and laughing and cheering, and they threw rocks and bottles crashing through the church's remaining windows, their faces red and demonic in the light from the blaze. Kate lingered for a moment at the back of the crowd.

How could they do this? she wondered. Where could so much hatred come from? These were children living here; they'd done nothing wrong!

Kate felt anger welling up inside her; she wanted to lash out at the mob, to hurt them; and it flickered through her mind that this must be how Rafe felt all the time.

Forcing herself to focus, she ran around the mob to the cross street behind the church. There was a wall separating the church from the houses on the block, and Kate ran alongside it. The heat from the fire was tremendous and stung her face. Beetles was throwing himself against a flaming door, again and again. Kate pulled him back.

"Stop! It's too dangerous!"

"He's still in there!" Beetles sobbed, struggling to get free. "Jake's still in there! Lemme go! I gotta—"

The door exploded outward. Black smoke billowed forth, and figures stumbled out, a dozen children, seventeen, eighteen, bent over and hacking, their faces blackened with smoke. Kate led them away, checking each one to make sure that he or she was okay. Jake was not among the children, and Kate turned and saw Beetles shielding his eyes and edging toward the door. She caught the boy as he made to leap.

"Let go a' me! I gotta—"

Just then another figure emerged from the smoke. Kate saw that it was Rafe and he was holding a child in his arms.

Beetles went limp against Kate.

"Is that . . . ," he said. ". . . Is he?"

For it was Jake whom Rafe was carrying, and the younger boy's face was smoke-stained and his eyes were shut. Kate felt her heart clench like a fist. No, she thought, please no.

Then the boy coughed thickly and blinked, his eyes red and watery. He saw Kate and Beetles.

"Hey."

"Hey," Beetles said, crying and smiling at the same time.

Kate reached out and touched the boy's hair. "What were you doing in there? Thinking about opening a shop?"

Jake smiled and said, weakly, "Yeah, the Burning-Down-the-Church Shop."

Rafe set the boy on his feet, and Beetles put his arm around his friend.

"That's all the kids." Rafe's face was smoke-black and his voice raw. "Where're the ones who're already out?"

"Abigail led them downtown," Kate said. "To the Bowery Theater. She said the manager's a friend of Miss Burke's."

Rafe looked at Beetles. "You heard that? You can take these other kids down there?"

"Course!" Beetles said, all his old confidence restored. "Hey, listen up! All you Savages follow me!"

And with Jake's arm over his shoulder, he led the children away.

Kate and Rafe were alone for only a moment when there was a crashing inside the church, then a loud metallic *clang* that was audible even over the roaring of the flames.

"One of the bells," Rafe said. "It fell outta the tower."

He started back into the church, but Kate caught his arm.

"What're you doing? All the kids are out!"

"I'm gonna get Miss B." He pulled free and disappeared into the smoke.

Kate didn't hesitate, but plunged in after him. Indeed, even if she'd thought longer—about her responsibilities to Michael and Emma, to her parents, about the fact that despite everything Rafe might still become her enemy—she would've acted the same. Just like Dr. Pym and Gabriel and King Robbie McLaur, Rafe had put himself in danger to protect her and, through that, her family. Now he needed her help.

She kept her head down and one arm up and before her face. The heat scorched her skin, the smoke burned her eyes, but then she was through to the main hall of the church, where the ceilings were so high that the smoke collected far above. She pulled off her coat and dropped it to the floor. The air burned her throat and lungs, and she wondered how long till the whole church came crashing down.

She was grabbed by the arm and yanked about.

"What're you doing?" Rafe demanded.

"I'm not leaving you in here alone!"

Rafe looked furious, but then part of the ceiling collapsed over the door that Kate had come through. Her exit was blocked.

"There's no time to argue!" Kate shouted. "We need to find Miss Burke and get out!"

He seized her hand. "Don't let go of my hand! No matter what!"

He took off through the church, dragging Kate behind him. At the base of the tower were the two enormous shattered bells. As Kate and Rafe clambered over the broken pieces, Kate's boot slid and her hand slipped from Rafe's. Instantly, smoke scorched her lungs, and the heat became unbearable. Kate began to cry out, but Rafe snatched up her hand, and she felt a cocoon of cooler air descend around them.

"I can protect you!" he shouted. "But you have to hold my hand! Come on!"

Kate nodded, and they started up the corkscrewing, rickety stairs.

The falling bell had ripped out huge sections of the staircase, and what remained was being consumed by fire. Still, Kate and Rafe charged upward, avoiding the planks that seemed most likely to collapse and leaping hand in hand over the spots where there were no stairs at all. Kate kept thinking that not only did they have to come back down these same stairs, which the flames were devouring with each passing second, but there were still two more bells hanging above them. How long till they came crashing down?

Then she and the boy were scrambling up through the trap-door and out onto the open platform of the belfry.

Kate had been expecting to find Henrietta Burke either dead or trapped under a collapsed beam. It turned out to be neither. The woman was standing at the edge of the belfry, her upright figure silhouetted by flames, staring calmly down at the street below. The cold night air made breathing in the belfry bearable, and Rafe released Kate's hand and ran across to the woman. Kate watched as Henrietta Burke turned to face Rafe, and she heard the boy's voice, demanding, pleading. Then Henrietta Burke shook her head, and she said something that Kate couldn't hear.

What was she doing? Kate wondered. They were wasting time.

Above her, the bells clanged against one another as the heat rising from the tower wafted them back and forth.

Rafe came back to Kate and he was wiping away tears and wouldn't meet her eye.

"She wants to talk to you."

"What?"

"She wants to talk to you. Go! This place is gonna fall apart any second!"

Unsure of what was happening, Kate crossed the belfry. It seemed to her that the entire tower had begun to wobble. Henrietta Burke had her shawl drawn around her shoulders and was staring down at the mob in the street. Kate could see the torches, like fireflies, moving about in the darkness.

"Rafe tells me all the children got out."

"Yes."

"And you sent them to the Bowery Theater? That's good. My friend there knows what to do. I made arrangements long ago in case this sort of thing happened. There's a place upstate. The children will be educated. Grow up in safety. And to think that we were so close to being safe forever. But regret is futile. Life is lived forward, even for time travelers such as yourself."

"Miss Burke—"

"No, listen to me." She turned then and looked at Kate. "People think me a hard woman, but the truth is much deeper. I gave up my own child long ago. I thought he would be safer among those who knew no magic, raised as one of them. I was wrong. His nature revealed itself; and when he needed me, I was not there. I have been paying that debt ever since. Rafe is the son I should have raised. But I can no longer protect him."

Kate felt the awful weight of the woman's words. Henrietta Burke stepped closer. "You remember our agreement? I help you to get home, and in return, I ask for payment at the time of my choosing. That time is now."

"But we need to go! The fire—"

"Child," the gray-haired woman said, "I am going nowhere."

She opened her shawl, and Kate saw the dagger-like shard of glass protruding from the woman's side. Blood was dripping off the glass and down her dress.

"Rafe wants me to escape. He still believes magic can fix everything. But all magic comes with a price, and the price to heal me would be too high. I am staying."

Kate opened her mouth, but no words came out. The horror of the situation and the woman's calm resolve had left her speechless. Henrietta Burke went on:

"I know who Rafe is. Scruggs thought I didn't, but I have always known the role that awaits him. Still, he has a choice."

The woman seized Kate's shoulder; her gray eyes were fixed and intense.

"Love him."

"Wh-what?"

"That is why you're here. That is why you came. You've already changed him. You can't see it, but I can. You are the only hope he has. You must love him."

Kate stared at the woman. The tower swayed, the bells clanged, shouts carried up from the street, flames swept over the roof. She shook her head.

"You don't understand . . . you don't understand who—"

"I know exactly who he is. Who he is destined to become. But you can still save him. Love him, child. Love him as he already loves you."

"Please . . . don't ask me that."

"But I must. It is the only hope we have."

Then the woman leaned forward and whispered in Kate's ear. "And here is my half of the bargain: you do not need a witch or a wizard or anyone else to help you access the power inside you. You never have. Stop fighting and let it out."

Instantly, Kate knew the woman was right. The power was in her; she could feel it even then, feel herself fighting against it. She'd been fighting it for months, ever since she'd taken the

Countess into the past and something in her had been changed forever.

The *Atlas*'s power was *her* power. She could not deny it any longer.

"Now go." And the woman, still staring in Kate's eyes, called out, "Take her!"

Kate felt her arm seized, and Rafe dragged her toward the trapdoor. Just as they prepared to descend, there was a crash, the floor shuddered, and Kate and Rafe looked back to see the corner of the belfry crumble. Like that, the woman was gone.

The journey back down the bell tower was even more perilous than Kate had imagined. More steps had collapsed, and Kate could feel the cushion of cool air that Rafe had created growing weaker and weaker. Still, Kate felt like she was in a dream, that nothing about her was real. Her mind couldn't process that the stern woman was really gone, much less the things she had said.

Then, at the last flight of stairs, Kate heard the sound she had been dreading, and it pulled her back to the moment. She and Rafe both looked up and saw the dark, gaping mouth of the bell crashing down toward them, splintering through the wooden stairs. At the same moment, the stairway they were standing on collapsed. As they fell, Rafe hurled Kate toward the door. She landed on her side, slamming into the wall, landing so that she had a perfect view of Rafe, in the center of the tower, lying unmoving on the floor.

Then Kate screamed his name as the bell crashed down.

CHAPTER NINETEEN
The Battle of the Volcano

Bands of Imps and Screechers were charging up the slope, carrying siege ladders they'd fashioned from trees chopped down in the forest. As soon as they came into range, the elves along the battlements began pouring arrow after arrow into the creatures. The archers were terrifyingly accurate, but the moment one Imp or Screecher would fall, another would leap to take its place, and the ladder would continue forward.

Already, the air was thick with a reeking, mustardy haze as the fallen Screechers dissolved into the rocky slope.

And still there were more and more. . . .

And the awful shrieking rebounded off the canyon walls.

"This is stupid!" Emma cried. "We should be down there helping!"

"We'd just be in the way," Michael said.

"And we are helping," said the elf princess. "We are inspiring those below to fight more valiantly. Though I do wish I had a scarf to wave."

On Gabriel's orders, the three of them were watching the battle from the top of the decapitated tower. Of course, Wilamena had told the children, their friend had no power to order her anywhere, but she was not about to be separated from her rabbit.

Michael had spent the first few minutes atop the tower trying to assess the defenders' chances. The fortress itself, apart from being built on a volcano, was well positioned. The slope on either side fell away sharply and was composed of a fine scree that gave no footing at all. This meant the attackers had to launch a frontal assault, which in turn meant the elves had only one wall to defend. This slight advantage was all that was keeping the fortress from being overrun. But Michael knew it couldn't last. Rourke's army was simply too large. So the question was, could the defenders hold out till Dr. Pym arrived? Or reinforcements came from the elf colony?

"Look!" Emma shouted.

From the slope below, something rose into the air, growing larger and larger. Michael stared, unable, perhaps unwilling, to understand what he was seeing; then the boulder smashed into the wall, sending a shudder through the fortress. Michael scanned the slope till he spotted one of Rourke's trolls bent over and wrapping its arms around another massive stone. Already, elves were showering arrows upon the creature; but the missiles barely scratched the monster's hide, and, moments later, a second boulder blasted through the top of the wall, spewing rocks and debris into the courtyard.

The first siege ladders had now reached the ramparts.

Michael silently downgraded his assessment of their chances.

"We can't just stand here!" Emma was nearly beside herself. "We have to do something!"

Michael started to say that he understood her frustration but there was nothing they could do when he saw that Wilamena had taken off her golden circlet and was waving it about and crying (for some reason), "Troo-loo-loo! Troo-loo-loo!"

"Actually," Michael said, "I have an idea."

Gabriel swung his falchion at a Screecher clawing its way over the wall, and the creature tumbled backward, shrieking as it fell.

The battle was an hour old and still being fought along the fortress's front wall. The Screechers and Imps continued to hurl their ladders up, and the elves continued to push them back. Gabriel knew that as long as they could defend the wall, they had a chance. But if Rourke's forces broke through, they would have to fall back to the keep, which, considering the dragon-sized hole in the roof, offered little safety. Gabriel glanced at the sun. Days here were short, and they had perhaps two hours till nightfall.

And the black smoke pouring from the volcano looked more and more ominous.

Just then there was a loud thud, and the fortress gates shuddered. Gabriel peered over the wall to see a pair of knobby-armed trolls standing before the gates, wielding a giant tree as a battering ram. The elves were firing down arrow after arrow; the creatures' backs and shoulders were barbed like porcupines, but the trolls paid the arrows no mind and smashed the tree into the doors again and again—*thud—thud—thud*—as Rourke, standing safely out of bowshot, urged them on. A few more blows, Gabriel knew, and the doors would crack open.

He turned to the elf captain. "Get a rope."

"Why?"

"To pull me in after."

With that, Gabriel slashed at an Imp scrambling over the wall, took hold of the creature's ladder, and with a great heave and leap, threw it and himself down and away from the wall. Riding the ladder, Gabriel vaulted himself farther than he ever could have leapt, so when the ladder tilted over, he was directly above the trolls, and he heard Rourke's voice through the din: "There! On the ladder! Shoot him!" As he dropped down, Gabriel swung his falchion at the exposed neck of the nearest troll—who did not see him, focused as the creature was upon its task—and, with the added force of his fall, it was perhaps the hardest blow Gabriel had ever struck. Then Gabriel hit the ground, rolled, and was up and leaping out of the way as the now-headless troll came crashing down. There was a bellow of pain as the ram landed on the second troll's foot, and Gabriel could hear Rourke shouting for the Screechers to shoot and not worry about hitting the bloody troll. Gabriel placed one foot on the tree, leapt into the air, and with a two-handed overhead chop, buried his falchion in the skull of the second troll.

And there it stuck, four inches deep.

Gripping the handle, Gabriel pressed his foot against the creature's chest and tried to pull the blade free. It didn't budge. Gabriel had just decided to leave the falchion and run for the fortress when the troll—who did not seem especially bothered by having a giant machete buried in its head—let out a roar of fury and grabbed him around the middle. "That's it!" Rourke shouted. "Don't let him go!" Gabriel felt his ribs being crushed together, the massive, stone-hard fingers digging into his chest and back. With his remaining strength, Gabriel smashed his heel into the creature's nose again and again, till at the fifth blow, the monster abruptly released him. Gabriel fell to the ground, gasping, as the pain-maddened troll, black blood pouring down its face, stampeded through the ranks of the Screechers and Imps. Gabriel staggered to the wall, caught hold of the rope that had been thrown down, and was yanked up the side of the fortress. The elf captain helped him over the top, and Gabriel looked back to see Rourke step in front of the rampaging troll and, with one swipe of an outrageously long sword, lop off the creature's head.

Rourke's bullyish affectation of good cheer had been replaced by real anger, and he pointed his bloody sword directly at Gabriel. His intention was clear; the two of them would meet before long.

Gabriel showed no response and turned away to find a weapon.

"You won't even tell us?!"

Michael shook his head. "I spoke too soon. I should've analyzed all the pieces before I said anything. It's a ridiculous idea.

Let's just forget all about it, go upstairs, and watch the battle. Okay?"

Michael, Emma, and the elf princess were standing at the base of the tower, speaking in hushed tones, as the Guardian was only twenty yards away, still tied to a column. So far, the man had given no sign that he was even aware of their presence.

Emma looked at the princess. "He's afraid of something."

Wilamena agreed. "I wouldn't have thought it possible, but you are right. Something has stolen his fierce rabbit heart."

"I'm not afraid!" Michael protested. "Of anything!"

"Sure you are," Emma said. "You're so afraid you won't even tell us the idea."

"That's not true."

"Then tell us!"

"Fine. But it's a stupid idea." And he took a breath, resolving to race through the explanation as quickly as possible. "Seeing the princess's crown reminded me of the dragon bracelet. This one, remember?" He held up the severed gold bracelet he'd retrieved from the debris atop the tower. "And it occurred to me that if we fixed the bracelet, we could turn her back into a dragon and she could help us win the battle."

"You're right," Emma said. "That is a stupid idea. Wow."

"How would such a thing even be possible?" Wilamena asked.

"It's not," Michael said. "So let's just—"

"Hold!"

Michael already had one foot on the stairs, but Wilamena's voice turned him around. Her manner had changed. Once again, she seemed suddenly regal and commanding, like a true princess.

"Even now, elf soldiers are fighting for you, perhaps dying for you! You have an obligation to tell me what you know. How would we accomplish this?"

"There's an anvil and forge in the courtyard." Michael spoke without meeting her eyes. "We melt down your crown and use the molten gold to seal the cut in the bracelet; then we recast the enchantment so that I'm the dragon's master instead of the Guardian. That's assuming there has to be a master," he mumbled, "and you can't just, you know, be your own master."

"And how're you gonna redo some spell?" Emma demanded. "You're not a magician. You'd need Dr. Pym. Or—or—"

"Or my old master."

Emma looked at the elf princess, then across the chamber at the Guardian, then back at Michael. "The guy who tried to kill us? Who murdered all his friends? That's the guy you want to help us? Your plan's even dumber than I thought."

"Actually," Wilamena's blue eyes were shining in the gloom, "it's brilliant."

Michael stared at the ground and said nothing.

"Yes, I see it now," the elf princess said. "There is a way to get Xanbertis to help, and the clever rabbit has figured it out. But for some reason, the idea scares him."

"Wait," Emma said. "So the plan's *not* stupid?"

"Look at me, Rabbit."

Michael raised his eyes. The princess's manner had softened. She laid a cool hand on his arm.

"I do not know why this thing scares you and I do not ask. Only hear this: I do not want to become the dragon. It means returning to a prison, one I thought I would never escape. But as long as elves are dying, I will do my duty. Will you do likewise?"

The elf princess could not have picked a word more likely to turn Michael around. The idea of duty ran through every aspect of dwarfish life. To accuse a dwarf of neglecting his duty was to accuse him of not being a dwarf. But how much of Michael's decision came from that, and how much from the princess's cool hand on his arm and her blue eyes gazing into his, Michael could never have said.

He straightened his shoulders. "Go build up the fire in the forge. Start melting the crown. I'll be there as soon as I can."

Wilamena squeezed his arm. "Thank you."

"Okay," Emma said. "But no one tell me anything. 'Cause that would be, like, a disaster."

Wilamena led her away, whispering, "I will tell you, but you really are very impatient, you know that. . . ."

Left alone, Michael wasted no more time, but walked immediately to where the Guardian was tied. He knew he couldn't allow himself to hesitate. And he'd promised now. Still, his hands were trembling, and he gripped the strap of his bag to stop their shaking.

"I need your help."

The man did not look up, and gave no sign of having heard.

"There's a battle going on. Our side's going to lose. When that happens, Rourke's army will kill the elves, kill you, and take the *Chronicle*. I need you to help me fix the bracelet that turned the princess into a dragon."

Still, the man did not look up.

"Do you hear me? They're going to steal the *Chronicle*! And kill you!"

Finally, the man raised his head. The red glow from the hole in the center of the floor gave his eyes an evil gleam. He glared at Michael with undisguised hatred.

"Good."

And he dropped his head back down.

This was, more or less, the reaction Michael had expected.

So get on with it, he told himself. You know what you have to do.

Michael knelt, shutting out the shrieks of the Screechers and the sounds of the battle and focusing on the man before him.

"I think you weren't always like this. It was all those years, all those centuries; it was too much. I need the man you used to be."

The Guardian lifted his head, and, just for a moment, Michael thought he saw something flash across his face—a plea, perhaps? He remembered looking into the eyes of mad Bert the night before and seeing the same look of entreaty.

Then it was gone, replaced by a sneer. "That man is dead."

"No," Michael said, hating the quiver he heard in his voice, "I think he's still inside you somewhere." And he opened his bag and drew out the *Chronicle*. "Wilamena—the princess—said the book can heal people. Like it healed my sister. And I think you're sick, is all. And maybe you don't want to get better because then you'll have to face the things you did. But the *Chronicle* can help. I . . . can help."

The man lurched forward, hissing, "Don't be a fool! Remember what happened with your sister! You took on all her pain, and it was too much! The pain of a child! Now you would do the same with me? I, who have been alive for almost three thousand years? I murdered my brothers! I betrayed my oath! Write my name in that book, and it will be you who murdered! You who betrayed! The pain will break you, boy. I promise. Your heart is not strong enough."

"You think I don't know that?" Tears were blurring Michael's vision. "You think I'd be doing this if I had any other choice? I don't even want to be here! I wish I was in Cambridge Falls. Or back at the Edgar Allan Poe Home in Baltimore, which is saying something, believe me." He rubbed his knuckles across his eyes and took a long breath to settle himself. "But I am here. And Kate put me in charge."

Then he snapped free the stylus and opened the book to the middle. His hand was shaking so badly that it took him three tries to prick his thumb and draw blood.

"I'm warning you, boy. Don't do this."

The tip of the stylus was smeared dark red. Michael gripped the shard of bone. Then he paused, unsure. . . .

"Do you spell Xanbertis with an X or a Z?"

"What?"

"I bet an X. Anyway, the book'll figure it out."

And Michael lowered the bloodied tip of the stylus to the page.

A shiver rippled through his body, and, as had happened with Emma, the Guardian snapped into razor-sharp focus. Michael could pick out the thousands of individual hairs of his beard, he could hear a beetle scratching at the inside of a pocket, smell the weeks of packed-on dirt and sweat (he had been able to smell that before, now it was just much worse). He began to write, the letters smoking and bubbling upon the page. He felt the power of the book rise up. . . .

Michael stopped writing. Half the Guardian's name lay scorched upon the page. He could feel the man watching him, waiting. And perhaps it was the desire not to look weak, or the memory of his silent promise to Wilamena, or just plain stubbornness, but somehow Michael made himself scratch out the last letters, and the magic rose up and swept him away. . . .

Michael was a young man, arriving at a walled city beside the sea. The city was all low-roofed red-brown buildings, clustered about a single high tower. It was to the tower that the young man directed his steps, for he had been called to the Order; and his excitement and pride and fear were Michael's excitement and pride and fear. . . .

And Michael felt the young man's love for his new brothers; he felt the young man's awe for the great trust given to him and the other Guardians; and, when Alexander's army attacked the city, Michael felt the depths of the young Guardian's rage and grief and shame as he and three others fled with the *Chronicle*, leaving behind their wounded and dead brothers. . . .

And Michael was with the man, no longer young, as he and his remaining brothers carried the *Chronicle* across the southern seas; he felt the man's iron determination as they marched over the ice, and Michael was with them when they arrived at the snowbound valley of the elves, and he felt the man's wonder as they used the *Chronicle* to wake the sleeping volcano and bring the valley to life. . . .

And then years, decades, centuries slipped by. . . .

And it was then that Michael felt the madness take root and grow, twining like a weed around the Guardian's mind. It was not greed that possessed him—that now possessed Michael—it was fear. Fear that someone would steal the *Chronicle*. At first, the fear was directed at the world outside. But as the years fell away, the fear found enemies closer by. He—the man, Michael—saw in his brothers their desire for the *Chronicle*. He knew that he alone could keep it safe. He alone could protect it. It was his duty, his responsibility. And then Michael was standing behind one of his brothers, and there was a knife in his hand. . . .

Michael felt himself falling into an endless darkness, and he tried to pull back, to save himself, but there was nothing to cling to; he was drowning in the man's grief and guilt, and it was too much; the man had been right, he wasn't strong enough; and Michael's last thought was of Kate and Emma and how he'd failed them. . . .

"Michael!"

He opened his eyes. Emma was leaning over him, holding a bucket. Michael's head and chest were dripping wet. Emma tossed aside the bucket and seized him in a hug.

"You're okay! Oh, I was so worried!"

For a few moments, Michael could do nothing but submit to Emma's hug. He did, however, manage to get his bearings.

First off, he was not dead. Secondly, he was no longer in the lava-lit chamber of the keep. Someone had moved him to the courtyard.

"I . . . I need to sit up."

Emma helped to prop him up. Michael felt trembly and hollow, as if the smallest jolt might shake him to pieces. He started to think about what had happened—then stopped himself. He wasn't ready to relive it. Not yet. Perhaps not ever. He was alive; that was enough.

He saw he was in a wood-roofed shelter along the fortress wall. To his left was the forge. He felt the heat radiating from the fire. And he could hear, beneath the din of battle, the steady *clink-clink-clink* of hammering.

"How did I get here?"

"How do you think?" Emma said. "He carried you."

"Who?"

"Him!" She moved, and there was the Guardian, standing at the anvil. He wore a heavy leather apron and thick leather gloves. His unruly beard had been bound up with string. In one hand, he held a pair of tongs. In the other, a hammer. The tongs gripped the golden bracelet, now throbbing red with heat, and the man swung the hammer down, striking the bracelet again and again. He was chanting softly. For a moment, Michael was too stunned to do anything but stare. As he watched, the man lifted the smoking bracelet and plunged it, hissing, into a bucket of water.

Michael scrambled to his feet. "He brought me here?! Him?!"

"Yeah. When I saw him carrying you, I thought he must've

gotten loose and killed you or something, but— Hey, what is it? What's wrong?"

Spotting his bag on the ground, Michael had snatched it up and was dumping out the contents. His camera, his pens and pencils, his journal, his compass, his pocketknife, a half-eaten pack of gum, his badge from King Robbie—everything tumbled forth, including the *Chronicle*, with the stylus snapped neatly into place. Michael didn't understand. He'd passed out in the keep; then, somehow, the Guardian had gotten free. Only rather than escaping with the *Chronicle*, the man had put the book into Michael's bag and carried him here. Now it appeared he was repairing the bracelet. It didn't make sense.

Unless . . .

Michael picked up the book, turning it over in his hands. Was it possible?

"So it really worked," Emma said.

"Huh?"

"The Guardian guy, when he brought you out, he wasn't crazy at all. He was totally nice. Your plan worked."

"Yes," said a voice, "he healed me."

The man stood beside them. He'd removed his leather apron and gloves, but his cheeks and forehead glistened with sweat and were stained black from the fire. He looked more demonic than ever. Except for his eyes. Michael found himself staring into them and thinking of Dr. Pym's eyes. They had none of the wizard's merriness, but there was in them the same sense of great age, and wisdom, and kindness. Michael felt some of his panic ebbing away.

"You're wondering how I got free," the man said. "When you collapsed, you fell toward me. I was able to get the knife from your belt."

"Okay, but . . . why . . . ?"

"Why did I not escape with the *Chronicle*? As I said, you healed me. I am again the man that I was." Then he knelt before Michael and raised his voice to ring out over the clamor of battle. "Bear witness all that I do pledge my breath, my strength, my very life, to your service. So I swear till death frees me of my bond."

Emma whispered, "Whoa."

"You brought me back to life," the man said. "You are the Keeper."

Fractured and empty as he felt, Michael could only shake his head. It wasn't that he didn't believe he was the Keeper; he didn't want to believe.

The man held out the golden bracelet. "It is done. The spell is complete."

Michael took it. The metal, so solid and warm in his hand, helped to steady him. He ran his thumb over the spot where his knife had cut through. The new gold had formed a faint, raised scar.

Okay, he told himself. Don't think about the *Chronicle*. Don't think about what happened. Think about this. Think about what you need to do now.

But he was like a wounded man trying not to think about the gaping hole in the center of his chest.

He managed to say, "Where's the princess?"

"Here."

Wilamena stepped into the enclosure. Her eyes were red, as if she'd been crying, and it occurred to Michael that the princess hadn't been there when he'd woken. But he didn't ask what she'd been doing. There was no time.

"The bracelet's ready."

The elf princess held out her arm. "And so am I."

Gabriel was fighting atop the wall when a roar in the courtyard spun him around. Gabriel recognized the sound, knew the creature that had made it, and told himself it wasn't possible. Then a golden blur shot past him, and he looked up to see the last rays of the sun glinting off the dragon's hide. A great silence fell upon the fortress as attackers and defenders alike stopped fighting and gazed skyward.

Footsteps pounded up the ladder from the courtyard, and Michael and Emma, breathless and flushed, ran toward him.

"Gabriel!" Emma cried. "Did you see? We did that! You see?"

She pointed to the sky, but Gabriel was staring at the children.

"You did this?"

"Well, it was mostly Michael. But I helped with the fire."

Michael, standing there, could feel the man's eyes upon him and understood his concern. Gabriel didn't know about the change in the Guardian, or that he, Michael, in being the one to place the bracelet on Wilamena's arm, was now the dragon's master.

"It's okay. She's on our side."

Michael hoped he sounded confident. In truth, the elf princess's transformation had rattled him. It turned out to be one thing to know that someone is going to turn into a dragon, and quite another to have it happen before your eyes.

Michael had been sliding the bracelet over Wilamena's wrist, and reflecting—he hadn't been able to help himself—on the perfect, honeyed softness of her skin, when his fingers had brushed a patch that was actually a little dry. Curious, he'd looked down and seen golden scales blossoming along her arm; he'd watched as her fingernails grew and thickened into claws, and he was just beginning to feel a tad uneasy, to think that perhaps they'd rushed into this, when a deep, serpenty voice hissed, "Get back, Rabbit," and Michael had looked up to see Wilamena's blue eyes turn the color of blood. The Guardian had yanked both him and Emma out into the courtyard, and a moment later, the wooden enclosure around the forge exploded, and the golden dragon, in all her terrible glory, stepped forth.

Wilamena was now hundreds of feet above the fortress, and Michael was staring skyward, wondering what he was supposed to do, how the bond between them worked, and just then the elf princess spoke to him. He didn't hear her voice in his head; it was nothing so precise. It was more a feeling: she was there; he was not to worry; she had the situation well in hand.

For the first time since Emma had woken him with the bucket of water, Michael began to feel better.

"Just watch."

The mass of the attacking army was clustered hundreds deep against the fortress wall, while a dozen siege ladders, studded with

Imps and Screechers, stood wedged against the battlements. No one had moved since the dragon's appearance. All were waiting to see what she would do. Then the dragon wheeled about and tore down out of the sky. Michael felt a hot wind as she flew past, heard the sound of ladders snapping, of Imps and Screechers being thrown to the ground.

"See?" Emma cried, grabbing at Gabriel's arm. "You see?"

Rourke's forces were in disarray, unsure whether to continue their assault upon the fortress or turn and face this new threat. The elves took advantage and poured arrow after arrow into their midst. The dragon, meanwhile, swung about and dove at the army, breathing out a rippling swath of flame. Disarray became chaos, and for a few minutes, those upon the walls watched as the dragon ravaged the attackers. At one point, she landed in the center of the force, breathing fire in a great circle all about her; then she chased down and crushed the burning creatures that tried to flee.

"Wow," Emma said. "She seems . . . really angry, huh?"

Michael silently agreed, and glanced about to gauge the reaction of the elves. It was then he noticed how few of them manned the walls. Puzzled, Michael looked into the courtyard, and saw, beneath a wooden shelter, more than a dozen elves lined up on the ground, their cloaks drawn tight about them. A cold weight settled on Michael's heart, and he understood where Wilamena had been when he'd woken beside the forge, and why she'd been crying, and that now she was taking her revenge.

Then Gabriel said: "Rourke is coming."

Some while before, Rourke had retreated to the base of the

volcano, where an Imp had set up a table and chair and proceeded to serve him lunch, which Rourke had eaten without any sense of hurry while watching the progress of the battle. Now he was charging up the slope, an enormous spear clutched in his hand. Wilamena was hovering ten feet in the air, torching a troop of *morum cadi*. She seemed to feel Michael's panic and turned; but she was off balance, and Michael gasped as the point of the spear drove deep into the joint of her shoulder.

"Watch out!" Emma cried. "He's got another!"

Again, the warning came too late; and all those upon the wall heard Rourke's second spear puncture the dragon's chest. Michael felt another searing jolt of pain, and his connection to the elf princess was severed. For a moment, it seemed that Wilamena would fall among the Imps and Screechers and be set upon. But then, struggling on one wing, she pulled herself higher into the air, and Michael watched as she careened down the slope, out over the plain, and crashed into the depths of the forest.

It seemed to Michael as if he too had been stabbed.

She's dead, he thought. She's dead, and it's my fault.

Rourke, meanwhile, had bounded forward, snatching up the battering ram that had been dropped by the trolls and charging toward the gate.

"The keep!" Gabriel shouted, pushing Emma and Michael toward the ladder. "Make for the keep!"

Michael felt numb. He was hardly aware of climbing down. In the courtyard, the blue-eyed captain was forming his elves into a line. Gabriel swept up Emma and shouted for Michael to follow. There was a loud splintering and the doors of the fortress burst open. Michael saw Rourke, wielding Gabriel's falchion, step through the wreckage as black-garbed Screechers and Imps swarmed past him into the courtyard.

He could hear Emma calling to him, but her voice sounded far away.

Wilamena was dead, and it was his fault.

Michael watched as the elves met the invaders. The blue-eyed elf captain clashed with Rourke in the center of the melee, their blades flashing and clanging; then something spun through the air, and Michael saw it was the captain's sword; he was down, and Rourke, laughing, moved in to finish him off. Michael wasn't aware of making a decision, but suddenly he was running forward, a rock clenched in his hand. For once in his life, his aim was perfect, and the rock thudded off the bald man's head. Rourke stopped and turned, giving the elf captain a second to recover his dropped sword and spring to his feet. Michael felt a momentary surge of triumph.

Then Rourke pointed at Michael, shouting, *"The boy! Get me the boy!"*

Three Screechers broke from the fighting. Michael turned to run, tripped, and fell. He scrambled to his knees, then glanced back, expecting to see dark shapes closing in; but the Guardian had rushed between him and the Screechers. The man's sword was a blur as he parried strikes from all sides, and Michael watched as he cut down first one Screecher, then another. As he fought, his back seemed to straighten, and his movements were swift and sure.

Michael knew that the man was buying him time to escape.

Get up, he thought. Run.

But then the ground trembled and he fell again. At first, Michael thought the volcano was finally erupting, but the quaking was strangely rhythmic, and he looked and there, charging toward him through the gates, came the last remaining troll.

He tried to stand, but his limbs refused to obey.

He could only watch as the troll thudded nearer, blacking out the sky.

The Guardian leapt into view, throwing himself at the monster. He seemed almost to embrace the troll; then the troll flung the man away, and the Guardian flew through the air and collided with a wooden post. Michael waited, but the troll made no move to seize him, and then he saw the hilt of the Guardian's sword protruding from the creature's neck. He rolled away as the monster pitched forward.

A second later, the Guardian pulled Michael to his feet.

Shielding Michael with his own body, the Guardian ran with him past the smoking corpses of the Screechers, past the battling elves, and up the steps to the keep. Once inside, the man released him, and Emma threw her arms around Michael's neck and clung to him, even as she scolded him for staying behind. For a moment, Michael simply stood there, panting. The red glow from the tunnel was brighter than ever, and the sounds of the battle were muffled by thick stone walls.

He heard Gabriel barring the door.

"What're you doing?" Michael pulled away from Emma. "The elves won't be able to get in!"

"The elves will make their stand in the courtyard."

"But—"

"It is their choice," Gabriel said. "We will climb to the tower. Help may still come—"

"*No!*"

Michael, Emma, and Gabriel all turned to the Guardian. He had fallen to one knee. Long ribbons of blood stained his arms and legs. Michael hadn't even realized he'd been wounded.

"There is a way out." The man's breath was strained, his face beaded with sweat. "You must go through the volcano. Past the cauldron, there is a path that will lead you out the other side. It is the only way."

As he finished speaking, he slumped forward, and Michael ran to the man's side. He was already pulling out the *Chronicle*.

"Hold on! I can heal you—"

"No . . . there is no time."

"But—"

"No!" The man seized Michael's arm; his voice had fallen to a whisper. "Beware. The book will change you. Remember who you are."

Michael nodded, though he had no idea what the man meant.

"Please, let me help you. . . ."

"Just tell me, have I fulfilled my oath?"

Michael had to speak through the knot in his throat. "Yes."

"Then I can meet my brothers with honor." And Michael watched as an immense, invisible weight slipped from his shoulders. With the last of his strength, the man pushed Michael away. "Now go. Go."

Michael followed Gabriel and Emma down the stairs,

stopping only once to look back. The man lay without moving, his eyes staring at nothing.

The Guardian. The elves in the courtyard. Wilamena.

How many, Michael thought, will have to die for me?

Then he slid the book into his bag and turned toward the volcano.

CHAPTER TWENTY
Into the Fire

The tunnel split in two.

Emma said, "Which way do we go?"

She and Michael and Gabriel were deep inside the mountain, well past the cavern where Michael had first met the dragon Wilamena. With each step, the heat had grown worse, while the air had thickened to a poisonous, hazy red. Twice, the volcano had shuddered so violently that Michael and Emma had had to brace themselves against the walls, and Emma had remarked that the bald guy had better hurry up or the volcano was going to kill them before he got the chance.

Now they were at a crossroads.

"We cannot afford to be wrong," Gabriel said. "Wait here." And he plunged into the right-hand tunnel.

The moment he was gone, Michael sank to the ground.

Emma knelt beside him.

"It's not your fault."

Michael said nothing.

"You wanted to save him. He wouldn't let you."

"He . . . he was right not to let me."

"What're you talking about? What do you mean, he was right?"

"He betrayed his brothers. Betrayed his oath. Carried the guilt around for centuries. We gave him a chance to redeem himself. He even passed on the book. He was ready to die." Michael looked at Emma. "I know it sounds strange."

The fact was, however briefly, Michael had shared the Guardian's life. He still had the memory of the man's guilt. Even if he couldn't make Emma understand, he knew what it had meant for the Guardian to set that burden down.

"Michael? What did he tell you back there? I couldn't hear everything."

Michael thought of the man whispering to him on the floor of the keep:

The book will change you.

But change me how? Michael wondered. Change me into what?

He shrugged. "Just to protect the book."

They were both quiet for a moment, then Emma said:

"Hey, do you have to be next to someone to heal them?"

"I told you, he didn't want me to. And it's too late—"

"I don't mean him. I was thinking"—Emma gripped his arm—"how do we know the princess is dead?"

Michael let out a cry and scrambled to pull the *Chronicle* from his bag, even as he cursed himself for not thinking of it before. He snapped free the stylus and was about to prick his finger when he paused. As much as he wanted to save the princess, the idea of taking on one more person's pain terrified him.

He remembered the rest of the Guardian's message:

The book will change you. Remember who you are.

"Michael? What is it? What's wrong?"

"Every time . . . every time I write someone's name in the *Chronicle*, I take on their whole life. I feel whatever they've felt. With the Guardian, when he murdered his brothers, I felt what it was like. I feel everything."

"Did . . . did that happen with me?"

Michael looked at his sister. She was staring at him with wide eyes, a reddish halo about her head. He gave a jerky nod. And then the words began spilling out, a torrent that had been building inside him ever since he'd freed her from the Guardian's spell. "I thought I knew what I'd done, betraying you and Kate to the Countess, but I didn't! I had no idea! I understand that now. And I promise, whatever happens, I'll make you trust me again. Like you used to. I promise."

And before Emma could respond, before he could hesitate a second time, he pricked his finger and wrote Wilamena's name in smoking, bloody letters, and the power rose up and swept him away.

Michael had thought the book would take him to where the dragon Wilamena had crashed in the forest, but he found himself in a world of ice and snow. He recognized the curve of the valley walls, the towering ring of mountains; but there were no trees, no birds; everything was cold and silent and white. He realized that he'd gone back to the beginning of Wilamena's life. And it was beautiful, for the elf princess was able, and Michael was able, to see the difference in every snowflake, in every crystal of ice. . . .

Then the world changed; the elf princess was swaying on a thin branch atop one of the great trees, and Michael was with her; and just as every snowflake and shard of ice had been different, so every leaf and needle on every tree was different, and the birds all answered Wilamena's call, and she raised her face to the sun, and Michael had never imagined his heart could be so full. . . .

Then darkness. Michael recognized the cave, the pool of lava, the tunnel leading to the keep; he felt how the dragon's body was a cage for the princess, how she fought, day after day, to hold on to her memories of the snow and the trees and the sun, but it was like shielding a candle on a dark, windswept plain. . . .

Then, without warning, Michael was lying on the forest floor, surrounded by splintered branches and trees, and he felt Wilamena's heart, his heart now, pumping out black blood onto a bed of crushed ferns. . . .

Live, he thought. Oh, please, please, live. . . .

"Michael!"

He was in the tunnel. The book open upon his knees, Wilamena's scorched name fading into the page. He felt hollowed out and shaky. Emma and Gabriel were both staring down at him.

"I'm sorry," Emma said. "Gabriel says that tunnel's a dead end. We gotta go the other way."

"But I don't know if she— I have to try again—"

"There is no time," Gabriel said. "We must go. Now."

"But—"

"Michael, they're coming!"

And then, finally, he heard the shrieks echoing down the tunnel.

Running, the screams of the Screechers at their heels, the air throbbing red; they rounded a corner, the tunnel opened up, and then, suddenly, they were in the great, smoking cauldron of the volcano. Below them, a hundred and fifty feet or more, was a roiling, churning lake of magma; above them hung the blue-black disk of sky. Michael felt as if they were perched on the side of some giant's enormous stewpot.

"Look!" Emma cried.

And Michael, squinting through the smoke, made out the mouth of a tunnel on the far side of the cone. He also saw, as did Gabriel and Emma, that the ledge they stood on was part of a path that ringed the whole inside of the volcano and would take them all the way around. The Guardian, it seemed, had not led them astray.

"Come," Gabriel said. "We must hurry."

Emma took the lead. They went as fast as they dared; the ledge was narrow and uneven and one wrong step would send them plunging to their deaths. Breathing was painful, as the air scorched their lungs, and the fumes from the lava made them nauseous and light-headed. When the children tried to steady themselves against the wall of the cone, the rocks burned their palms. And all the while, the volcano quaked and rumbled, and huge bubbles exploded out of the magma, sending globs of lava shooting upward.

Michael tried to focus, but as with a dream that lingers after waking, he couldn't shake off the feeling of being caged by the dragon's body.

They were halfway around the cone when there was a shout behind them. Rourke had emerged from the tunnel and was striding toward them along the path, Gabriel's falchion clenched in his right hand.

Gabriel drew his own sword. "Go. I will catch up."

Without a word, Emma grabbed Michael's hand and pulled him on.

Gabriel braced himself along the widest bit of ledge, and waited.

The children had gotten within forty paces of the tunnel when the volcano gave a violent jolt, and Michael, stumbling, twisted his ankle badly. Right away, he felt it start to throb, and he knew that any more running was beyond him.

"Michael—"

"I'm okay. I just—"

"No! Look!"

She was pointing past the mouth of the tunnel, to where a figure was coming toward them along the path. The figure was a skeleton, its bones blackened and smoking. It clutched a jagged-edged sword and moved with a jerky lope the children recognized.

"It's one a' them Screechers the dragon torched!" Emma

exclaimed. "But its body's all burned away. How's the stupid thing still alive?"

Michael didn't know and didn't care. The creature had circled the path from the other direction and was about to cut off their access to the tunnel. If that happened, they'd be trapped. Michael stood, putting all his weight on one foot.

"Emma, I can't run. You have to go on—"

"What?! No! I'm not leaving you here!"

Michael was about to say that he was the oldest and was ordering her to run when two more Screechers appeared on the path. They also had been burned, if not so completely as the first—which in some ways made them even more horrible, with the bits of charred flesh and muscle still clinging to their bones—and all three were closing in.

"You can climb, can't you?" Emma demanded.

"What?"

"And I do trust you, you idiot! Who else ever fought a dragon for me, huh?!"

Michael shrugged. ". . . No one?"

"That's right! And you're my brother! I'll always trust you! Tell that to your stupid book! Now look!"

Fifty feet above them was what appeared to be the opening of a small tunnel.

She pushed him toward the wall, shouting, "Climb!"

The rough, porous rock of the volcano made for ready handholds and footholds, and Michael found that he was able to climb with one leg, though not as fast as Emma, who quickly outpaced him. Indeed, the real pain was in his hands, which were soon raw and scorched. But the sounds of their pursuers coming up behind them, of bony fingers scraping against rock, helped him ignore the pain and climb even faster.

And Michael couldn't stop thinking of what Emma had said and wondering if she really meant it. The thought filled him with new hope and strength and chased away the shadows clinging to his mind.

Suddenly, the volcano gave a shudder, and the rocks Michael was gripping came loose in his hands. He scrabbled madly at the wall as he plummeted downward; there was a hard *crunch*, and he caught hold of what felt like a twig or stick poking from the rock. Only it wasn't a twig. To his horror, he saw he was clinging to the dismembered arm of a Screecher. Turning, Michael saw a one-armed skeleton disappearing into the lava. It seemed he had landed on top of the creature, the impact breaking its arm, even as its hand had remained clenched around the rock. Michael made a mental note to wash his own hands properly the first chance he got—Screecher bones probably carried all sorts of germs—and he looked up to tell Emma he was okay, only to see a second monster grab hold of her boot and try to yank her off the wall.

"Emma!"

He started toward her, but he hadn't gone more than a few feet when the skeleton tumbled past, clutching Emma's boot. Michael looked up. Emma smiled and waggled her foot.

"I undid the laces."

Then her smile vanished. Following his sister's gaze, Michael saw that the smoke over the lava pit had cleared, and Gabriel and Rourke were visible across the cone. The men stood toe to toe, their weapons a blur, the sound lost in the rumble of the volcano. Gabriel was not attacking, but merely parrying Rourke's strokes, which rained down in a continuous onslaught, as if the bald man had not one weapon but many, all in constant motion. Then a new cloud of smoke hid them from view. Michael looked up, expecting to see Emma climbing down to help her friend.

But Emma hadn't moved, and Michael realized that she wasn't leaving him, that she wouldn't leave him, that she had indeed meant every word she'd said.

"Quit daydreaming!" she shouted. "That thing's right behind you!"

Michael scrambled upward. He could hear the Screecher clawing at the rocks below his feet, and he told himself that Gabriel would find a way to win; he always did.

Emma called down, "I'm here! There's a tunnel! Hurry!"

The volcano seemed on the verge of breaking apart. Chunks of rock had begun blasting off the wall as jets of hot gas pock-marked the cone. Michael's arms quivered with fatigue. As he approached the ledge where Emma waited, the cone tilted in, and Michael's bag hung below him like a pendulum. Emma lay down on her stomach and reached toward him. Michael knew the Screecher was close.

"Don't look down! Take my hand!"

Michael strained upward and caught his sister's hand. Just as he did, the Screecher leapt and grabbed hold of his legs.

"Michael!"

He was pulled completely off the wall. Emma was flat on her

stomach, holding his hand with both of hers as the Screecher clung to his knees. The creature was almost all bone and weighed very little, but Michael could feel Emma's sweaty fingers slipping through his own.

"Michael! I can't hold you! Michael—"

The skeleton was climbing up Michael's body, the bones of its hands digging into his thighs. Michael fumbled for the knife in his belt.

"I need—"

"Michael—stop moving—I can't—"

And then his hand slipped through Emma's fingers.

Rourke seemed to have no weakness. He was stronger than Gabriel, faster, better rested; and he wielded Gabriel's own weapon, rescued from the skull of the dead troll, more easily than Gabriel ever had himself. Indeed, the man's only weakness, if it could be called a weakness, was that he liked to talk, and did so incessantly, even as he rained down blow after crushing blow.

"Don't get me wrong, boyo, you've got pluck, and I like pluck—almost had you there—but you're still just a man, while I—oh, now that one gave you a haircut—I am so—much—*more!*"

Rourke's blade clanged off Gabriel's sword, and Gabriel lunged forward, pressing him into a clench. It was an act of self-preservation. Gabriel had had no rest since the start of the battle, many hours before, and his movements were growing sluggish, his sword arm heavy and slow. He could not ward off many more blows.

Rourke laughed. "Why, lad, you're dead exhausted! Shall we take a break? Have a spot of lemonade? Get someone to massage your toes?"

Gabriel said nothing and tried to drive the man back. But Rourke wouldn't budge. Nor did he resume his attack. He just stood there, smiling grandly, the hilt of his blade locked with Gabriel's. Gabriel realized that the man was taunting him.

"Tell me," Rourke said, "how does it feel to know that the Dire Magnus will soon return to this mortal plane? That his footsteps will once again grace our sweet, gentle earth? Does it not fill you with awe? With wonder? With gratitude?"

Gabriel continued to strain against the man. The longer Rourke talked, the more time it gave the children.

"I think he is a fool. Pym beat him once. He will do so again."

"Oh, will he? And who will help him? His magician allies are dead. I killed them myself. And Pym alone is no match for my master."

"We have the children."

"Yes, of course," Rourke said, "the children."

The bald man shoved him away; Gabriel saw a flash of steel and raised his sword. Too late, he realized it was a feint, and Rourke's kick caught him full in the chest. He felt ribs snap, and he flew backward, bouncing off the wall, as his sword spun away and he tumbled off the ledge.

A moment later, Gabriel was dangling, one-handed, over a sea of lava.

Rourke came and crouched above him, the falchion balanced casually on his shoulder. "Well, lad, you put up a good fight and have nothing to be ashamed of. I just have one question before we pop you into the cooker."

Gabriel had managed to find a grip for his other hand; his legs still hung free.

"Did Pym ever tell you what will happen to the wee children when the Books are finally brought together? I'm curious, for you see, I asked the tykes' parents and they didn't know. It made me wonder how much the old fella has been keeping to himself."

Gabriel looked up. He knew it was what Rourke wanted, but he couldn't help himself. The fact was, Pym never had told him what would happen when all three books had been found and brought together. He'd only ever said that it was necessary to the children's safety. And Gabriel had accepted it. So what did Rourke know that he didn't?

"Ah," Rourke said, the glow from the lava shining off his bald head, "I thought not—"

Just then the entire volcano lurched to the left. Rourke was caught off balance and fell backward. In a flash, Gabriel had pulled himself onto the ledge. His broken ribs scraped together, filling him with a dull, sapping nausea. But he knew this was his one chance. He kicked away the falchion, knocking it into the pit. Then he stomped, with all his strength, on the man's wrist. Bellowing, Rourke threw his shoulder into Gabriel, then charged forward, pinning him against the wall, where he pounded Gabriel with elbows and fists. Gabriel felt more ribs crack, and he whipped up his head, the back of his skull colliding with the bald man's chin. Rourke cursed and slammed Gabriel into the rock wall, again and again. Gabriel felt his vision blur, and he kicked out blindly. He felt a sort of thick crunch; there was a cry of pain, and the man released him.

Gabriel leaned against the wall, panting, waiting for his vision to settle. Rourke was bent over, cradling his knee.

"You rascal, I think you've bloody crippled me!" He pulled out a long, gleaming knife. "I was going to let you go easy, but now I have to hurt you."

He lunged forward, and Gabriel, too weak to defend himself, felt the blade slide between his shattered ribs. More than anything, Gabriel hoped that Emma was away, out of the volcano, and not seeing what was happening.

"I want to finish what I was saying." Rourke pulled out his knife and stabbed Gabriel yet again. "When the Books are finally brought together—are you still alive in there, still listening?— when the Books are brought together, the children will die. That's the truth, my lad. It's been prophesied and it will happen. So all this time you've been protecting the little lambs, old Pym's been leading them to the slaughter. I thought you'd enjoy knowing that as you die."

And he drove the knife in again, and deeper still.

Gabriel felt the steel point reaching inside him, and he felt the volcano make its last and greatest shudder, and he called up his remaining strength and locked his arms around Rourke as the ledge crumbled beneath their feet. At some deep level, Gabriel believed what Rourke had said. But did that mean Pym had used him all these years? Gabriel didn't know. He only knew that

Rourke had to be kept from the children. The man fought him, but Gabriel held him fast till they were both falling toward the lava, releasing him only when he knew that Rourke, like himself, was doomed.

And neither man, Gabriel nor Rourke, saw the large shape shooting past them into the smoke.

After his fingers had slipped from Emma's, Michael had thought that was that: he was finished. But he found himself bumping and skidding down the wall of the cone, shredding his clothes, bruising and skinning the whole front half of his body; and when he crashed onto the ledge fifty feet below, it turned out that he'd done nothing worse—beyond all the scrapes and bruises—than sprain his other ankle.

Then something snapped tight around his throat, and his head was jerked back. He realized he was being choked by his own bag. Michael managed to roll onto his stomach so the strap was against the back of his neck, and he peered over the edge of the path. There, dangling over the pool of lava, was the skeleton.

Honestly, Michael thought, I really do hate these things.

The bag's pouch hung between Michael and the creature, and Michael reached down and pulled the Chronicle free. The skeleton was clawing upward, trying to reach him, but Michael drew his knife and—saying goodbye to his journal, his compass, his pens and pencils, his camera, his pocketknife, his badge from King Robbie—he cut the strap and watched his bag, its contents, and the Screecher all fall and be swallowed by the lava.

Michael flopped onto his back. Emma had been calling his name, and he could see her face, far above him, and gave a weak wave.

Okay, he thought, enough lying about. You're not on vacation. Stand—

That was as far as he got before the volcano spasmed and the ledge he was on collapsed. Michael felt himself falling and shut his eyes, clutching the *Chronicle* tight to his chest, as if the book might somehow save him. And because his eyes were closed, he felt, rather than saw, the great claws that seized him about the middle. When he did open his eyes, they were seared by the fumes and heat rising from the lava, and he saw only a blur of golden scales, and already the dragon—for it was her, Wilamena, her golden scales, her body healed and whole—was turning, swooping upward, and Michael saw two more figures falling toward the lava, and Wilamena snatched them both out of the air and climbed higher; and Emma was above them, screaming with joy and jumping up and down, and without stopping, the dragon plucked her from the ledge; and then there was an explosion, and Michael looked down and saw the entire cauldron of lava blasting toward them; and they flew before it, out of the cone, Michael feeling the cool night air on his face, looking back to see the lava shooting into the darkness, and the dragon turned, diving down the side of the mountain, and there was the fortress, with lava flooding about its walls, and, silhouetted atop the tower, a small cluster of figures.

The dragon hovered just above the tower, and the elf captain and six exhausted, wounded elves fell back in astonishment.

Setting down Michael and Emma and Gabriel, Wilamena perched upon the wall, Rourke still clutched in her talons.

"Your Highness, you're alive!" The elf captain dropped to a knee. "I would compose a sonnet—"

"Perhaps later," growled the dragon. "Are you all that remain?"

"We are. The bald devil slipped past us to the keep. We fought our way here, expecting to find the children. Then we ourselves became trapped."

Suddenly, the dragon gave a roar of pain, and Rourke tumbled off the side of the tower. Rourke's knife was stuck in the dragon's leg, shoved between the armored scales. Michael yanked it out, and peered over the wall.

"He's gone! I can't see him anywhere!"

Dark blood ran down Wilamena's leg.

"Are you okay?" Michael asked.

The dragon Wilamena seemed almost to smile. "I'm fine, Rabbit."

"Michael!" Emma was kneeling beside Gabriel, panic in her eyes. "Gabriel—he's hurt really bad! You gotta help him!"

But as Michael started to open the Chronicle, the tower shook, and the elf captain said there was no time, they would help their friend once they'd reached safety. And the elves lifted the unconscious Gabriel onto the dragon's back, and Emma climbed up behind him, and Michael sat before him, so that together they pinned the wounded man in place. Then the dragon snatched up the remaining elves and, beating her great wings, leapt into the air. When Michael looked back—they were already high over the plain—he saw the entire fortress sinking into the volcano.

"Hurry!" Emma shouted, a sob breaking her voice. "I think—I think Gabriel's dying!"

"Your friend is strong," said the dragon. "He will not die. We will not let him."

"Where're you taking us?" Michael asked.

"Home, Rabbit. I'm taking you home."

CHAPTER TWENTY-ONE
Separation

The iron bell crashed down. Rafe lay without moving, beams from the collapsed staircase piled on his back. Kate was on her side in the doorway, unable to reach Rafe in time to save him. She could only cry—

"*STOP!*"

—and shut her eyes.

A second passed. Two seconds. Three . . .

Where was the crash? The thud that would shake the floor? Everything was silent and still, and the only thing Kate felt was her heart pounding in her chest.

Slowly, she opened her eyes. Nothing had changed. The bell was exactly where it had been, twenty feet above Rafe's head. Only it wasn't falling; it simply hung there in the air. She looked around. The tongues of flame climbing the walls were frozen in place. Then Kate realized how utterly quiet it was. The roaring of the fire, the popping and breaking of glass, the snapping of beams: all had stopped.

She got to her feet and stood there, afraid to move.

Henrietta Burke had said that the magic of the *Atlas* was a part of her; she only had to stop fighting it. The moment the woman had said it, Kate had known she was right. Ever since Kate had taken the Countess into the past, she'd felt the power inside her. But she'd pushed it down, denied it.

Then, as she saw the bell plummeting toward Rafe, all the barriers she'd erected had come tumbling down.

But what was this eerie stillness?

Even as she asked the question, Kate knew the answer:

"I stopped time."

She could feel the strain inside herself. It was as if she had dammed up a river and it was struggling to break free. She knew she could not hold it back much longer.

She took a step toward Rafe—and stopped.

A terrible thought had taken hold of her.

Rafe was destined to be the Dire Magnus—the reason her family had been divided, the reason she and Michael and Emma had spent the last ten years in orphanages, the reason they'd grown up without knowing their parents. She only had to relax, to let time flow; the bell would fall, and her family would be together once more.

She stood there a second longer, then said a silent apology to her family.

I'm sorry. I'm sorry, I just can't.

She stepped forward, took Rafe by the wrists, and pulled him out of the rubble.

She was barely aware of dragging him through the main hall of the church. All her strength and focus was required to hold time in check. The longer it was stopped, the greater the pressure became. She pulled him through a hole in a half-destroyed wall and out into the dark, empty street. There she dropped his arms and collapsed at his side.

And let go.

She felt a roaring inside her, and the world's noise returned. She heard the crackling of the fire, the crash and clanging of the bell as it struck the bottom of the tower, the shouts of the mob around the corner. She was on her hands and knees, gasping, her dress soaked with perspiration.

"What—where—"

Rafe had opened his eyes, the cold air jarring him awake. He leapt up, stared at the street, the burning church, at her. . . .

"Did you—how did I get here?"

Kate was still trembling from her effort. She took several shaky breaths and got unsteadily to her feet.

"She was right. . . . Miss Burke said I had the magic in me. I'd just been . . . afraid of using it. I stopped time. I pulled you out of the church."

"You pulled me out?"

"Yes."

"You saved my life."

"Yes."

For she had; whatever happened from this point on, for good

or ill, she had chosen to save his life. Behind them, the church continued to burn, and Kate could hear the mob shouting and cheering around the corner. The boy stared at her.

"And you can go home now. Back to your brother and sister."

Kate nodded.

"And Miss B is dead."

She could feel the anger and sadness coming off him, like heat from the fire.

There was a rumbling, and they both turned as the bell tower began to sink and tilt, the base of it eaten away by flames, and there was a cheer from around the corner as the tower tipped over and crashed through the roof of the church in a great explosion of smoke and sparks.

With a cry, Rafe ran to the crumpled iron fence, yanked free one of the bars, and took off running around the side of the church.

Legs trembling, Kate went after him, shouting his name.

When she came onto the avenue, there were now perhaps forty men armed with torches and clubs, cheering and laughing, their faces ghoulish in the firelight. None of them saw the boy racing toward them. There was no magic in Rafe's attack; it was all animal pain and anger. He struck a potbellied man full in the head—a distinct *clonk* Kate heard from twenty yards away—and laid him out cold. Then he tore into three young toughs, all of them older and bigger than he was. He struck the first across the shoulders, and the young man dropped his torch and fell to his knees with a grunt. Rafe jabbed the end of his pipe into the stomach of the second, doubling him over, then brought his knee up into the man's face, so that his head snapped back. The third tough was fast and had his knife out and slashed Rafe across the arm. The pipe clattered to the street, and the tough kicked it to his friend, the first one Rafe had attacked, who grabbed it as he staggered to his feet. The other tough was up as well, though bleeding from his nose and mouth, and he too had his knife out. The trio surrounded Rafe, and Kate was about to dive into the fray when Rafe snatched a torch, spoke a silent word, and flames leapt off the torch and engulfed the three men.

"No!"

Kate knocked the torch from Rafe's hand. The flames attacking the men died away. At the same moment, there was a sound of approaching bells and sirens, someone shouted that the police were coming; instantly, the mob melted away, including the three young men, who fled into the darkness, calling back threats as they ran.

Rafe made to go after them, but Kate grabbed his arm.

"Stop it!"

"Why? You saw what they did!"

"But you can't! I won't let you!"

She wrapped her arms tight around him, hugging him to her. He pushed and struggled, but she held on to him with all the strength she had, her head buried against his shoulder, till, finally, she felt the fight go out of him. She held him a moment longer, limp in her arms, then let go. He dropped to his knees in the snow. She could see his shoulders shaking. Kate knew what he was feeling: His mother, Henrietta Burke, Scruggs—all of them were dead. The children he cared for hunted. She felt how easily his anger could consume him. And she remembered what Henrietta Burke had said:

Love him as he already loves you.

"Come with me."

Rafe looked up, tears shining amid the smoke and ash on his cheeks.

"What?"

Kate thought her voice would tremble, but it didn't. She knew this was right; this, finally, was why she was here, to stop him from becoming the Dire Magnus.

"Come with me."

He shook his head. "I can't. Someone has to look after the kids."

"They're going to a home upstate. Miss Burke set it up; they'll be okay. Come with me."

He stared at her, searching her face. The bells from the fire and police wagons were getting closer.

"What is everyone afraid of? You. Scruggs. Miss Burke. You're trying to keep me away from something. Why does the Dire Magnus want me?"

Kate couldn't resist the pleading in his eyes.

"He . . . he wants you to take his place."

"What?"

"I can't explain. But you won't be you anymore! You'll be him, and all the ones before him! He wants to use you! You have to come with me!"

As she said it, Kate realized that not only was this what the *Atlas* wanted, this was what *she* wanted. And it had nothing to do with him not becoming the Dire Magnus; she just wanted him with her.

Love him as he already loves you.

"I want you to come. Please."

Rafe still hadn't risen from his knees, and he stared down at his hands. Kate saw they were burned and blistered. "She told me to choose. Miss Burke. She said I could choose who I would be. The same thing my mother said."

"So choose. Come with me."

She held out her hand. Rafe looked at it, at her. It seemed to Kate that the whole world held its breath. Then, slowly, he reached up.

"You!"

The voice came from down the street. Kate looked past Rafe's kneeling form to where a shape had emerged from the darkness.

"I knew you'd be here, you freak! I told you you'd get yours!"

Kate saw it was the pinch-faced boy who'd chased her and Abigail and Jake and Beetles down the street earlier that morning and that he was holding a gun and it was aimed directly at her.

There was noise all around them, the roar of the fire, the clanging of the approaching bells, the shouts of the fleeing mob; still, Kate heard a small, distinct *pop*, and the pinch-faced boy turned and raced off into the darkness. Rafe had already leapt to his feet, but he seemed unsure about what to do, and looked from the disappearing boy back to Kate. Kate wanted to tell him she was fine and to stop staring at her like that, but she felt suddenly wobbly. Without realizing she was falling, she felt her head strike the cobblestones. Even then, she was surprised to find herself lying in the snow. She tried to get up and found she couldn't. Rafe's face appeared above her.

"What . . . what happened?" she said. "He missed me, didn't he?"

"Shhh, don't talk."

She could see the fear and worry in his eyes and that scared her more than anything. With a great effort, she lifted her head and saw, blossoming on the front of her white dress, a large red stain.

"Rafe . . ."

"It's okay. We can fix this. It's okay. . . ."

Her first thought was of Michael and Emma. She had to get to them. She couldn't die here; they would never know what had happened to her. She had to get back to them. And she reached for the magic inside her, but she was too weak. She couldn't focus enough to command it; the magic slipped from her grasp.

"I have to . . . ," she murmured, ". . . I have to . . ."

Rafe was lifting her in his arms. "I'll get you to someone who can heal you. Scrug—no, not Scruggs . . . We just need someone powerful. A powerful magician . . ."

She could hear the panic in his voice, and she found herself wanting to reassure him. "It's okay. I don't feel that bad. Only . . . cold."

Rafe's face changed. "I know who can fix you. Just hold on."

And he was running through the street, with Kate pressed against his chest. They passed the police and fire wagons that were sliding around the corner, and Rafe was running as if she weighed nothing at all, and indeed, it seemed to Kate that she was growing lighter, that all the weight, all the heaviness, was slipping from her. And Rafe was sprinting down the avenue, and she could hear the singing of New Year's revelers; it was getting close to midnight. And there was more shouting, but no, that was Rafe, he was shouting at a horse-drawn cab and leaping in before the man could stop, yelling out an address, telling the driver to go as fast as he could, and Kate heard the snap of reins and felt the jolt as the cab jerked away, and she was aware of how tightly Rafe held her and how cold she was and she couldn't actually, really, be dying.

"My brother and sister . . . they won't know what happened. . . ."

"You'll tell them. You're gonna be okay. I know who can fix you. Just hold on." Tears rolled down his cheeks. "I'm not losing you too."

And then, she couldn't be sure, she might have imagined it, but she thought he leaned down and kissed her.

The cab raced up the avenue, sliding around corners, the cabman shouting for people to make way, and Kate felt herself drifting off, lulled by the steady pounding of the horse's hooves and the swaying and rocking of the cab, and Rafe was holding her and murmuring, "It's gonna be okay. I'm not gonna lose you. . . ."

And then the cab was slowing, the driver calling for the horse to turn in, damn it, and Kate couldn't see where they were, but Rafe was kicking open the door, leaping out of the carriage with Kate in his arms, landing so softly that she felt no shock at all, and he was sprinting forward, and she heard a shout, harsh-voiced and brutal, that penetrated the cloud around her mind.

"No—Rafe—you can't—"

"There's no other way. If he's as powerful as you say, he's our only hope."

Rafe was moving too fast to be stopped, and he'd passed the sentries and was inside the mansion before he was trapped by a circle of four snarling Imps.

"Back away," said a voice that Kate knew, and the Imps parted.

Kate saw Rourke step forward, massive, bald, dressed in a dark suit with a white shirt and tie.

"Your boss needs to fix her," Rafe said. "I'll do whatever he wants. He just has to fix her."

The giant man looked at him for a moment, then nodded. "He said you would come. Follow me now. She doesn't look like she has much time."

To Kate, it was like being in a dream. She had no control over it; she could only watch as events unfolded around her. Rafe was carrying her up the stairs behind Rourke, and they were passing through the double doors and into the ballroom packed with men and women and other, shadowy creatures, and the crowd parted to reveal the ancient Dire Magnus, dressed in a long green robe, and Rourke bowed, and Rafe kept walking till it was just Kate and Rafe and the ancient sorcerer in the center of the candlelit ballroom.

"I knew," the Dire Magnus murmured. "I knew that you would come."

"No." Kate was clawing at Rafe's shirt, which was already wet and dark with her blood. "No, please, just leave . . . run. . . ."

She wanted to fight him, to force him to leave, but she had no strength; her life was ebbing away. She heard Rafe's voice as if from a great distance, telling the Dire Magnus to heal her, that he, Rafe, would do whatever the Dire Magnus wanted, be whatever he wanted, but only heal her.

She felt the sorcerer's wrinkled hand on her forehead.

"She is slipping. She is even now beyond my power. There is only one thing that can bring her back. I can send her there. I can use the power inside her. She must go back to her own time. But she will live."

"Do it," Rafe said. "Do it, and I'll do whatever you want."

"Nothing else? That's all you ask?"

"And I want the humans to pay. I want to make them pay."

"Oh, my boy, that I can promise."

And Kate felt the Dire Magnus calling up the power of the *Atlas* inside her, and she heard him whispering, "Your brother will find the *Chronicle*. You must go there. He will save you."

And she looked up into Rafe's face, and saw his green eyes looking down at her from the smoke-stained darkness of his face, and she tried to say, ". . . Don't," but he shook his head and whispered:

"It's too late. It's done. You'll live, that's what matters."

And she could hear the bells tolling midnight across the city, the magic world was pulling away, and she heard the Dire Magnus, his skeleton's head leaning close, saying, "Do not worry. You will see her again. We both will. . . ."

CHAPTER TWENTY·TWO
In the Trees

Michael woke to the sound of birds singing.

He saw blurry treetops and pieces of blue sky.

He was in a bed, the softest of his life.

Beyond that, he had no idea where he was or how he'd gotten there; but something told him just to enjoy the moment and his ignorance.

Then he smelled . . . a pipe?

"Feeling rested, my boy? You've had quite the long sleep. It's nearly midday."

Michael flipped over to see Dr. Stanislaus Pym sitting in a chair. In every way but one, the wizard looked the same as always. He was dressed in the same rumpled tweed suit; his white hair still stuck out in all directions; his tortoiseshell glasses still wanted mending; his pockets were heavy with odds and ends; indeed, only the wizard's smile was different: it was somber, muted, lacking any of its usual merriment. And had Michael not been puffy-brained with sleep, he might've noticed the change.

"Where—where am I?" he asked, accepting his glasses from the wizard and looking about.

The room, now properly in focus, seemed to Michael like a sort of large wooden cave. There were no boards or planks. The walls, floor, and ceiling were one continuous gnarled block. The only furniture was his bed and the one chair. There was no door. But across from the wizard, where the wall opened onto what could have been a balcony, Michael saw a wide, flat branch, extending outward.

"Am I in . . . a tree?"

"You are, my boy. You're with the elves at the end of the valley, and they make their home in the trees. I do hope you're not queasy about heights. Though what am I saying? My goodness! You arrived here on the back of a dragon!"

At this, Michael's memory of the night before returned. He recalled the feeling of flying, of the wind rushing by, of the forest below, dark and silent and still; he recalled the heat radiating from the dragon and the muscular beating of her wings; he recalled trying to prop up Gabriel even as his own strength began to fail, and Emma shouting that they needed help, and the dragon diving down into the trees; and he recalled being surrounded by a hundred singing voices as gentle hands lifted him to the ground.

"Did I pass out?"

"The elves sensed that you were very weak. Their song put you to sleep."

"But where's Emma? And Gabriel—"

"They are both here and have both been tended to. Emma had only cuts and bruises and minor burns on her hands. Gabriel's wounds were serious, but the elf physicians are highly skilled. He is out of any danger."

"But I was going to heal him! With the *Chronicle*—"

"A generous offer. But the power of the Books must always be the avenue of last resort. Sleep and rest will heal Gabriel now. Oh, and if you were wondering, the *Chronicle* is beside you."

Michael leaned over, and there on the floor was the book. He had grown so used to its pull that only now, seeing it, did he become aware of the tug at the center of his chest. Secretly, he was relieved he would not have to heal Gabriel. As far as he was concerned, he'd be happy if he never touched the *Chronicle* ever again.

"You can pick it up, if you like," the old man said, eyeing him closely.

"Thank you, sir, that's not necessary. I did want to ask about Princess Wilamena. Is she still a dragon or—"

"The Princess has been returned to her normal, lovely form. And let me say"—there was a hint of the old sparkle—"you have quite an admirer there."

"Well, that's a relief to hear. The first part, I mean. Listen, Dr. Pym, I need to talk to you about the *Chronicle*—"

The wizard held up his hand. "I'm sure you have many questions for me, just as I have many for you. But I think I see your breakfast."

An elf was approaching along the branch, carrying a tray

laden with covered cups and bowls and a tiny porcelain kettle. The elf wore green breeches, high white stockings, black shoes with bright gold buckles, and a tight-fitting, short-waisted green jacket that had a kind of gold brocade and was buttoned to the neck.

Really, Michael thought, the amount of time they must spend getting dressed.

Then he thought of the elves he'd seen wrapped in their cloaks in the courtyard of the fortress and felt ashamed. Never forget what they did, he told himself.

"Thank you," the wizard called. "We'll sit outdoors."

A low table and several large cushions had been set out on the branch, and the elf spent a few moments carefully arranging the breakfast, then plumped up the pillows and, with a bow, carried away the empty tray.

"Shall we?" the wizard said. "We can talk after you've eaten. Your clothes are at the end of the bed."

As the wizard stepped outside, Michael picked up his folded shirt and pants, which had been cleaned and mended during the night, and got dressed. He found the blue-gray marble, still attached to the strip of rawhide, and slipped it over his head. He noticed that his hands were no longer burned, and his cuts and bruises had all but vanished. He flexed his ankles and felt no pain. The elf doctors, it seemed, had healed him as well.

"Come along, my boy!" the wizard called. "The day is fine! Oh, and bring the book."

With some reluctance, Michael picked up the *Chronicle*,

pulled on his boots, glanced about for his bag—remembering only then that it was gone—and headed outside.

The day was indeed fine, with a cool breeze drifting through the trees and the sunlight warming them from above. The meal was simple: nuts, berries, cream, honey, some sort of tea made from flowers. But the berries were like none Michael had ever seen: strawberries as big and red as apples, blueberries so fat and deeply purplish blue that they looked like plums, giant raspberries spongy with juice. . . .

"You don't mind sharing, do you?" the wizard said, reaching over to dunk a fist-sized strawberry into the cream. "Oh my, yes, delicious."

Michael didn't reply. He was already cramming handfuls of almonds and walnuts into his mouth. He hadn't eaten anything since Gabriel's stew the day before, but until sitting down, he hadn't realized just how ravenous he was. For a few minutes, he forgot about everything else and focused on breakfast. Soon, his fingers and lips and teeth were stained a dark purple-red. And it was only when the wizard pressed him to try the tea—the first sip like drinking sunshine, a glowing, golden warmth spreading through his still-exhausted body—that Michael began to eat more slowly, and to savor each bite.

The branch that Michael and the wizard sat on was perhaps ten feet wide and perfectly flat. Glancing over the edge, Michael put the ground—half hidden in the gloom of the forest floor—at a dead drop of three hundred feet. Closer by, he could see rooms, similar to his own, dotting the surrounding trees and accessible by staircases that corkscrewed up and down the great trunks. But most amazing to Michael—and what made him long for his lost journal and camera—was how a branch from one tree would reach out and wind about the branch from another tree, then continue on to connect with a branch of a third tree, creating a complex web of pathways along which Michael could see dozens of elves moving about fearlessly. There was a whole city up here, Michael realized, suspended in the sunlit reaches of the forest.

He turned back and saw the wizard staring at him.

"What is it? Do I have something on my face?"

"Oh yes. Quite a bit. However, I was looking at you and thinking of the boy I knew, and thinking also of the boy who's performed such amazing feats these past few days. Your sister and Princess Wilamena have told me everything. Michael, I'm very proud of you. And I hope *you* are proud of you."

Michael considered this carefully. He knew that in times past he would've been pompously telling the wizard that it was no big deal even as he not-so-secretly believed that it was a big deal and that no one else could've pulled the affair off quite so well. But he didn't say that now. He was thinking about the Guardian and his brothers, and the long, long years that they had spent protecting the book. And he thought about Wilamena and the elves putting themselves in danger to defend him and his sister. And he thought about Emma, staying with him in the volcano as Gabriel fought for his life. . . .

He said, sincerely, "I had a lot of help."

"True. But still you recovered one of the lost Books of Beginning! You returned a princess to her people! You brought yourself and your sister through fire and war to safety! Resourcefulness. Bravery. Coolheaded intelligence. Credit where credit is due, my boy. How right that you should be Keeper of the *Chronicle*!"

"Dr. Pym, before you say any more, all this Keeper business—"

"And how doubly appropriate," the wizard went on, as if Michael hadn't spoken, "that tomorrow is your thirteenth birthday. You truly are growing up."

"Wha—*gugh!*"

"Are you all right, my boy?"

In his surprise, Michael had first inhaled, then choked on, then coughed up a blueberry the size of a robin's egg. He managed to say, "What?"

"Don't tell me you've forgotten your own birthday?"

"I . . . excuse me . . . I guess I did. Anyway, isn't it kind of silly to think about birthdays with everything that's going on?"

"Again, I disagree. These markers are important. Leave it to me. I will think of something appropriately festive. But now I promised you a talk."

"Right, well, like I was saying—"

"Why don't I begin by telling you what I've already told your sister, hmm? Where I've been, the things I've discovered, et cetera, et cetera."

Michael was getting the distinct sense that Dr. Pym knew what he intended to say and was putting him off. Fine, he thought, but sooner or later, the wizard would have to hear that Michael had no intention of remaining Keeper of the *Chronicle*.

He and the *Chronicle* were simply a bad match; there was no use pretending otherwise. But for the time being, he took another sip of tea and gave the old wizard his attention.

"You last saw me in Malpesa, struggling with Rourke on the rooftop. Well, after the building on which we stood collapsed into the canal—I was not injured, thankfully—I immediately made my way to the chamber where you and I discovered the skeleton. To my dismay, I found the chamber had already been ransacked by Rourke's minions. I then had a choice. I could either follow Rourke as he pursued you and your sister, or . . ." Here the wizard paused and pulled out his tobacco pouch. "Tell me, my boy, what do you know about the reading of minds?"

"Not much," Michael said. "In *The Dwarf Omnibus*, G. G. Greenleaf calls it 'wizard sneakery.' No offense."

Dr. Pym huffed. "First off, *sneakery* is not a word. Secondly, I do wish Mr. G. G. Greenleaf would not hold forth on subjects about which he is so appallingly ignorant. In point of fact, to gain access to another's thoughts is a very difficult and sticky business. With someone like Rourke, it can even be quite dangerous. Luckily, when we clashed on the rooftop, his attention was so fixed upon destroying me that I was able to slip past his defenses and glean several valuable pieces of information." He stuck the end of the pipe in his mouth. "Your parents are no longer prisoners of the Dire Magnus."

"*What?!*" Michael's shout carried through the trees, startling a flock of birds in the canopy.

Dr. Pym nodded sympathetically. "I had much the same reaction. But consider what occurred just before your battle at the volcano. Why would Rourke have presented you with a fake father if the real one had been available? It raises the question, does it not?"

Michael admitted the wizard had a point. "But are you absolutely sure? Not that I don't believe you—"

"No, no, you are quite right to ask. As it happens, in my nauseating trip through Rourke's mind, I also was able to learn the location of your parents' prison—"

"That's where you went?!" Michael exclaimed. "When you left Malpesa? Where was it? I bet it was some desert where it hasn't rained in a hundred years! Or a jungle filled with cannibals and giant poisonous insects! Or—"

"They were held in New York City."

Michael stopped, thinking he must not have heard Dr. Pym correctly.

"For ten years," the wizard went on, "your parents were kept prisoner in a mansion on the island of Manhattan. And to think of the time Gabriel and I spent scouring the far-flung reaches of the globe, pushing out the very corners of the map! I even knew the house where they were held! A hundred years ago, the Dire Magnus's followers operated from its premises. Yet never once did it cross my mind that our enemies would be so bold as to use that house as your parents' prison. Oh, Michael, there is no fool like an old fool."

And he sighed, looking very old indeed.

"But you did go there?" Michael prompted.

"I did. The mansion is cloaked, but I found it easily enough.

It had been abandoned. My suspicion is that once Richard and Clare escaped, their captors fled, perhaps imagining that your parents' friends—that is to say, myself and others—would seek retribution. Whatever the case, I was free to do a careful search. So to answer your question, yes, I feel certain that they were there and have now escaped."

"When?"

"My guess, and it is only a guess, is quite recently. Within the last few weeks."

"Then . . . where are they?"

"Where are they? Who helped them escape? Sadly, my boy, I am as in the dark as you."

The wizard fell silent and blew a large smoke ring, watching as the breeze lifted it away. Michael knew it was a good thing that their parents had escaped, but what had it actually changed? The Dire Magnus still wanted him and his sisters, still wanted the Books. They still didn't know where their parents were.

"It did make me think," the wizard went on, "that perhaps they have tried to contact us. I am referring to the glass orb that arrived at Cambridge Falls, the one you now wear about your neck."

Michael's fingers caressed the marble, and he felt a shiver of excitement. The wizard was right; it was more likely than ever that the marble had been sent by their parents. But then he remembered how it had been addressed to "The Eldest Wibberly," and something in him pulled back. He was not yet ready to take that title from Kate.

"Maybe."

The wizard shrugged. "Of course, it is yours to do with as you please. Now, while searching the mansion, I made one other discovery that is worth mentioning. Do you remember my saying that the Dire Magnus has been a presence in this world for thousands of years?"

Michael said he did.

"Well, interestingly, there is only one known way of achieving immortality—"

"You mean the *Chronicle*?"

"Exactly so. And we know in his case that was not an option. So how did he do it? It has always been my belief that discovering his secret is essential to defeating him once and for all."

"But you've been alive just as long! How'd you do it?"

The wizard shook his head. "That's not important."

"But—"

"We are talking about the Dire Magnus. Let us not get sidetracked."

"But—"

"Oh, very well. I wrote the *Chronicle*."

Michael opened his mouth, then closed it. Whatever he'd expected, it wasn't this.

"Don't look so surprised. The Books didn't write themselves, and you know I was part of the council that created them."

"You . . . wrote it?"

"Transcribed it, would be more accurate. The knowledge and power in the *Chronicle* are far greater than my own. The wisdom of the entire council of magicians passed through me, and I committed it to paper. In the process, some small sliver of the *Chronicle*'s power stayed with me. Now can we discuss the Dire Magnus?"

Michael nodded. He was still somewhat dumbfounded.

"First, we must look at the particular nature of his longevity. Do you remember Dr. Algernon referring to him as the Undying One?"

Again, Michael said he did.

"Well"—and here the wizard smiled—"far from never dying, the Dire Magnus has died many times."

"But you said—"

"And each time, he has been reborn. He dies and is reborn, dies and is reborn, over and over."

"You mean he's reincarnated?"

"Not exactly—"

"So it's more a rising-from-the-ashes thing?"

"Nor that either—"

"Does his spirit possess some poor kid's body? I saw that in a movie—"

The wizard held up his hand. "We could speculate all day. That has been my dilemma. Many theories, but no proof. However, all magic, especially powerful magic, leaves traces, and in that mansion, I finally found what I needed."

Michael was doing his best to remember every word the wizard said, but oh, how his hand ached for pen and paper! There was just no substitute for a written record.

The wizard blew another smoke ring and then asked, abruptly, "My boy, what do you think happens when the universe dies?"

"Huh?"

"You can't imagine that all this will just go on forever. The universe is a mass of constantly expanding energy, and one day it will collapse upon itself. Like a cake left too long in the oven. Then what? Nothingness?"

Michael shrugged. He had no idea.

The wizard leaned over the table. "It will be reborn."

Michael almost said "Huh?" again.

"The life of the universe is not a straight line. Rather, imagine a circle. And along that circle, the universe is born, destroys itself, and is born again, over and over, endlessly. You understand?"

"I . . . think so."

"Well, here is the truly amazing part. Just as the universe is reborn over and over, so is everything in it." The wizard waved his arm in a broad, encompassing gesture. "This forest, the valley, the world outside, all the creatures who inhabit it, have all existed before, and will all exist again."

"You mean, we've all . . . been alive before?"

"Exactly so. You, me, Emma, Katherine, Gabriel, this tree—in a pattern repeated for eternity. Who knows how many times you and I have sat here, having this exact conversation? And what the Dire Magnus did was to make contact with those earlier versions of the universe, to reach into them and pluck out his other selves and bring them here. How many times he did this, how many copies of himself he gathered together, I cannot say. But he then threw these other selves out across time, each further than the last, like stones tossed into the ocean, so that every few hundred years, another would be born into this world."

"But . . . why?"

"Because long ago, it was prophesied that the full power of

the Books would not be unleashed for thousands of years. And without the power of the Books—all three, you understand, working in concert—he had no hope of achieving his goal. So—"

"Dr. Pym," Michael interrupted, "do you realize that you've never said what exactly his goal is?"

"I haven't?"

"No."

"Never?"

"Never."

"Why, to usher in an age of magic in which he wields ultimate power! In which humanity is enslaved! That is his goal! And has been, these many, many centuries!"

"And he could do that?"

"Could he do that? My boy, the power of the Books is inseparable from the fabric of existence. Think of it this way—each time Katherine used the *Atlas*, each time you used the *Chronicle*, the world about us was changed. And that was done unconsciously. Imagine someone who *wanted* to change the world. Oh yes, if the Dire Magnus controls the Books, he can achieve his goal."

Michael nodded, wondering what he had done, what he had changed, each time he'd used the *Chronicle*. No wonder Dr. Pym called the Books an option of last resort.

"As I was saying," the wizard continued, "by means of these other selves, the Dire Magnus created a living bridge to carry himself across time. Now—and here we come to what I discovered in the mansion—it was always the duty of the current Dire Magnus to locate the next and confer on him the memories and power due him."

"What do you mean, confer the memories and power?"

"These individuals are not born with knowledge of their true origin. It is not until the memories of the previous Dire Magnus—indeed, of each previous Dire Magnus—are transferred that the new Magnus gains the knowledge of who he is.

"And the last Dire Magnus came into being, or awoke, you might say, in that mansion at the turn of the twentieth century. That was what I discovered. And it was he whom my fellows and I fought and vanquished—or so we imagined—forty years ago. Since then, no other has risen to take his place. I believe that he was the last of those taken from the other worlds."

"Then if you killed the last one, shouldn't it all be over?"

"You would think. But even in death, his spirit has continued to drive his followers. And now that the prophecy is close to being fulfilled, the Books found and brought together, he is determined to rejoin the world of the living and reclaim all his old power."

"How is that even possible?"

"My boy, the answer lies beside you." He nodded at the red leather book resting on the branch. "Which is why the *Chronicle* must be kept from him." Dr. Pym knocked the smoking tobacco from his pipe. "Now I think it is time to see your sister."

Michael nodded. "I assume Emma's with Gabriel—"

"Actually," the wizard said, "I was speaking of Katherine."

Kate was in a different tree, and to get there, the wizard led Michael across several of the bridges formed by the entwined branches, then down a harrowing staircase that wound around one of the massive trunks. As they walked, Dr. Pym explained how he had arrived in the valley just after the volcano had erupted, emerging from the tunnel beneath the mountains in time to see the dragon fly past, with all her passengers. He'd followed them to the elf colony.

"The scene was chaotic, as you might imagine: between the elves' joy at their princess's return, their grief at learning of those who had fallen in battle, Emma shouting for someone to help Gabriel—I'm afraid my own arrival did little to calm things down—and then, without warning, Katherine was in our midst."

Dr. Pym abruptly stopped walking and turned around. They were on the stairs, Michael two steps behind and above the wizard, one hand clutching the *Chronicle*, the other the trunk of the tree. He'd been staring at the old man's back as a way of ignoring the plunging drop to his left. Now he found himself and the wizard eye to eye.

"Michael"—the wizard's voice was somber—"there is no way to prepare you for what awaits, but do know we will make things right." Then, without explaining further what he meant, the old man turned away down the stairs.

Rounding the curve of the tree, they came upon a room very like Michael's own, a deep alcove in the trunk set above a wide, flat branch. The wizard paused at the entrance and gestured for Michael to go ahead. Inside were three figures. The elf princess Wilamena stood to Michael's left. She wore a dress of dark green satin, embroidered with golden thread in the design of a great tree that seemed—if one did not look at it directly—to be moving its branches in the wind. The princess's hair had been washed and braided, and it shone brightly in the dim light. She looked at Michael, her eyes full of sympathy, but did not speak or move toward him.

Across from her, to Michael's right, was Emma. She had neither changed clothes nor washed nor slept since the previous night, and, seeing Michael, she leapt up from where she was kneeling and ran and threw her arms around his neck, sobbing. Michael made the motions of holding her and patting her back, but something in him had shut down. His eyes were vacant; his body no longer seemed his own.

Directly before him, Kate lay on a low bed. Her eyes were closed, and she was wearing an ivory lace dress with a high neck. A blanket had been pulled up to just below her shoulders, and her arms lay outside the covers, her hands clasped about their mother's golden locket. Her face was very pale.

Michael didn't have to ask; he knew his sister was dead.

Gently, he disengaged Emma's arms from around his neck, took her hand, and went and knelt beside Kate. He paused a moment to gather himself before speaking.

"When . . . when did she . . ."

"Just after she appeared," the wizard said from the doorway. "The elf physicians and I tried everything we could. I'm very, very sorry."

Michael reached out and touched his sister's hand. The skin was cold.

It wasn't real, he thought. It was some trick. This wasn't Kate; she couldn't be dead. And yet he knew it wasn't a trick, and this was his sister.

Emma seized his arm, shaking it as she sobbed.

"Michael—bring her back! Use the book! You can do that, right? Bring her back! You have to! You have to!"

Michael didn't have to be told. He already had the *Chronicle* open, the stylus in hand, and was getting ready to prick his thumb.

"I'm afraid that is not going to work."

Michael looked to where Dr. Pym stood, framed against the forest.

"Your sister's spirit has crossed into the land of the dead, the same place where the Dire Magnus has been trapped for forty years. His power there is very great. He will not release her."

"What're you talking about?" Michael demanded. He was impatient and scarcely heard the wizard's words.

"There is a shadow over her," the elf princess said, speaking for the first time. "It settled on her the moment she died."

"Your sister," Dr. Pym said, "is a prisoner in the land of the dead."

CHAPTER TWENTY-THREE
The Ghost

Michael insisted that he at least be allowed to try to bring Kate back. The wizard agreed, but said that if he felt any resistance, he must not force it. Michael barely heard him. Pricking his thumb, he placed the bloodied tip of the stylus on the page, felt the familiar current run through him, saw Kate's face snap into focus, and began to write.

He couldn't get past the second letter of her name. It was as if an invisible force stood against him, and when he tried to push back—directly disobeying the wizard's orders—he felt a crack start to open in the stylus. He stopped, panicked.

And that was that. Dr. Pym urged the children not to give up hope, saying he was going to consult with Princess Wilamena's father and the elders among the elves, that they would find a way to free Katherine; then the wizard and the elf princess left, and

Emma collapsed against her brother, sobbing; and Michael, who felt as if he were at the bottom of a dark well, and receiving only dull vibrations from the world above, put his arm about her and let her cry.

The two of them stayed by Kate the rest of the day, hardly speaking. Twice, Emma left to check on Gabriel, returning each time to say that he was still asleep.

When night came, there was singing in the forest. It was sad and beautiful, and an elf who brought them dinner said it was a death song for the elves who had fallen in the battle; and the children listened and felt comforted. But neither was hungry, and without Dr. Pym to tell them to eat, the food remained untouched. The wizard returned sometime later. He told them he had not yet found a way to free Kate from the Dire Magnus's hold and he pressed them to get some rest. Michael said he wasn't going anywhere, but he joined the wizard in demanding that Emma go to bed. Emma tried to argue, but having stayed up with Kate all the previous night, she was mumbling and heavy-lidded and almost trembling with fatigue. Eventually, she gave in.

Her room was in a different tree, and she hugged Michael before she left.

"It's your birthday soon, isn't it? I guess . . . happy birthday."

As Emma stepped out onto the branch, Dr. Pym called for her to wait, saying he would guide her through the dark. He turned to Michael.

"What is it, my boy? I can see you have a question."

"Could I . . . could I have brought her back? Did I do something wrong?"

It had tortured him all day, the idea that it might have been possible to bring Kate back, if only he'd been strong enough or clever enough, and that the wizard, to spare his feelings, had placed all the blame on the Dire Magnus.

Dr. Pym seemed neither troubled nor surprised by Michael's question. "No, my boy, you did nothing wrong. You never had any chance of reviving your sister. I only allowed you to try so that you could understand what it is we face."

"But I almost broke the stylus."

The wizard shrugged. "Worse things might have happened. The stylus is a crutch, nothing more."

The elf who had brought dinner had also brought candles, and in the flickering light, Michael studied the old man's face and tried to divine his meaning. The answer, if there, was impossible to read.

"Tell me," Dr. Pym said, "did the Guardian give you any warnings about using the book?"

"He said . . . he said it would change me."

"How could it not? Each experience we have changes us. And when you use the *Chronicle*, you live another's entire life, share their hopes and fears, their loves and hatreds; it would be very easy to become lost. You must always remember who you are."

"That's what he said. But what if . . . what if I'm not—"

"Michael"—the wizard kept his voice low and private—"I know you do not wish to be the Keeper of the *Chronicle*. You tried to tell me so this morning and I would not listen. The fact is, the *Chronicle* chose you for a reason, and I believe the choice was correct. I myself would have chosen no other."

"Dr. Pym, I appreciate your trying to make me feel better, and I know it's good for team morale—but I'm just not the right person."

He had finally managed to say it; the words were out.

The wizard, however, was shaking his head. "You are so, so wrong."

"But—"

"Michael Wibberly, you have a fire inside of you."

"I . . . Wait, what?"

The wizard placed his wrinkled hand over Michael's heart. "It is the fire of true feeling, of love and compassion, of sorrow. It is the flame that ignites the *Chronicle*. Without it, you could never have used the book as you have. True, as yet you do not command the full power of the *Chronicle*; but even Katherine needed time to master the *Atlas*." He reached up and gripped Michael's shoulder. "You have so much more to give than you imagine."

And so saying, he left, taking Emma with him, and Michael was alone with Kate.

He tried to lie down beside her, but his heart was beating wildly, and he stood and began pacing, the *Chronicle* held tight to his chest. He walked back and forth in the small room for an hour or more, glancing again and again at his sister's face, as if he might catch some sign of life. The rain began all of a sudden, a fierce, pounding rain that came streaking down outside the room. Michael walked out into the darkness, still clutching the book, and allowed himself to be drenched. The rain was cold, almost freezing, but it did nothing to cool the fever burning through him, and his heart still beat as if to break free from his chest. He knew only that he couldn't go back into the room.

He hurried down the winding stairs, water streaming from his glasses, his feet slipping on the wooden planks. He was being reckless, he knew, but still he went faster and faster, growing dizzier and dizzier as he circled the great tree. Then he was on the forest floor and walking quickly, not knowing or caring where, pushing his way through the thickets of ferns as his feet sank in the mud, his arms locked around the *Chronicle*, his heart thudding.

After a while, he realized he was hearing, through the constant shushing thrum of rain, the faint sound of voices. It was the singing that he and Emma had heard before—the death song of the elves. Michael hurried toward it. Soon, lights appeared, wavering among the trees, and he came upon a procession. Thirty or more elves, wearing dark cloaks and carrying candles (whose flames seemed somehow impervious to the rain), were moving slowly through the forest. Michael hid behind a tree and watched them pass. Once again, the song comforted him, and he felt his panic begin to ebb. Then, just as the elves disappeared among the trees, the rain stopped.

Michael stood there, taking long, deep, slow breaths, and listening to the water drip from the branches. He put his hand to his chest and his heart was no longer pounding. He found himself fingering the lump of glass under his shirt. It occurred to him that the time must be well past midnight. He was thirteen. By any measure, he was now the eldest Wibberly.

He took the marble from around his neck and placed it on a thickly knotted root. Michael stomped down and felt the glass crunch beneath his heel. There was a hissing, and Michael stepped back as a silvery-gray mist rose into the darkness. The outlines of a figure began to take shape, the smoke molding itself into feet and legs, a torso, arms, shoulders, a head. And, as Michael watched, the swirling mist resolved into the familiar features of his father.

The misty figure was identical in every way—how he was dressed, the glasses he wore, the shagginess of his hair and beard, even the fatigue in his eyes—to the figure Rourke had produced before the fortress walls. The only difference was that the figure before him was made of nothing but smoke. Michael could see straight through him to the trees beyond.

"Incredible," the figure murmured, gazing at its own ghostly hands, its voice thin and echoey, as if coming from far away. "It actually worked. But then . . ." The figure turned and caught sight of Michael. "Oh my . . . are you . . . you can't be . . . Michael?"

Michael nodded. At the moment, nodding was all he could manage.

"But . . . you . . . you're so big!"

Michael had been holding himself perfectly still. He hadn't known what to expect when he'd smashed the orb, but finding himself face to face with his father—or some version of his father—for the second time in as many days had left him reeling.

"Oh, my boy—" And the figure rushed forward, as if to embrace him. Michael didn't have time to move, and anyway, it proved unnecessary, as the specter passed right through him. Michael turned and saw the figure standing two feet behind him, looking confused and a little embarrassed. "Well . . . that was stupid."

"Listen—" Michael knew he had to regain control of the situation.

"Are we in some sort of forest?"

"What? Yes, but—"

The figure waved its hand impatiently. "Never mind that now. There're things I have to tell you. This may be difficult to believe, but I am in fact—"

"I know who you are."

"You do? You mean you recognize me? How could you remember—"

"I saw a picture." Michael had recovered, though his voice was still shaky. "What kind of proof can you offer that you are who you . . . look like?"

"Proof? You mean like ID of some kind?"

"I don't know! I just need proof!" Michael felt himself becoming frantic. "How do I know you're my dad?"

"Well, as it happens, I'm not."

Of all possible responses, this was not one that Michael had seen coming, and it momentarily checked his rising panic.

"Is your father a strange, smoky apparition? No. Your real, flesh-and-blood father is somewhere else. At least, I hope he is. I'm a reflection of Richard; only instead of reflecting just his face, I reflect everything: how he looks, his memories. For instance, I remember the last time I saw you—or rather, he saw you. It was Christmas Eve, ten years ago, he carried you and Emma out of the house and into Stanislaus's car. You were both sleeping. And both so small." The figure was quiet for a moment, then said, "And I have his thoughts and feelings. If he was here now, looking at you, he'd be thinking exactly what I'm thinking."

"What's that?" Michael asked hoarsely. "Just . . . out of curiosity."

"How much he wished to have seen you grow up." The figure stepped closer. "Michael, in giving you up, your mother and I did what we thought was best. But every day for the past ten years, we've lived with the pain of our decision. Compared to that, captivity was easy." The figure shrugged. "Is that proof enough?"

Michael was frozen with uncertainty. He wanted to believe that this was his father, or a reflection of him, but how could he be sure?

"So you have all my dad's memories?"

"That's right. Ask me anythi—"

"Who is King Killick?"

". . . I'm sorry?"

"Who's King Killick? If you've got my dad's memories, you should know. I'll give you a hint. He's a famous elf king."

The figure stared at him, a confused look on its face. "I . . . have no idea."

Michael felt something crumble inside him.

There, he told himself, that'll teach you to hope.

"Of course," the figure continued, "if you'd asked about the *dwarfish* King Killick, that'd be another matter. But I've never heard of an elf named Killick. Seems odd for an elf to have a dwarf's name—"

"What—"

"There's actually a quote of Killick's I've never forgotten. The dwarf Killick, I mean. He said, 'A great leader lives not in his heart—'"

"'But in his head,'" Michael finished.

"Exactly! You know it too! Then why did you think Killick was an— Oh, I see, you were testing me! So, have I passed?"

Michael nodded; he didn't trust himself to speak.

"Good." The figure knelt before Michael. "Then here's what I have to tell you. Your mother and I have escaped. How and who helped us aren't important. We're sending you and your sisters this message so you know we're okay. We think we know where one of the books is hidden, and we're going to look for it—"

"But you don't have to!" Michael blurted. "I've already got it!"

"What're you talking about?"

"We went to see Hugo Algernon! We found the tomb in Malpesa! We came to Antarctica! I've got the *Chronicle*! See?"

He held out the book. The figure reached for it, then stopped. Tendrils of smoke rose from the tips of its fingers. "Oh dear."

"What's happening?" Michael asked.

"I'm running out of time. This body isn't built to last. Listen to me." The specter placed its evaporating hands on Michael's shoulders. "That's wonderful that you have the *Chronicle*. But we're looking for the last book."

"The last—"

"If we fail, listen, if we fail, or if you find it before we do, don't let Stanislaus bring all three books together. They must be kept separate. We've learned things. They may or may not be true, but it's not worth taking the chance." Michael started to speak, but the figure cut him off. "You don't have to understand. Just promise me."

Michael nodded. He could see through the figure more and more clearly.

"But . . . you can't go. . . ."

"I'm afraid I don't have much of a choice. I can't tell you how proud I am of you, and how proud your actual father would be, if he were here now."

Michael couldn't believe that this was it. There was so much he wanted to ask, so much he wanted to say. Then Michael realized that anything he told the apparition would vanish when the apparition vanished. It would be like whispering to the wind.

"I lost the *Omnibus*."

"What?"

"*The Dwarf Omnibus*. You gave it to me the night Dr. Pym took us away. I've been keeping it all this time. I wanted to give it back to you. But I lost it. I'm sorry."

"Oh, my boy, that doesn't matter. Honestly."

But Michael was shaking his head. He knew he was avoiding the thing he had to say. He took another breath.

"I . . . betrayed . . . Kate and Emma." The words were heavy and stuck in his throat; he had to push them out. "Last year, in Cambridge Falls, I betrayed them to the Countess. She promised she would find you and Mom. She lied, of course. And I knew . . . I knew what I was doing. But after, it was so awful. It hurt so much, I just . . . I never wanted to feel like that again. I never wanted to feel anything again. . . ."

He was crying quietly, and he wiped his hand across his face, which was still wet from the rain. The figure said nothing.

"But the *Chronicle*," Michael went on, "it makes you feel things! And I don't want to! I can't! No one understands that! I just can't!"

Then he dropped his gaze and clutched the book even tighter to his chest.

"Michael." The figure had to say his name twice more before he looked up. "That quote from King Killick, do you know why I've never forgotten it?"

"Because," Michael said thickly, "it . . . makes good dwarfish sense?"

"No. Because it was how I used to be. Before you and your sisters. Before your mother. I lived entirely in my head."

"And it was better, right?" Michael said. "Things hurt less?"

"No! I mean, yes, I felt less pain. But the point of life isn't to avoid pain. The point of life is to be alive! To feel things. That means the good and the bad. There'll be pain. But also joy, and friendship and love! And it's worth it, believe me. Your mother and I lost ten years of our lives, but every minute of every day we had our love for you and your sisters, and I wouldn't trade that for anything. Don't let the fear control you. Choose life, son."

Then the figure put its ghostly arms around him, and Michael closed his eyes, and it seemed that his father's shade became more solid, more real. Michael could feel his father's chest against his cheek, hear the beating of his heart, and then Michael opened his eyes, and he was holding nothing but air.

Suddenly, he was aware of a golden glow, and he turned and saw the elf princess. She wore a cloak with the hood thrown back, and her hair shone in the darkness.

"Were you . . . watching?"

She nodded, unashamed. "Yes." She stepped forward and took his hand. "Come with me."

"Why?"

"I am going to show you how to bring back your sister."

CHAPTER TWENTY-FOUR
The Rise of the Dire Magnus

Hand in hand, Michael and the elf princess raced through the forest. Wilamena led the way, the sodden arms of the ferns swinging back to let her pass before closing on Michael and drenching him, which they did again and again. He hadn't asked where she was taking him, nor had she offered any hints, and so it was a surprise when they arrived at the canyon wall and Michael saw a dozen cloaked figures standing about with candles. He recognized them from the procession through the forest, and indeed, they were still singing, though so quietly now that Michael had to strain to hear the song. The figures were gathered before a triangular crevice, and, as Michael watched, one of the elves extinguished his candle, stepped into the crevice, and disappeared.

"My people came to this valley thousands of years ago," the

princess whispered, "when all was ice and snow. Have you not wondered why we chose to make such a wasteland our home?"

Michael thought about saying that he couldn't begin to fathom the workings of an elf mind; then he decided that the correct answer was "Yes."

"We came," Wilamena said, "because our race is drawn to the places where the mortal world and the spirit world overlap. Imagine two circles, their edges touching, and a narrow space that belongs not to one world or the other but to both. That is what exists in this valley. What exists here." And she nodded at the crevice in the wall.

"You mean," Michael said, "that cave takes you into the land of the dead?"

"Yes and no. The true land of the dead is a place the living do not venture. The cave leads to the in-between place, where the circles touch. And there the dead can come to us. Did you not feel this when you first entered the valley? A presence you could not explain?"

And Michael realized that he had felt it, that when he and Gabriel and Emma had come into the valley, he'd had the sense that they were not alone, that something was looking over their shoulders, but he'd dismissed the feeling as nerves.

He watched as a cloaked elf extinguished her candle and entered the crevice.

"What are they doing?"

"They go to say farewell to those who died in battle. None can stay long in that place, but there is time enough to say the things that must be said. Then each will return to their own world, the living to the living, the dead to the dead."

Michael looked at the elf princess. "I should have tried to bring them back. The elves who died. I should've used the *Chronicle*. I wasn't thinking. I'm so sorry."

Wilamena shook her head. "Death is part of nature. This was their time, and they died bravely. Your sister is different. Her journey among the living is not yet finished." She looked toward the crevice. "And if the enemy will not allow her to come here, then you must go there."

Michael understood. He swallowed and tightened his grip on the *Chronicle*. "Does Dr. Pym know about all this?"

"Certainly, he knows of this place, but he does not know I have brought you here. Indeed, in counsel with my father and the elders, he has spoken against sending you into the Fold."

"The Fold?"

"That is what we call the place where the worlds overlap. The wizard knows you must travel there alone, and that he would have no power to protect you. He is searching for a safer way to free your sister; but there *is* no safer way."

"Why do I have to go alone? What about the elves who're already in there?"

"You will not see them. Even if you and I were to enter side by side, we would find ourselves far apart. You might discover yourself in a city, while I would be on a vast, empty field. The Fold changes for each of us and is always different."

Michael felt that the more she told him, the more confused

he became. He just wanted to know one thing. "How do I find Kate?"

"Simply hold the idea of your sister in your mind, and she will come to you. But be warned: others have stayed too long and been unable to find their way back. You must be quick, Michael."

"That's the first time you've called me by my name."

Wilamena smiled. "I think you are not a rabbit anymore."

Michael looked at her, and the memory of that brief time when he had shared her life came back to him. He remembered the darkness and despair she'd suffered during her long years as a prisoner, but he also recalled the deep, unquenchable joy she took from the world around her; and he knew that given the choice, Wilamena would suffer through all she had and more rather than sacrifice one day of being alive.

It was just as his father had said. She chose life, all of it.

Then Michael did something that surprised even him. He leaned in and kissed the elf princess. Her lips were soft, and he couldn't tell if it was magic or not, but he felt a warmth spreading over his cheeks and ears, down his neck, and across his chest. He said, "Thank you," and turned and walked past the gathered elves and into the cave, taking the warmth of the kiss with him.

After only a few feet, he could see nothing but blackness. He stumbled repeatedly on the rocky floor but continued creeping forward, one hand held out before him, the memory of Kate clear and strong in his mind. Then, in the distance, Michael perceived a dim gray light. He made for it, and the darkness around him faded, and the floor became smooth. He realized he was no longer in a cave, but a corridor of some kind.

Then Michael stepped into the light and gasped.

He was standing in the great hall of an old stone church. He took in the rows of columns, the stained-glass windows, the vaulted ceiling. Strangely, instead of pews, there were lines of cots running down the center aisle. The church appeared to be empty.

Then Michael heard, faint and echoing, the sound of a violin.

Emma woke and knew that something was wrong. She sat up and looked about. Her room was similar to her sister's, but in a different tree, several hundred feet away. Pulling on a pair of soft leather shoes (a gift from the elves, as she had lost a boot in the volcano), Emma walked out onto the branch that served both as a balcony and a bridge to the rest of the forest. Water was pooled all about. More dripped from the trees. Clearly, there'd been a rainstorm. How had it not woken her? Emma had the terrible thought that she'd slept through an entire day and into the next night.

She started off toward the tree where she'd left her brother and sister. She forced herself to go slowly, as the branches were slick with rain and the night was murky and black. Arriving in Kate's room, she found her sister exactly as she'd left her, and Michael nowhere to be seen. But standing beside Kate's bed was Gabriel. He looked to be completely recovered from his injuries, and as he turned, Emma ran forward and hugged him. She said his name over and over, and he held her and she felt safe in a way she had not felt since she'd arrived at the elf village; and even the darkness about them seemed to recede just a little.

Emma stepped back and wiped her eyes.

"What're you doing here? I thought you were still asleep!"

"I woke and was much better. When I heard about your sister, I had to come."

Still holding Gabriel's hand, Emma knelt beside the bed. Her sister's brow was smooth. Death had erased the furrow of worry.

"Where's Michael? He's supposed to be here."

Gabriel shook his head. "There was no one here when I arrived."

"Something's wrong. I knew it. Michael should be here."

Gabriel was silent for a long moment. It was as if he were listening to something far away; though all Emma could hear was the steady dripping of rain. "I think he has gone to try and bring back your sister."

"But he already *did* that! He tried writing her name in the book and he couldn't!"

"There is another way. A dangerous way. He can seek out her spirit directly. The wizard could have shown him how."

"What? Why wouldn't he tell me?"

"No doubt he was trying to protect you."

"But she's my sister too! We gotta find them!"

"Come then. I know where to look. It may be they need our help."

Emma leaned down and whispered to Kate that she loved her and would be back soon, then she rose, and she and Gabriel hurried from the room.

• • •

Michael followed the music down the nave of the church past the rows of cots and through a door in the back wall. He found himself at the base of a tower. In the middle of the floor, a large bell lay on its side, its iron shell cracked in two. A rickety-looking wooden staircase spiraled upward along the walls. Michael stood there, listening to the song of the violin echoing through the tower; then he began to climb.

The elf princess had said that the Fold was different for everyone. But where had this old church come from? And what did it mean? Was he right in following the music? Would it lead him to Kate? And who, he wondered, was playing it?

The staircase ended, and Michael found a ladder leading through a trapdoor in the ceiling. Tucking the *Chronicle* under his arm, Michael headed upward, emerging onto a wide wooden platform atop the tower. Stone columns around the edge of the platform supported a peaked roof, and three iron bells hung suspended in the rafters. There was a hole in the center of the floor where, presumably, the fourth bell had fallen through. The church stood in an endless field of mist.

Am I still in the cave? Michael wondered. Or am I somewhere else?

He felt confused and frightened and very alone.

Kate was nowhere to be seen. But he had found the source of the music.

A boy, a few years older than Michael, with unruly dark hair and dressed in worn, vaguely old-fashioned clothes, stood at the edge of the belfry, playing a battered violin. His fingers were dirty, but he played with an easy, fluid precision, and his eyes were closed, as if he was lost in the music. Michael stood there, unsure, waiting.

The song died away; the boy lowered the violin.

"My mother taught me that. I used to play it for her. My name's Rafe."

"I'm Michael."

"I know."

"What . . . what is this place?"

"The church?" The boy reached out to one of the columns supporting the roof. There was something sad and loving in the way he touched it. "This is a place that no longer exists in the living world. It was where I came to know your sister. The Fold—to use the elves' word—can be manipulated if one has the will and power. When I felt you coming, the church seemed an appropriate choice. But perhaps it's merely sentimental."

He looked at Michael; his eyes were a startling shade of green, and Michael knew then who he was, and that he was not a boy at all; he was their enemy.

"Where is she?"

"Behind you."

Michael turned. A large desk stood where none had stood before, and his sister lay upon it, wearing the same high-necked, white lace dress that Michael remembered. Her eyes were closed, her face pale, and her hands were folded on her chest. He walked over and touched her arm. It was solid; she was real.

"You're keeping her here, aren't you?"

"Yes. I am."

"Why?"

"I think you know the answer to that."

Michael said nothing. He sensed the boy had come up behind him.

"My followers in the living world have preserved my physical body for decades. They are waiting for it to rise. For me to rise. As Keeper of the *Chronicle*, you have the power to restore me to life. Release my spirit, and I will release your sister. Otherwise, she stays with me."

Michael felt a cold weight settle in his stomach. This was why Dr. Pym hadn't wanted him to come here. He'd known that Michael would be faced with this exact choice: either to bring his sister back and also bring back the Dire Magnus, or to leave Kate trapped in the land of the dead, forever.

Only there was no choice, not for Michael. He didn't care if the Dire Magnus returned to life and regained all his old power. He didn't care that he would be responsible for all that happened afterward. Kate was what mattered; she was all that mattered. Michael would bring back the Dire Magnus a hundred times over if his sister would just open her eyes and speak to him.

And perhaps that was what the wizard had truly feared.

It seemed to Michael he could hear another violin in the distance, playing a different song from before, one that was both faster and more haunting, less human.

"Come. Make your decision."

"I already have." Michael opened the *Chronicle* on the desk and snapped the stylus free from the brackets.

"Your hands are shaking. There's no need to be scared."

"I'm not." It was true: he wasn't. The shaking was nerves, the knowledge that he was doing something both momentous and wrong, but which he couldn't help. He wanted his sister back and he would pay any price. And letting the Dire Magnus return to the world was only part of the cost. Michael knew that everything he'd experienced before—Emma's feelings of betrayal, the elf princess's despair at her long imprisonment, the Guardian's guilt and madness—was nothing compared to the darkness and hatred he would find inside the Dire Magnus; and the moment he called on the magic of the *Chronicle*, all that darkness, all that hatred, would become his. There was no way he wouldn't be changed.

Michael knew all that, and again, he didn't care.

He held his thumb on the table and pricked it with the stylus. He turned to the boy. "Release Kate. Then I'll bring you back."

The boy smiled. "This isn't a negotiation. I go first, or I take your sister away to a place where you can't follow, and that will be the end."

"How do I . . . how do I know you'll let her go?"

The boy who called himself Rafe reached out and gently moved the hair off Kate's forehead. "Because I want her to live just as much as you do."

And Michael looked at the boy's shining green eyes and believed him.

The boy gripped Michael's arm, his voice suddenly cold and commanding. "Now write my name."

And Michael set the tip of the stylus on the page and wrote, in smoking, bloody letters, *The Dire Magnus*. . . .

The next instant, he was a man, lean and hawk-featured, but with the same startling green eyes, living in a dusty, war-torn land. The man was a village sorcerer; he was hard and proud, but Michael felt his love for the people he protected, and for his own young family, his wife and child, and indeed, Michael felt that they were his people, his family. And when the man returned home to find his village burned, his family murdered, it was Michael's heart that turned black with hatred and guilt. Together, Michael and the man hunted down and punished the men responsible, and Michael reveled in the suffering the man caused, that he caused; and when their revenge had been taken, the man's rage then turned upon all men, all humans, and Michael felt himself burning with the same anger. . . .

Michael gripped the stylus tight in his fist; he was trembling badly, struggling to hold on to himself. . . .

The magic pulled him down once more. . . .

He was old. He had traveled far, learned much, gained more power, and now he was dying. It was night; there was a fire, and Michael stared across the flames at a boy with emerald-green eyes, and heard himself, in a hoarse, wavering voice, speak of three books of unfathomable power, and tell the boy that they, that he—for the man and boy were one—would use the Books to change the world. Then the man took a knife and drew it across his own throat, and Michael became the boy. . . .

More time passed. The boy who had sat across the fire was long dead, his bones dust. Yet still he was alive, just as the first man was alive, as Michael was alive, in the body of another, a man with the same blazing green eyes. The man was whispering in the ear of a youthful conqueror as they sacked a city on the sea; and Michael stalked through streets filled with fire and screaming, and he felt a terrible, high joy at being so near his goal. And then Michael and the man descended to the vaults below the tower and found the Books already gone, and Michael felt a thousand years of anger rise up and consume him. . . .

Michael felt himself falling deeper and deeper into darkness, and there was nothing he could do to stop it, no part of himself he could cling to. . . .

Centuries passed. The world changed. Michael died and was reborn, died and was reborn. The Books eluded him, but he gained power, and with power, followers. And with every year that passed, Michael felt the faces of the first man's wife and child becoming more and more blurred and indistinct. . . .

He was another man, this one tall and fair-haired, but with the same emerald eyes, carrying inside himself half a dozen lives, half a dozen deaths, and he was listening to a prophecy about three children who would find the Books and bring them together. Three children who would be sacrificed so that a new world might come into being. . . .

And more deaths, more lives. Michael became aware of a strain inside the man, inside himself, as each life was coupled to the one before. . . .

Then Michael was an old man, older than he had ever been. His bones were twisted, his breath weak and watery. He stood in a candlelit ballroom, surrounded by dark figures. Then the crowd of figures parted, and a boy stepped forward. Michael recognized Rafe, and saw he held Kate in his arms, and a forgotten part of

Michael came alive at the sight of his sister; she was wounded, bleeding, and Rafe was trading himself for Kate, his life for hers, and there was anguish in the boy's face; then suddenly Kate was gone, and it was happening again, Michael was dying, and he felt the Dire Magnus's spirit attaching itself like a cancer to the boy's soul. . . .

But something was different from all the times before, and the difference, Michael realized, was in Rafe.

"That will do, I think."

The stylus was plucked from Michael's hand. He collapsed against the desk, gasping and covered in sweat. He felt as if he'd been poisoned. Hatred and anger still coursed through his body. He struggled to stay on his feet.

The boy's green eyes glittered. "Did you enjoy your trip through my various lives? I imagine it was a bit overwhelming. I can't tell you how much I appreciate this, Michael. But before I go—" He clenched his hand, and the stylus snapped.

"What're you—"

"Oh, I fully intend to let you bring Kate back to life. Just not today. I need to take care of a few things first, and I can keep a closer eye on her down here. You, however, should leave. I would say that you've already stayed too long."

The boy was fading from sight, becoming misty and insubstantial. Michael lunged forward, but his hand passed through the boy's arm. *"Stop! Please!"*

"Goodbye, Michael. We'll meet again soon."

The pieces of the stylus clattered onto the floor, and Michael was alone. He scrabbled at the fragments, but the tower shook, and one of them rolled away, disappearing between the boards of the platform. Michael let the remaining shards fall from his hand. It was hopeless. He looked and saw the mist rising up and rolling in waves toward the church. He'd failed. More than that, he'd made things worse. And how could he bring Kate back now? What would he tell Dr. Pym? What would he tell Emma? He turned to the desk and took Kate's hand. It was cold.

"I'm sorry," he whispered. "I tried. I really did."

Michael felt a darkness welling up inside him, and his despair turned to rage. This wasn't fair! This shouldn't be happening! Not to Kate! Not to him! It was Dr. Pym's fault! It was their parents' fault! They should be the ones here! He wished they were dead, not—

A voice spoke inside his head: *The book will change you. Remember who you are. . . .*

That's . . . not me, Michael thought. That's the Dire Magnus. It's not me.

And he looked at his sister's face, focused on her, and he felt the rage and the darkness recede. It was still there, deep inside him, the same way the other memories were there, Emma's and the Guardian's and Wilamena's, but he remembered who he was.

Seconds passed. Michael knew he needed to go, but he wouldn't leave his sister. Indeed, he couldn't. He'd used the last of his strength beating back the Dire Magnus's poison. That, on top of everything else—the loss of Kate, the meeting with his father, Michael's simple, human exhaustion—it was too much; he was finished; and something in his chest seemed to crack open, and all the feelings he'd been bottling up for months, all the guilt and the sadness and the shame, came surging forth.

Michael rested his head against the still-open book and sobbed.

Sometime later—a few seconds, an eternity—he heard a strange sort of hissing. Michael rose up and wiped his eyes. His tears were sizzling on the page. Nor was that all. The book itself was on fire. Flames licked around the edges of the cover; they crawled across the page, but the book, and Michael's hand that rested on the book, remained unharmed. Michael pulled his hand away, and the flames died.

For a long moment, he was too stunned to have any thoughts at all.

Then the tower shuddered, the bells clanged, and his brain jolted to life. He thought about the pattern of flames carved into the book's cover, the way the letters would bubble and smoke when he wrote someone's name; he thought of the wizard saying, *You have a fire inside of you.*

Did that mean he had caused the flames? Or had the book sensed something in him and the flames were its response? Either way, somehow, without using his blood, without the stylus, he'd tapped into the power of the *Chronicle*. And he'd done so, he sensed, at a deeper level than ever before.

But what good did it do him? Without the stylus he couldn't write Kate's name.

Another memory came to him. He was in the elf village, and Dr. Pym was saying that the stylus was a crutch, nothing more.

At the time, Michael had had no idea what he'd meant. But what if—Michael felt the excitement of the idea surging through him—what if the stylus was like the photos they'd first used to tap into the power of the *Atlas*? Eventually, Kate had been able to command the *Atlas* at will. Could the same be true here? Could the stylus be just a means of accessing the *Chronicle*'s power until one had mastered its workings? He thought about the fact that the Dire Magnus, having broken the stylus himself, still meant to bring Kate back to life. The stylus couldn't be the only way of using the *Chronicle*!

The tower shook. Fingers of gray mist slithered over the lip of the platform.

Michael placed his hand on the open page and focused all his attention on his sister. He was seeing things with an eerie, perfect clarity. He realized that all the time the *Chronicle* had flooded him with the feelings of others, of Emma and the Guardian and Princess Wilamena, it had wanted his feelings, his heart. On some level, Michael suspected that he'd known this all along, that this was the reason he'd tried so hard to push the *Chronicle* away. Except that the *Chronicle* was his responsibility; Michael understood that now and accepted it. *Remember who you are.* I'm Michael Wibberly, he thought. I'm the brother of Kate and Emma. And he reached down to the feeling that formed the very bedrock of his life, his love for his sisters, and offered it up.

His eyes were closed, but he heard the *whup* of flames.

Suddenly, Michael found himself in a high-ceilinged, narrow-windowed room filled with twenty or more beds in neat rows. There were Christmas decorations on the walls, and Michael recognized the dormitory of the orphanage in Boston where he and his sisters had lived just after their parents had disappeared. Kate held Emma in her lap, and Michael saw himself, three years old and already wearing glasses, sitting at the end of her bed. Kate was telling them that one day their parents would return and they would all have Christmas together but that Michael and Emma had to believe it would happen, that only then would it come true. Kate was five years old, and Michael marveled at her strength. . . .

He was in Richmond, Virginia, the orphanage in Boston having burned down years before. Their parents still had not returned. Their Richmond orphanage was in an old tobacco warehouse on the banks of the James River. It was summer, and Kate had taken her brother and sister to the river, and they were splashing each other and leaping from high rocks into a deep pool, and Michael felt Kate's own happiness at seeing her brother and sister happy and carefree. . . .

Then they were in a different orphanage, this one next to a fancy private school, and Kate was sneaking them into the school's library to read them stories in the dark, empty corners of the stacks. . . .

And he was with Kate as she fought with one orphanage director after another who tried to split them up; he stayed up with her half the night before his and Emma's birthdays, putting together presents that she had worked on and saved for month after month, all so that he and Emma would have something special to open; Michael saw the million small ways she tried to make their lives a little better, most of which he'd never acknowledged or had taken for granted; and though the orphanages changed, and they all grew older, Michael felt how Kate's love for her brother and sister remained as strong and constant and fierce as ever, and he understood that there was nothing he could do to lose it, and when he took his hand away from the book, his vision was blurry with tears, and he watched as his sister's body grew faint and ghostly and, finally, disappeared.

He stood there taking long, ragged, trembling breaths. He felt emptied out, but also complete. The Dire Magnus's darkness no longer threatened to rise up and consume him. His sister had given him new strength; more than that, she *was* his strength.

The tower swayed and shuddered. Mist clawed at his ankles, and Michael knew he had to go. Snapping the book closed, he raced for the trapdoor. He leapt down the tower stairs three at a time. When he reached the bottom, he heard a crashing and splintering from above and knew that one of the bells had broken free. He didn't look up but kept running and was already in the great hall when there was a deafening *clang* and the floor shook beneath his feet. The church was disintegrating, the walls and ceiling fading into mist. On either side of him, past the rows of cots, there was nothing but fog, stretching on and on. He could still see the doorway that led to the tunnel, and he raced toward it as the floor turned to smoke.

Michael dropped to his knees just beyond the mouth of the crevice, taking gulps of cool, clean air. He had stumbled along in darkness, tripping again and again on the rocks that jutted up from the tunnel floor. Finally, there'd been a light in the distance, and he'd made for it, knowing what it was, knowing who it was. Now the golden glow was all about him as the elf princess leaned close and her shining hair fell forward.

"Are you all right? Are you hurt?"

Michael felt her hand on the back of his neck, and he sensed the other elves waiting nearby. He stood slowly, uncertain of his legs.

"Yes. I'm okay." But his hand trembled as he adjusted his glasses.

"Did you find your sister? Did you bring her back? Where is the stylus? What happened? Speak to me."

Michael looked down at the *Chronicle*. His fingers were curled tight around the spine. Yes, the stylus was gone, but his connection to the book was stronger than ever. The *Chronicle* was a part of him now. He looked at the elf princess.

"I need to see her."

Hand in hand once more, Michael and the elf princess hurried through the forest. The ferns were still wet from the rainstorm, and Michael was drenched all over again. When they reached the elf village, there were lights moving in the branches far above. The princess led him to his sister's tree and up the spiraling stairs. Just outside her room, Michael stopped. The elf princess turned toward him, her face illuminated in the candlelight shining through the doorway.

"What is it?"

"What if . . . ," Michael whispered. "What if she's not . . ."

Wilamena squeezed his hand and smiled. "Come."

Two more steps brought him into the room, and there was Dr. Pym, bent forward over his sister, speaking softly; and there was Kate, sitting up, her eyes open, nodding as she listened; and Michael didn't hear the cry that erupted from his throat, he only knew that a moment later, he was in his sister's arms, sobbing; and he could feel Kate's cheek against the top of his head, and he could hear the beating of her heart, and he could hear her voice saying his name, over and over.

Michael wanted to tell her how much he'd missed her, how much he loved her, that he had kept his promise, that Emma was safe, but he couldn't speak; and finally, it was Kate who drew away. She put her hands on the sides of his face and lifted it so he was looking into her eyes. There were tears on her cheeks, but she was smiling.

"Michael, did you bring me back? Dr. Pym said you were the only one who could. How did you do it?"

Michael took a deep breath and wiped at his eyes. He could feel the wizard watching him. Kate was back; she was alive. It was time to face the consequences of what he had done. And he opened his mouth to tell them about the green-eyed boy, about the Dire Magnus, when the wizard said:

"I also am eager to hear the story. But let us save the explanations till Emma arrives. I sent for her as soon as Katherine began to stir. She should be here in a moment."

"No. She is gone."

And Michael and Kate and the wizard all turned to see Gabriel enter and step past the elf princess.

"I went to her room, but it was empty. She is gone."

"Gabriel, are you sure this is the right place?" Emma asked. "There's no one here."

"I am sure."

They were at the edge of the clearing where, two nights before, Emma and Michael had watched the elves have their picnic, where Emma had been abducted by the dragon Wilamena, and where Rourke had built the portal to bring through his army.

The portal, its fire quenched, stood in the center of the clearing, half a dozen felled trees fashioned into a rough arch.

"We must be patient," the man said.

Since leaving the elf village, Emma had several times been on the verge of mentioning her fear that no matter what they did, Kate was lost for good. Mostly, she just wanted to be reassured. But each time she thought of her sister, lying there so pale and still, it took all of Emma's strength to keep from crying. And beyond that, there was something in her friend's silence, some new unsettling quality, and it kept her from speaking.

Without warning, the wooden archway burst into flame.

Emma gasped. "Did you know that was going to happen?"

"Yes."

"What's it mean?"

"This portal leads to a stronghold of the Dire Magnus. It was from that stronghold that the army came through yesterday.

And it is where, for decades, the body of the master has been preserved."

Emma wanted to ask what master he was talking about, and what did some stupid portal have to do with bringing back her sister—she was confused and starting to feel a little bit scared—when, from deep in the forest, she heard shouting. Emma listened. Someone was calling her name. But the voice . . . It couldn't be. . . .

Then a hand gripped her arm. There was a shimmer in the air.

And Emma saw that the face beside her was no longer her friend's, and screamed.

Afterward, they put together what must've happened, how Rourke must've survived the fall from the fortress tower, how he must've entered the village under the cover of a glamour, disguised as Gabriel, and lured Emma away. It even came out that the pair had been seen heading into the forest.

But that was all later.

Immediately after Gabriel failed to find Emma, Wilamena roused the village, and elves streamed out into the valley. Word soon came back that the wooden archway in the clearing was on fire once again.

They were too late, of course. By the time Kate and Michael and the wizard arrived at the clearing—Gabriel had sprinted ahead with the elves—Emma was gone, and the wooden arch had collapsed into a smoldering jumble. Anton, the blue-eyed elf captain, had gotten there first, just in time to see Rourke carry a screaming, kicking Emma through the portal. He said there had been another figure as well, but it was strange, for at one moment the figure had seemed to be a man, and the next a boy. Both man and boy, the elf captain said, had the same startling green eyes.

Then Kate grabbed at Dr. Pym, crying, "It was him, wasn't it? It was Rafe!"

But the wizard didn't reply. For Michael had run forward and was pulling at the burning timbers with his bare hands and shouting his sister's name, and the others had to come and lift him away.

JOHN STEPHENS is also the author of *The Emerald Atlas*, the first installment in the Books of Beginning trilogy. John received his MFA from the University of Virginia, and went on to write and produce television for ten years. During this time, he read His Dark Materials by Philip Pullman and fell in love with fantasy for young readers. He spent the next several years waking at 4 AM every morning to write *The Emerald Atlas* before heading to work for the day.

John lives in Los Angeles with his wife and sons and their dog, Bug. Visit BooksofBeginning.com to find out more about *The Fire Chronicle*, the Books of Beginning, and John.